MW00892913

HOUR OF TRIAL

By Lena Robin

Cover photo by Joel Filipe on Unsplash

Copyright © 2018 Lena Berchielli a.k.a. Lena Robin

All Rights reserved. No part of this book may be reproduced, or stored in a retrieval system, or transmitted in any form or by any means, electronic, mechanical, photocopying, recording, or otherwise, without express written permission of the publisher.
This book is a work of fiction. Names, characters, places, and incidents are products of the author's imagination and are used fictitiously. Any resemblance to actual people living or dead, events or locales, is entirely coincidental and used in a fictitious manner.

ISBN: 9781730780479
Imprint: Independently published

DEDICATION

I would like to dedicate this book to my husband Al who keeps me laughing and my girls, Sophia and Rowen, who keep me on my toes, give me a ton of hugs and love and make my life a blessing.

TABLE OF CONTENTS

Hour Of Trial

CHAPTER 1

Day 1

As Alex stood alone, the smell crept past the menthol rub smeared under her nose, causing an involuntary shudder. She thought about how the pervasive stench of garbage, debris, and human excrement could overwhelm even the most tenacious volunteer helping in the area. The years she spent coming there told her the smell would only minutely diminish as the cooling days of autumn set in. She blinked and raised her arm to protect her eyes from the rays of fading light as it pierced through cracks and joints in the concrete overhead. The place looked as decrepit as it smelled. Occasional rustling noises from cats chasing rodents broke up the sound of leaks and the drip drop that constantly echoed in the background and gave life under the bridge its own lonely rhythm. Alex gripped her shaky cart, then maneuvered around the giant, stinking couch that nobody was sleeping on at the moment, more evidence of the desolate nature of the place.

Suddenly, one of the cart's wheels caught into a crevice in the concrete. Alex sighed in exasperation. She hit that same crack so many of the times she came, and never learned. Although she appeared small to other people, she knew, she could move even the heaviest cart out of the crack. Years of kickboxing had developed her strength. Today, almost finished with her rounds, the near-empty cart easily jerked out of the shallow cavity - an inconvenience, not a difficulty.

Where the heck did Rebecca go? Glancing around, she imagined that this dilapidated environment was an inescapable walk through Hell. Under the bridge, limitless dark shadows and perplexities screamed of its secrets. Many of its residents existed solely trapped in their own minds, doomed to relive their past traumas and horrors every day. The appearance of the living nightmare under the bridge provided the residents a safe zone, one in which they lived out their self-imposed punishments in relative peace. It sent chills up the back of Alex's neck each time she

1

tried to comprehend the bridge residents' aversion to the outside world, as each was determined to live within their dread, under the bridge.

Alex wished she didn't feel so guarded every time she stepped into the area. Each man and woman living there had stories to tell, and she eagerly provided the listening ear they needed. Once she began talking to the residents her anxiety evaporated and she became more and more enveloped in their lives and stories. The residents escaped the reality of their world, even if only for a moment, by telling their stories. It reminded her of why she risked volunteering in such an uninviting place.

Over the years, tents replaced the cardboard boxes the residents lived in, yet some, like David, still preferred the security and familiarity of their tired, worn boxes. Every time Alex tried to talk him about moving into a tent, he completely ignored her arguments of rain protection and fewer bugs. He'd pat the outside of his box then squawk, 'Less likely to be stolen, and the cats like it better.' Alex smirked thinking about it, then braced herself. Even though she knew he was kind-hearted, she never knew what his state of mind would be, "David it's Alex, I've brought you dinner." Alex eyed the two joined boxes that David slept in, the rickety crack between them with two flaps served as David's door.

The box shuddered slightly as a big brown eye darting back and forth materialized in the crack, "Alex is that you? You alone?" David barked with a hint of a drawl when he spoke, and asked the same question every time she came, and it always made her chuckle.

Alex gingerly squatted before the boxes, "Yes David, it's me, and you know I don't come alone, Dr. Rebecca is here with me today." She waited for his reaction. Sometimes he seemed to intensely dislike Rebecca, and other times he merely reacted in jest, either way, he needed her help. The infection on David's arm grew continually worse until Rebecca came with medical care and treatment. Rebecca hated coming down here, but Alex somehow guilted her into it. She grudgingly joined Alex's endeavor, even though she had made it clear that she despised working on anything more consequential than an amoeba. Talking patients simply argued too much. Alex sighed, without someone to check on these poor souls, they could easily rot away without anyone noticing, and it broke her heart. Her job at HUD was important, but she did not see its immediate effects. Alex felt comfort in knowing that her presence here made a significant difference in people's lives, one she saw and experienced on a personal level.

Interrupting her thoughts David's box wobbled and his one eye that peered through the crack squinted in mischief, "Whoo-wee, that witch?" He hid his humor and smile behind the cover of his box, "No, no, no, your dinner ain't worth getting poked and pricked."

Alex smiled then wiped the side of her face with her shoulder; she always seemed to have an itch when she couldn't scratch it, "Yes it is, now come on, she simply wants to help you stay healthy." They debated the same argument every time she brought Rebecca, and while he eventually consented to medical treatment, he liked to tease first. Alex sighed, "She is checking your vitals, changing your bandage, and asking you a few simple questions." When he didn't respond she knew it was time for a little tough love, he seemed to respond well to that, "So quit your whining, get out here, and get your dinner. It's your favorite, and I helped mash the potatoes myself." She hadn't since she'd rushed over from work, but he didn't need to know that.

A scruffy, matted, brown-haired head poked out, "With butter ?" David grinned, exposing his teeth through a mass of unkempt beard and hair. Something about the soft look in his big brown eyes kept the guise of a wild man at bay, but everything else about his appearance screamed unstable and almost barbarian. She didn't understand the bond they had developed over the years, yet she cared for him, even on his off days, but today his humor and good nature showed through the dirt and grime of living under the bridge. Today was a good day.

The sight of David's head poking out of the box caused laughter to unexpectedly bubble up from inside her, "Of course, and lots of salt too." Alex kept the rest of the mashed potato ingredients to herself. As the residents' favorite staple of most the meals she delivered, potatoes easily disguised the multivitamin powder added to it. Rebecca developed the vitamin powder, especially for the indigent population. Now she and the research company she worked for donated it to soup kitchens locally as well as all over the United States. Rebecca said she did it entirely at Alex's request, but Alex could see the pride in her friend's face at her contribution.

David crawled completely out of his box, wearing the green camo military jacket he wore all year, no matter the weather. It added to his charm in Alex's eyes. He had served in the military but rarely talked about it. Alex had looked up his service records and glowed with pride at his contribution in saving the lives of an entire village of women and children, though she never said anything to him. David's head bobbed up and down as she placed the box of food into his outstretched hands. He sported a huge grin and grunted, "Uhh, huh, huh." David's momentary joyful demeanor abruptly shifted, as he narrowed his eyes and pursed his lips looking over Alex's shoulder, "Hee, hee, hee, hee, I thought a house dropped on that one." Alex glanced over her shoulder and laughed. Rebecca resembled an angel more than a witch. Alex's short, dirty blond bob and pale, Irish blue eyes made her feel plain in comparison to Rebecca. Rebecca's long silky, rich brown hair accented her flawless skin and floated through the air like a wave as she tossed it over her shoulder. Her large, beautiful chocolate brown eyes calmed and seduced any man, woman, or child when she chose. As long as she wasn't sporting her RBF (resting bitch face), she appeared to be an ethereal dream. However, when that RBF emerged, David was right, she was scary, and smart people ran or at least cowered in fear.

Like a five-foot-ten-inch gazelle towering over Alex's barely average height, Rebecca gracefully moved in closer. She scrunched up her face at David in a mock sneer, "Very funny, but that won't get you out of your checkup, bahahahaha." Rebecca's maniacal laugh echoed loudly against the cement. She snapped on her gloves, and comically raised her eyebrows up and down to emphasize her point, "Not so smug now, huh?"

David stuck out his tongue, reached out his arm, then turned his head away; his gruff voice playfully whined, "Pththt, scary witch, I only put up with ya because ya come with Alex." She took David vitals then started to unwrap the bandages on David's arm to check how the wound was healing.

Alex loved hearing David's stories, still squatting, she wrapped her arms around her knees, "All right why don't you finish telling me about your fishing trip with your dad?" He scrunched up his face and snarled at Rebecca, but Alex distracted David by reminding him, "You know you were telling me about fishing on the St. John's River, in Florida."

David beamed, and ignored the manhandling he received, "Oh yeah, now where was I?" Rebecca flashed a grateful smile while she finished bandaging up his arm. As he finished his story, Alex stood up to continue with her last delivery; David abruptly grabbed her arm and pulled her back down. Desperation laced his voice as well as the expression in his eyes, "Now don't you go wanderin' over near that Doug." Suddenly, realizing what he had done, he quickly released his grip on Alex. Rebecca moved in to separate David from Alex by jutting her arm between them and scowling.

Alex stumbled back, breathing in staggered breaths from the surprise of it. David acted out, silly and sometimes a little paranoid but he had never grabbed her. Fear and adrenaline flooded Alex with a momentary memory, but she was not that person anymore and she pushed it away, "David! What has gotten into you?"

David shamefully lowered his head, "Now you know I would never do anything to hurt you, and I'd never hurt a girl." As if he was unable to look directly at Alex, he stared right through her, toward Rebecca, "You know Ay'ed never do nothin' to hurt ya, right Alex?"

Alex nodded her head then grimly smiled, "I know David, but you shouldn't startle me like that. You tell us about Doug every time we're here. We are always careful, and he has never done anything but poke his head out and grab his food."

David bowed his head in humiliation and peeked up with narrowed eyes, "Humph, he is a bad man I'm telling ya, and I wish ya wouldn't go over there." He pouted then scurried back over to his box home with his food. The cats waited, impatiently meowing and brushing up against him, begging for their food. He poured out a line of dry cat food on the ground as several strays who had adopted David over the years raced over to eat.

Alex stood up straight but was still a little shaky from the sudden shift in David's behavior. As her favorite under the bridge resident, she felt almost a kinship with him and loved hearing his stories and listening to his relaxed little drawl, but she wasn't a fool and never extended the relationship beyond their current friendliness. Not allowing herself to be scared off by his crazy rants, she dismissed his warning, but they were short on time and they needed to leave before dark, so Alex quickly put Doug's food in front of his tent then called his name. They did not hear or see Doug, but he often chose not to show his face or even speak to them.

Could the place smell worse than usual today? She must be imagining it. Alex wanted to hurry if she was going to make it for her visit. Luckily, Rebecca helped push her along. Her sarcastic friend rolled her eyes and sneered, "You know, I'm so happy to help you but how do you do this all the time? I don't get it, couldn't you help at the soup kitchen or in the shelter? They should go there to eat instead of dragging the food over here."

While she knew Rebecca was only saying what was on her mind, sometimes Alex wanted to reach over and shake her, "You know these people will never leave this place to go over there, besides nobody else wants to come here. You want them to starve?" Like a lightbulb went off in her head, Alex brightened up then snickered and grinned at Rebecca, "Ahh, maybe that is why David thinks you are a witch."

Rebecca raised her eyebrows and glared, then gave Alex a gentle push, "Ba-ha-ha-ha, maybe he knows something you don't."

Alex was driven by an innate need to better the lives of others, but she had to negotiate or bribe Rebecca to accompany her on trips under the bridge. Today, to enlist her help, Alex played chauffeur and drove Rebecca to her parents' house where she parked her car. Before stepping over the threshold, Alex looked down to the worn welcome mat at the names Mr. and Dr. Martin, which were barely visible after years of use. Some things never changed. Together, they walked in, to the familiar sight of Rebecca's dad lounging in his recliner, listening to the news, several octaves too loudly, and her mom, Moira bustling around the house. Recently, Moira had taken up crafting to fill her time, and Alex saw the supplies strewn all over the dining room table. Rebecca grew annoyed every time she saw it, so Alex pushed her past it to the family room and kitchen. She did not want to hear Rebecca lecturing her mom again about going back to work. Rebecca glanced over at the table but ignored it, and instead of criticizing, said, "We brought you dinner!"

Rebecca's dad glanced up and smiled but staying seated, "You girls were careful, weren't you?"

"Yes Dad, we always are." Rebecca rolled her eyes at the question and gave each of her parents a kiss before walking to the kitchen to pull out four plates from the cabinet.

Alex knew Rebecca expected her to go to the gym that evening and had avoided saying anything about her own plans, but time was up and she needed to say something now. Alex looked down and prepared herself to deal with the snarky remarks that always sat at the edge of her friend's lips, "Not for me thank you; I am visiting my brother today, I need to get going."

Rebecca hesitated as her face contorted into a resentful scowl, "So you're taking your dinner to go? I feel used. Can't you go on nights when I don't plan for us to attend the kickboxing class? I didn't spend my afternoon exposing myself to hell and a shit ton of venereal disease so that I could spend the evening at the gym by myself." Alex noticed Moira roll her eyes at the comment and bite back a snicker. Not even Rebecca's own mom wanted to deal with the sarcasm and feisty debates her daughter's annoyance would bring for the rest of the visit. Alex should be used to it by now because both her brother and Rebecca regarded communication through sarcasm, argument, and heated debate a much more effective technique than polite conversation. Sometimes, Alex did not have the mental energy to tolerate it.

"Hey, you see this? Isn't that where your brother is incarcerated?" Everyone looked over at Moira pointing to the television as the camera panned over the scene across the front of a building where several people waited at the entrance.

Alex's shoulders slumped, and her face slacked, it felt like all the energy she had, instantly drained out of her. She nodded and sighed, "Yes, Moira." Even after all his months of incarceration, she hated admitting to herself or anyone else that Tristan was in prison.

The camera settled on the news reporter, a pert blond dressed a tight, low cut shirt and short skirt. Her big, perfect-toothed smile practically leaped off the screen. The camera zoomed into a close up of her perfect hair and slightly overly made-up face; she squeezed her microphone as she intently eyed and flirted with the camera, "According to sources at the Fulton Federal Penitentiary, visitors and family members of the incarcerated were turned away at the gate. These terrified loved ones received no explanation for the suspended visitation and had no recourse. Rumors run rampant about the facility and its current locked down state. What is the cause?

Have racial tensions risen to unmanageable levels or are we dealing with a murder? Is a full out riot imminent? Are rival gangs taking over the prison? This reporter reached out to the warden, assistant warden, and the chief of security for the prison, but as of yet, I've received no response. What are they hiding? This is Christy Gallagher reporting live, from Fulton State Penitentiary, more to come as this puzzling story unfolds."

Rebecca sneered in triumph in Alex's direction, "Well, I guess you aren't going there today. Now you can join me at the gym."

Thwap, thwap, thwap, Alex, powered herself toward the punching bag that Rebecca clutched and perspiration dripped down her face then ran off the tip of her nose. Gina squawked in the background, "Find your inner strength. Each punch should come from your core and follow through the bag. You don't need huge biceps to take down someone bigger than you. You can do it if you let your core do the work for you." Concentrate, Alex took a deep breath and closed her eyes. Then, as she punched the bag, she felt the power surge through her body and follow through the bag, with such force that Rebecca grabbed the bag to maintain her balance. Gina laughed in the background, "Now that is what I am talking about!"

Rebecca scowled and dismissively shrugged, "I guess I wasn't paying attention." She hated to lose, and Alex knew it. Rebecca defiantly widened her stance then put her shoulder into the bag, "Now try again, my little friend."

Alex grinned knowing exactly how to get under Rebecca's skin, "Uh huh, I am sure your lack of attention was the problem. Just admit you hate to lose, especially when the person beating you is a shrimp." She focused again on her punch then hit simultaneously with each word that came out of her mouth, "Size. Doesn't. Matter." Pausing to take a breath, Alex adjusted the headband holding the hair out of her face. She pulled down a small section of the sweat-laden hair to cover the scar on her cheek near her jawbone.

Rebecca sighed with an exasperated glare and put her hand on her hip, "Why do you do that?" Rebecca also knew how to get to Alex; they seemed to spend their time together trying to see who could annoy the other the most. Rebecca usually won.

Alex tilted her head and sighed, "Oh stop. You are annoyed that I almost knocked you down. You know why I keep it there, so you better grab that bag again before I knock you right on your butt."

Her stubborn friend shook her head. Rebecca refused to let the subject go, "It is there whether you cover it or not. If you hate it, get it taken care of, it is only a reminder to you." Rebecca hastily grabbed the punching bag, knowing that Alex would follow through on her threat, and heaven forbid she end up on the gym floor.

Alex held back a laugh at the thought of Rebecca sprawled out on the floor then; she refocused her energy toward her core muscles, squeezed, and rapidly punched, thwap, thwap, thwap. She hit the bag, continually, to the beat of the background music, hoping Rebecca would stop talking and concentrate on holding the bag. Alex wanted to brood and punch in silence but needed to defend herself, "Why do you think I leave it?"

Rebecca's forehead now glistened with perspiration from the effort of holding the punching bag, which inspired Alex to throw in a few kicks in as well. To Alex's relief, her friend said nothing for several minutes. The scar was a sore subject for Alex, and Rebecca seemed to bring it up every so often. Alex couldn't tell who the scar bothered more, her or Rebecca, maybe that was why she continued to bring it up. Finally, Rebecca spoke up but decided on a change of subject, "So, they aren't allowing any visitors in?"

Unfortunately, the topic of her brother's incarceration agitated Alex even more than the scar conversation. Rebecca knew how sensitive she felt about those topics, yet she continued to press her buttons on purpose. Alex wanted to scream at her friend that it was time to work out in silence, but managed to hold her annoyance inside and answered anyway, "The warden shut down the place and nobody will tell me anything, except, there wasn't a riot, yet they are still taking safety precautions, which means, no visitation. Now, I'm plagued with even more questions. They should make a public statement for everyone, instead of letting the news stir up such speculation. "

Rebecca adjusted her grip on the bag, "My company is contracted with their medical facility, and they may know what is happening in the rest of the prison. I know a few people in Facilities, and even though they don't love me, I will see if I can find out anything. I'll let you know about the shutdown tomorrow."

Alex wished she could kick herself sometimes. She realized that Rebecca wasn't trying to provoke her, the questions were meant to help. Sometimes Rebecca's snarky attitude caused others to assume the worst about her intentions, and at this point in their relationship Alex should know the difference, "Why did you wait to tell me that, can't you call them now?"

Rebecca shook her head, "Alex, when I told you they don't exactly love me over there, I put it mildly. The Facilities director hates me. I will need to make several calls. You know, I call someone, who knows someone that is friendly with the director, and then they call me back, on their schedule. I will find out something, but I have to wait, which means you wait too." Rebecca stared at Alex for a moment, then sighed, "Fine, don't give me that look; I guess I'll call someone tonight." Rebecca smiled and gestured to Alex encouraging her to continue with the workout, and grudgingly, Alex half-heartedly complied. Thwap, thwap, thwap, "Alex, you are pulling your punches. Focus."

Alex narrowed her eyes into little slits as she continued to hit the bag, "I am having a very difficult time doing that. I can't fully focus on anything while I'm thinking about Tristan in there. I need to know what is going on. He could be in the middle of trouble, and I wouldn't be able to do anything about it."

"Yeah, you won't be able to do anything if you know or not. It's too bad he got caught."

Alex shouldn't get angry when Rebecca only wanted to help but why couldn't she keep her mouth shut or at least show a little compassion; Alex dropped her gloves, "Jeez Rebecca! Heartless much?"

Rebecca let out a sigh and rolled her eyes slightly, "I didn't mean it like that. I know he is a hacker, not a murderer."

Alex's jaw dropped, "I am well aware of his crimes. After all these years, your insensitivity can still surprise me. If something is going on at the prison, people could get injured, and Tristan, as well as all the inmates, could potentially get hurt, especially if the problem is facility-wide."

Rebecca scoffed at her friend, "You are telling me you are worried about everyone, not just Tristan? Ugh, your bleeding heart is almost more than I can take. You know we are going to disagree on this matter. People make their own choices and get what they deserve in there." Rebecca leaned in closer before whispering, "After what happened to you, you should want every criminal shithead alive to suffer."

Breathing heavily, Alex turned and punched the bag, "What is wrong with you?!" She angrily stared at the confused expression on Rebecca's face before stomping off toward the shower room.

"Hey, it is my turn to hit!"

CHAPTER 2

Day 1- Later

Alex whipped open the gate to her apartment building, then marched herself through the courtyard. Usually, its tranquil ambiance provided in an immediate sense of relief from the outside world. Although a small space, it resembled a lazy village more than a condo courtyard in the nation's capital. The scent of the flowers and vegetation, the neatly arranged benches shaded by the large, full trees, the raised plant beds and the gentle trickling of the fountain usually soothed her soul. Today, even this beautiful little courtyard reminded Alex that she felt anything but peaceful. With a sigh, she held back the tears building up in her eyes and tried to ignore the clenching in her chest as she trudged forward toward her door. Alex mumbled to herself, "How could Rebecca be so insensitive? She tries to provoke me then pushes me away. She takes all her crap out on me, and sometimes I don't know how we've continued this friendship for all these years. She's my best friend yet she loves to push my buttons and torture me mercilessly. Rebecca is overly opinionated and judgmental. Her timing is awful, and she constantly reminds me that my brother is a criminal. What if he's in real trouble? What happened at Fulton that they'd stop letting visitors in?"

"Hey Alex, who are you talking to? Is that your phone ringing?"

Alex turned her head toward the voice, "Huh?" Completely caught up in her thoughts and the conversation with herself, Alex didn't hear the phone ringing or notice her neighbor Erika, sitting there. Her beautiful friend had perched herself on the edge of the courtyard fountain, and dangled her foot in the water, teasing the fish. Alex often joked with Erika that men purposely went to the E.R. just to get treated by her, so they could gaze up into her big brown eyes and hear her sexy accent. Alex pleasantly smiled even though it was difficult for her at the moment,

"Uh, oh thanks." She preferred that Erika not think of her as rude, then waved good night. Clumsily, she fumbled for the phone without glancing at the incoming number. Hustling into her apartment, she slammed the door with her foot before answering.

"Hey Alex, I only have sixty seconds."

"Tristan, oh my God, are you okay?" Alex haphazardly dropped her bag near the front door in the hall. She'd been waiting for this call. Her hands shook revealing her nervousness, as she tried to grip her phone.

"Calm down lil' sis, I'm fine."

"What is going on? I heard the news about suspended visitation and the Fulton office confirmed it but wouldn't tell me anything else."

"I am sorry, baby girl, but I don't even know what is going on. I can only repeat rumors, and they suggest that the high-security side of the prison is having trouble, not mine. I am in club fed, which is much safer than you feeding the homeless under that bridge. You're careful, right?"

"Seriously, Tristan? I'm going crazy, clueless about what is happening to you and you change the subject to lecture me? I am not a little girl anymore and can take care of myself. You, on the other hand, are stuck in prison and are a little girl compared to some of those, those, giant thugs in there. They could eat you alive."

Tristan casually grunted, "Whoa, watch the harsh language. Don't worry; they all stay away from me because they think I am crazy." He chuckled trying to break the tension, "The place is practically locked down, so nothing is going to happen to me. Besides you aren't supposed to worry about me, it is my job to worry about you. You are the best thing I have left in this world. You are stuck with me lil' sis and while I can't physically be there for you right now, I will always want to watch out for you. Ugh, my time is up, I love you lil' sis."

Alex gripped the phone harder and took a deep breath, as she thought to herself, then you shouldn't have been doing something to get yourself locked up. The line suddenly went dead, "I love you too Tristan," she whispered, gently ending the call. Tristan probably lied about everything on the other side of the prison to make her feel better. She looked down at her hands and began to pick at her cuticles. His idea of safety and hers conflicted, and a little of the rage from earlier in the evening budded toward her brother, *Asshole.* How dare he question her choices? His weren't stellar and now look where he is. They were supposed to stick together. Both their parents spent their lives helping others, so why should she or anyone else do any less? They weren't here anymore, and he got himself locked up, and now the responsibility to help others lay on her. Alex shook her head trying to let go of the clenched feelings that had built up in her stomach and chest over the last hour. She had almost missed the call because of her brooding, and besides, he was okay, or at least he said so. She realized her frustration had nothing to do with Rebecca or

Tristan and she overreacted to both of them. Her feelings reflected the overwhelming sense of helplessness over this entire situation, and she detested all her overblown internal drama because of it.

Alex showered and changed into her comfy yoga pants, then curled up under her blanket in her cozy little living room. Cozy, the word Tristan used for small, but she loved it, and not just because it was hers but because he bought it for her. Sometimes she experienced radical pangs of guilt that she lived in this adorable little place while he was stuck in prison. His whole situation confused her. Tristan's reputation in the I.T. world commanded respect. Wasn't success enough? Why did he break into government computer systems? She clenched her jaw every time she thought about it, but prison was only temporary. He plead guilty, got 18 months, and would be out before she knew it.

She snuggled deeper into the overstuffed couch, a place she sometimes slept. It cuddled her like a big bear hug. Alex looked over at the potted dwarf orange tree Tristan gave her that hid the humidifier and sat in the corner near the south-facing window that contained her small herb garden. The smell of the fruit turning from green to orange filled the living space, and when she closed her eyes, she imagined herself outside, in the country. Tending to her plants helped her feel at peace with the world, especially when the world slept away and her own sleep needs dictated getting only four hours a night. She hated to waste time waiting for the rest of the world to wake up, and tending to her plants helped her feel her time was well spent. One day she would get a large plot of land similar to Rebecca's and care for an entire garden of plants and vegetables.

Alex sighed, she detested fighting with Rebecca but sometimes the woman overstepped. She didn't need constant reminding that her brother was a criminal. Rebecca also did not need to remind her of what happened all those years ago when she got her scar. The event had burned itself into her memory. *Rebecca is just insensitive and didn't mean anything by it.*

Alex began to think about the important stuff in her life, a habit she used to avoid dealing with immediate issues. As a young girl, she feared growing up to be a mediocre person living a mediocre life. She'd focus on it, pontificate on it, and wrote comprehensive plans about achieving a remarkable life in her little journals. Alex chuckled to herself; the poetry in her journals explored what she considered, at the time, "the depths of her soul." Ridiculous, but at least it filled her with a sense of purpose. If the world improved because of something she did, then she'd escape a life of mediocrity. However, all of her dreaming and planning was a foolish extravagance with what soon followed in her life. Daddy died because of his desire to assist others and at the hand of men who lived a world away, by people who needed the most help. She couldn't forgive those terrorists, yet still, she needed an alternative to defeat the mediocrity. When Alex suffered her attack, she lost her bravery and knew that no amount of dreaming would help change the world to a better place, so she settled on assisting those nearest her. Now she was living the very ordinary life she feared most. Even knowing she made a difference, it still felt empty, especially on a night like tonight when she fought with her best friend. The loneliness was exaggerated. Rebecca, beautiful, huge-hearted and exceptional at everything she did, except interacting with people or relating to their feelings. She and Rebecca were polar opposites but together they would make one outstanding individual.

Arrgh, Alex, such a hypersensitive, emotional pain in the ass. Rebecca gripped the steering wheel of her car. The headlights peered down the road and flashed by towering oaks and pines that lined the highway. The nighttime drive to Dashcorp's facility flew by quickly compared to her daytime trip, and the drizzling rain and empty roadways sheathed the dark in mystery. At night, nobody came out to this part of the countryside. Countryside, the term did not really apply to any place located so close to D.C. but it appropriately described the landscape. Anywhere with nature and the woods, Rebecca's favorite place, second only to her lab, inspired her creativity and calmed her soul. The roads in the area lacked streetlights, which gave it a lonesome aura, a perfectly invigorating atmosphere for Rebecca. She spent hours and hours in the quiet of her lab, superlatively content; thus the wet, empty road lined with an expanse of woods, filled her with glee. The peaceful drive gave her time to think.

Rebecca knew Alex thought of her as a savior, but she couldn't be whom Alex wanted. She happened along to the right place at the wrong time. She needed Alex though, without Alex as her friend she would feel utterly alone. The fools she worked with only tolerated her because she delivered. They understood very little about what she did, and the more she thought about it the more irritated she became. Rebecca absent-mindedly rubbed the pendant hanging around her neck as she pulled up to the one traffic light between the town and the facility, located right before the oddly placed restaurant and funeral home. It's location never made any sense to her. Studying herself in the mirror while she waited for the light to change, her slender fingers smoothed down her long dark hair into its ponytail then she applied some lipstick, "Good enough." She pushed the visor mirror closed before the light changed, "I don't understand, we know Tristan is in jail, it isn't a secret. She says I am judgmental, but I'm making an observation, not a judgment." Rebecca glimpsed at the car next to her, a strange sight at this time of night. The driver stared at her and smiled as she kept talking to herself. She raised her hand to her ear pretending she was speaking to someone on the phone, "We all have to live with the choices we make in life. I live with mine. Why is it so difficult for others to live with theirs? They should just accept the fact that, when you do stupid things, you may be caught. Alex got caught by thugs, I got caught in the middle of bombs, and Tristan got caught hacking. Nobody cares about all the good stuff you do. Alex is the perfect example of that." Rebecca audibly sighed and stepped on the gas as the light changed.

As she sped toward Dashcorp, she wondered who had called the emergency meeting. In her mind, the only thing that would warrant an emergency meeting was a breach in her lab. Otherwise, why not wait until morning? Seven years in her current position and she was rarely called in for emergency meetings. Most the time the emergencies did not apply to her or her projects. At least Rebecca wouldn't need to feign sleep tonight; there was always too much to do to, and besides, she didn't need it anyway. It was an attribute that she, Alex, and Tristan all shared. For the most part, Rebecca enjoyed being awake for the long hours, although sometimes her headaches increased in frequency when she stayed awake for too long. Lately, the debilitating headaches had been interrupting her work, absolutely unacceptable.

Rebecca pulled into a parking spot not far from the front door. Now she needed to put on the pleasant face because meetings required cooperation, a trait she wrestled with, and the RBF just got in the way. As long as she remembered that nobody gave a crap about her, she could easily distance herself from her feelings, and everything would proceed more smoothly.

Tristan abhorred lying to Alex especially when she knew it but she worried too much already. If anyone in the low-security side of the prison developed whatever spread throughout the other side of the prison, anarchy would ensue, not only inside the prison but outside with Alex as well. Tristan's unrestricted bluntness extended to everyone on Earth, except Alex, so he lied to her to protect her. He felt the need to protect her since he failed so miserably in the past. The guilt had persisted all these years, and he didn't expect them to dissipate any time soon.

Closer to a dorm than a real prison his side of the prison was considered low-security, but with cells instead of dormitory style like other club-fed prisons. If a riot occurred, everyone there was in trouble. Remarkably, only a few guards worked there to maintain order if things got out of control and the cells wouldn't be able to protect anyone unless the cell doors were locked with each inmate safely inside. Tristan hung up the phone, peered back at the line of prisoners waiting their turn to use the phone, and then sighed before heading back to his cell. Surrounded by white-collar criminals, the tedium of the daily routine wearied even the most resilient, and he had never considered himself resilient. Back at the row of cells, Tristan plopped himself down on his bed then pretended to sleep.

Some days he didn't know how to survive his sentence. He envied the inmates allowed on the internet and near computers. His conviction was a mere a slap on the wrist but its parameters limited the use of computers while he remained incarcerated, and probably during his parole if he received it. His only recourse during parole would be to work for one of the government agencies that tried to recruit him for years before he was caught. For now, all his plans and ideas existed entirely in writing, or he mentally stored them. Unfortunately, by the time he got out, all his projects might suffer the same fate as the dinosaurs and die. Foolish miscalculations and languidness got him caught. Not the work itself, but the choice of clients, break your own rules and you suffer the consequences every time.

He heard someone talking to him. Men were continually talking to him when he tried to concentrate. He never had any privacy. One of the other inmates worked his way around the room gossiping and now stood before Tristan, trying to engage him. The poor fool evidently feared the unknown and dealt with it by talking to everyone and anyone with listening ears. Did they not understand he was trying to concentrate? Sometimes, these inmates acted more like cave dwellers than white-collar professionals, not because of the violence but in how clueless they were about everything around them. The guy gave the impression he was a complete pushover in here because he trusted the wrong people. Tristan empathized with him for some unknown reason, so he nodded intently and pretended to listen to the harmless guy, even if his constant chattering ground on Tristan's nerves. A million and one ways in the world to spend the day yet listening to trivial gossip tortured him the most. He couldn't wait until his verbose new friend left as the man jabbered on, "You know, all the other inmates say you are completely antisocial, and a bit of a loon but I don't think you are. We've been having a lovely conversation, and I think we will become great friends if the bug on the other side of the prison doesn't get us first that is. We could walk around the yard tomorrow if you like."

Tristan knew he was lonely when he realized his desperation for a friend caused him to not only listen but to defend himself when he usually didn't care, "I am not antisocial, I am socially resistant, meaning I prefer to spend time thinking by myself, nothing personal against you of course."

The guy laughed at Tristan's joke, "Oh, sure, I understand, I talk too much. You aren't the first person to say that, you just aren't mean about it that is all. Well, I will let you get back to your pondering, thanks for the chat." Humph, the man picked up on the hint and left, without getting insulted, maybe he is tolerable. If only he could take all the talk and quietly run it through his head, he'd be great.

Rebecca walked into the conference room, casually pulling on her lab coat. Fahim glanced up as she entered, but her usually calm, patient demeanor was nowhere in sight. Rebecca grew apprehensive at the woman's frantic pacing and the contorted expression on her face looked almost comical when Fahim pursed her lips before speaking, "Rebecca, so kind of you to join us." Rebecca intentionally lost the pleasant face she had pasted on before entering, and her stern grimace dared anyone else to question her. Fahim impassively ignored the glare and nodded her head toward the empty seat at the conference table. She admired the woman and allowed Fahim to manage her all these years because of that admiration, but the expression on her supervisor's face evoked serious concern.

Fahim straightened the bottom of her shirt as she inhaled slowly and deeply. Closing her eyes, she exhaled using the same theatrics, "The situation at Fulton Penitentiary is receiving a gross amount of local press. Our counterparts at the CDC feel the viral outbreak is a minor flu virus and we will resolve the matter over the next few days. Since our facilities and personnel can easily manage a small outbreak, they don't need to involve themselves. I am sure you saw the local press coverage of visitation suspension at Fulton Penitentiary. Christy Gallagher is stirring up all kinds of trouble before we've even investigated the situation, and now I will fill you in on what I know."

"Seven days ago Fulton Penitentiary, whom Dashcorp is contracted with to service their medical care, had one of its prisoners refuse to report to work duty. He declared he was suffering headaches, felt weak, feverish, and his muscle ached, by all accounts common cold or flu-like symptoms. By the time, he reported to the infirmary he had developed additional symptoms, and within several hours, another prisoner had reported symptoms following the same pattern. These two prisoners did not interact at any time during their normal routines. Within two days, fourteen more prisoners reported to the clinic and our on-site medical personnel, unable to manage the onslaught of patients checking into the clinic, contacted the main office about the situation. Since then, new uncharacteristic viral symptoms emerged, and fatalities began yesterday. We don't want to lose control of the situation, or bring in the CDC."

Every time Fahim mentioned Fulton Penitentiary, Rebecca drifted to the fact it was Tristan's facility. These meetings took far too much time, but as soon as the special committee or assemblage of verbosity, as Rebecca called it, established itself, each department typically returned to normal duties. She simply needed to sustain her patience long enough that each of the long-winded department heads, vying for attention could have their voices heard. Their completely annoying desperation wasted everyone's time, and her exasperation required containment if she wanted to return to her own projects quickly. Did they not understand the more they said, the higher the probability they volunteered themselves for the assemblage of verbosity? Each one of them thought of her as an intolerant bitch. If she spoke up trying to effectualize the meeting, it undermined Fahim, which she didn't want to do, and it also encouraged her blathering co-workers to continue their rants.

Rebecca acted like she was listening intently to the conversation. She knew the assemblage of verbosity only needed to choose and assign its members, and Fahim seemed like she was ready to hear input, "...as directors of your departments...," Fahim stopped mid-sentence and peered toward the open door of the conference room. As each director turned, CEO, Dr. Brent Adams leaned against the door jam, listening. "Call me Brent," he always said, when someone addressed him formally. Some found his perfectly starched shirt and contrasting casual attributes like his wavy, slightly rumpled hair and cocky smile, charming, but Rebecca avoided him like the plague. He never appeared to have a care in the world. How did a man with the number of remarkable responsibilities he had let himself appear as such a lackadaisical leader? He slowly took a deep breath, and delivered a dazzling smile, "Go on, I don't mean to impose."

Fahim nodded and continued momentarily, only to be abruptly interrupted as Brent cleared his throat. Fahim looked up as all the department heads, except Rebecca, turned toward Brent. *Go on he says, why doesn't he just join the meeting?* "Do we really need all the department heads for a little viral break out?" Rebecca turned toward Brent, whom she saw at least made a little sense today. Brent was staring directly at her, and she glared directly back at him. The corners of his mouth went up as he cocked his head, and Rebecca responded with the tight-lipped smile she used during meetings to seem less intimidating. Brent continued, "Facilities and one or two others are perfectly capable of managing the situation. Publicity will also work to clean up the ugly face Christy Gallagher has put on of our facilities department and everyone else can get on with their evening."

Rebecca smiled to herself. He single-handedly saved them all from butting heads and wasting time. As everyone exited the room Brent remained in the same spot, people needed to walk around him to get out, and he nodded pleasantly to each person as they scooted past. A dominance play? As Rebecca turned and started for the door to make her escape, she caught Brent staring at her, again. He smiled his charming grin, "Rebecca, I think you will join the special committee team."

Stopping abruptly, Rebecca faced Brent, "What?" Everyone else stopped to watch too, and some turned around and peeked back in the door. Rebecca smiled inside, instantly seeing an opportunity to help herself and Alex. *Hmmm, maybe Tristan could get a small reprieve from his cell at Fulton.* "Me? Why do you want me to join this team?" Everyone knew she'd never readily agreed to work on a special committee so she couldn't agree without a fight and openly glared, "I am never on these teams for a reason and I'm not an Epidemiologist." She glanced over at Judy and Nithi and sensed her nostrils flare. Her scrunched up in pure disgust, and try as she might she couldn't pull it back.

"Just because your degrees and work aren't currently in Epidemiology or Virology doesn't mean you aren't well suited to work in that field. I know you resolved several seemingly complex situations for us in the past, and I want the bad publicity to disappear, immediately."

She huffed, "I did that stuff when I was a tech many years ago, and nobody else can do my research, it will bring my project to a halt." Seeing Judy and Nithi reminded her why she never wasted time on special committees, no matter what the benefits were. Judy bumbled around organizing papers and talking quietly to Nithi. It surprised Rebecca that such methodical work could be capably executed by a complete scatterbrain, but Judy's meticulous work spoke for itself. The two looked ridiculous standing together, similar to a ball and a bat. Judy, short and round with pasty white skin and mousy hair, chittering away as though she was waiting for her knitting club to start. Everyone else liked her. Externally, her pleasant attitude and constant hugging ingratiated most people but she talked incessantly which perturbed Rebecca. And Nithi, skinny and while not tall still towered over Judy. His dark skin and hair blatantly contrasted with his mentor, and he constantly bowed his head submissively at Judy's blathering. He followed her around unable to make a decision without her. Ugh, best friends, more akin to co-dependent symbionts feeding off each other's neediness. Rebecca's private little joke forced an unintended half grin on her lips, too bad nobody would ever hear it.

Rebecca hated having to listen to their ineffective discussions and liked to get the job done quickly. She usually used her wit and sarcasm to alienate people, and then laughed about it later, even though inside she wished to act differently. Rebecca's self-imposed autonomy paved a more natural path for her than the verbal filter and time it took to work well in these committees. Her schedule required too much to deal with other people's petty egos, so she bared the self-imposed autonomy defiantly.

"Wonderful, this investigation will be simple for you then, since I am sure your expertise has grown these past years. Occasionally getting out of the lab is good for a researcher," Brent pompously leaned in, "and we all know that you work on much more than Bioinformatics in that lab of yours. I certainly don't want to slow down your project, but this little viral outbreak will only take you a few days, then you can run back to your lab."

In her most condescending look and tone, Rebecca took a step toward Brent and lowered her voice, "The work I do is far too important." Then, to emphasize her point, Rebecca narrowed her eyes and glowered before she continued, "My work is classified and nobody can fill in for me. We will fall behind schedule." The audacity of her abrupt arrogant comment shocked everyone in the room including herself. Rebecca stole another glimpse at Judy and Nithi. Their mouths hung open. Rebecca wanted to be assigned to this committee and found Judy and Nithi's reaction humorous, but they didn't need to know why. Judy's expression betrayed the woman's seething inside. Their strong objection to working with her was evident, but she probably could stop objecting now. She'd already put on a good enough show. Judy caught herself with her mouth agape and delivered Rebecca a friendly grin, and Nithi responded with a smile and tight-lipped bow. Rebecca coldly nodded in their direction.

Brent smirked, but she saw the irritation growing in his eyes, "Not a request." He sauntered over toward the table and pulled out a chair right in front of her, Rebecca turned to sit in acquiescence but quickly saw he wasn't pulling the chair out for her. Another power play? Brent settled himself down in it then plunked his feet up on the conference table. He lazily leaned his head in the direction of the door and others still in the room and with a hand swipe shooed the uninvolved staff on their way. "In fact, I think you would make the perfect leader of our little focus team." With a chuckle and a grin he added, "I can see a great growth opportunity for you and maybe your colleagues as well."

Even better, but after their display toward her, she resolved to torture them as soon as the opportunity arose. She knew Brent wasn't changing his mind; she could see the resolve in the expression in his eyes but had to add at least one more dig at Judy and Nithi. She leaned on the table and bent toward Brent, "I am sure you do, however, if you utilize a researcher more accustomed to the methodical nature of tedious facility projects, we will all be happier. One whose skills are more apt to benefit an institutional environment." She saw Judy and Nithi nodding in the background, they didn't get her humor but at least they agreed with her.

Brent smiled again as he shook his head, "I always put my best on special projects and committees, no matter how joyous they feel about a project, and I heard you are an extremely competent researcher with experience in resolving problems quickly." He tapped her hand matter of factly, smirked, then stood up and sauntered out of the conference room, conversation over.

Rebecca felt a surprising admiration for the man. She had no idea he was so sadistic, "Alright, Judy and Nithi today has been a long day already. Let's not make it a long night too." With the boss gone Judy didn't bother to hide her animosity, and delivered an icy cold stare as she dropped a pile of papers on the table in front of a seat.

CHAPTER 3

Day 2

Rebecca glimpsed behind her and sighed before entering the Medical quarantine tent. She spotted Judy and Nithi ambling in from the parking lot behind her, toting rolling suitcases behind them. They looked like they were going on a vacation. She played nice, well, as nice as possible, but found their tedious discussion on procedure and unnecessary detail draining. Nobody loved an exhaustively verbose conference as much as those two. They demanded a discussion on the probable scenarios and what-ifs, ad nauseam. Why did they waste their time with such useless information when decisions needed to wait until all the information on the situation was thoroughly examined? After listening to the two of them for hours, Rebecca could no longer choose the proper diplomatic response to listen attentively, as the effort to steer the conversation toward constructiveness met its end. She felt like she was experiencing the beginnings of her own personal hell in that meeting.

Around midnight, Rebecca authoritatively stepped in and delivered a thorough breakdown of the following day's strategy. The appalled expressions on their faces satisfied her bursting annoyance, but her patience had faded ages before she interceded, and her declaration took about two minutes. Rebecca knew she could be a difficult person, but she wasn't cruel and didn't feel like she should be subjected to cruelty either. Compromising her time when she knew of a much more efficient option was brutality at its worse. The promise of future meetings and discussions after the next day's investigation pacified them, but that too required discussion. She'd endured enough, and couldn't stand another word. As she stood up to leave, she pointed to the paperwork on the table and asked, "You got this right?" She couldn't tell if they were happier to play with more paperwork or get rid of her, but she didn't care because today was a new day and it was now time to focus on critical developments. She had re-adjusted her plans and work enough already, but she wasn't going to change her style of working too.

A grumbled voice from the past interrupted Rebecca's thoughts, "Aye! We've not seen ye since ye got promoted ta projects research. Ye slummin' here with us today, huh?"

Rebecca recognized that rough Scottish accent anywhere and she turned and grinned widely, "Oh I am getting to relive my days as a lowly tech and figure out what is going on here since the current staffing is so inept." Several techs turned and glared at her comment, making it even funnier to her. She couldn't help if they weren't capable of dealing with the problem and management requested that she lead the investigation. Eventually they'd warm up to her or she'd scare them into compliance, either way, they'd respect her brilliance in the end. If only people found her as funny as she found herself, she'd say the thought aloud, but people rarely understood her sense of humor.

Abe was the man that everyone wanted to work with, including all the techs, but to Rebecca, he was more of an uncle than a co-worker. Always a hugger, he leaned in for a giant bear hug and despite Rebecca's hatred of such emotional displays, she tolerated it from him because she'd known Abe for as long as she could remember. He worked in infectious pathogen research with her mother, even when Rebecca was a child. He taught and trained her when she interned as a graduate student then supervised her when she interned as a postgraduate. Abe taught her to look beyond the evidence of strains and samples to the lives of the infected. His sparkling green eyes and easy smile softened his sizeable beast-like presence and big hairy face. Abe grunted, "You mean the inept, like me? Rebecca always a smart arse! It is nice to see ye but must ye scare my techs as soon as ye walk in?"

As if arriving home after a long trip, Rebecca admired the temporary medical tent's interior that Dashcorp erected outside of Fulton Penitentiary's infirmary. Every object, all the materials, and scientific apparatus were neatly arranged and belonged in the same place it all had since she interned many years ago, "I see nothing changed since my last visit." The glint in his eyes divulged more than he was saying, and he glanced over to a workstation set up exactly the way Rebecca liked it. It was obvious he had anticipated her arrival. Rebecca knowingly squinted, "You can't fool me, old man. You knew I was coming, didn't you? How is that possible, did you request me? How does a lowly tech such as yourself acquire such an immense amount of pull?" Every lab technician coming into Dashcorp knew of Abe and wanted to work with him, management respected him, but still, she loved to tease him.

Abe roared with laughter, dipping his head back and holding his middle. He resembled a Scottish Santa in a lab coat, "I knew ye'd figure out it out, but I figured ye'd take at least a few minutes longer though."

Judy waddled over with Nithi following her, and the pair stood behind the Abe and Rebecca listening in. Judy's face morphed into with a contorted, confused expression, as she cocked her head to the side and blurted out, "You requested Rebecca?" She quickly covered her mouth at her conspicuous snafu. Rebecca knew Abe heard it and even understood why Judy had said it. Rebecca's personality often turned people off; however, her results always impressed both management and techs alike. Rebecca knew she appeared indifferent to others' opinions of her, but Judy was concerned about how people perceived her and would probably spend the rest of the investigation trying to ingratiate Abe after that slip-up.

Abe and Rebecca glanced at each other and snickered as Judy blushed. She did not understand their past but knew she had blundered. Abe pointedly looked at Judy then nodded, "It is nice to meet you in person Mrs. Samanski and Mr. Almeda. Yes, I did request, Dr. Martin, Rebecca is,..." Abe paused, searching for the right words, "...uh, quite direct and decisive, but she also deciphers and solves field issues more expeditiously than anyone I've ever met. I wish I could talk her into coming back to my department permanently, but she got promoted into her current position at such a young age because of those investigative abilities. Not like us old folks slaving for years just to be noticed, huh?" Abe elbowed Judy in a friendly gentle manner, emphasizing the inclusive 'we.' Then he motioned to a table in the corner, "Ye can set up your paperwork over there. Will either of ye join us in the infirmary today, or do ye prefer to analyze the data from the corner? Ye seem like such a people person Mrs. Samanski; I bet those inmates would love visiting a friendly las such as yourself."

Judy and Nithi's faces reddened and she turned away as they both simultaneously shook their heads. Neither were experienced in Epidemiology or any other type of biohazardous environment or fieldwork. Did Abe know that? Sheepishly, they hauled their wheeled luggage behind them, over to the table in the corner. Rebecca smiled, "You didn't need to say all those nice things you know. I've been assigned to this facilities flub, and I can't get out of it." Rebecca paused and studied Abe's face, "But you know all about that don't you?"

Abe placed his hand on Rebecca's back and gently guided her to the hazmat closet and prep station, "Oh, I spouted lies, all lies, and I didn't mean a word of it. Ye are far too much work for me to want ye back here. I only said it to make dealing with Twiddle Dee and Twiddle Dumb over there easier for me."

The banter with Abe lifted Rebecca's spirits every time they were together and she snickered, "Ha, those names are going to stick for a while, but as long as you had a sufficient reason for all the lies. How did you get me assigned here? I noticed that you ignored my question before."

"Ahh, ye got me there. I hoped to keep the secret to myself a little longer, though I guess you're goin' to get it out ah me, eventually. I've known Dr. Adams since he was a wee lad. His father and I went to school together, and now the boy consults with me regularly." Abe leaned in closer and proudly nodded, "I am a mentor to him."

Unable to resist the fodder, Rebecca snorted, "There are so many funny things about all you just said. Where do I start?" She affectionately put her hand on his shoulder, "If you're his mentor and he consults with you as often as you imply, why don't you use your pull to get into a more prestigious job?" Rebecca knew Abe would never leave fieldwork, he shined in this environment, "And most importantly, boy? You call the CEO of Dashcorp, a huge multinational research company, located all over the world, boy? Ha, I cannot wait to get down to the water cooler to spread that one about."

"Ha, ha, ha! We sure do miss your sense of humor around here," his laughter stopped abruptly, "and by we, I mean me, of course, nobody else likes it." She grinned at his little dig while he continued, "Ahh, but my dear Rebecca, you're meant for much bigger things than us lowly techs. Ye know I loathed my days in the office, same as your mum. I live for days in the field and the lab, researchin' and figurin' out problems. However, most importantly, I will call that boy anythin' I damn well please. Why don't ya spread that at the water cooler, the one I am sure ye frequent?"

Rebecca giggled and motioned subtly with her head toward Judy and Nithi, "Not everyone over in corporate appreciates my sense of humor either."

"Pthh, those two? Your humor is merely over their heads, and ye've changed if ye started carin' about others appreciatin' your sense of humor. Don't change a thing or I'll think one of those bacteria ye are so fond of has crawled into yer brain and takin' over."

Rebecca scrunched up her face, "Don't worry, I still don't care, but I keep getting stuck with the Twiddle Dees and Twiddle Dumbs of the world, which is why I prefer my bacteria."

He nodded, paused and firmly pressed his lips together, "Uhh, not to change the subject, but I am dying to ask, how is yer dad?"

The conversation eventually turned to her family every time they spoke, yet still, she loathed answering the questions, "My dad is still sitting in the same chair that he has been in since he got out of the hospital after 911, he can't stop watching the news, waiting for another terrorist attack."

Abe scratched his beard and shook his head, "Oh, I am sorry to hear that. Seventeen years is a long time to sit in a chair, PTSD can ruin you. How about yer mum? We miss her around here."

Rebecca sighed, wishing she had better news of her mom, "She is at home taking care of my dad. He is useless since 911, and now she can't ignore the problem anymore. I worry about her since she retired."

24

"Ye worry about her, now? Now that she is home? " Abe paused and netted his bows with a confused look on his face, "All those years in the field and lab handling infectious viruses and bacteria and ye worry about her now?"

Rebecca sighed, "She thrived working in the field. She never wanted to be anywhere else, and she got to help people. At home, she has taken up baking, wood burning, crafting, and scrapbooking. Who does scrapbooking anymore? Everything is digital."

The conversation went the same way each time and Abe sighed as he gently placed his hand on Rebecca's shoulder, "Well now she is helpin' your dad by being there. Your mum never took on anything she couldn't handle, except ye of course." He grinned at his last dig, proud he got another one in before the conversation changed.

Rebecca ignored his attempt to lighten the conversation. Rarely did she allow her emotions to show, but Abe understood even if Rebecca resented it, "She shouldn't need to take care of him."

Rebecca's thoughts drifted back to the day that changed everything. She was sitting at the breakfast table and her Dad grinned as he placed the omelet on her plate, proud of himself, "Don't tell mom I let you sleep in now." The smell of the onion, potato, and egg omelet filled the kitchen and the television played in the background. The dishes piled up in the sink like they always did when Dad cooked.

Rebecca moved the food around on her plate, "Aren't you late for work?" Rebecca didn't care because she enjoyed their time together but she needed to at least act concerned. She'd be happy if he never went into the office ever again, "Weren't you supposed to go up last night and meet them this morning?"

Her Dad smiled a loving grin filled warmth, "Don't you worry about that sweetie. I'll shuttle up to the city for the meeting this afternoon. I am going to take the train in so I can get some work done. I am meeting your Uncle and Grandfather at their office in the twin towers, I'll get home somewhat late, but I will see you in the morning. It was silly to stay overnight when I can easily move the meeting, and then I also get to eat breakfast with my favorite little girl."

Rebecca rolled her eyes. She loved it when he said stuff like that but still protested, "Da-a-d, I am almost fifteen, practically a grown woman, you can't keep calling me your little girl." She grinned at him, "but I appreciate the eggs and the extra shut-eye. I will miss my programming class this morning, but I can easily do that one in my sleep."

"You will always be my little girl Rebecca, no matter what or how old you get. But I think you sound a little over-confidence with talk like that. Can't you take it down a notch?" She grinned and shrugged her shoulders. Then, he shook his head, "I know you and your mom were up late working on some project. I don't understand why you had to work so late on it when it isn't due for weeks. Didn't you just get it?"

"Oh come on Dad, you know I get too excited to wait. I have to make my projects as extravagant as possible. I am the youngest senior this year, and they expect fantastic things out of me, not to mention, my teacher is amazing!"

"Ha, ha, ha. You sound the same as your mom did when she was in school. When she discussed her grad work, I didn't understand what she was saying most the time. Try to keep your old man from feeling lost as you get older and tell me about it in English instead of science-gab when you're done." Her Dad abruptly stopped and dropped open his jaw while staring at the television. He staggered into the family room and it turned up. The News report showed a close-up video of an airplane crashing into the World Trade Center and flames engulfing the top floor and erupting from all sides. His ragged breath caught in his throat as he panted, "Is-is-is this real?"

"What's wrong?" Rebecca turned around to see what he was doing and dropped her fork as the news replayed the first plane crashing into the World Trade Center. That day changed everything for the world but hit Rebecca even closer to home, her uncle and grandfather died in the tower; shortly thereafter, her father had a heart attack on the floor of the family room while watching the news coverage.

Rebecca's dad's spirit died with his brother and father that day and to make matters worse, he suffered a break down along with his heart attack. He lost the core of his family and countless friends. After that, haunted by his memories and the demons that took over his mind, they rarely discussed much of anything. Rebecca's anger and guilt after all these years morphed into a sense of sadness when her mom retired to take care of her dad. She sighed and dismally looked at Abe while she shook her head to push the memory from her mind, "After seventeen years, I don't think dad's self-imposed confinement will ever end."

Abe frowned, "Aye but he's a good man, and Moira loves him. Ye aren't the only one he deserted ya know. Are ye tryin' to tell me I should stop by and see her?"

Rebecca sneered to accommodate the change in conversation, "It took you long enough to get the hint, now let's get these pansy paper suits on."

As Rebecca eyed the suit, Abe teased her, "Pansy huh, ye remember how to do that, right?"

"Oh, I don't know if I can deal with these low tech suits, maybe I should have brought my big girl suit and showed you what a real hazmat suit is supposed to look like." She held it up and curled up her lip, "How do you not infected daily with these things?"

Abe laughed, and played along, trying to goad her, "Alright Miss High and Mighty, ye need me to help you with that suit, don't ye?"

The right side of Rebecca's mouth curled into a half-smile as she gently elbowed Abe, "I've missed you too." Rebecca tucked in her necklace under her shirt before she and Abe slipped their PE hazmat suits on over their clothing, careful not to poke holes or pull too hard even though the suits' material was quite sturdy. Before going through the heavy plastic door into the infirmary, Rebecca and Abe stood under the fans to blow outside particulates off their suits. She marched into the infirmary ready to work. It had already been converted to a series of individual isolation tents where the patients read, slept, and talked over-loudly to each other through the plastic. She pursed her lips second-guessing herself and wishing she'd reviewed the giant stack of reports, or at least listened to Twiddle Dee. Rebecca had no idea where they were at with the investigation. She'd put it out of her mind when she went home the night before.

Rebecca picked up to the first patients' chart as the prisoner smiled at her with a creepy, serial killer grin. He pulled against his restraints and reached toward her then stuck out his tongue and suggestively wiggled it, "Well, unless the protruding tongue and animalistic behavior is a symptom, which I doubt, he seems to suffer the symptoms of a juvenile miscreant, which is purely idiotic, since I am here to help him." His eyes darted back and forth, and he laughed maniacally at his own behavior.

Shaking his head, Abe scowled at the prisoner. "Try that again buddy and you will need several casts to go along with your antivirals." The man slowly pulled back, lay down on his bed and closed his eyes. The prideful look on Abe's face beamed of satisfaction until he glanced over at Rebecca, who stood holding a hypodermic needle in her hand and a grin on her face. He chuckled, "And here I thought I was still intimidatin' Ye shouldn't enjoy tranquilizin' patients that much ye know."

27

"Oh, he deserved it. I work on microscopic research for a reason, I prefer my patients quiet and less perverse."

Abe stepped between the obnoxious prisoner and Rebecca just in case he woke up but she reassured him, "Don't worry, with what I gave him he won't bother anyone for hours. Now let me see, the symptoms present as quite minimal, other than a slight flush and fever, several with Exophthalmos, and possibly Telangiectasia, no obvious signs of a unique or dangerous pathogen or any slow-acting poisons, especially a fatal one." Rebecca looked at Abe, "I see several antivirals and antibiotics listed here, so I guess you ruled out poisons, but I don't see which ones you tested for. Did you get involved with this before or after the med trucks came yesterday?"

He rolled his eyes at her, "Ye may be brilliant, but ye should seriously consider readin' a report once in a while, deary. I wrote those reports ye didn't bother to read. Ahh, it reminds me of the old days when ye were here. Of course, we tested for all known poisons, and the infirmary staff sent those tests to out the main facility days ago, all came back negative. In fact, nothing we can identify is showing up in their blood work. We started administerin' antivirals, as the antibiotics were ineffectual, but we cannot exactly figure out what the cause is. I wouldn't have requested your help otherwise." He grinned again and Rebecca knew he was about to say something snarky, "Ye know since your mum's not available." He paused, proud of his little jab and looked disappointed when Rebecca ignored it before continuing, "We excused the staff, then quarantined them in the main Dashcorp facility that you pretend to work out of. None show any symptoms, as of yet. The strange thing is we can't figure out how the pathogen is spreading. It seems improbable that the transmission is person to person. All the men's roommates were also quarantined separately. Several developed the fever and have since been moved into here, but just as many are completely symptom-free. We can't figure it out, hence the first testing series we did for poisons."

"Okay, I need fresh blood samples from each man quarantined, as well as all the expired patients, and the staff including guards who've been in contact with..."

Abe sighed, looking like the conversation with Rebecca exhausted him already, "Now before ye get your panties all in a bunch, why don't ye try reviewing the reports I already wrote up. I've done this a few times before ye know."

"That comment wasn't condescending or sexist at all, but fair enough, I should know better. Twiddle Dee and Twiddle Dumb have surely memorized all the information on every report by now. You know I prefer not to taint my conclusions with someone else's information, and I want the new samples for progressional comparisons to your previous work. Why don't you give me a quick rundown of those reports? I only want the relevant data and those things are so clogged up with extemporaneous information, I didn't even to bother reading them. I will compare the information to my own once I get the new samples back."

Abe scrunched up his face in disgust, "A fine waste of my time, it was. We followed standard protocol, and the reports contain the contact, transmission, contraction and fatality models. The symptoms, for the most part, follow the course of a fever one day, the next a slight flush, headaches, and then the veining begins to appear on the side of their face but does not develop into the full Telangiectasia until the third day. At that point, headache severity increases and the eyes begin to bulge. The patient suffers a stroke no matter what treatment we've tried and within a few hours or days, complete organ failure and dies. The only exceptions were the two fatalities in which the onset of a violent outburst coincided with immediate stage three symptoms, stroke then death. One man over in the corner has been alive for seven days without symptom progress past the Telangiectasia. The headaches have faded, and he seems fine."

"All personnel working and exposed to the patients were quarantined?"

Abe sighed, "Of course, all guards, as well as medical and administrative staff, this isn't my first rodeo. Have you forgotten who you are working with? Maybe I understand why Twiddle Dee and Twiddle Dumb can barely tolerate you, huh?"

"Ugh, I am sorry. I am accustomed to explaining each point to every person in exhausting detail. I forget who trained me. Let me examine a few of these men, especially the man with the halted symptoms and take a few of my own samples."

Abe grimaced, "Pthapt, ye aren't going to let the sample thing go are ye?"

Rebecca flashed the sweetest smile she could manage, "You know how I work Abe, what body part locations did you take epidermal scrapings and samples from?"

Abe looked a little uncomfortable, "Uhh from several spots on the veining, stool, blood, urine, as well as the inside of their noses and mouths."

Rebecca nodded her head, "Okay good, and I also want under their fingernails and ears."

"Those aren't procedural typicalities. Why would you consider those spots with these symptoms?"

"YOU trained me, remember? You must be getting lazy in your old age." Rebecca smiled at her joke, "Under their nails to see what they touched," she scrunched up her nose in disgust, "Men don't wash well. In their ears, because it is close to the veining site, and all the men present with veining in the same area, so maybe the point of contact or infection site is their ears."

Rebecca handed Abe a sheet of paper then acted as if her request were a standard part of the investigation, "I also want this prisoner sent over to the on-site quarantine isolation facility."

Abe perused the request, "He is not one of the ones exposed to the pathogen or showing symptoms. He isn't even on the exposed side of the prison."

She nodded and pointedly peered at Abe, "Yes, but I think he would be helpful in our case."

Abe grimaced at Rebecca, "A friend of yours?"

Rebecca stared down at her pad as if she was studying the information intently, and then shrugged her shoulders, "Important to a friend."

Abe smiled, "Nice to have you back Rebecca."

Rebecca glanced up from her pad, "Yeah, lucky for you, this pathogen is fascinating, so you are probably stuck with me a while."

CHAPTER 4

Day 2

E very day at work, Alex searched her heart to figure out if she was making a difference, and every day it felt like an uphill battle, with very few wins. At least when she fed the residents under the bridge, she got to see the looks of appreciation and knew they got at least one good meal a day. She knew the importance of her day job, why didn't everyone else see how vital housing was for everyone? Shelter, safety, and food were the basic necessities everyone needed to grow as a human being and develop into productive members of society. The vets, homeless families, and even addicts and criminals saw hope in the future when adequately housed. Although housing didn't help her brother, maybe if Tristan saw hope for the future, he would've taken a different path. No, she would not let her frustrations discourage her.

Alex ran into her friend, Katie, on the stairs. Katie was always such a pleasure to be around, happy with just enough wit. She smiled as Alex greeted her, "It feels like I haven't been to work forever."

Katie giggled as she held the stairway door open, "Seriously? I feel like I just left here. I must be doing something wrong."

Alex smiled in response, and she looked around the desks and cubicles lined on the slick tile floor of the office perfectly in a row. As if the department's trim, efficiency replaced the haphazard direction of the people's lives they helped. At least the waiting areas boasted some comfy leather couches and lamps to mirror a homey environment. She responded to Katie with one of her standard evasive replies, "Oh, I keep busy."

Stacey's freckled face shot up from her behind her cubicle wall as they walked by, "Oh did you go out on a date? I never hear about any of your romantic endeavors Alex." She imagined Stacey as a teenager, chasing after boys then grinned to herself.

Even as an adult, the woman wanted a man in her life all the time. Alex loved her work friends; their positive attitudes raised her spirits every time she saw them. If only she also loved her boss. Alex snickered and shook her head; she didn't need to tell them she hated dating.

Katie, not a woman who needed a man, yet she seemed to regularly enjoy the company of one, cocked her head to one side, "Really? Why not? You get asked out don't you?"

Alex bit her lip. She shunned conversations focused on her personal life, but it was inevitable when the other work conversations were so heavy and intense. These light discussions helped everyone maintain their upbeat outlook, "Oh, I guess I am picky."

Katie swung her hair over her shoulder, "You know I am going to tell you a secret, and I am not bragging here, but I get asked out all the time." Alex scrunched up her face about to try and redirect to another topic, but Katie cut her off, "Seriously, I know I am a little 'curvy', " Katie motioned finger quotes in the air, "but I know a secret, I know how to get them to overlook, all this." She smoothed her hand down over her waist and full hips, and then smiled an outlandishly toothy grin.

Alex grimaced, she had no use for dating but decided to humor her friend, just in case it was all leading to one of her preposterous jokes, "I think they want 'all that,' but okay, I'll bite, what is your secret?"

Grabbing a lock of her long, shiny brown hair, she ran her fingers down the length of it, stopped, then seductively gazed into Alex's eyes as if she was flirting with a man, "Men are easily distracted, and suckers for long pretty hair and a naturally made up face. They think I am gorgeous and we all know that if you act interested in what they say, they think you are brilliant. They don't care about anything but themselves, so I fain interest in their babbling, and I am usually the most interesting person they ever met because of it. You don't talk about yourself much, so it will be easy for you, all you do is ask a couple of questions, and they will chat your ear off all night long." As she finished, a grin overtook her face, and Alex couldn't tell if she was being serious or facetious.

Alex snorted out the laugh she had tried to hold back and could tell that the others in her office were startled by the sudden fit of giggles. Katie and Stacey joined in, which elicited an even more outrageous cackle from Alex. She still wasn't sure if Katie meant anything she just said, but it was too funny to dismiss. When Alex finally managed to stop snorting and giggling she asked, "I've heard that before, but don't you think men are a little more sophisticated than that?"

Again, Katie grinned then pointedly nodded and raised her eyebrows, "You would think so, wouldn't you, but don't be naive, if you want a date that is all you need to do."

"I think I'd rather remain alone. Forever. What did you do last night?"

"Okay, Little Miss Finicky, have it your way. Everyone, besides you, went for drinks, and you missed out! Ryan got hammered then sang Karaoke like a kid just out of college, Sheryl hooked up with a senator's aid, and I sat back, watched and laughed the whole night. Though, it is much more fun to sit with my buddy and make drunk sarcastic comments. It's a great way to blow off steam. You have to come with us next time."

"No date?"

"Uh no, I wanted some real fun, but of course, you didn't show."

"Ha, ha, ha, sorry I missed it, next time."

Katie paused at the conference room door and sighed, "Are you ready for this one?"

Alex shook her head and walked into her boss, Chad Power's, conference room. She knew the meeting would be arduous, and paused to prepare mentally. Her creepy boss and the new administration's policies were not supportive of HUD, but the department helped more people than the president could understand if he cared to.

That evening, Alex held out her glove for Rebecca to check, but didn't converse at all and instead stare blankly. The gym's hardcore group, as Rebecca liked to call it, never missed a class. Alex and Rebecca weren't part of the hardcore group yet still came as often as possible. Alex hit the bag weakly as Rebecca held it, droning on about something but Alex pretended to concentrate on her hitting, instead of listening. She wanted to escape, not be at the gym, enduring reality. She wanted to go home and take a nap, or at least pretend to, so she could temporarily ignore the drama of the last couple of days, and also avoid thinking about chad Powers and his repugnant request. Suddenly, filled with rage and all the strength she could muster, she swung at the bag with such force that Rebecca almost fell over, "Bastard!"

"What?" Rebecca's face scrunched up in a mix of confusion and annoyance, "You're really that mad at me? Come on. I said I was sorry, and I even put chocolate in your locker, time to get over it."

Alex looked at her friend quietly for a moment, "Says the woman who thinks everything is about her, at all times." She regretted snapping at Rebecca immediately and hoped it didn't bait her into another argument. Rebecca eyed her suspiciously but kept any response she may have had to herself. Relieved, Alex shook her head, "Oh it's not you."

"Well obviously."

Rebecca appeared more ornery than usual lately and Alex thought for sure they'd fight again before the evening ended, but when nothing happened, Alex sighed gratefully and went back to her rhythm of hitting the bag, thwap, thwap, thwap. Maybe the gym is the best place for her now, even better than a nap, getting out her frustrations and pretending the punching bag was Chad Power's face felt very therapeutic. Rebecca continued to babble on about something that Alex ignored. That manipulative, sexist, swine knew precisely which buttons to push and liked to wave that promotion over her head. She should be out of his slimy little reach by now, but without his recommendation, she'd never get the promotion. He wanted to keep her under his thumb, but with this new position, she could genuinely help people, in her way, and if Chad Powers tried to derail her again after his absurd request, she would take him down.

"Alex? Are you listening to me?"

She shook her head to bring herself back to reality, "Sorry, too busy concentrating." Rebecca's aggravated scowl penetrated her self-pity. Alex should feel bad about ignoring her friend, but she didn't for some reason. Maybe some of Rebecca's toughness rubbed off after all these years.

Rebecca's mouth hung open in faux astonishment, "Have you heard a word I said or do I need to repeat myself?"

They were both acting too surly, and Alex wasn't in the mood to be the ever patient listener, so she changed the subject, "Well, working out with you is an exciting way to spend an evening."

Distraction only worked when Rebecca allowed it, she never missed a thing, but today she seemed to welcome the change of subject, "Yes, I am fabulous aren't I?"

Rebecca loved to hear how extraordinary she was. For such a seemingly arrogant individual she constantly needed stroking. Alex rolled her eyes, "Ha! You have been completely unavailable for the last couple of days. You annoyed me, remember? You are supposed to kiss up to me more for being such an insensitive trollop yet you haven't made much of an effort."

Rebecca cocked her head to the side then scrunched up her face, "Funny, I brought you chocolate and even ignored your feeble attempts to divert my attention. I think I am kissing up extremely well." She never admitted to making a mistake nor allowed her true feelings to show, lest someone think she had a heart, but Alex knew the point would be lost on her best friend. Rebecca thought logic and rational, straightforward information paramount to all other interactions, no matter the cost, even if everyone around her hated her. "Work is busy," Rebecca wanted to change the subject now, shocking.

"Uhhmmm, okay." Ugh, time to move away from that topic, "You know, the chocolate you left for me isn't enough to buy me off. I want more, you know, if I am to ignore your insensitive nature."

Rebecca grinned, it was precisely the kind of interaction she craved, light debate coupled with sarcastic remarks, "Okay princess, how may I accommodate your highly sensitive nature so that we can get on with our lives?"

"Well, you can start with more chocolate and maybe a foot rub, a good one, and I also believe an opening is available in the schedule at the soup kitchen on Saturday."

The expression on Rebecca's face looked like she'd just bitten into a lemon, "Great." The tone sounded anything but excited, "Forget the foot rub, get yourself a boyfriend or hire a masseuse for that one. I know you threw that one in there just to sucker me into another round of Sister Rebecca helping the homeless, didn't you? When?"

Alex felt a satisfied smile spread across her face, "Bright and early at 8 A.M., and I know you love it."

"Oh yes, especially the lovely smells and pervy homeless men ogling me."

"Too bad, you conceded, and now you're committed to it." Alex paused and pouted a little, "Hey, you haven't even asked me about my brother, and we haven't spoken since the night of our little spat."

Mischievously, Rebecca half smiled and practically sang out the words as flirtatiously as possible, "I don't need to."

Alex leered at Rebecca and sighed. She could tell by the look on Rebecca's face there was no way out of a guessing game either, "What do you mean?"

Cryptically, Rebecca looked away, "I can't say."

Rebecca loved to make a dramatic show of leaking out information at her own pace. For information about Tristan she could temporarily forget her annoyance, so she jumped up and excitedly pushed Rebecca, knocking her down, "You found out something?"

The look of Rebecca's long arms and legs sprawled out on the gym mat like a fallen gazelle and the shocked expression on her face almost caused Alex to erupt with laughter. Both girls looked over in the direction of Gina who eyed them suspiciously. Rebecca innocently waved, and Gina shook her head, and then refocused on the students in front of her. Alex dropped down on the mat beside Rebecca, "Tell me!"

"Whomever do you speak of?" Rebecca shrugged her shoulders then pretended to adjust her gloves and smiled. Alex waited patiently while her friend tortured her, Tristan must be fine, then Rebecca reached out her gloved hand as if she were royalty waiting for assistance. Alex scrambled up, knocked her friend's hand out of the way, and waited with her hands on her hips. Finally, Rebecca conceded, "Any implications of such contact is considered breaching confidentiality and not in compliance with HIPPA laws or company procedures and therefore should get me out of volunteer work."

If Alex hadn't had boxing gloves covering her hands, she would have pulled her hair out while anxiously waiting, but the gloves made her feel like she was swatting herself, "You know I have been sick with worry." Rebecca smiled at the comedic display, and Alex understood why, she knew she looked ridiculous and awkward, but her heart was beating so rapidly it felt like it would jump out of her chest if she didn't get a direct answer soon.

"Sometimes Alex, you simply need to ask the right questions. Unfortunately, under serious repercussions from my company, I can only say I found nothing."

Alex fell back on the mat, covering her heart with her gloved hands and rolled her head around, "Uh, now you're just cruel."

"I may have submitted a request that certain patients move to a certain facility, one that I may or may not work at."

Alex jumped back up again and moved in Rebecca's direction, almost head-butted her friend, "Oh my God, is he sick? I saw the news report."

Rebecca put her hands up to protect herself but also smiled and shook her head, "Nope."

Alex began to lose her patience with her friend's evasiveness, "I can't believe you won't come out and tell me what is going on! Is he okay? Tell me more before I lose my mind!"

Rebecca rolled her eyes but finally surrendered, "Shhh, he is fine and at my facility. I can keep an eye on him while the facility shut down sorts itself out. I am trying to make arrangements for you to go see him."

Jumping on top of her friend, Alex accidentally smacked her in the head with her glove as she gave her a huge hug, one that Rebecca patiently tolerated, "Really, when? How long before you know?"

Rebecca sneered at Alex and rubbed the side of her head, "I will let that pass, but my little abuse of power at work and the punch in the head should get me out of playing Sister Rebecca Saturday." Alex obstinately shook her head and made a face at Rebecca's request, "Fine, I play Sister Rebecca, and I will let you know something when I do. Now shall we continue? Please get off me, grab the bag and let me have my turn to swing at it!"

She jumped up, "Just waiting for you." Alex clutched the bag then widened her stance, readying herself for the coming onslaught of punches. She would get to see Tristan soon, and as the relief washed over her, time slipped away with Alex in a daydreamy state. Whap, whap, whap, the punches were soft at first, but before long,

Alex needed pay attention and hang on tightly to the bag because of the intense force coming from Rebecca's punches. Alex shook her head to clear the inattentiveness, "Whoa, what did I miss? Five minutes ago we were rolling on the floor all happy, and now you are punching like you want to hurt someone. Since when are you so bipolar?"

"What?" The confused look on her friend's face morphed into conveying a sudden realization, Rebecca smacked her forehead with her gloved hand, "OMG, I am such an idiot."

Alex decided to humor her friend, after all, they were best friends, and she was helping with her brother, "Why is that? I thought you were omniscient."

"You smacked me too hard in the head then choked me while you hugged me, and it must have caused a small aneurysm. My infinite intellect repaired my brain telepathically but it took a couple of minutes, I am back to myself now. Thank you for that lovely smack in the head, but not even you and your dangerous hugs will take me down. I completely forgot to tell you, and it has been aggravating the heck out of me, guess who took an assignment to a dreaded assemblage of verbosity."

Rolling her eyes, Alex wanted to laugh, "A special committee?"

Rebecca scrunched up her face in disgust and nodded. Alex tried to hold back her grin, but could not, "Ha, ha, ha, and I thought you always got out of those." Rebecca prided herself on never serving on the special committees. Rebecca and her obnoxious renames, she needed to tell herself she was too important and superior to work on a trivial committee but apparently, she wasn't.

"I do, usually, but Fahim ran the meeting until Dr. Adams, Mr. Bigshot CEO, hijacked it. I had my reasons not to object, but now I get to work with two 'intellectual giants,' and they would prefer to work with anyone else in the company, other than me. I call them Twiddle Dee and Twiddle Dumb."

Alex could tell Rebecca was complaining just to brag about what she went through to help out with Tristan yet Alex appreciated it, "Ha, ha, ha, well that sounds like a disaster in the making, you are going to eat them alive. But why did Dr. Adams assign you, aren't you working on a special project of your own?"

Rebecca stopped for a moment, "Yes, but someone with influence requested my assistance in the matter. Now I am going to picture Twiddle Dee and Twiddle Dumb while I punch this bag." Whap, Whap, Whap.

Alex shook her head slowly and rolled her eyes, "You..."

Rebecca grinned, "Are you done gabbing so I can get to the point?" Alex nodded and motioned for her to proceed. Heaven forbid she interrupt with her own snarky comment, but she needed to let Rebecca continue, "Someone qualified needs to direct Nithi and Judy. They work well enough within the lines of clearly defined rules, but neither has ever worked on a pathogenic outbreak. I make them uncomfortable with my non-conformist approach to problem solving and my devastating wit; I am such a rebel. Brent needed someone direct, logical, and of extraordinary intellect, to speed the little investigation along and solve all their problems for them. You know, to show Twiddle Dee and Twiddle Dumb how managing a committee is properly addressed."

Alex gagged, "I think I just threw up in my mouth a little, keep telling yourself that."

Rebecca furrowed her eyebrows and scrunched up her face, "What are you twelve?" Both Alex and Rebecca burst out laughing.

Gina glared over at them, "Girls! Are we giggling or working out?"

Then, from the corner of her eye, Alex saw the news pop up on the television with a perky blond grasping onto a microphone filling the picture of the television screen.

Like clockwork every day, Judy drove home from work, stopped at the grocery store on the way home, and started dinner. Then, she'd have time to switch on the computer to review her emails and watch the news before her husband came in. He'd usually drop into his lounge chair until dinner complaining that being a mailman was such a physically exhausting job. Dealing with Rebecca on the special committee pushed her patience to its limit, but having to listen to her and Abe from the corner of the tent like a child in timeout completely humiliated her. All day, she looked forward to sitting down to her little evening routine. Judy scrolled through her emails, Nithi, of course, checked in on her; she could say almost anything to him. Concentrating on the emails became too difficult as thoughts about the special committee kept popping into her head. Ugh, she couldn't believe that Rebecca was leading the investigation. Judy resented Brent's decision because she just wanted the opportunity to prove herself. How was Rebecca the proper leader for a Facilities investigation? That woman! She probably didn't even go to church yet somehow God blessed her with everything, looks, smarts, and luck. Well, almost everything, nobody really liked her because she was kind of bitchy. Judy thought the two were becoming friendly last year when Rebecca came over for dinner, but no, nothing else happened. Rebecca went back to her snippy ways and they barely ever spoke. Most people liked Judy but Rebecca, that little heathen, went to work, to her lab and left, sometimes without talking to anyone. Maybe it was all a test, and greater things were still to come.

Judy closed out her email then clicked the news on her home page, and Christy Gallagher, her favorite news reporter, so perky and exciting, filled the screen. Christy went to Judy's church, and though they weren't friends, they were friendly. Staying within the legal parameters of confidentially, she occasionally let a comment or two slip, but Christy never outed her. Judy loved having a celebrity seek her out. It made her feel important.

The most recent report showed Christy standing in front of Fulton Penn and smiling into the camera in her flirty way, "Christy Gallagher, reporting from Fulton Penitentiary, again. And the news looks grim; we can now confirm that the lockdown at the Fulton Penitentiary is due to medical concerns. A medical truck pulled up only moments ago then closed off traffic to and from the prison. Dashcorp, the company contracted to run the medical aspects of the facility, deployed medical trucks and we can also see what looks like quarantine tents erected on the infirmary's side of the prison. Currently, the warden, assistant warden, and even the Dashcorp facilities management have all refused my interview requests. What are they hiding and why won't they talk to us?" Christy turned and motioned to a small crowd, one larger than the day before, "These family members waiting to visit their loved ones have been turned away again. Now, let's hear what they have to say..."

The publicity department didn't contact Christy? Maybe she should do it for them? Judy scrolled through the comments of the news report while she listened to the interviews, most were spouting off about the injustice of visitation restrictions. She shook her head. Those ungrateful people should be happy to see their criminal family members at all, yet they complain about a couple of days of restriction. Why didn't those people understand, God punishes those not following his word.

Judy continued scrolling through the comments and stopped at one under the name Viralist, "God is just. (II Thessalonians 1:6-10)." Judy paused, why didn't the writer use the whole verse? She grabbed her Bible located on the corner of her desk, "God is just: He will pay back trouble to those who trouble you and give relief to you who are troubled ...They will be punished with everlasting destruction,... This includes you because you believed our testimony to you. (II Thessalonians 1:6-10)." She sat back and thought for several moments, then looked back at the past several days of comments and each day Viralist commented the same, "God is just. (II Thessalonians 1:6-10.)"

Judy's curiosity got the better of her and she 'Googled' Viralist, Viral list, the most viral content, no, Viral lists website script written in PHP that lets you build a viral content website, no. She browsed through the first search page and then, finally at the end of the second page found a Viralist Justice Blog page, and selected it. On her screen popped up,

> *You are here not by chance, but by God's choosing,*
> *He made you exactly as you are by His choosing.*
> *You are one of a kind, unique, and you lack nothing,*
> *You are here, at this time in history, to fulfill His special purpose.*

Judy sighed, filled with a strange sense of relief. She knew she had a purpose and she was only being tested with Rebecca. She heard keys jingle in the doorway, so she closed out her computer, then quickly scurried into the kitchen to finish dinner. She would read more on that blog later that night after dinner. Her phone rang, Christy Gallagher, calling her. Dinner might be late tonight.

CHAPTER 5

Day 3

Melissa wrung her hands together, looking back and forth, obviously torn between helping Alex and walking out the door, "Alex are you sure you don't need me to go with you?"

Alex waved it off, "No, don't worry. Go home to your kids. I won't be long, and I'll text you when I'm finished."

Melissa smirked gratefully, grabbed her bag and ran out while Alex packed up the box of prepared food containers for the under the bridge residents. The fading autumn light left less time to deliver to the bridge before dark, but the kitchen was located only a couple of blocks away, and Alex convinced herself that plenty of daylight remained to finish, a quick run by car. The area didn't frighten her as much as it used to, but she carried on cautiously wherever she went. Attacks and muggings could happen anywhere, at any time. Many volunteers declined the under the bridge delivery route unless they were provided serious protection, Alex made the conscious decision not to live her life in fear of it, as such beliefs surrendered to the hysteria that grew crime's power.

Feeling braver than usual, as well as working in the quiet Alex, became absorbed in her own reflections and contemplated profound thoughts, a past time that fulfilled her and passed the time. Several under the bridge found their way home and others found love, and love gave them a passionate desire to improve prove their lives, and they did. With her humanitarian passions ignited, she confidently loaded the food to bring to the residents under the bridge. She smirked and shook her head at her own pretentiousness before she continued with her work.

The plan to expeditiously deliver food alone meant that Alex had no time to socialize with the residents. They craved human interaction and respectful treatment, and to drop their food and run did not feel like she had properly fulfilled her work, but today she had no choice. She left the food containers near the front of tents and giant boxes with quick announcements, "Good afternoon, Gerald, your dinner is here. Hello, Mindy dinner is here. David, your dinner is here."

The daylight had faded more quickly than Alex had anticipated and as she hurried past David's box, he poked his head out through the opening. She turned to face his ramshackle cardboard home and saw a twisted look of confusion on his face. Before Alex could move on, David scrunched up his mouth, adding to the contortion of his face and asked, "What's the hurry? You don't want to talk to me today?"

Alex smiled, "I always want to talk to you, but I need to hurry today."

David eyes darted about as he looked in several directions, and scowled, "You alone?" Then, his box shook as he stealthily started maneuvering out of it, disturbing a cat sleeping on top.

Alex took a step back her confidence waning and slowly maneuvered backward so she didn't startle him, then gently warned, "David, please stay there so I can finish what I am doing." It was David, and she shouldn't worry, but she came alone.

David paused, "I ain't going to hurt you, see?" He halted his exit from the box, "I won't come out anymore, don't be scared."

Alex looked around and saw nobody else, even the other residents from under the bridge were out of sight preparing themselves for nightfall. She took another step back and looked toward Doug's tent; with only his dinner left to deliver, she needed to decide the best way to proceed.

David scratched his face and jerked it around, "I would never hurt ya, Alex, although I don't want ya to go down by Doug's tent today, I can deliver it for ya."

Alex cocked her head and sighed, "Uh, thank you, David, but he needs to eat too if you want more food for yourself I can bring extra."

David reacted by narrowing his eyes and furling up his eyebrows into a ferocious scowl, "I don't want his food. He steals mine sometimes, but I ain't no thief." David's face reddened, "I ain't no thief."

Alex squatted down, which went against everything her experience taught. She should have dropped the food and run. David never made her feel like he would hurt her, but feeling too safe put volunteers into the most dangerous situations, "I am sorry David, you don't scare me, but I am a little jumpy today. I didn't mean to upset you."

David rubbed his face some more, "Ahh, I'm not upset, just embarrassed that you are scared of me. Don't go down to Doug's tent, he was on a crazy tirade earlier this week, and I heard him yelling more than usual. It won't be safe. Look, he ain't even been eating his food, and yesterday's is still there."

Alex looked over toward Doug's tent and wavered back and forth in her mind about what to do. She didn't know if David would actually deliver the food but it was already dark out, so she acquiesced and put the food down next to the other container, "Thank you, David. That is very kind of you."

He shoed her away like she was one of his cats, "You should go its already getting dark, now git."

Alex backed away before turning to hurry to her car; she should never have gone alone, especially not this late in the day. She turned her head fully expecting David to grab the food and retreat to his box but instead, he cautiously crept in the direction of Doug's tent. He placed the food container about 10 feet from the opening of the tent and yelled, "Doug food is here," then he ran back to his box and dove inside. David poked his head out and waved at Alex before she trotted off toward her car then locked the doors the moment she got in.

Alex put her forehead against the steering wheel of the car and breathed heavily. What a stupid risk, all to prove her bravery and confidence. Her preparation over the last decade to deal with confrontation and unsafe situations did not mean she should intentionally put herself in jeopardy. Her thoughts drifted back to her life at the age of fifteen, when she used to accompany her brother to his community service. The first time Tristan got caught hacking he'd been a minor and merely served community service hours, at seventeen, the authorities took it easy on him. While he was busy, she sometimes wandered off, she thought herself invincible at the time, and was completely unaware of the dangers around her, even though she had been warned thoroughly. She walked around the neighborhood and even to the bridge back then, sometimes alone.

Her last moments of innocence came on one of those walks. She had always loved her long hair and adored it in a pretty ponytail back then. The boys that grabbed her were in a gang, and it was initiation time. A mammoth sized boy grabbed her long ponytail, pulled her back using the ponytail like a leash, and smashed his hand over her mouth. He wrapped his arm tightly around her neck and lifted her. Stunned, she didn't know what had happened. She inhaled raggedly trying to catch her breath but gagged at the smell of sweat and cheap, overly applied aftershave. He dragged Alex so quickly that she couldn't get her feet underneath her to cooperate, and she struggled against him. Alex slammed her head back into his face thinking he'd drop her so she could get away, but he did not loosen his grip and only seemed angered by her resistance attempt, "Bitch! You will pay for that!"

Other boys she hadn't realized were there laughed and called out to her, and her loudest scream came out only as a faint, despondent moan. The big one's thick, calloused fingers crushed her mouth and pressed the skin of her lips into her teeth, and as the inside of her mouth ripped open against her teeth, she tasted the metallic flavor of blood building against her tongue. Unable to move her head, she clawed at his arm and reached for his face, only to be thrown down onto her back, knocking the wind out of her.

Alex's breath stuck in her throat and she wasn't able to catch it or even scream out. The big boy dropped down on top of her with one of his knees, landing directly on her arm. She heard a crunch, and it sounded like he broke her arm, but Alex didn't feel it. She felt only terror. He pushed her other arm that she was thrashing about to the ground and kneeled on it with his other knee. She squirmed with all her might, but couldn't move. He was too strong. Finally, after he released her mouth and she was able to get air into her lungs, she screamed her loudest, most desperate plea. Someone had to help her, didn't they? How could this happen? The boy forced his oversized meaty hand aggressively against her face, and over her mouth, before she screamed again, then he pulled a giant knife from the back of his pants. Alex tried to bite his hand but he was pressing down too hard. Flailing but still unable to get him off her, his size and power overwhelmed her, and she could do nothing to stop him. The struggle spurred laughter in the background and he showed off, waving the knife around and using it to trace around her face, neck, and breasts. The realization struck Alex that he intended to kill her. Alex succumbed to her fate and peered directly into his face, his dark hair, and unshaven skin glistened with a film of sweat and grease. Why was this happening? Tears burned her eyes and she felt them drip down her cheeks.

Looking up past the boy, she saw an alley, one that smelled of urine and garbage, but she couldn't believe the alley would be the last memory of her life. The big boy pressed the knife into the side of her jaw and she heard a whine in the background, "Don't slice her up, I can't do her if she's all bloody and gross." The boy on top of her pulled the knife slowly, along Alex's jaw near her ear in a slicing motion, at first, she felt nothing, but then, it began to burn, and she sensed the blood running down her face and off her neck.

The big boy with the knife laughed, "Aww the poor baby can only do it if the girls look pretty. I am done playing with her anyway. I go first, and then you all get your turn, now hold her down so I can take what I came for."

Two other boys grabbed her arms as the big boy released his hold on her and he got up to undo his pants. The pain in her crushed arm almost blinded her and

Alex screamed as loudly as possible, with all the death wrenching desperation she felt. Almost to quickly to see, the boy now with his pants down jumped on top of her. This time he landed on her ribs and he swung his fist brutally into the side of Alex's face. She thought her eye exploded from the punch. A white light replaced her vision on one side, as the other eye watched blurs and heard muffled babbling, then white snow drifted around the edges of her vision and it faded in and out of the blackness. Alex convinced herself that this travesty wasn't being inflicted upon her as her pants and shirt were ripped from her body. Her breasts were mauled and pulled at by rough hands and fingers, and vomit filled Alex's mouth. Confusion, adrenaline, and panic took over her body, but nothing in her life prepared Alex for the feeling of being ripped in two. She couldn't escape panting rancid breath that covered her face and she felt the jerking motion of the sweaty body on top of her, knowing others were waiting their turn. She did not want to die, and her mind raced trying to develop an escape from the hell she was experiencing, but blackness took over.

Muffled screams and exploding echoes brought Alex back to awareness. No longer being punched or battered, her head rested against softness as someone with smooth hands stroked her forehead. Tears streamed down Alex's face as she realized where she was and what had happened, and an anxious voice cried, "I think she is waking up."

Alex moaned. She hurt all over and had a difficult time breathing, as calloused, rough hands gently clasped her hand and a low, gruff voice whimpered, "Ohhh, I am so sorry I couldn't get here sooner sweet girl, I ran as fast as could."

Sirens wailed in the background, and the gruff voice rumbled, "I oughtta git goin' now." Alex glanced over but only saw a blurry shadow scurrying off, and when she looked up, she stared into a blurry face so beautiful, she could have sworn it was a forlorn angel, crying.

Bam!! Bam!! Bam!! Alex jumped and twisted toward the car window, startled back into the present. David's face peered into the window, "I thought you was goin' home, git goin'."

Her heart raced and she pressed on her hand against her chest. Alex took a few deep breaths and shuddered trying to rid herself of the memory. She never wore her hair long enough for a ponytail after that day. Alex nodded and waved to David as he stood with his arms crossed, his protective nature from those years in the military never faded. He looked like a scowling hairy barbarian watching guard over her. She grabbed her gear shifter to push it into gear, and then with one more deep inhale to settle herself down, she drove off, satisfied in braving that which terrified her the most, even though the attempt was a foolish one.

Rebecca watched as Alex tentatively approached the table in the corner of the restaurant where she sat. She hated fighting with Alex. They had been through so much together, and these petty spats were a waste of time. Even though the time at the gym together seemed like the end of the dispute, Alex made Rebecca work for forgiveness when she stepped over the line. She didn't mind, for without Alex keeping her in line Rebecca's stop filter got clogged, and everyone around her suffered including her friend, who got resentful. Alex stopped short of the table, and slowly Rebecca pushed a dark chocolate bar, her favorite, across the table. Alex eyed the chocolate before addressing her friend, "Well that is a good continuance of yesterday, you insensitive wench, but you aren't getting out of Saturday."

Alex nodded to emphasize her point but remained standing waiting, and Rebecca pursed her lips in response, "You know apologizing is difficult for me, I don't enjoy upsetting you. That," Rebecca waved toward the candy, "is practically me on my knees." When Alex still didn't sit Rebecca sighed, "Fine, I'll still go on Saturday, just take the offering and sit down so we can eat. Look, I even ordered for you already, I can see it calling your name."

Grinning widely, Alex swiped the candy off the table and pulled out a chair to sit, "I guess two days of groveling plus your assistance under the bridge is enough punishment." Alex wasted no time when she sat down, and shoveled the food quickly into her mouth without hesitation, and all conversation halted while Alex finished eating.

Rebecca watched her friend stuff salad into her mouth, thoroughly entertained at the speed Alex ate. Everything appeared back to normal, and when Alex stopped long enough to breathe Rebecca thought it would be safe to talk, "Well, what have you been doing since yesterday?"

Alex tried to swallow and took a sip of water, but started talking with her mouth still half-full, "You know the normal stuff; I went to work, fed the residents under the bridge-."

"Wait, you don't usually go down there today."

At first, Alex didn't respond and took another bite of food, but after chewing for ages, she continued, "Well, Terrance needed to change days with me."

Rebecca glared as she sat back in her chair and crossed her arms, "Who did you go with?"

Alex shrugged her shoulders uncomfortably, but Rebecca would not let it go, "Seriously? You mean you went alone?!" The intensity and command of her voice distracted people at the tables nearby, and they stopped their conversations to stare at the disruption.

Alex reached across the placed her hand on Rebecca's arm, "Calm down." Then she smiled and looked around self-consciously, "I think people around us think we are in a lover's spat." A waiter dropped a tray of dishes with a loud crash, they all stared at the waiter and his mess, nobody paid attention to them anymore.

Rebecca, hated that Alex could be so stubborn and she wouldn't be sidetracked, "You can't distract me Alex. Why would you go by yourself? Why take that risk?" Alex stared down at the napkin in her lap but didn't answer. Rebecca heard only the sound of her ragged breathing at that point and felt as if she was on the verge of an anxiety attack. The horrors she faced in her past still haunted her even though she tried not to let it show and when she thought one of the few people she cared about could get hurt she practically fell apart inside. First, her family in 9-11, then, Eliana in Israel; the pain shrouded her heart and left the sting of more loss. She'd hid away at the research facility in the Antarctic to clear her head and came back to the states only to once again find herself in the middle of another unjust attack, the one that ended up with Alex in her lap. Alex survived and always seemed to accept the attack as part of her growing up, but Rebecca could not. She couldn't lose Alex too.

Finally, Alex responded with a sigh, "I filled in; Melissa's daughter came down sick, so I told her to go home."

"She went home and left you alone? Oh, don't tell me, you conveniently left your baton in the car?" Alex looked away which told Rebecca all she needed to know, "What is wrong with you? You aren't invincible, and you could get hurt, attacked, or worse."

Alex inhaled deeply and she narrowed her eyes, then she leaned in and peered intently into Rebecca's eyes before quietly saying, "You need to stop now, you don't get to speak to me like that. I made my decision to go, and am willing to live with the consequences. Most people down under the bridge have merely lost their way, and aren't dangerous. In fact, a man like David is a hero living with PTSD. Someone needs to feed and take care of them. I am sorry it scares you, but it is my decision to make."

Rebecca felt her face burning and her hands trembling. She did not know how to react to her turbulent emotions and slammed her fist on the table in anger, "I don't know how you can keep doing this. I won't lose you too. Finding you the way I did was the most heartbreaking thing I ever experienced. I didn't know if you'd survive and couldn't bring myself to leave your side for weeks."

"Try months, but someone chased off those creeps, and now the area is different, it's changed. I won't do anything I can't handle. We don't want YOU to go through that experience again now do we?" Alex pointedly stared down her nose at her friend, "Be careful Rebecca your emotions are showing and someone might think you have a heart."

Rebecca flicked her napkin at Alex and with a snarky smirk she matter of factly stated, "If you tell anyone, I will end you." With the tension abated, they both snickered and Rebecca grunted, "I don't know why I put up with you."

Judy squirmed in her seat while she listened, "Since this reporter first brought you the devastating news…," she hadn't really given away any confidential information, only common sense deductions. Christy continued, "My anonymous source states that visitors have been turned away and will continue to be turned away until the illness is cleared from the building. This is Christy Gallagher and now I will show you some footage taken earlier today at the White House. Military and secret service guards have doubled-." Judy turned off the news. Politics bored her.

Judy switched web pages to the Viralist for Justice Blog so she could continue reading. She scrolled down and carefully read each uplifting and even provocative message he'd posted about justice and God preparing for His return to the world. She licked her lips with satisfaction, as she would be one of His chosen. Her religiousness assured it. She scrolled down to a section she hadn't read before, wondering how she'd missed it, "To learn more about how you can assist God in bringing beauty and justice to this world, enter your email or phone number here for messaging." Judy entered both and immediately, she heard the ding of her email notification and quickly opened it to a couple of lines of text. "Spread the news to those who can help the world. The fruit of the righteous is a tree of life, and the one who is wise saves lives" (Proverbs 11:30, NIV)". She had no idea what she was supposed to do with that information. She heard the jingle of keys entering the lock. She quickly jumped up and ran into the kitchen, unpacked the roasted chicken she purchased, and put the potatoes she microwaved onto a platter so he would never know that she'd cheated in her dinner preparation.

CHAPTER 6

Day 4

"Another day of playing Sister Rebecca, what a fantastic way to spend a Saturday morning." She sniffed the food and made a face before closing up another food container, "I can't believe you talked me into this!" Alex treated the kitchen like it was a second home, but it made Rebecca feel uncomfortable in its cloak of neediness. The old converted warehouse contained storerooms, a large industrial kitchen, as well as tables and chairs past the counters that made it resemble a third world cafe, but the walls needed paint, the floors were concrete, and while some found it charming, the terrible events that occurred in the area conflicted with the homey feel and couldn't fool Rebecca.

Alex smirked and plopped another helping of potatoes into a new box, then she closed it and picked up a marker to draw a little picture on the side. She called the drawings a 'special personalized message' for each resident. She grinned in Rebecca's direction, "Yes, you are such a saint, but I didn't talk you into anything. Just quit complaining and do your job so we can load the boxes or we will spend the rest of the day here. Is that what you are aiming for?"

Sneering at her friend, Rebecca recalled Alex blackmailing her to volunteer, and while she reluctantly agreed to come, at least they got the joy of playfully torturing each other the entire time. Maybe if Rebecca pushed hard enough, Alex would stop asking her to go on these humanitarian escapades. She laughed internally knowing that scenario would never happen. While Rebecca detested the place, Alex appeared at ease performing the menial tasks of preparing food and organizing the deliveries, but she really blossomed when she got the residents to start talking. Why Alex worked that dull job at HUD in the sea of bureaucracy was beyond Rebecca. She said did it to help people but there is no way such a dreamy person found it satisfying. What the heck did she plan on doing with her life? Rebecca decided not to lecture her again, and instead raised her eyebrows in an indignant expression, "You love ordering me around don't you? That is why you always want me to come here with you."

The gleam in Alex's eye gave her the answer, yet she still heard her friend proudly announce, "Yes Rebecca, yes I do." She casually chucked an empty food box in Rebecca's direction that hit her on the arm.

Rebecca laughed and was about to return it when her phone rang in her pocket, and she signaled to Alex to wait a moment, "Good morning Nithi. Are you sure? Now? Okay, I will be right there."

Alex stopped drawing the picture on the side of the box and put it down. Disappointment painted her face as she placed her hands on her hips and furrowed her brow, "You figured a way to ditch me and need to leave, right? I can't believe you are bailing on me."

"I am sorry Alex, it is the assemblage of verbosity and there is no way out of it. Do you have anyone else to go on deliveries with you?"

Alex pouted and crossed her arms, "I will be fine."

Rebecca shook her head. This girl required a lot of work, "You are acting like a child, and that is not what I asked, is anyone going with you?"

With an exaggerated sigh, Alex answered, "Yes, Saturday is the easiest day to get the volunteers to help me. Well, other volunteers. Not you, of course." Alex stuck her tongue out then crossed her eyes at Rebecca.

Rebecca rolled her eyes, happy that her friend wasn't upset about being deserted last minute, and then she shrugged, "Work is nothing I can help." Rebecca delivered a tight-lipped smile to her friend, and nodded, "I will see you soon." Sooner than you think, she thought. She hoped Alex didn't feel close to whoever it was. If it were David, today would be an extremely long arduous day, and Rebecca didn't want to deal with it on top of all she was about to do. No, definitely not David, she and Alex would have noticed something this week.

She needed answers; Rebecca tentatively approached the tent, apprehensive about the unknown. She peered through her plastic mask at Abe, and he nodded before motioning her forward. Abe furrowed his eyebrows in confusion at her behavior, "Are ye feeling all right girl? You know techs can help me with the site collection."

Nobody else called her girl and got away with it, but his observation about her ridiculous behavior embarrassed her, astute as it was. She had conducted many of these searches in her life as a field researcher and displaying trepidation about its unsavoriness didn't make any sense. She shook her head, "I'm fine and I need to be the one to do this. I am just wary of a pathogen so prolific that it appears one day then moves right on out of the facility the moment we discover it. What is this thing, and how is it already running rampant? It could be airborne, Abe. Somebody sneezed a week ago, and now it is everywhere."

"Aye, don't even say somethin' like that girl. That scenario is extremely unlikely. Why do ye need to jump to worst case scenario immediately?"

"Because that is my job." Rebecca's flimsy hazmat suit and breathing apparatus blocked the smell of the surroundings. The habitat was not even suited for animals, yet men and women lived here, and while the filth could not get beyond the seals of her suit, it crept in, slowly, in her mind. Abe examined the outside, searching and taking samples from the exterior of the tent, and its surroundings. She bent over to enter the tent of the bridge's most menacing resident, Doug. Inside, Rebecca surveyed the small space. Garbage and boxes lined the edges of Doug's shelter. Built up in piles like walls but ordered, and rolled up against one wall lay a sleeping bag and several blankets. She took pictures before cataloging anything then opened plastic evidence bags to place some of the more mundane items from the top of the piles and swabbed surfaces to test later. She deposited the bagged items into a collection box, but from the sheer amount of garbage and number of objects in the tent, she knew she'd require several more boxes.

She cataloged pieces of sausage skin, piles of newspapers, dozens of clean looking ice cream wrappers, used tea bags, and empty soda cans. Rebecca found sixteen different ID's belonging to women. What the hell? She called out, "Abe, uhh please have one of your techs check on the status of the women on these ID's." She returned to bagging the items in the tent, and the garbage walls were filled with utility bills from around the country, new and used empty plastic garbage and re-sealable bags, two cut up gallon jugs, dirty rags, towels, cassette tapes and a player that ran on batteries, several empty food cans, a cooler with clothing and shoes, and stacks of both empty and partially full food containers. While the chaotic atmosphere of the over-filled tent looked like a huge heap of garbage, each item appeared to have been meticulously placed into its spot, and at the bottom of the garbage walls, wedged into place, two wooden boxes that looked as if they were slid in and out on a regular basis caught her attention. Rebecca continued cataloging and although a tech could bag these items, she needed to discover what this mysterious vagrant hid from the world. After over an hour Abe poked his head in to see the progress and grunted, "How does such a little tent not burst from so many belongings in it?"

Rebecca shrugged, "Almost through, but I will need another oxygen change." The walls were no more; only the two wooden boxes remained, which she had saved for last. He must have treasured them because they looked well cared for and guarded. Shivers run up her back and into her neck. Abe waited while she opened them, one was filled with more cassette tapes and the other was filled with cardboard jewelry boxes. Rebecca glanced up, "Maybe the guy was a millionaire in hiding, and these are filled with priceless gems, huh?" Abe smirked and shook his head, and she chuckled at the disgust on his face, "No?" She opened the first box. In it, a small rubber banded swatch of fine blond hair lay on top of cotton, "This appears to have belonged to a child, maybe he had children." Rebecca lifted the cotton, shuddered, and hastily dropped the box as if it had burned her.

Abe scowled, "Hey be careful." Under the layer of cotton sat a tiny dried out child-sized finger with a ring on it. Abe stuttered, "Oh dear." This finger was not the first she'd seen ripped from a body.

Bile filled Rebecca's mouth as her thoughts drifted back to the time she spent in Israel before she met Alex, one day in particular. The sights, smells, and sounds of the small alleyways, old narrow streets with a mix of well-kept and dilapidated courtyards stirred her memories. Walking with her best friend Eliana, they perused the local art galleries, studios, boutiques and craft shops filled with a variety of Christian, Muslim, and Jewish vendors that welcomed all. At the time, it imbued Rebecca with a sense of hope for the future. After their long walks down the dry, dusty streets, Eliana and Rebecca would settle in for food and drinks at a different cafe each day. On the day that still permeated her nightmares, they chose a lovely Mediterranean cafe, one with open seating on the street and flowers in magnificently carved stone pots all around them.

After finishing their meal, Eliana called the waiter, and Rebecca pulled out her purse to pay, but it slipped from her hands. They were still slippery with the grease of the meal and both Eliana and the waiter giggled at her clumsiness. As she bent over to pick up the handbag, a man shouted some panicked Arabic words. She could not see him because he was behind her and didn't understand him because she didn't speak Arabic. Then, Rebecca felt it. She knew immediately that it was an explosion. The planter must have protected her from the severity of the blast but it blew her all the way down to the ground, and only her ears hurt. The noise around Rebecca deafened initially, followed by a blank, hollow ringing in a sea of silence. Soon, she heard the muffled, horrendous sound of people screaming, abruptly interrupted by a second explosion, a massive one, even bigger than the first. Clouds of smoke and a plasticky smell overtook the small area, and it became increasingly warm and painful to breathe. Some people dropped to the ground and others ran. Rebecca's first intuition was to escape, but she couldn't leave without Eliana. Eliana must have been terrified because she lay very still. Rebecca screamed her name but Eliana didn't move, and a blank look filled her eyes. Rebecca reached desperately for her best friend's hand; instead, a piece of debris hit her, only it wasn't debris, but bits of fingers that dropped one by one right near where Eliana's hand had been. The skin was ripped open with fat and bones showing through where the finger pads should be. The rancid air caught in Rebecca's lungs, as she tried to call out her friend's name again, but her friend couldn't hear her. Eliana would never respond again.

Rebecca knelt on the ground, paralyzed, looking around and realized that blood covered everything. People had lost legs, she could see their bodies, but their legs weren't attached and everywhere, bodies were without heads. A woman screamed and cried out, 'where is my baby?' The shock must have blinded her to the fact that she was holding a baby that lay limply in her arms, no longer breathing. A man's chest lay completely open, and next to him a second man whose body shook violently. Two men lay face down with blood pouring out of their heads, and glass stuck out of everything. She should have been helping people with their injuries, yet Rebecca's focus kept returning to her friend and the fingers scattered around where her friend's hand should be. So much blood filled the air she not only smelled it but tasted the metal of it. It gagged and cloistered around Rebecca's head as if it had nowhere else to go, taunting her.

She tried to clear her head after the tragedy by running off to research in the Antarctic but didn't help. Losing Eliana, and the image of the fingers haunted her in the few hours of sleep she got each night, even after all these years. The size of the finger brought her back to reality, the animal! Her heart beat so rapidly she got lightheaded, "I-I wasn't expecting it. I don't think I contaminated it." Rebecca reached up to anxiously rub her pendant but it was neatly tucked behind the protection of the hazmat suit she wore.

Abe's appeared confused by her reaction. She'd seen worse working in other quarantine areas, but he empathized and changed his tone, "Dearie, I would have done the same. Don't fret. Let me help you sort through the rest of that box. Now we are engaged in more than a medical quarantine investigation. It is also a crime scene."

Rebecca shook her head, "It was startling that is all. I can manage."

Abe ducked out of the tent to inform authorities about the situation, and Rebecca couldn't stop herself. She started frantically opening the boxes hoping to find jewelry but sadly, each small cardboard jewelry box held a small, banded clipping of hair and another unthinkable horror. She found tiny dried out child-sized fingers with rings on them, small earrings with dried out parts of an ear still attached, baby teeth with bits of gum and dried blood, and a tiny pair of pink princess glasses with a rotted eyeball in a bracelet sized box. By the time she got to the last box, her heart felt as if it had shriveled away and what was left was filled with an all too familiar despair.

Brandon shifted the weight of the food carton boxes he carried for Alex, "I haven't been out on delivery before, thank you for asking me, Miss Alex."

Alex smiled at the tall, skinny, wiry muscled teen, "I told you, call me Alex. Are you ready for this? It is not a glamorous job."

"I can't help it, ma'am, I was brought up to call my elders Miss or Mr." Brandon paused and quickly stuttered, "I-I don't mean you are old ma'am, I am very sorry. I simply mean that you're a little bit older than I am."

Laughing at the sheepish expression on Brandon's face, Alex waved it off, "Okay, well Miss Alex is fine then. Here, let's grab the cart I usually use."

Brandon adjusted the box and placed it into the cart. His deep brown skin glistened with sweat from the weight of the box and trek from the edge of the parking lot. Alex held a jar of menthol rub toward Brandon, "Put it right under your nose, trust me, it helps and you're going to need it." He smiled, and reached into the jar, "They told us about the smell in the orientation, but I am sure it will be okay. I lived right near these areas my whole life, and believe me, and I know how bad they can smell. Thank you." He spread a bit of menthol rub above his lip and wrinkled up his nose, "It stings a little."

They turned the corner from the parking lot, and Alex paused as she glanced around, "What is going on?" The whole area was sectioned off with police tape. Big white trucks and tents lined the perimeter, and a couple of news vans sat parked in the distance. Usually deserted, except for the residents, it never saw this much activity. She glanced over at Brandon and saw his mouth hung open, and his big brown eyes stretched so wide they looked like saucers pasted on his face. Alex shrugged her shoulders and said, "Stick by me, and I will find out what is going on." Alex called the soup kitchen to request a return truck; the residents would not get their food this morning. She spotted a police officer guarding the area, but he was quickly dispatching everyone approaching him. Alex needed to get information without getting dismissed, so she marched up to him and started talking before he could bark orders at her, "Sir, I am with the Feeding the Homeless soup kitchen and this area here is my normal route. Where did all my people that live under the bridge go?"

The police officer glanced at her, the cart, and Brandon then nodded and said something incomprehensible into the walkie-talkie on his shoulder. She never could understand the static-laden conversations on walkies. Then he turned to Alex and politely barked an order, "Ma'am, please wait here for one moment."

Alex's stomach clenched and her voice felt momentarily lost, so she only nodded and croaked out, "Uhh okay." Her stomach increasingly knotted up, but about ten minutes later two figures, a man, and a woman walked toward her, Brandon, and the police officer. She instantly recognized Rebecca and the RBF she sported, today though, something more hid behind her mask, and Alex found the look troubling. She had never seen the man walking beside Rebecca before, but noticed that his perfectly pressed pants and starched button-down shirt conflicted with his sauntering approach and messy hair. He walked straight up to Alex and did not wait for Rebecca to do introductions. He cheerfully stuck out his hand, which was odd for the scene, and began speaking with authority, "Hi, I am Dr. Brent Adams, but just call me Brent; I am pleased to meet you." He gestured over to Rebecca, "Behind me, is my colleague Dr. Martin."

Alex paused for a moment. Why was Rebecca acting as if they were strangers? She looked over toward Rebecca, but her friend waited, saying nothing. A sad darkness filled her eyes. So, this man was the man Rebecca referred to Mr. Big-shot CEO. She wondered what he was doing here. She heard about him in Rebecca's occasional rantings but still, why hadn't Rebecca at least said that they knew each other. Alex reached out and shook his hand, "Nice to meet you, uhh Brent, I am Alex Donaghue, and this young man beside me is Brandon Johnson." She nodded toward Rebecca, "Nice to see you again Rebecca." Rebecca only half smiled at Alex, but her eyes lost some of their dark cast as she winked.

Brent smiled, reached over the tape and placed his hand gently behind Alex's back herding her towards where Rebecca stood as he held up the police tape, "How do you know Rebecca?"

Alex stepped back out of his reach. His charm oozed but who did he think he was trying to guide her in his direction without even telling her what he wanted? "What are you doing?"

Brent dropped his hand and cocked his head to the side, as if her question confused him, "I hope you can answer some questions for us about some of the people that live here under the bridge and I was showing you the way to our tent."

"I'd be happy to help, but I can't leave my food cart or Brandon." Alex motioned over to Brandon and the cart, and Brandon smiled and waved.

Brent looked at Alex, then Brandon, then the cart, "You're here passing out food?" Brent smiled in a kind, slightly surprised way, and the smile caused his eyes to crinkle up and reveal a mischievous quality to it. He glanced at Rebecca who stood watching but still said nothing.

Is this guy for real? He tried to maneuver her into joining him when she had no idea who he was, and he didn't even know why she was there, but instead of voicing her annoyance, Alex innocently smirked, "What else would we do here?"

"I am sorry; I only heard that someone was here who knew the residents. I had no idea know why you were here or what you were doing. Hello, Brandon." Brent reached over the police tape to shake Brandon's hand, and Brandon trotted over to grab it then energetically pumped it up and down. Brent appeared entertained by Brandon's reaction, "It is a pleasure to meet you. I am impressed by the work that you and Alex do here, I had no idea."

Why was Brandon smiling like a Cheshire cat? Alex jutted out her chin trying to exude confidence, "If you need me to answer questions, you only needed to ask. I've called a truck to pick up Brandon as well as the box of food and I will assist you after it arrives and Brandon is safely on his way back to the soup kitchen."

Brandon eagerly stepped forward, "I can stay if you need me to Miss Alex."

Turning toward Brandon, Alex put her hand on his shoulder and gestured toward the truck already pulling into the parking lot, "I think you should go back to the warehouse with the truck for now Brandon." His face filled with disappointment, but she ignored it as she glanced over her shoulder to speak to Brent and Rebecca, "I am going to walk Brandon back to the truck then I'll come back and see if I can help you." Brent and Rebecca both nodded as Alex continued on her way, she leaned in and whispered, "Why do you look like you just won the lottery?"

Brandon's excitement shone all over his face, "Do you know who that is?"

Alex shrugged and shook her head, "Rebecca's boss?"

Practically jumping up and down Brandon grabbed her hand, "That is Dr. Brent Adams, and he is the CEO of Dashcorp, the man is thirty-two and runs one of the largest multinational research organizations in the world. Everybody wants to work for him." Alex grunted to herself, not Rebecca, she complained about the man constantly. Brandon continued to blab about his accomplishments and philanthropic undertakings. He sounded impressive but usually with big accomplishments came even larger egos, yuck. Brandon finished his ramble, "He was even listed on D.C.'s top fifty most-eligible bachelors last year."

Her face twisted up, "I am confused. I thought you had a girlfriend."

Brandon vigorously shook his head and snickered, "No, that is not what I mean. I read about him in that article." As they reached the truck Brandon finished, "His career path is the type I want to take. If you get a chance, can you ask if he has any internships in his office, and mention me? Please!"

"Okay, okay, I will see what I can do. You got him, Joe?" Joe smiled and waved; Brandon nodded and gave Alex the thumbs up.

Brandon gave Alex a quick hug then jumped into the back of the truck, "Don't forget okay?"

"I won't forget, don't worry." Alex smiled reassuringly, but as she turned back toward the police tape, her stomach sank, knowing she headed into a foreboding situation.

CHAPTER 7

Day 4 - Later

Judy pulled into a parking spot and spotted Rebecca's car across the lot, and wondered how long she'd been there. Christy Gallagher stood outside the police tape setting up to report from the scene. Judy wanted to talk to Christy and give her some news but would have to wait until Sunday at church. She should go over and at least say hello, it would be rude not to wave, but somehow she resisted. Judy couldn't have anyone thinking she had given a reporter inside information, so she acted like she was unpacking her car and watched out of the corner of her eye. Rebecca appeared and her face was contorted with rage. She marched over to Christy, so Judy moved in a little closer to listen, this time kneeling to adjust her shoe, but Christy started her report before Rebecca reached her.

"Christy Gallagher reporting from one of the most historic yet roughest neighborhoods in D.C., Columbia Heights. It's rustic beauty, and beautiful Victorian buildings are not enough to chase away destitution and bring justice to this place. The seediest area being this forgotten overpass where the homeless live and seem to thrive in wretched conditions, a place simply known as "under the bridge." Normally, the death of a homeless man would go unnoticed in the nation's capital, but not today. Rumors from the local residents nearby tell a sad, yet scary tale of a homeless man who died with mysterious symptoms. The Dashcorp medical team is investigating the recent death of the Columbia Heights homeless man. Has the illness from Fulton Penitentiary spread to the city? Will authorities respond to the down and out of our society or will the overcrowding, substandard medical care within our system, and apathy to the incarcerated and homeless be the perfect storm, for the beginning of a prison's extended isolation as well as the extermination of the homeless? Will the CDC decide this killer disease and these poor souls are worth their time?"

Rebecca paused for a moment and waited until the cameraman walked over to the news van and put his camera away. Judy had inched closer, half-hidden by a line of cars, as she didn't want to be seen by either woman, when Rebecca started her rampage on poor Christy, "How could you? You are only stirring up panic and fear with these irresponsible, sensationalized reports."

Christy flung her hair over her shoulder and indignantly replied, "What, apologize? The public has the right to know what is going on around them, and I am performing my duty to the public."

Rebecca clutched her hands into fists by her side, and Judy feared she was about to hit Christy, but Rebecca didn't move toward her, "No, you are merely grabbing your fifteen minutes of fame at the expense of the victims and their families. How did you even know we were going to be at this location?"

Judy's eyes widened and she tensed as Christy's head shot up, "I am sorry, how are you involved in this investigation? What is your name?"

Rebecca ignored Christy's questions and growled as she marched off. Judy sighed with relief that she wasn't outed and decided the whole exchange felt immensely satisfying to watch. This incident is what Judy's last email from the Viralist referred; the Viralist really is a messenger from God.

Brent waited patiently behind the police tape for Alex to return. He looked around for Rebecca who had disappeared the moment Alex walked away. Abe tried to maintain his composure as he told Brent what happened, and most people would have broken down, but not Rebecca. He often found Rebecca aggressive and emasculating, exuding cold sarcasm and biting hostility, sometimes with only a glance. Many of the scientists he worked within the research department were perceived as antisocial or cold, but solely because of their intellect or laser focus, Rebecca was an entirely different animal. Of all his researchers and department heads, nobody achieved the label of pain in the ass to the extent Rebecca did, but her work over the years had won them several government contracts, so everyone put up with her "quirks". He'd spent hours laughing with Fahim about her effect on others and introducing arrogant or cocky new hires, inspectors, or new board members to

Rebecca was one of Brent's favorite past times. Her beauty befuddled every man she met then within minutes yet with barely a word they'd want to run and hide under a desk. Rebecca reappeared next to him, now her blank-faced stare oozed with anger, the kind that left a palpable perimeter.

Brent held the police tape up for Alex, and stared at her as she walked through. He noticed Rebecca eying him, and he tried not to gawk, but Alex did not fit the image of a typical volunteer. She appeared together and confident without the over-directive attitude of someone who thought they were doing such important work that everyone else lost their significance. Instead of the typical super short, masculine haircut or long scraggly hair pulled back into a ponytail that most of the volunteers sported, Alex, wore a short, smart bobbed haircut that framed her adorable face. Her clothes reflected a practical yet feminine, casual style instead of workout clothes or hand-me-down hippie looking outfits that the big-hearted volunteers usually wore. Brent's distracted eye followed Alex, and he felt extremely unprofessional. Then he saw Rebecca still watching him, but he'd welcomed the torturous remarks he'd receive later from his most annoying scientist, all to have a look into Alex's welcoming pale blue eyes. She smiled, and nodded to him, "Thank you, you know you made quite an impression on Brandon." Again, he noticed Rebecca watching, something about her demeanor had changed, no longer angry, she seemed amused and probably was waiting to make fun of him at the most embarrassing moment possible.

He turned to Alex, "Really how is that?"

The three fell into stride as Rebecca and Brent escorted Alex toward the tents. The area smelled so offensively that Brent felt like the interiors of his nostrils burned, yet somehow Alex hadn't mentioned it. She appeared completely unphased by everything going on around her. A small smile curled up on one side of her mouth, "Oh, he told me you were one of D.C.'s fifty most eligible bachelors last year." Huh, Alex was making fun of him, not only was she attractive, but she had a sense of humor too. Rebecca rolled her eyes then shook her head, the humiliation over that bachelor article had only recently died down, and now she would harass him about that later also, if not sooner. Somehow, Rebecca never cared who a person was, nor their position, she delivered her little jabs and sarcastic comments without fail. She usually entertained him with her antics, except when she directed the remarks toward him. Then, his endurance needed to outlast their conversations.

Raising his eyebrows, Brent smirked, "He thinks being a bachelor is an impressive feat, huh?" He shrugged, "It is really quite simple."

Alex's subtle laughter lightened the air around them, "Funny. No, he wants to follow your career path. In fact, he knew quite a bit about your resume and wants me to ask you if you have any internships available in your office."

Trying to smile as charmingly as possible, Brent reached into his pocket and handed her his business card, "You think he will know what to do with this? I know kids use those fancy apps on their phones for these things, but tell him to call me." He beamed when he felt a spark of electricity from the touch of her finger, but Brent averted his eyes so she wouldn't see how dorky he felt. Of course, Rebecca noticed that too. Ugh, he could try to avoid her for a while, or maybe he'd fire her to prevent the drama altogether. The thought made him smile to himself.

Alex glanced at the card, nodded to him, and slid the card into her pocket, "Oh, he is a bright boy, I think he will figure it out." Brent knew he was acting like an obsessed schoolboy, and Rebecca watched silently, probably waiting to pounce. She almost smiled which was conceivably even more terrifying than her previous angry vibe.

As they approached a large white tent, screaming visibly startled Alex, "What is going on?"

"Unfortunately one of the residents is-"

Rebecca stepped forward and cut off Brent, "It is David, your little war hero. He lost control when we put him in the truck and I tried to speak with him, but he barely tolerates me under normal circumstances."

Brent glared at Rebecca and muttered, "You know the residents too?"

Rebecca grabbed Alex's arm when she began walking toward the truck. Alex tried to pull away and objected, "Rebecca, I must talk with him, you know he is a kind, gentle, man. He shouldn't be locked up in a truck. He must be terrified."

"You can't go over there right now." Rebecca pulled Alex back toward the tent before responding to Brent, "I know some of the residents, but barely. I help out with some of the medical needs, occasionally. You know Dashcorp funds the vitamin powder added to their food, right?" She knew he had personally approved the project, as well as the donations to the other soup kitchens across the country but he remained quiet waiting to see where she was taking the conversation. Rebecca motioned to Alex, "Alex regularly comes down here, what, four times a week?" Alex watched her and nodded as Rebecca continued, "She knows who they are and all their stories."

Rebecca pushed through the tent flap dragging Alex behind her, with Brent in tow. Inside the tent, several tables and chairs filled the area. At the side, Judy and Nithi leaned over a pile of files, papers, and a laptop and both glanced up when Alex, Rebecca, and Brent walked in. Judy quickly waddled over toward them holding a few papers in her hand and opened her mouth to speak, but Brent put his finger up to halt her, so she paused. Brent pulled out a chair for Alex and watched as the corner of Rebecca's mouth lifted slightly as if she knew some private joke, "Alex I'd like you to meet another member of the team, Judy Samanski, is working with us on the situation."

"What situation? I still don't know why I am here. Is David okay? Why is he in that truck, did he hurt someone?" Alex sighed, "Why is your company even here?" She glanced around at the faces staring at her, "I am sorry Judy. I am pleased to meet you." Alex turned toward Rebecca, "Well?"

"Medical protocols and HIPPA restrictions limit what we can legally brief you on." Rebecca stared down her nose at Alex, "but we still need your cooperation."

"Really?" Alex pursed her lips, "You're going to play that card?"

Brent maneuvered up next to Alex, and handed her a cup of water then sat down beside her. She played with the edges of the paper cup and sipped at the water, but he saw that she was trying to hide her nervous energy. The whole scene must be quite intimidating for her, and he was surprised she didn't get up and run away at such craziness. Judy cleared her throat and tried to show Brent a paper, but he impatiently pushed it back at her and instead gazed at Alex with what he hoped was a calming smile. Rebecca tried to take the paper, but Judy pulled it away, flattening it against her chest. Rebecca pressed her lips together trying to hide her smile, without much success. Brent took a deep breath and shook his head before turning his attention back to Alex. She must think his group is full of idiot children, "I am sorry Alex, I know how frustrating these confidentiality and privacy issues can be. We wouldn't take up your time today if we didn't absolutely require your assistance."

Alex glanced over at Rebecca who impishly smirked, "Oh? I am used to hearing it."

Noticing their interactions, Brent raised eyebrows and smiled, their relationship must be much more than casual acquaintances, "Hmmmm, Judy please go grab us some confidentiality contracts. Alex, you obviously care about these people, and it seems cruel to keep you out of the loop, but I can't divulge any personal medical details about the individuals involved without their consent." Judy squeezed in beside Alex trying to maneuver between she and Rebecca, but Rebecca glanced away as if she were unaware that Judy's girth was in any way an obstacle. Brent watched, and to hide his smirk, rubbing his forehead with his thumb and index finger. He needed to scold them, but Rebecca would just laugh while Judy would cower in humiliation, the opposite effect he wanted. Judy reached in, finally managing to place a confidentiality contract in front of Alex, and pointed to where Alex should initial and sign, and then scuttled off glaring at Rebecca as she went. Rebecca smiled sweetly at Judy, again acting clueless, and Brent noticed as Alex took in every minute detail of the exchange.

Alex scowled at Rebecca, "Seriously? You can't take it easy on her?"

With a smile and a wink, Rebecca looked over at Brent who had been watching the interaction between them. Then, she angelically replied, "I took it easy, but I need to have a little fun once in a while. Now that you've signed confidentiality contracts we can be a little more forthcoming with information." She was overtly flaunting her power for Alex's sake, which meant Alex held some kind of power over Rebecca. He had never seen that before, intriguing.

The exasperation in Brent's sigh said more than words, "Obviously you two know each other quite well, much more than casual friends I'd say. Why did you choose to keep that information to yourself, Rebecca?"

He watched the impish grin on Rebecca's face shift to feigned innocence, "Objectivity, of course."

"Right," he sneered and changed his expression as he peered over at Alex's sweet face, "Let me explain why we need your assistance Alex. I am going to show you a photograph, please tell me if you know this man." Brent held out a photograph, and Alex stared down at it. The picture wasn't gruesome, but the man in it was obviously dead and exhibited all the telltale signs of the pathogen. His eyes bulged even though they were closed, strange dark lines resembling tattooed veins ran all up and down the sides of his face emanating from his temples, and his grey tinged skin was swollen around blueish-green lips. Alex shuddered and quickly looked away. Rebecca said nothing but her expression changed from mischievous fun to somber and angry.

Alex's eyes filled with tears, yet none spilled, "That is Doug, what is wrong with him?"

"And how do you know Doug?"

"You never answered any of my other questions. What is the condition of the other residents that live under the bridge?" Alex leaned in and grabbed Brent's shoulders, earnestly pleading with him, "I need to know, some of these people have nobody and are probably scared out of their mind." She promptly let go, but the look in her eyes still expressed acute concern.

Rebecca stepped in, "I am sorry Alex, but Doug passed away from complications of an unknown pathogen. Most of the residents here were examined and showed no symptoms, but they are required to stay in quarantine for now. David is highly agitated, and we cannot examine him, and we will use a tranquilizer on him soon if he does not calm down."

Again, Brent's annoyance with Rebecca welled up inside him; apparently, she knew much more than she let on, and now she told Alex far too much information. All the while Judy and Nithi cowered in the corner like little rats, no wonder Rebecca tormented them. He turned to the upset woman, "I am sorry did you know Doug well?"

Alex shook her head, "No, in fact, he scared me, as well as everyone else around here. I am sorry to get so emotional, but I am very concerned about the other residents. Let me speak with David, he will listen to me. Please don't tranquilize him. He'd hate to be treated like an animal."

"You mean the man in the truck?" Brent shook his head, "We can't."

Rebecca stepped in close to Brent and leaned in, then, with the most sincere pleading look her eyes she calmly implored, "Of all the people I know, nobody can reach a person the way Alex can. David would never consider hurting an innocent, especially not Alex. He is strapped down, and the protective doors will shield her, if he reacts poorly then we can tranq him."

Her plea was so sincere that Brent paused for a moment in shock before nodding and gesturing toward the door, almost slapping Judy, who somehow stealthily appeared by his side. Taking a deep sigh, Brent said, "Judy, I will be with you in just a few moments, please."

"But-"

Brent dismissed Judy without even listening to her but Alex didn't have time to wait for him. Rebecca abruptly grabbed Alex's arm and quickly led her out of the tent. Rebecca whispered under her breath, "Individuals not exposed or showing signs of infection were sent to our corporate quarantine facility, for their own safety." Alex cocked her head in confusion as Rebecca's cryptic comments continued, "I've suggested we move anyone exposed to Doug, individuals such as David, to our research facility. Similar to some other individuals you may know of." Alex opened her eyes wide, and Rebecca purposefully nodded her head. Alex's eyes teared up a little, but she refused to let the tears escape. She grimaced and sighed with relief then squeezed Rebecca's arm in gratitude. Rebecca protected her, as always and that protection extended to Tristan and David.

Alex looked over her shoulder and watched as Judy squeeze the papers in her hand into a wrinkled mess as Brent exited the tent. Rebecca dismissed herself as Brent took the lead and Alex followed behind. She saw Rebecca duck back into the tent, so Alex was on her own for this part. Several trucks lined the side of the parking lot several hundred feet from the bridge, but David's petrified screams alerted her to which truck he occupied. Brent gently wrapped his fingers over her shoulder, and it sent a small shiver down her arm and into her neck, but his calm, deep voice soothed her jitters, "I am deeply moved by your concern for these men and women who live here. Your grace and compassion in such a difficult environment is remarkable." She pressed her lips together in a tight-lipped smile at his complimentary words. They were meant to console and maybe distract her, but the emotion she felt from Rebecca's news almost overwhelmed her. He aimed to comfort her distress but didn't see the relief in her eyes. Brent continued, "Alex, your friend has been restrained and sedated, just enough to run tests but you can't go near him, he is under quarantine. You may only speak to him through the window, and you will need to be suited up even to enter."

Alex wasn't sure what he meant by 'suited up' and stared up at the truck before entering, it resembled a large enclosed blood donation bus with the entrance steps that lead to a small closet area filled with biohazard suits. Alex wrinkled her nose at the strong smell of antiseptic that hit her like a wall; it even made it past the menthol rub she'd smeared under her nose earlier. First, Brent directed her to wash her hands in the bathroom that was fully equipped with a shower, and then he helped her to put on a hazmat suit over her clothes. The confined area left barely enough room for the two of them to maneuver around. As he assisted Alex in carefully pulling the white suit over her shoes, her heart started to beat faster. She wasn't accustomed to being in such an intimate proximity with a man she didn't know. He gripped her leg gently as she used his bent-over back to balance herself, "I think I can get it by myself."

Brent stood up with his face inches from hers, "Sorry, but unless you're properly trained in donning a hazmat suit, I must assist you." Alex nodded and turned for him to zip the back, then held out her hands as he pulled the gloves over them. His slight grin enveloped his whole face and crinkled up the skin around his deep brown eyes, "We can't risk exposing anyone else, especially someone as helpful as you."

Was that flirting or did he treat everyone so carefully and pleasantly, "So, what brings a CEO down here to the middle of a quarantined area? Isn't this a little below your pay grade?" Alex pressed herself up against the wall to give Brent some room to move and dress in his hazmat suit.

Expertly pulling up his suit, Brent smiled, "I prefer to keep track of everything going on in the company, and you saw the fun going on in the tent, I am needed here. I can better oversee the investigation if I am directly involved, especially if the investigation does not stay within our company." His smile faded as the words came out of his mouth.

Confused, Alex furrowed her eyebrows, "What does that mean?"

Brent ignored her question as he smoothed the hair out of her face and plopped the headpiece over her head. It looked like a windowed bucket with flaps that attached to the suit. Unsure of how she felt about the situation Alex walked toward the window to talk to David, and a fan blew down on her. It sounded similar to a hurricane and startled her, but her reaction may have been to the anxiety building up over the morning's stress. David hadn't stopped yelling the entire time. She had never heard him say anything for so long or so loudly. Inhaling deeply, she slowly exhaled trying to relieve the tension she felt before she gently tapped on the glass with her gloved hand, "David, it is me, Alex."

Behind the small room's window, David still wore his military jacket and appeared no different from every other day except he lay strapped to a rolling stretcher. He jerked his head toward the window, trying to get a better look at who was speaking to him, "Alex? Is 'at you? You look like one of these yahoos. Why am I in here? I did nothin' wrong." He struggled back and forth against the straps, "Get me out." Alex ached at seeing the anxious expression on his face and watching him struggle.

She pursed her lips to hide her emotions, and noticed he appeared glassy-eyed and tired, "David, I could hear you yelling outside."

"Yep, that's the idea." He let out a few more hoots and struggled against the straps some more, then made snapping noises like he would bite anyone that came close to him, "They shot me up with something and threw me in here. I bet they are stealin' all my stuff right now."

Turning to look at Brent who stood right next to her, Alex mouthed the word "What?!"

Brent shrugged, "Unfortunately when a patient poses any kind of threat to personnel or others, the protocol demands we subdue the victim with a mild sedative. The effects are merely temporary, until he calms down, although it doesn't seem to be working on your friend here. The investigation will probably claim many of his belongings, but eventually, he may get some of them back."

With a deep sigh, Alex decided to ignore the question about his stuff, most of it was garbage, yet he remained attached to it. She hoped his cats weren't seized and put down. It would break David's heart. She thought about how she could best handle David's agitated state, and blunt honesty always worked well for her in the past, "Well, if you want to stay sedated and strapped to a table, keep acting crazy."

David's mouth dropped open, and he scowled, "I ain't crazy and I can't let them take me. I gotta be here, just in case."

In case what? She leaned her bucketed head against the glass not sure of what he meant, "I know you aren't crazy, but right now your behavior suggests that you are and nobody is going to believe anything different until you start acting like a civilized man. You need to let these doctors and nurses do their jobs and stop snapping at them. If they think you'll bite, they will treat you like an animal."

Snorting, David shook his head, "Never you mind, I only look crazy 'cause they got me all drugged up."

"Until you start acting calm and reasonable, they will keep you strapped down and continue drugging you and probably with something much stronger; then, you will be a lump unable to make choices or even speak. They merely need to take some samples of your blood to make sure you aren't sick, and I need you to be okay."

With a high-pitched squeal, David lifted his head and squawked at the medical staff, "I ain't sick!"

Alex crossed her arms hoping to relay that her patience was running out, even though it wasn't, "Doug died you know, and they need to test you to make sure you aren't sick too."

David smiled at Alex, and momentarily stopped struggling, "I never liked that bastard."

Alex knew he couldn't stand Doug and he wasn't shy about expressing it, "That is not a very nice thing to say no matter what you thought of the man."

David pouted and scowled before he barked, "He's never been right in the head, and I sensed danger being around him."

Alex thought she could enlist his cooperation if she compared the two. He'd hate anyone to think he was anything like Doug, "You know, right now, you don't look too right in the head either, do you?"

"The man was garbage, I could tell, and I never hurt nobody I wasn't supposed to."

Brent glanced at Alex with raised eyebrows, and Alex shook her head, "David was a marine, a hero, in fact."

Leaning in to speak to David, Brent held up his finger to Alex to signal her to give him a moment to talk, "Well, we can't treat our heroes this way, can we? David, please be my guest at Dashcorp's facility, it has very nice accommodations. Unfortunately, we cannot let you go until we clear you of the illness Doug died from, and I'd like to get you un-strapped."

While Alex appreciated Brent's attempted assistance, David's reaction looked panicked instead of reassured, and he struggled more violently against the straps and shook his head around, "I ain't goin' to no funny farm!"

Alex tapped rapidly on the window, afraid he'd be tranquilized, "Please, nobody is taking you to a mental hospital. Brent is talking about a medical research facility, a nice one, the one that Rebecca works at. Brent is her boss so whatever he says goes."

David eyed her suspiciously, "Huh, sounds like a funny farm to me and I can't go to no funny farm, especially if that witch is there."

Alex had a difficult time expressing herself with the suit and bucket hat in the way, so she tried to convey her feelings emphatically through the tone of her voice, "Oh come on now."

Brent snickered at the witch comment, "Oh, you must know Dr. Martin. You aren't the first to call her a witch, but I can keep her away from you if you prefer."

The conversation distracted David enough that he spoke and acted more normally. He liked the attention on his jokes about Rebecca, "Naah. I's jokin' 'bout the witch part, sort of, but she is a pain in mah tush. You're her boss, huh? Well, I won't know a soul and will get lonely. I don't want some stranger stickin' needles in me, better the witch."

"I have an idea that may help. We usually only allow family to visit, but I can stretch the rules for you to see Alex and the witch of course."

Brent seemed to enjoy calling Rebecca a witch and the joy he expressed in delivering the label got a snicker from both David and Alex, which lightened the tension enough for her to continue, "Yes and I will come by and visit as often as I can."

David turned abruptly back to the window, and picked at the straps with his fingernail, "Ya will? That is mighty kind of you Alex. You are always such a sweet girl. I don't want to go without my stuff and how am I gonna look out for this place if I'm not here? Now boss man, tell me how long I gotta stay there and what about my mashed potatoes? I don't feel comfortable with a stranga pokin' at me, and I'd rather the witch even if she is a bit rough. Can't you go get her now, so I can get out of these straps?"

Brent nodded his head, "Yes sir." He looked at Alex and shrugged, "I will make sure you get mashed potatoes, as much as you want and I will let the technicians know you are my special guest so they will treat you like a king. And the witch," Brent smiled while he said it, "can draw your blood when necessary if you prefer. As for the area here under the bridge, nobody will have access to it, everyone that lived here, is quarantined and a guard will remain here until further notice, it will be safe."

The expression on David's face slackened, "Okay, but don't let them trap me there Alex. I'm trustin' you."

CHAPTER 8

Day 5

Brent met Alex at the security station the next day, and a sizeable muscle-bound guard took her fingerprints. Brent waited patiently through the entire process. Wow, he certainly thrusts himself into all aspects of the job. He is nothing like Rebecca described him. She said he strutted around like a peacock getting in the way of her work, but he seemed quite helpful to Alex. Why did Rebecca find him so annoying? Yes, he tried a little hard to lay on the charm, which Alex never entirely trusted, and he also treated that poor Judy a little insensitively, but Rebecca did too. In fact, he seemed very pleasant and even patient with Rebecca and all her antics.

The empty Dashcorp halls echoed as Brent lead Alex through white hallway after white hallway. She was relieved she had a guide because she'd undoubtedly lose her way without one. Brent explained the purpose of each new area they walked through, showed Alex to a locker room and once again helped her carefully dress in a hazmat suit, before leading her to see Tristan. He explained that the hazmat suits were merely a precaution because the area was initially set up for drug trials, and while it remained secure, the filtration systems were being upgraded to work safely with the unknown levels of toxicity. Dashcorp took the highest level of precaution possible.

They entered an area filled with rows of plastic walled closets yet on closer inspection, the closets were actually compact rooms, and they stopped at the one Tristan occupied. The room looked like all the other ones each with a bed, a desk, and chair, but he had a television set on the desk. The door to a small bathroom area stood ajar and contained a sink embedded into the tank of a toilet and a shower head poked out of the wall. A wet room? Tristan must have sensed that he wasn't alone because he looked up from his bed, raised his eyebrows, and grinned, Alex placed her gloved hand on the window and started talking, but Tristan didn't respond. Brent leaned in to switch on the comm, "I'll be back in 30 minutes. I am trusting you with the rules because well, Dr. Martin told me to and she scares me." He smiled and casually walked down the hall out of sight.

"Noted." Alex turned to her brother, "Did I wake you?"

"Ha! You know I never sleep, I merely enjoy thinking about new ideas." Tristan rolled out of his bed then dragged a chair over to the window, "Thirty minutes?"

She felt a little odd standing at the window looking in on her brother like he was merchandise, and she didn't know what to do with her hands, "Yes, Rebecca managed to get as much time as possible without causing a stir, at least it is something. New ideas? What kind of ideas?"

"You know me, sis, my mind is never quiet." He tapped his temple and made a silly face, "In fact, it keeps me entertained for hours. I never get bored and have the most stimulating conversations. Who is your friend? He doesn't look like any of the techs or guards I've seen around here before."

Alex gestured down the hall to where Brent had walked, "Brent? I just met him yesterday. He is Rebecca's boss, Dr. Brent Adams."

"She has her boss escorting you around? Wow, that woman has moxy!"

Bursting with laughter, Alex shook her head, "No, I met him when he and Rebecca were under the bridge investigating. He offered to escort me."

Tristan huffed and narrowed his eyes, "How many times do I have to ask you to please stop going down there! Wait, investigating what?"

Here it came, Alex didn't want another lecture about how she spent her free time and tried to change the subject, "You still haven't answered my question."

"What question?"

"What kind of things were you pondering?"

"You know, ideas, hey, stop changing the subject. That is my trick. Why do you insist on putting yourself in harm's way? I repeat, investigating what?"

"I am doing what I feel I need to do, but it won't be a problem anymore, the area is shut down."

The tone of Tristan's voice changed, he was losing patience for Alex's evasive answers, "Why is it shut down?"

Alex peered down at her hands unable to pick at her cuticles so she cracked her knuckles instead, "They moved the residents out."

"Why?"

"Come on Tristan, don't worry about it, I came here to visit you and catch up." She wanted to spend her time with him laughing and talking not dwelling on something she wouldn't change about her choices. Yesterday's drama had drained her enough, and she didn't want to add to it by wasting their limited time together talking about quitting, it wasn't going to happen.

Tristan folded his arms and erased all the expression from his face, a sure sign that he was seconds from exploding, "You came to see me. There isn't much to catch up on. I was in jail, now I am in another kind of prison, although this one is much quieter, thank goodness. Now, what aren't you telling me, Alex?"

Alex's ability to hide information from her brother was nonexistent. He was like a detective and always knew when she was holding back. His persistence upset her and now when she spoke, her voice wavered, "I didn't come to fight with you. Can we have a normal conversation? Please, tell me what kind of ideas you were thinking about so we can get this visit back on track." Alex hated fighting with anyone, let alone her brother; it made her anxious and uncomfortable.

Tristan scrunched up his eyes then cocked his head in confusion, "I didn't think we were fighting, I thought we were having a discussion, one in which you were being very evasive. Listen lil' sis, you know you will tell me eventually, so you may as well tell me now. I have so little happening at this time in my life, except sitting in a cell, that I spend much of my time thinking and worrying about you, at least give me the respect of being honest with me."

Alex wrinkled up her nose, reluctant to divulge the previous day's events, "One of the residents got sick and died, so they cleared out the area under the bridge. And before you ask, don't worry, I never went near the resident that got sick, nobody did."

Tristan stared blank-faced, "Okay." She hated when he responded that way. It gave her no insight into what he thought or felt. He glanced over his shoulder to the television on the desk, she felt her anxiety rise at the tension level, and her stomach felt like it had a rock in it. She opened her mouth to say something but changed her mind, clamping it shut. She had not envisioned their visit being an argument, and she wanted to cry then start all over. He looked back at her and smiled, one of his warm, toothy grins that lit up the room, as well as Alex's heart, the smile that always made her feel like everything was going to work out, "I am glad you came Alex. You are my favorite person in this world, and I miss you when we can't talk to each other."

With a sigh of relief, the tension decreased and Alex smirked, "So what kind of ideas were you pondering?"

"I'm considering a speed limitation device for vehicles, a device attachable to cars that regulates..." Tristan excitedly explained his newest idea and Alex wondered if it was another far-fetched dream or if he'd pursue it. He had plenty of ideas, but he liked the design and disliked the implementation phases. The thirty minutes flew by, and Brent appeared by Alex's side, with an uncomfortable half-grin, he introduced himself to Tristan, and they all said their goodbyes. As Alex and Brent walked down the corridor, Brent lightly took Alex's arm, "Would you like to eat lunch before visiting with your friend David?"

Getting unsuited and re-suited again would be a lot of work, but she'd enjoy her visit with David much more on a full stomach, "I'd love that, thank you."

On the way to the cafeteria, Alex's phone rang and she wanted to ignore it but briefly excused herself instead. The soup kitchen manager. She'd forgotten to call the kitchen about the changes in deliveries but didn't want Brent to see her as irresponsible, so she tried to make the call quick. His gruff exterior and gruff voice matched perfectly, and in her mind, she saw him barking into the phone as he spoke, "What is happening with your delivery route? Should we make food for the residents under the bridge?"

She grinned in Brent's direction and hoped he didn't think her rude, "No, the bridge route is temporarily suspended because it is under quarantine and all the residents were moved into a quarantine facility for an indeterminate period of time. I will keep you updated with any changes in the situation." The kitchen manager grunted an incomprehensible response and hung up.

Brent watched her with a curious expression on his face but said nothing and she wondered what went through his brain when he looked at her like that. After they got their food and selected a table in the corner of the almost empty cafeteria, he started eating. She had ordered one of her favorites, an open-faced turkey sandwich with mashed potatoes, corn and a side of cranberries. She longed to take a giant bite but decided against it and nibbled instead. Alex assumed she'd inadvertently spit food at him if she ate and tried to talk at the same time. Brent paused while he watched her before blurting out, "Do you think that feeding these people is helping them?"

She didn't know what to say or even quite understand what he meant by the question, so she hesitatingly answered, "Well, of course, starving them isn't going to help them." As Alex glanced down at her full plate, as guilt enveloped her, she lost her appetite. She knew she gave the residents more than food on her visits and hoped they were being well-taken care.

Brent peered deeply into her eyes as if he looked for something, then matter of factly responded, "What about the adage, a handout is a handout, and people sit back and wait for more when they can get it for free. They've lost their self-respect, and charity doesn't help them, it demeans them. Why else would they choose to live in such a drastic way?"

Alex momentarily paused to work through her confusion. She had thought Brent prided himself on being some kind of philanthropist and didn't understand the conversation, "Huh? They've definitely lost their self-respect, and for whatever reason, they ended up there without a home or a path in life. They shouldn't starve because they've lost their way."

"But as long as you help them, they will never help themselves. They will choose to live under the bridge, day after day, not doing anything for anyone, and merely taking up space and creating waste. You help them do that. I believe in helping people, don't get me wrong, but they need to pull themselves up by their bootstraps and stop wasting away. You only get one chance at life."

Alex rolled her eyes and felt her face flush as the annoyance then anger built up inside her. Through a clenched jaw she tried to control her words, "Are you so blind to see only your side of life? How is a person supposed to pull themselves up by their bootstraps when their hunger blinds them or their psyche is riddled with addiction or mental health issues? I don't know if any of them will ever make changes to their lives, but if they waste away to nothing, they'll never get a chance. You're correct, they only have one life they get to live, but do you think that any of these men and women grew up thinking, when I grow up I want to be homeless and hungry?"

Brent smiled, seeming to enjoy the conversation, "No person chooses that." Was he baiting her?

With a smug smile, Alex paused, "You just won this little debate for me. Lost is lost, they don't choose to lose that way. I am feeding them so that if they ever a see another option, they can make a change. I don't give them money or drugs; I give them food. They rarely experience kindnesses and trust almost nobody." She won that debate far too quickly. What was he up to with this conversation?

"If nobody fed them they'd still need to procure food to eat, that little act of living could help them make other choices to move their lives toward self-respect and an actual life."

He wasn't finished, and her frustration with the conversation increased, "Really? I feed them once a day. Have you ever been hungry? I mean starving? You cannot even get your thoughts straight in your head. Feeding them gives them an opportunity to see straight, something they won't do if they starve. I've seen tremendous kindnesses from the most destitute and the greatest cruelties from people with the most. I choose to feed them because my conscience will not allow me to do anything else."

Alex swore she could see the corner of Brent's mouth twitch like he was holding back a smile, yet he continued to question her, "But why there? Why those people? Why not children or people who at least attempt more than living as the refuse of our society?"

She didn't understand why he frustrated her so much, yet it enticed her to persist with the insane debate, so she tried to explain it on a personal level, "A friend convinced me to go down there at the lowest point in my life. She took me there, and I saw a light in the eyes of some of them, a light that could extinguish if we forget about those people. I've seen that light ignite into friendships, hope, and even love when there was none before. If we can find a way to help them survive until they can solve their own problems then they can accomplish anything?"

"That is a little idealistic, don't you think?"

She wanted to scream at him but knew from experience she needed to remain calm for him to take her seriously, "It is extremely idealistic, but feeding them keeps them alive and I prefer that to their other options."

"Each time I'm almost convinced that your way of thinking is worth considering you say something like that. They haven't yet figured out a way to resolve their issues. Why do you think there is any hope of a change for the better just because they survive? And what about mass murderers and rapists? Do you think they deserve the chance to make their lives better? You don't know what those people you are helping may be guilty of."

Alex struggled with the question because of her history, but she knew the right answer, "If a person changed shouldn't they be allowed to make amends? If they haven't and live under the bridge wouldn't you rather they stay there?"

Brent shook his head and grunted, "I'd rather see violent criminals pay for their crimes, but I understand your sentiment. You are truly a romantic at heart aren't you?"

Alex shook her head. She couldn't tell if his comment was complementary or condescending to her, "Not at all, I am a realist. I know the statistics for these men and women, but what requirements does a person need to possess to be treated like a human being? If someone hurt you, and a stranger stepped in and saved you, would you feel their lives worthy then?"

Brent's face contorted a little in confusion. Alex knew her response didn't make much sense without the context of her past but he conceded anyway, "I am still not a believer, but I see your point, a little."

"Whether you do or not, it makes no difference. Our responsibility in our one little life is to make the world a better place and those who don't, always feel as if they've missed out on something and grow to regret their choices at some point and it leaves a void." She raised her eyebrows and pointedly eyed him, "Unless you are a complete narcissist of course. They try to fill the void with stuff or distractions, and those tactics never work for long, then they must move on to the next thing trying to fill the void. I use my time in a way I can live with to fill my void, and it never grows old in its thoroughness, unless you look for immediate results. I am not a fool. I know what results can be expected." Alex lost her appetite. Inside she yearned to shout that she knew it was the right thing to do and she didn't need to prove it, but something about this man grounded her, which helped to argue less emotionally. It was a soapbox sermon to be proud of, and Brent looked pleased instead of annoyed like she felt. She longed for a kickboxing class at that moment.

Judy attended the early sermon at church and most of the time her husband escorted her. Dressed in her Sunday best, she said hello to all her acquaintances and made time to speak with the pastor while her husband waited patiently near the church building's exit. Judy urged her husband to get home quickly so she could attend to her emails and the private message board of the Viralist Justice Blog. He whined when they got in the car because today they were supposed to go out for pancakes after church. As sweetly as she could she reassured him, "Darling I want to make them for you myself. It is from the heart when I make them." He stopped complaining and the rest of the drive was in silence.

Judy quickly prepared her husband a massive stack of pancakes, cut him up some fruit and whipped up some cream for his fruit after making his coffee. She turned to leave the kitchen and heard him ask, "Aren't you having any? You love pancakes."

"No dear, I am not hungry." She quickly waddled over to the computer. Judy wished she had the cute little prance of Christy or the authoritative strut that Rebecca had, but no, she waddled. With a big sigh, she plopped down into her chair, turned on the news and saw a prerecorded investigative report from Christy. Wow, she is expanding her work, no wonder she wasn't in church today!

The camera was pointed at Christy and the background behind her was a blur, she was in a moving vehicle, "This is Christy Gallagher reporting on our investigation of the incident in Columbia Heights and it has led us here." The camera rotated in the direction they were driving, following behind large white vans, "As you can see we're following the Dashcorp vehicles, none of these vans are going to the morgue. We seem to be heading in the direction of Dashcorp's main research facility. It is one of the best-equipped research facilities in the world today. This reporter contacted Dashcorp's CEO Dr. Brent Adams for comment, and I have not yet received a reply." The caravan reached the fenced perimeter of Dashcorp, and all the vans proceeded in, but the news van was halted at the guarded gate. Christy reached her microphone out to the security guard, "Sir, do you know what is happening behind these walls?"

"Ma'am, I am going to need to ask you to leave, you are on private property."

"Well, there you have it; Dashcorp confiscated a body that rightfully should have gone to the morgue. The Dashcorp medical facilities management has denied my repeated requests for an interview, as the Fulton Penn situation grows out of control. What are they hiding?

For the first time in a long time, Judy knew she was doing important work.

Alex walked along the long white hall and tried to remember the name of tech escorting her. His lanyard had twisted up with other key-cards and made his ID card impossible to read. The pleasant enough fellow didn't say much and his hair looked like he just woke up in a true absent-minded professor style. If his movements jerked any more abruptly, she could have easily confused him for a crazy-haired robot. Great, now she'd call him her crazy-haired robot escort, in her mind, all day. Ugh, it had better not slip out. The hall accommodated an endless number of even more hallways, as well as mysterious metal doors with electronic locks. Ceaseless white upon white, like some scene from a science-fiction movie. Tristan said that sci-fi inspires all scientific advances. He might be right, as the Star Trek shows he regularly subjected her to her entire life flaunted electronic work pads, computer voice software, and communication devices that resembled cell phones. She couldn't even recall how many sci-fi movies in which she'd seen this hallway.

The walk with Brent seemed to speed by much more quickly; he talked to her the entire time, but this guy only spoke when necessary. Crazy-haired robot stopped and punched a long code into the keypad before swiping his key card, then led her back to the locker room that Brent had brought her to earlier and directed her through the doors on one side, Alex nodded and paused, "Don't you need to help me?"

Crazy-haired robot scrunched up his face, apparently confused, "Why would I do that?"

"But I thought, there were protocols or uh, Bre--, Never mind." She felt her face burning. Hmmm, interesting, Brent was a real player, and she fell for it. She scampered into the room so she wouldn't need to look crazy-haired robot in the eye, found, then donned a hazmat suit. Brent's help made putting it on easier, but she managed by herself.

Alex met crazy-haired robot back in the main locker room area, still trying to avoid looking him in the eye, but he barely noticed her presence. She wondered if his crazy hair got scrunched up in the hazmat suit or was his hair so resilient that it popped back up when he removed his helmet. He silently led her through some air locked doors to another white hallway, "The patient you are visiting has been sleeping on the floor under the bed."

Alex shrugged, "He is accustomed to sleeping in a small space on the ground, so the bed might feel odd to him." She stared in, unsure of what to say. A clean-cut man in scrubs sat on the bed with his head shaved almost all the way to the scalp and she didn't recognize him. Robot escort must have brought her to the wrong room.

The clean-cut man turned, noticed her, and smiled a giant welcoming grin, one that, from the way his posture relaxed, expressed relief, "Alex!"

She knew the warmth of his eyes no matter how the rest of his appearance had changed, "David?"

Self-consciously David looked up to where his hair used to be and rubbed his head, "Yeah, they said I had lice and they shaved off all my hair. What do you think?"

David had never shaved his beard or cut his hair before and the change shocked Alex, "You look very different, but I like it. Are you okay?" Now she could see David's face was handsome beyond his big brown eyes. Slight scarring on his cheeks gave him a rugged but friendly appearance, although his ears stuck out and were slightly different sizes, it added to his charm. He wasn't wearing his green military jacket, and she had never, in all her years visiting under the bridge, seen him without it.

He rubbed his face as if he needed to wake himself up, "Yeah the bastards medicated me too, so I am a bit dopey, but besides the grogginess I am okay. They feed me as much as I want and a man brought me this here television, he said I was special, and he needed to take good care of me. I have been watching all kinds of stuff; television sure has changed over the years." David got closer to where Alex stood, like being closer would help hide what he was about to say, then he

77

whispered, "You think they really put my stuff in storage or do you think they chucked it all?"

Trying to smile reassuringly, Alex whispered back, "I am sure if they said they would keep it for you, they did, I am sorry you are here."

"Me too, it is a little quieter than I am used to, so it is creepy, and I miss my cats. They used to sleep with me, and I can barely get any sleep without them. Now that Doug is gone, I should sleep like a baby. His demons finally got him. He'd been squawking about those demons for years, and he knew they were goin' ta kill him."

"I don't think his demons killed him, David, a disease did."

David adamantly shook his head, "Oh no, his demons got him, he was an evil man, and I won't miss him one bit. I am just glad the demons never got you or that witch you hang around with." Alex chuckled, but when she opened her mouth defend her friend, David grunted, "Oh, I know ya like her and all, but I can see it in her eyes, I ain't fooled by that pretty face. There is a witch behind them eyes, and it terrifies me."

She snorted at that comment, "You aren't the first to find her intimidating."

"Nope, she's a witch. Now, what'd ya bring me? I can see ya got something there behind yer back."

She held out a fluffy stuffed cat and felt her face burning. Bringing a stuffed animal to a grown man made her feel foolish, "Don't think I am too silly, but I know how you love your cats, so I brought you one you could have here." She shrugged as she half-smiled, "I couldn't resist when I saw it, and now you won't need to sleep alone."

David's his face lit up, "Alex that is the nicest thing anyone has given me in years, except the mashed potatoes ya bring me, you know how I love those. Well, gimme!"

Alex dropped the stuffed cat into a chute in the wall, and David reached in to grab it. He immediately hugged and stroked it, its super soft fur begging to be touched. He turned to her and she saw tears welling up in his eyes, "Thank you, Alex, this here kitty is quite a thoughtful gift, maybe now I can get some sleep." Somehow, David appreciated it, and Alex's relief swept away her earlier embarrassment. Then, suddenly his eyes grew large as his face filled with anxiety, "What about my cats? Who is gonna feed them? They must miss me."

"Don't worry, I already got food and poured some out for them this morning. They also they keep the area clear of rodents and bugs. They have plenty to eat and I'm sure they'll be fine.

The answer seemed to appease David, so he returned his attention to the stuffed cat. From the corner of her eye, she spotted movement and turned to see Brent. Huh, he came back. She thought their little debate scared him off. Visible through his hazmat suit's mask He flashed her a huge grin with sincerity expressed not only in his smile but also in his eyes. He greeted David, but David only grunted at him and nodded before returning his attention to his stuffed animal, petting it slowly. Alex turned to Brent, "I am surprised you came back."

"Why? I told you I'd catch back up with you." His eyes filled with mischievousness as he flashed another of his brilliant smiles.

Alex glanced down at her gloved hands and fiddled with them, "Well, I thought after our little debate..."

Brent raised his eyebrows in surprise and chuckled, "No."

She felt her stomach swirling and against her better judgment decided to take a chance, "Well, maybe we could have a more agreeable conversation over dinner tonight?"

"Now that is a fantastic idea; however, I can't."

Instantly, her stomach went from swirling with excitement and nervousness to feeling like a big block pounded its way through her insides toward the floor, "Oh, okay." Alex felt foolish for asking. Of course, he was only being polite by asking her to lunch. She had no sense with men, and she usually never asked them out. They were usually either gay or interested in Rebecca. She was going to rage at Rebecca for this one! Just because he was pleasant toward her did not mean he wanted to spend time with her. He probably went out with a different beautiful woman every night of the week.

Brent led Alex down to the locker room, and neither said much on the way before they both changed out of their hazmat suits. In the lobby, Alex pushed out her hand to shake Brent's, "Thank you for taking the time out of your day to escort me to see Tristan and David."

Brent smirked, reached in for her hand, and pulled her a little closer staring directly into her eyes, "The pleasure was mine." After several moments, he released her hand and gestured toward the exit. Alex's embarrassment grew into annoyance at his last flirtation. Ignore it, it didn't mean anything. Near the door, Alex glanced over to Brent; he rubbed his forehead and took a deep breath, "Tomorrow is going to be an extremely difficult day."

Questions circled Alex's head, but before she could ask anything of him, he said goodbye and left.

CHAPTER 9

Day 6

Rebecca sped straight into her parking spot, slamming on her brakes and screeching her tires. What could be so crucial that Judy needed to call a meeting first thing in the morning? She slammed the door to her car, oops, not the car's fault. She marched up to the conference room and saw through the window that Judy and Nithi sat on one side of the table and on the opposite side Brent had just pulled up a chair to sit. Before stepping through the door, Rebecca took a deep breath and pasted on her Mona Lisa smile to hide her annoyance. All three glanced over at Rebecca as she paused in the doorway. Judy and Nithi would shortly feel the brunt of her agitation. Brent might escape, but only as long as he didn't waste her time.

Neat piles of papers lay in front of each person's seat; Brent's on one side, and three others across from him. Rebecca ambled over to her pile picked it up then sat next to Brent, circumventing Judy's attempts to assert her importance. Rebecca read over the paperwork in front of her, dated with Saturday's date. Doug's initial DNA connected him to multiple unsolved rape, child molestation, missing person, and murder cases across the country. His tent contained the boxes of rubber banded hair clippings with other "mementos" from his crimes, 78 horrors in total. Great. Rebecca couldn't believe Alex had fed the monster. Brent cleared his throat to speak, "Judy, why wouldn't you share this report with all of us on Saturday when we had someone there who could answer questions about the victim?"

Placing her hand over her collarbone, Judy haughtily replied, "I tried, but you and Rebecca were too involved in speaking with her friend to listen." Judy smirked in Rebecca's direction and gestured over the paperwork, "As you can see, I compiled all the paperwork necessary to discuss the progress of the case.

Rebecca's nostrils flared, "You refused to show me because you wanted Brent to see it first?"

Judy shrugged one of her shoulders, "You should have let me talk, Rebecca knows the-"

Brent's breathing grew audibly louder, and he interrupted in a voice, so calm it even unnerved Rebecca, "We don't have time for this kind of bureaucratic incompetence. What were you trying to do?" Nithi sunk into his chair and Judy's pallor paled, clearly conveying the fear of her political miscalculation. Brent leaned in, and the volume of his voice slowly increased, "Dashcorp is dealing with a fatal pathogenic outbreak, and you hold back critical information to show me first? Rebecca could have used this yesterday, while SHE was working." Brent turned to Rebecca, "I saw you needling her too, and while you may find it funny, but it is completely unprofessional. You are both acting like children, and I have no tolerance for it. You do realize that the world is watching Dashcorp and every move it makes? I need professionals working together so we can quickly resolve this fatal outbreak. As it is, the CDC has stepped in, now that the pathogen is beyond our facility."

Judy sputtered, "I-I've never been questioned about my administrative or management skills."

"This isn't about you. Tell me you understand, and you will stop playing these games because this investigation is not a game. In. Any. Way." Brent slapped his forehead, "I feel like I am back in the lab dealing with interns and their petty, self-serving behavior." Disgust filled Brent's face, as his voice rose, "People are dying! You were supposed to lead the administrative aspect of her investigative research team, and I put you both together because I thought you could complement each other's work expertise. I am not messing around here!"

Judy voice wavered as she pointed to Rebecca, "She is making it very difficult to do my job."

Brent practically screamed at the top of his lungs, "I give up! If your actions impede others' work on a special committee, I don't want you on it at all. Judy, you are excused from the committee and will not join another until you can exhibit more than a passing proficiency in administrative duties, as well as in dealing with difficult colleagues."

Judy stared open-mouthed then squeaked, "I don't know what to say." She managed to nod her head before glaring at Rebecca and scurrying off.

Brent turned to Nithi, "I take it from the expression on your face that you understand we work as a team, not as individuals vying for promotions or acknowledgment." Nithi straightened in his chair, and vehemently nodded his head, but before he could even get a word out, Brent turned to glare at Rebecca and continued, "I put you on the special committee because I wanted to get you out of the lab to flex your creative problem-solving abilities. I did not put you on a committee to torture your teammates."

"And also because Abe requested me?" She felt a little less sure of herself but needed to remind him that she did not openly request the appointment to the assemblage of verbosity.

"Yes, and because Abe said you would resolve this issue, but treating your colleagues with respect, no matter how you feel about them, is a much more effective way to get things done. Acting like an ass won't get you out of the committee, which is what I think you were aiming for, but I won't tolerate the unprofessional behavior."

She shrugged before smugly replying, "I never treated Judy with any disrespect. I simply pushed her passive-aggressive buttons." The expression on Brent's face grew even more outraged, and while she wanted to gloat, it rattled Rebecca's confidence enough that she conceded, "Fine, I will play nice, but I cannot help it if you put incompetent people on a committee with me." She looked over at Nithi whose blank face showed no emotion at all, he must have been afraid to move or even breathe too loudly.

"You sound like a complete narcissist." Brent closed his eyes and shook his head while he breathed deeply for a moment, "You had a moment to review the reports. Any theories?"

"Oh, who's replacing Judy?"

"Do you ever answer a question?"

"Do you?"

Brent's voice adopted the eerily calm tone again, and he chuckled in a non-humorous manner, "I see why you usually work alone, and I warned you I'm not messing around. Stop being so difficult, and trust me those words are far milder than the ones I want to use. None of the situation that you are so flippant about is a joke. If you weren't extremely competent at your job, I'd fire you just to get you out of my hair. I will replace you as lead and oversee the investigation myself, and you will only lead the research aspect of it. Nithi will take over Judy's administrative duties, and I expect complete professionalism from here on out." Brent raised his eyebrows still waiting for his answer.

Half-smirking at what felt was a win, Rebecca cocked her head, "Only extremely competent? Well, I can do what I need to do. Nithi and I will do just fine together won't we?" Before Brent could say anything else, Rebecca scooted over toward Nithi and started dividing the reports. Nithi continued to sort the full gamut of data, and she turned to Brent with intense seriousness, all the humor gone from her face, "No matter my approach to dealing with others, my work is never a joke." She glared at Brent waiting for a reaction then, after a moment continued, "The data collected does not show any common denominators amongst pathogen victims with respect to contact or contraction, especially now we included the bridge fatality. Pulling the blood work analysis," Rebecca handed the report to Brent, "It shows no known detectable pathogens although we detected higher mineral levels within the infected blood. Transmission is an unknown as is all analyses regarding pathogen cell identification. The pathogen is unlike anything ever encountered. We can't find it."

Nithi tentatively spoke up, "We also have no further information about the one survivor. Rebecca interviewed him on Friday, and took follow-up samples, and according to reports, as of this morning, nothing has changed. He has developed no more symptoms beyond the initial fever and veining on the sides of his head and neck. The veining has not faded and has permanently discolored his skin. The hyperpigmentation is almost like a tattoo, except done with his own body's pigments and tissue, akin to a scar. Biopsies reveal that unlike tattoos, the hyperpigmentation permeates the depth of the skin and cannot be removed." Rebecca nodded her approval at Nithi.

Brent heaved a sigh then sat back with his hands interlaced behind his head, "That is not what I was hoping to hear. The CDC will be here soon but was hoping to turn them away when they got to our door. There is nothing I can do now to keep the investigation solely within Dashcorp, so get ready." Brent scowled at Rebecca, "Now you will both need to work with their staff and even though the investigation will proceed within our facility, their staff leadership will supersede our authority."

Rebecca lamented. Things were moving too fast. Saturday's discovery guaranteed that the CDC would get involved, but she hated the idea, "Ugh, I was afraid you were going to say that. When did you make the decision, today or Saturday?"

Brent's eye twitched, "Once the pathogen left our facility we lost our control. I knew you would work on it yesterday and hoped you'd find something, but since we don't have a solution to report, the investigation will be turned over to the CDC, as of today. Dr. Sonso and I already worked out contingency plans for just such an eventuality." Brent leaned forward to put his head into his hands, "I thought by now we'd have figured this out, administered antivirals, and nobody else would die. What a publicity nightmare." Rebecca and Nithi watched as he walked out without saying another word to them.

Rebecca's felt her nostrils flare and her face burn with rage. Brent had the empathy of a rock. She forcibly flicked a page across the table and under her breath, she seethed, "A publicity nightmare, what a caring person he is."

Shrugging, Nithi bent to pick up the paper she had sent flying to the floor then gathered the reports, "I'll get this."

Rebecca focused and studied the blood samples on the monitor and considered her plan for the investigation, including how to manage the CDC, but one thought kept pushing its way to the front of her mind, this is only the beginning of a long nightmare. She needed to start by analyzing the movements of Doug, and David could probably help her with that. At least by keeping David at the Dashcorp facility instead of the temporary quarantine warehouse, she'd have direct access to him. Hopefully, David hadn't contracted the pathogen. She owed him. He saved hers and Alex's life by being there on that day. Shouldn't a war here get a pass on dying from a terrible disease? Alex claimed he was one, although who can really know what that means. After coming home a hero, he chooses to live in a box? Why wouldn't the man move out of that wretched box and into a tent like all the other homeless? His awareness of everything that went on under that bridge shocked everyone, including Rebecca. He must have spy holes all over that thing.

Concentration had a way of stealing all the other senses and Rebecca hadn't even noticed anyone entering the lab. Now they stood right next to her. How did she let that happen? From her peripheral vision, Rebecca could see they were waiting to speak with her. Maybe they'd go away if she ignored them. She waited a few seconds and turned to see Abe in front of her with several people she had not seen before, probably the CDC. She delivered her friendliest smile, "Hello, I apologize. I was so engrossed in my work that I didn't see you. How may I help you?" Abe smirked at her comment, but her recent reprimand from Brent helped curb her urge to respond with her real feelings.

Gesturing to each person as he introduced them, Abe did not take his eyes off Rebecca. "Dr. Martin, I'd like to introduce you to Dr. Sonso and her colleagues, Josie Johnson, and Hector Vazquez. Dr. Sonso and her support staff, from the CDC, will take lead on the investigation." Abe raised his eyebrows, waiting for Rebecca's reaction. Dr. Sonso, a tall, thin woman in her fifties, had a hooked nose, curly hair, and small, piercing eyes that were maybe a little too close together and board-strait posture. She looked down her nose and pursed her lips when she was introduced. Josie, a big-boned, athletic young woman glanced down at her hands, seemingly embarrassed by the attention of an introduction. Hector, a dark-haired, handsome-faced young man with shockingly stunning, muted green eyes, pushed the glasses up on his nose, and grinned at Rebecca. He gawked, starry-eyed, the way most men did when they first met her.

. She couldn't believe the CDC was already involved. Great, more people to get in her way The pathogen's spread into the general population hastened CDC participation, no doubt, but it was unexpectedly swift. The pathogen's progress had advanced much swifter than she had anticipated and now with the CDC as part of the investigation, her methods would surely be derailed. Rebecca nodded her head with what she hoped was a friendly smile at each introduction. She needed to handle the situation correctly, time to channel her inner Alex. She reached out and shook each one of their hands, placing her own over each of theirs, and stepping closer to each person as she greeted them, trying to express warmth, "Thank you, Dr. Dunkin, it is my pleasure to meet you all. Dr. Sonso I've heard fantastic things about your work, please accept my apologies for not recognizing you on sight. How may I be of assistance?" That should do it. Dr. Sonso appeared pleased, and Abe seemed thoroughly amused although maybe a little confused too.

"Good morning Dr. Martin, I am happy to make your acquaintance. I look forward to reviewing your efforts on the investigation. We at the CDC,..."

Rebecca zoned out as Dr. Sonso babbled on about herself and the CDC. At least Brent managed to keep the investigation based out of Dashcorp's lab. How, she couldn't fathom, but maybe because CDC facilities weren't quite as extensive as the Dashcorp facility. Private companies didn't house as many administrative burdens as public health agencies like the CDC did, and Dashcorp was able to use its resources more efficiently with the most advanced equipment and talented researchers and had the required housing for the quarantined.

Sonso continued to babble, "-Of the reports from the WHO, U.S., Afghanistan, Pakistan, Turkey, the UK, the Republic of Congo, Sudan, Guatemala, India, and South Africa have high rates of an unknown pathogen causing fatalities reported in high numbers. The WHO is worried about a possible global pandemic."

Suddenly aware of the conversation, Rebecca blurted out, "The W.H.O.? Dr. Sonso, releasing that information to us before now may have helped us. How are they keeping the news quiet?"

Sonso inhaled deeply and raised one eyebrow at the interruption, "Your company is a for-profit business, and the CDC's charter is disease control and prevention. As a government agency, we are privy to information a private company is not."

Wow, those kinds of condescending remarks made playing nice much more difficult. Sonso said that as if she was speaking to a completely ignorant civilian. Rebecca's reputation was world renown, and even without her status, the sheer number of Ph.D.'s Rebecca held over almost everyone usually demanded a modicum of respect in academia, and Sonso dared to speak to her like that? Why would Sonso choose to talk to her in that manner, especially at their introduction? She needed to reign in the dialogue before she lost control of not only the conversation but also the investigation. Rebecca glanced over at Abe gaping at the turn in the discussion, probably waiting for Rebecca to blow her top, and Josie hunched over like she wanted to hide. Rebecca smiled and graciously nodded her head, "Of course Dr. Sonso, pardon the interruption; I am overwhelmed by shock at the pathogen's spread. We need to support each other as much as possible during this investigation, and those kinds of interruptions won't help either of us. Please continue."

Grinning smugly, Sonso continued, and Rebecca smiled to herself. She'd managed to control her behavior as well as play nice, now she commanded the conversation. Abe's mouth hung open, and his face expressed a state of shock. He shook his head, and quietly excused himself. Ugh, Sonso is incredibly annoying. I will smile and nod my head and play along instead of indulging in territory games and dominate the investigation. Judy tried to play games across the departments and lost; she had played from a weaker position and without some of the vital informational components to win. Sonso had the power to knock her out of the investigation entirely if she chose, and Rebecca couldn't let that happen. Not yet. She needed to know what Sonso knew, and see what she saw.

"Is the body ready?"

Rebecca nodded. She hated being part of the autopsies, it reawakened unpleasant memories, but today the circumstances demanded she attend, "Let me show you the way to the lab."

Judy seethed, overcome with rage so intense that she knew others sensed the emotion emanating from her in waves as she walked by. She hid in her office for the rest of the day, hoping nobody needed to speak with her. Judy had never felt such humiliation her in entire life yet Rebecca was the focus of her hatred, not Brent. At the end of the day, she snuck out of the office to avoid talking to anyone. Judy didn't stop at the store to pick up groceries for dinner and went straight home. Then she went straight to the computer and impatiently watched the news.

"This is Christy Gallagher reporting from Fulton State Penitentiary with an important update. Our government has finally taken the illnesses and medical conditions of these poor inmates seriously. Behind me, as you can see, a CDC truck has joined the Dashcorp contingent in-." Judy switched off the news, turned to the private message room with the Viralist, and typed out a message explaining what happened at work. A reply came almost immediately, "I am so sorry you are experiencing such a difficult time at work. Do you mean the woman you told me about in previous chats?" Judy replied that it was, and the Viralist sympathized, "Then she works against our cause, which is to bring righteousness back into the world. Trust me when I say, you will not have to do anything to her because she will be punished, as He extracts punishment on the profane evils of the Earth. It has begun. Only the chosen and most devout will live with him and he needs soldiers here on Earth to work for him. Are you willing to work for Him?"

Judy leaned back in her chair, wondering what he meant. Every previous communique with the Viralist had been uplifting and made her feel essential, but a soldier? She replied, "Without a doubt, I am one of His soldiers, but I could never do anything illegal or that I'd get in trouble for. I love Him and want to see the world properly run, that is all."

"God will never ask you to do anything that is immoral, but He needs your help. Only His love will save the devout. We must warn people so they can come back to Him before it is too late." Judy did not know what to do, and she saw the direction that the conversation was leading and didn't know how she felt about it. If she chose to turn away, would she too be guilty? "Judy?" The beating of Judy's heart echoed loudly, and she thought it might burst its way through her chest if she didn't make a decision. If the conversation continued, there would be no turning back.

Judy placed her fingers on the keyboard, "I am here."

Alex spied Rebecca appear from behind the hanging punching bag. Rebecca adjusted her gloves and jumped from one foot to the other to warm up. Alex had persevered through the weekend that lasted forever and felt like they hadn't worked out together in ages when it had only been days. Grateful that the relationship between them had finally returned to normal, she put on a cheerful smile, and fist-bumped Rebecca with her gloves, "Hello friend, where were you hiding?"

Grinning back, Rebecca, still hopping from one foot to the other, punched her two gloves together, and prepared for practice, "Oh? Oh, you know, under piles of paperwork and a microscope."

Alex longed to ask her about Tristan, David, and Doug but did her best to keep the questions to herself. Rebecca would eventually get to those topics and would mercilessly tease Alex if she didn't get to lead the conversation, especially if she had big news. Instead, Alex held the punching bag tightly for Rebecca to swing at and wondered why their friendship had such strange, sometimes childish dynamics. Rebecca adjusted her gloves again, and swung with a few gentle punches, whap, whap, whap, "I have big news. Someone is no longer part of the assemblage of verbosity."

"Ha, they couldn't stand working with you and let you off?"

Chuckling and shaking her head, Rebecca paused then looked pointedly at her friend, "Nope, they can't do anything without me, someone else."

"What?" Alex let go of the bag, it swung and knocked her to the side, and almost to the floor, but she managed to stay upright by clinging on to it, "I cannot believe it! All your infantile behavior and they kept you? Then it had to be that poor Judy dismissed from the committee, you were kind of relentless on her. I am surprised she didn't run screaming from the tent on Saturday. I wanted to, and we're friends."

"Huh. You know you love me and my antics, and yes it was Twiddle Dee. Of course, I wasn't dismissed because am I absolutely irreplaceable. Moreover, those so-called antics are just me testing my colleagues to see if they were worthy of working with me. I merely use humor to entertain myself especially when illogical fools surround me. The work never suffers." Alex rolled her eyes, which got a sneer from Rebecca, and she walloped the punching bag in retaliation before continuing, "But that isn't all, another organization had inserted itself into the investigation."

Alarmed, Alex felt her heart beating in her chest, because Rebecca had told her horror stories about dealing with the CDC. She wanted the whole thing to be over with so she could get to her routine of regularly visiting Tristan until he got out and seeing David and the other residents when she brought food to the area. CDC involvement meant the outbreak was more than just minor, and she leaned in closer to Rebecca, and then whispered, "You mean the CDC?

Rebecca delivered a glare ferocious enough to melt Alex's eyeballs, "Shhh, a little discretion, please! Saying it aloud alerts even the most clueless, and that is how unfounded rumors begin."

Alex shrugged and scrunched up her face apologetically, "Oh, sorry, but I did whisper."

"Well, I got rid of one annoying idiot only to gain an entire organization of them, and to make matters worse," Rebecca's rant continued, "I now have to work with a completely condescending bitch! All I want to do is the science, but now I get to deal with the distraction of bureaucracy and sweet-talking."

With a snort, Alex snickered, "Yes, that must be quite difficult, having to speak nicely to someone. In true Rebecca form, I am going to say, welcome to the real world honey." Alex chuckled some more, to which Rebecca furrowed her brow and snarled. Rebecca continued her snarky sneer and it caused Alex to erupt in a cackle so loud, other people in the gym glanced over. Alex, through the mirth, spat out, "Stop, I can barely stand up." Rebecca outwardly struggled to maintain her annoyed composure, but as she watched Alex fall to the floor, holding her stomach, and laughing, the annoyed looking woman smirked. Finally, Alex collected herself, stood up and chuckled but still couldn't wipe the smile from her face, "Sorry, I really mean that too. Uh, who is she and why is she a condescending bitch?"

Rebecca stood like an imposing giant with crossed arms and a scowl on her face, and started relaying the tale from earlier that day, "...Can you believe she said that to me! I've taken to calling her Sonso. She is an educated woman and-" Rebecca stopped mid-sentence as Alex felt her face contort into another snorting, laughing fit. Agitated by the interruption Rebecca barked, "What?"

"She sounds quite a bit like someone I know. Hmmm, I can see why you're so annoyed." Alex lost control of herself again and laughed even louder than the music as she ignored the scowl on Rebecca's face.

Rebecca gently pushed Alex backward, "What is with you today? Are you high? We are nothing alike. Urrgh, I am happy my pain creates such joy and laughter for you."

Alex gently shoved Rebecca back, "Oh lighten up. Someone should get to enjoy your pain for all that you inflict on others, and it may as well be me."

"Lovely, since your interest in the issue is personal, I will tell you that both my boss and the other organization involved in the investigation will now lead and may not allow some of the freedoms previously allotted."

Alex got the hint and dropped her hands, all her giggles gone, "Oh, that is a good reason to be out of sorts." Her breathing slowed, and her stomach roiled, "It is serious?"

Rebecca shrugged her shoulders, "We can't take any chances, so it's probably nothing."

"Why discuss this here, we should talk in code or go somewhere else."

Rebecca grunted, "You blew that one already, here is fine, besides our schedules won't allow for anything else. If we don't meet here, we will turn into big lumps, who only work, eat, sleep, and never see each other. If this place is bugged or I am being watched, I am probably going to jail, and all for you."

"Maybe Katie is right, and we need to get social lives, something beyond work and meeting at the gym."

"Seriously? Avoid the topic much? You accuse me of hiding, yet here you-"

Alex interrupted, "Yes, but I am not hiding! I need time to process the information. And yes, seriously, we're young; we should date and have fun."

"Process? Well, you choose to spend your free time saving the world, instead of having fun. You could date if you wanted, I don't date because I suck at it."

"Yes, process, because the situation has turned more serious, and just as I was having some fun. I thought it was just some odd flu bug. Please give me just this one. Now back to social lives, men drool over you all the time."

"Yes, they love me until I open my mouth, then they either get angry or run screaming. I kind of enjoy it but," Rebecca swung her arm over her forehead in feigned dismay, "it has lost its challenge. You, on the other hand, have no excuse except you're just sooo picky. Still processing?"

Alex nodding her head and grimaced, "Yes, still processing. Men aren't interested in me; they're nice to me, and there is a difference."

"Ha! I never saw my boss pay that much attention to anyone. He wasn't merely being nice to you."

"Please, he had a job to do, and he only did what he needed to do, to get that job done." She hadn't told Rebecca about the rejection from the day before, her humiliation still stung a little, "He was listed on D.C.'s top fifty most eligible bachelors last year. You don't get that kind of attention from sitting at home alone. He probably goes out with a different woman every night of the week. Anyway, I've learned, people that charming are not usually that honest with you."

"You're an idiot, not to mention blind. The man works all the time. There is no way he has fit dating into his schedule too. Why do you think I kept my mouth shut during your little interview? I am not blind; I saw the way he watched you, and he even offered his business card to your little assistant. He was trying to impress you." Rebecca's voice intensified, "He even said you could go see David, which I might add, gets you in to see your brother too, so now I don't have to ask for any favors or pull any strings to make it happen. Why do you think I let you know whose screaming you heard? I seriously broke some rules there. I know you, and I knew exactly what you would do. He was obviously enthralled with you, and I bet on the fact. I knew exactly what he would do too."

Alex rolled her eyes at Rebecca's ridiculous statement, "Oh, come on! You can't seriously tell me you planned all that?"

"You lead a boring life Alex; don't you think I knew exactly when you were going down to that place? Even if I hadn't planned to be down there with you, your schedule is pretty predictable. I didn't know he'd spend the entire time drooling over you, but I did know you would find a way to go see David and somehow get him to let you in for some visits."

Alex felt her cheeks burning at the idea, but she didn't have the nerve to tell Rebecca that he made his lack of interest in her perfectly clear on Sunday. Her declaration that she planned it might be entirely true, but Alex refused to give Rebecca the satisfaction of saying it, "No way, not even you are that maniacal."

Luckily, Rebecca ignored the blush, but glared and replied in a snippy tone, "Okay."

Alex withheld what she wanted to say and changed the subject, "How does the other organization coming in affect your involvement."

"Oh good, I guess you've had time to process, that or you want to change the subject, again. You really are predictable you know. My involvement in the project will continue pretty much the same, but if the situation grows out of control, at least I won't be the only one responsible for trying to manage it. Once the situation moved out of your brother's facility protocol dictated that we relinquish control to the other organization immediately. Somehow, Brent managed to keep the research-based out of our lab. I still don't know how he achieved that feat."

Alex didn't understand how the CDC and Dashcorp worked together because Rebecca could never answer her questions with all the confidentiality and classification laws, but decided to press the issue anyway "I'm confused, why didn't you pass it over to the other organization immediately?"

Rebecca nodded like she knew the question was coming, "At first we thought we could control it, then we had to confirm that both the prison and the bridge issues were the same problem. Somehow, Brent also managed to be notified to investigate under the bridge, which completely overstepped protocol. He must have friends in high places to stay embedded at the center of this investigation. Can we return to the conversation about you and Brent? I liked it better."

Alex scowled but wouldn't allow Rebecca to deter her, "No, we can't, that conversation is over." If only she knew how foolish Alex felt even at the mention of Brent's name, "How will these changes affect visitation?"

"You mean regarding your visits?" Rebecca watched as Alex nodded before she said, "So far, not in any way that I know of, but I will definitely leak your visitation plans to Brent."

Alex sighed, her friend never stopped, "All right Rebecca, you are like a dog with a bone, let it go."

"Can't." Rebecca cackled like a witch and stared with crazy eyes, "You know I can't."

Chuckling and shaking her head, Alex grabbed the bag again and glared at her friend, "You need to get a life, now hit."

CHAPTER 10

Day 7

The morning slowly crept by as Alex awaited the impending sentence of her personal degradation and avoided eye contact with every person in the office by trying to look busy. She hated what her boss had asked of her, the entire act reeked of sexual harassment, and she wanted to slap herself for being party to it. It shouldn't be such a big deal, but nobody here knew of her past. At least Michael had the decency to be offended for her. As the time for her departure drew near, she felt Michael standing over her desk, staring down at her, "Are you ready for this Alex? I am going to let you do most of the talking."

Alex wanted to ignore him but he was her work ally and a good man who remained professional and courteous at all times. She didn't want to face him or his question, yet she managed to glance up to him as he blew his hair off his face. He always had one piece that hung down, as if it had escaped from the rest of his perfectly gelled hair. Alex wondered if he did it on purpose. He didn't quite comprehend her sense of humor, or her manner of dealing with uncomfortable situations. She couldn't stop herself and played off his question as if she was unaware of her assignment, "Why wouldn't I be?"

Michael's face twitched, and his long, lanky shape appeared slightly hunched over, which didn't match his usual board-strait posture or perfectly tailored navy suit. He hesitated, momentarily, as if he didn't know how to respond. The man thought far too literally, "Well, because Powers asked you to do what was necessary with Seth today to get him to sway the senator on our department's behalf."

Michael still didn't get it and wasn't going to, but acting flippant helped her mood, so she feigned a look of surprise, "Well, thank you for reminding me, I almost forgot." His warm, brown eyes, usually alive with energy, now hinted at awkwardness as he peered down at her with sincere concern. Alex too regretted her choice of words and her tone but wasn't in the mood to coddle him. She stood up and pulled her handbag from the desk drawer then pointed to the neatly arranged credenza, "Please grab that bag over there, if we will leave now and we can get over there early."

Michael lifted the bag up and down weighing its contents, then peeked inside, "Do you mind if I ask what is in the bag?"

She should have grabbed it herself so she wouldn't have to explain every move of her plan to him, "It is a bottle of wine and two tickets to the concert in the park."

Michael curled up one side of his face in an awkward grimace, "Isn't it getting a little cold out for a concert in the park?"

His knack for only seeing the obvious started to wear on her nerves, so much that she let more of her annoyance slip out, sighed and rolled her eyes. Realizing how rude she'd been she mumbled, "Sorry Michael. The concerts don't start until spring. This is to let him know that if he'll only get what he wants if he comes through. I won't follow through of course, but the implication is there, so there is a one-time chance of it working."

Michael's cheeks had turned pink as he shifted from one foot to the other, "Heh, heh. I see. Good plan."

Alex pressed together her lips in a tight smile. What she really needed right now was a good dose of snarky Rebecca style sarcasm to alleviate her nerves, but she'd have to settle for Michael's straight-laced approach. The conversation with Michael drained her while her stress levels were so high, and the contorted confusion on his face didn't help. She needed to reel in her emotions so she didn't alienate her kind-hearted friend any further, and wished she could take a nap instead of talk, but that wasn't a luxury she had at the moment. She decided to 'suck it up' as Rebecca would say and get on with her day.

Michael would probably avoid for a while in the future, like the time she said she had a crush on him when she'd had too much to drink. She had meant an innocent work crush. The man had a husband for more years than she could fathom being with one person, but he still took it the wrong way. He avoided her for quite a while after that slip. She admired him, and had only meant the comment as a compliment.

As Alex and Michael approached the offices of the conservative Louisiana senator, she adjusted her hair around her scar, a nervous habit she couldn't seem to break. The comfortably appointed reception area of the senator's offices boasted neatly arranged traditional furnishings and alluded to the typical political machine that ran the Senate. A well-groomed, middle age staffer glanced up from her typing. She looked like a fifties secretary with a perfectly pressed suit and slightly pouffed hair similar to a Fox News reporter, then she tilted her head, waiting for Alex or Michael to say something.

Putting on her friendliest smile, Alex strutted directly up to the desk, "Good morning, I am Alex Donahue. Michael Strickland and I are scheduled to see Seth Mitchell."

The staffer nodded, but still did not smile or project any friendliness, "Yes, he is expecting you and told me to send you back, his office is third on the right."

Alex nodded and walked toward her disaster of an assignment, down the hall into the cubicle pen. Desks and file cabinets lined up the way they did in every other political office, "Michael, why don't you go talk to some of the staffers and if the door closes give me about three minutes before you come in. He'll act overly friendly if he thinks he can get away with it, although he may be on his best behavior, if he thinks it will lead to something else, but please keep your eye on that door." The shut door to Seth's office gave Alex a moment to collect herself before going in. She inhaled a deep breath of air and sighed, knocked on the door and said, "Hi Seth" as she opened it. Seth lay, slumped over his desk. Hungover? She tentatively crept over to his desk to see if he was asleep and froze. His face appeared flushed, and marks that resembled veins shadowed his temples, similar to the photo of Doug.

Seth's head wobbled up, and he recognized Alex immediately, "I am sorry I've been looking forward to this meeting, but I think I may have the flu." Seth grabbed his head, "This headache is killing me."

Without thinking, she dropped the bag, scrambled out of the office, grabbed Michael's jacket sleeve, and dragged him toward the reception area, "Alex what is going on? Did he make a pass at you?"

Alex shook her head as she practically threw him forward at the reception desk. She hyperventilated as she tried to speak, "Call security, nobody can leave the office or building." She grabbed her cell phone and dialed Rebecca as Michael stared at her in confusion, so she pushed him forward and he picked the phone on the desk. The staffer tried to object, but she hesitated at the scowl and fear Alex knew was pasted on her face, "NOW!"

Rebecca answered the phone, "It isn't a great time right now. Can I call you back later?"

"NO!" Alex screamed, hyperventilated, "It's here Rebecca, it's here. Whatever got Doug is here!"

Minutes felt like hours before Alex heard sirens, and Michael jumped at the blaring sound, his eyes giving away the terror he felt. The reception staffer eyed Alex cautiously, but she stared out the window at the raucous. Alex turned to Michael and put her hand on his shoulder, "Thank you for not running off, I could tell you wanted to." As police and firefighters surrounded the building, he nodded in response but no words came out of his mouth. Several of the staffers nervously walked toward the front reception desk, but Alex put her hand out blocking their path, "I am afraid you will need to return to your desks. Nobody is allowed to leave their office or the building."

An angry sweaty-faced man at the front of the growing group stepped forward, about to push his way past her, "Who do you think you are?"

Michael stepped in and placed his arm across the doorway, scowled, and leaned toward the man, "Return to your desk." Michael's height and fastidious appearance implied authority and the man cowered back, intimidated by the aggressiveness of Michael's response. The man meekly maneuvered to the window with some of the other staffers. Immediate crisis averted, Michael pulled Alex aside, "What is going on here Alex? You never answered my question. I did as you asked, and now I want to know why."

"Your question is fair enough Michael, but I don't know what I am permitted to divulge, and I can't say anything until someone in authority tells me I'm allowed."

Frustration grew on Michael's face, "You expect everyone to abide by your demands without an explanation? I don't understand you. You spend your days at work hiding from others, and now without any explanation, you make one phone call and shut down an entire building. Who are you and what are you hiding Alex?"

She sadly shook her head, "I am nobody, but I signed a confidentiality agreement, and I can't say anything, yet."

Someone had switched on the news, and the ever-annoying Christy Gallagher stood in front of the camera in the middle of a report, "My private sources reported the disease at the Fulton penitentiary is unlike anything he has ever seen. The source states that the disease starts with cold or flu-like symptoms then progresses, ending in a gruesome death, and the only living victim of this unknown disease is marked with vein-like striations on his face and neck. He has not been produced for comment and has reportedly been in a meditative state since the onset of the disease symptoms."

Michael marched off to a corner and fumed. Moments later, as if responding to the news report, giant CDC trucks, and Dashcorp medical trucks joined the police and firefighters surrounding the building. Whimpering echoed through the silence that now haunted the office. Michael glared at Alex even more intensely and visibly huffed his annoyance. White hazmat-suited bodies resembling aliens swarmed into the building, and several minutes later the first one appeared at the door escorted by two more carrying riot gear and weapons and walked directly up to Alex. Rebecca's eyes peered at her from behind the mask.

Rebecca smiled inside the bucket-like helmet of the hazmat suit and calmly addressed Alex like they were chatting over lunch, "You seem to attracted trouble. What is going on?" Alex quickly explained walking in on Seth and Rebecca gently placed her gloved hand on Alex's shoulder, concern showing through the mask, "You were supposed to stay safe, not end up in the middle of craziness as soon as I turn around." Alex shrugged, holding back the emotion she felt, but before she could say anything, Rebecca handed her a box of facemasks to pass out.

Rebecca turned to go and Alex grabbed her arm. Instantly, the two escorts jumped up to intercede, but Rebecca put her hand up telling them not to bother. Motioning toward Michael, Alex asked, "Can I tell my co-worker what is going on here?"

Rebecca contorted her face but nodded, "He will soon learn about it anyway. Do it privately though, we don't need a riot on our hands."

Alex wandered over to Michael whose arms were crossed and handed him a facemask, "Alright Michael I can tell you now." She watched as he humphed, then unfolded his arms and nodded for her to continue, she took a deep breath to steady herself, "What I am about to tell you is strictly confidential, and even though I 've been authorized to tell you, I am not sure if you can repeat it yet. We may have been exposed to an unknown disease. I am not sure, but Seth's symptoms appeared similar to something I encountered over the weekend."

"What do you mean a pathogen you encountered? How would you-?"

"When I fed the residents under the bridge-"

"Feeding residents under what bridge? I don't know what you're talking about."

"I know you must feel very anxious right now, but if you want to know what is happening, you need to let me finish explaining." He gestured for her to continue, "In my spare time I feed the homeless."

Michael seemed unable to stop himself from repeatedly interrupting Alex's explanation, but she understood his nervousness, and tried to be patient as he interjected again, "That is what you do with your spare time? How do I not know that? What does that have to do with the situation here? Please, Alex, explain all of it to me."

"I am sorry Michael I will do my best to explain. I work with Feed the Homeless Kitchen in my spare time and do everything from meal prep to fundraising, to deliveries. I never told anyone about my spare time activities because I guess I don't want anyone to judge me. This weekend one of the men that lives under the bridge where I deliver died from an unknown illness with symptoms similar to what I saw on Seth."

Michael nodded his head as he listened, "Will it be fatal?"

She shrugged, "It was for Doug, yet David, another man who lived right near him did not seem affected. I'm sure they're only taking precautions, but I am not sure what kind of disease it is or anything else about it."

Adjusting his facemask, Michael furled his eyebrows, "How could you keep this to yourself?"

"Legally, I had no choice but to keep what I saw private, which is what you need to do now." Alex motioned over to the white suits leading people out, "Look, we're being escorted out of here, and I am sure we will all learn more soon enough." Alex glanced down the hall, "I hope Seth is alright."

Michael contorted his face at Alex's comments then protectively guided her toward the door, "I wonder where they'll take us?" Alex looked at Michael then grimaced as she shrugged her shoulders, but he didn't stop asking questions, "Why would anyone judge you for working at a soup kitchen? Everyone at the office constantly speculated about what you do when you aren't at work. You should hear what people came up with."

"Seriously? People talk about me when I'm not around? Don't they have a better way to spend their time?"

"Ha, ha, everyone loves a mystery, and you are the office's most private person. I myself don't bother with gossip much, but it is fun to listen to once in a while."

Alex shook her head while they waited to step into the line of people being escorted out of the office, "Great, just great."

Like a scene from an alien invasion movie, a suited hoard came down upon the scared victims as they arrived at a loading dock. Separated one by one, and led down the hallways sheathed in plastic, Alex tried to breathe, slowly fighting back the hyperventilation. Rebecca had explained the process, but the explanation did not accurately describe the terror of the experience. The stunned eyes of each victim peeked over the masks affixed to their faces. Trepidation seeped out in the tears that welled up in the pockets of their eyes, but Alex held it all in, the fear, the shock, and the dismay. She'd been through worse. She heard weeping but did not turn to see who had broken down. She did not comfort the afflicted or sooth the shaken. Alex's knowledge of the possible death that waited for them all somehow mollified her reactions; she looked ahead and said nothing. They were afraid for their lives, but some fates are worse than death. They knew nothing of the terror that lurked in the hidden corners of every street. The information, gift or a curse she did not know.

Now, no longer distracted by her conversation with Michael, Alex sat alone in her thoughts, sinking into the realization of her choices and possible future, or lack of it. She thought she'd made choices that would keep her safe but here she was. She didn't think she possessed the bravery to face the aftermath of her own tragedies, let alone the sadness of other people's heartbreaks, so Alex decided to spend her life working toward preventing problems and hopefully save someone from facing a tragedy similar to hers. She longed to find the forgotten and help them, rather than clean up messes after everything fell apart. She chose a job to help fix the ills of society before they happened, supposedly a safe job. All she knew and understood disappeared with each tragedy she faced, and now, she followed a different path, one down a white hallway.

She'd lost her father to terrorists then her mother to addiction, and her end would come in the form of a disease? Rebecca told her not to worry, but Alex saw the terrified look on her friend's face. Now she was stuck with all these other poor victims waiting for a disease to strike them down. She saw how it killed Doug as well as the effects of it on Seth, and now she wished someone would tell her what was going on. She put on a brave face through the initial alarm of it but now her thoughts wandered through the darker places in her mind, and she needed more information.

When the doldrums of everyday life set in, work, sleep, then repeat, the redundancy and stifling monotony would inspire a prayer for change but it became a fruitless struggle. An adventure or exciting affair only graced Alex's life, when new ordeals or trials set in, ones that tested her resolve and unnerved her very soul. With this last roadblock, life's ability to demoralize and unhinge her took over. Alex's feelings of self-pity overwhelmed her at that moment. She usually found beauty and grace in her challenges, but how many lessons did life need to teach her? Had she not learned enough already? The travesty of her inconsequential existence began to set in and she yearned for the familiarity of her boring life again.

The tears she had been holding back finally pushed their way forward, threatening to overflow at any moment. If only she followed her intuition and left the dirty jobs, for the obscene individuals, with whom they belonged, but she agreed to do the assignment and all for a promotion. Now, once again her life was in danger and this time Alex had pulled Michael down into the risk with her. Her need and desperation to move up in her work life tempted her and stranded her in this crisis. She never believed in knights on white horses nor fairy godmothers coming to save the day, but Alex knew Rebecca might rescue her once again, this time, from an unknown peril.

Uncertainty was nothing but an unpleasant louse, teasing her soul and dragging her into hidden depths of self-pity. She hated it and preferred solitude so as not to bring anyone down with her. The muffled cries and fearful energy surrounding her brought her back to reality and served as a reminder that loneliness often occurred in the midst of a crowd and exacerbated her feelings of self-pity. She shook her head at the ridiculousness of how she drew her mind into such self-indulgent thoughts. Then, like a prisoner being dragged back to reality and carted off to experience their last day on Earth, Alex stepped forward in the line of victims waiting to be examined. Alex breathed a sigh of relief as Rebecca's sarcastic tone interrupted her thoughts of desperation, "I see tears. You aren't going to get all dramatic on me are you?"

Alex laughed through the tears that now spilled against her will, "Yeah, you say that behind the protection of your little white suit, but you know me too well." Rebecca squeezed her hand and gestured that her work demanded her attention, Alex nodded and watched her friend walk away.

Escorted to a plastic lined cubicle, a hazmat-suited alien took blood, scraped out Alex's fingernails, took scrapings from all her exposed skin parts, hair samples, swabbed her mouth, nose, ears, and even her eyeballs. The technician gave only directive orders and ignored all her questions. Mentally she compared her situation to that of being mold, scraped and sampled for analysis during a biology class in high school. Eventually, she was directed to the showers, but all her clothing was confiscated and she sat under a UV light for what felt like hours. Alex balked at how unsettling being treated like a non-person felt but many of those she tried to help might feel this way regularly. She reminded herself she'd been through much worse, but still wished Rebecca would come back.

Another anonymous white hazmat suit directed her down an antiseptic smelling hallway separating her from the others being led back toward the loading dock. She ended up in a windowed closet, but the window faced the hallway, not the outside. Alex pulled on the door handle but the door was locked so she turned to face her little room. It contained a bed with white linens, some medical equipment, a white desk, and chair, as well as a stainless toilet with a sink on the top of the tank. It reminded her of a prison cell and looked just like Tristan and David's. Humph, now she knew how they felt. At least her little cell wasn't in the high-security wing like Tristan's, but they were both trapped and unable to leave. Terrified, Alex did not know what she should do, so she sat down on the bed then smoothed out her Dashcorp issued scrubs. Nobody told her what would happen next or what she should do and they were utterly tight-lipped about everything. Where was Rebecca?

The view of the white wall Alex stared at grew tiresome, so she pushed herself up off the bed and approached the window. It peered out into a long hallway of more white. She saw doors to her right and left, spaced at regular intervals, probably more little jail cells. On the opposite wall, two doors spaced far apart, and huge mirrored windows broke up the space, one-way glass. Great, they monitor every move. She leaned against the window and pressed her forehead into it. The coolness of the glass chilled her even more than her wet hair and triggered an involuntary shudder. Alex turned on the intercom but heard nothing. Quarantined with nobody would tell her anything, no clocks to watch the time and nothing to do but worry. Frustrated, Alex banged on the window before returning to the bed. With a huff, she dropped down, whipped her feet up onto the bed and crossed her arms over her chest. Fear crept in, and the build-up of the anxiety and turmoil she felt growing in her chest and belly swelled to intolerable levels and once again tears burned the corners of her eyes before streaming down the sides of her face and falling into little puddles onto her tiny inadequate pillow. She swore she would never let it happen again yet here she lay, helpless and at the mercy of others, and probably diseased and about to die alone. She knew pain and did not fear it, but this ignorance ate at her. Where were they all? They seemed to disappear behind their little doors, and she could do nothing but stare at more white.

The sound of a door close and the muffled padding of shoes hitting the white floor woke Alex. Quickly, she sat up on the bed and rubbed her face, which was undoubtedly swollen from the crying, but she could do nothing about it now. A quiet knock rapped on the door before the clank of the electronic lock opened and echoed through the little closet jail cell. Two anonymous hazmat-suited bodies entered the room. Inside the suits two women, one a little older and one younger about Alex's age looked her up and down, their appearance was a mystery through the windows of their suit helmets. The older one barked, "We need to take some more blood samples then obtain as much information as we can about your recent whereabouts and interactions."

If Alex hadn't been so upset and stressed she would have laughed at the lack of bedside manner, instead she stuck out her hand to greet the woman with a handshake, "Hi, I'm Alex."

The older woman peered down at her pad, "I am aware. Do you have any questions?"

Alex smiled, indifferent to the sharp and clinical retort. She had already figured out the older woman's identity and kept her hand out for the handshake, "Yes, I have plenty of those but why don't we start out with some basic introductions."

The older woman stepped back recoiling her hand and protecting herself with her pad, "Ah yes, I am Dr. Sonso, and my assistant here is Josie. No touching, please." Josie nodded and from the scrunched up look around her eyes she appeared to be smiling, but then she quickly ducked her head at the eye contact, "Josie is going to take a few more blood samples while we talk." Josie went about the business of taking more blood samples from Alex as Sonso began and riddled Alex with questions, and Alex did her best to answer them.

After dozens of questions, Alex could no longer contain herself, "Excuse me, aren't interviews normally conducted by a technician? How do I rate your attention, Dr. Sonso?"

With an annoyed but smug look on her face Sonso nodded, then straightened her already board straight posture, "Correct, normally a technician would conduct the interview, but Dr. Adams asked me to see to you personally." She quickly added, "And while I do not work for him, I am with the CDC, I decided to appease my colleague's request."

Wow, and people thought Rebecca was cold. Her friend had quite accurately described the woman, such a people person. Alex refused to react to her extremely condescending attitude and remarks, and smiled her warmest, most welcoming grin, "Well, thank you for taking the time out of your schedule."

Sonso paused and smiled, "Your welcome. I've been asked to explain your situation to help alleviate some of your concerns. You encountered an individual infected with an unknown pathogen. Now don't be alarmed, new viruses are discovered every day.

Alex shifted uncomfortably, "Yes, but I saw the effects of this virus, and I am pretty sure it killed one of the homeless men I feed. What is the chance I am going to contract it?" She started to twitch and pick at her cuticles.

"You will stay in quarantine, and if any symptoms develop you will be administered our most up to date treatment as it becomes available."

Breathing heavily and fighting back more tears, Alex swallowed hard, "How long before you know if I am developing symptoms?"

Sonso pursed her lips and responded with a look of distaste, "We have not yet determined the incubation period for the disease."

"You mean I am to be locked away for an indeterminate amount of time?" Alex should feel comforted dealing with a high-level doctor, especially one who mirrored her best friend's reactions to emotional situations, but she wasn't at all comforting. Rebecca dealt with uncomfortable situations using biting wit and humor but cared deeply behind her cold facade. Perhaps Sonso did as well, although Alex didn't see it. Concern enveloped Rebecca's eyes even as she acted annoyed or cold, but behind Sonso's coldness, the woman's eyes gave Alex the shivers. She was all business.

"At this time, I cannot give you a definitive answer. Do you have any other questions for me?"

Alex shook her head and stared down at her hands in her lap. She had a million questions but had already spent enough time with the woman. Sonso and Josie nodded and left the room, closing the electronic lock behind them with a clank and an echo.

CHAPTER 11

Day 8

The night lingered on forever, and hours crept by as Alex's stare drifted from the white walls to the white ceiling to the white door. Emergency lights kept the halls bathed in an eerie red glow that lasted through the night, but with no windows to tell her the time of day or if the sun had risen, she didn't know how long she'd been there. Alex tried to practice a little yoga to calm her nerves, but even that did not help alleviate the knotted feeling in her stomach, which now growled as well. She skipped eating because her anxiousness made eating the lunch and dinner brought to her unappealing, but now she suffered from hunger pains on top of anxiety and exhaustion. She felt forgotten and wanted to scream into the intercom that somebody needed to come and let her out.

Alex tossed her legs over the side of the bed and she sat up with a sigh, then from the corner of her eye, she spotted movement in the window. Funny, she hadn't heard any doors but realized she'd left the com off. A white-gloved hand holding several chocolate bars waved back and forth, and a small duffle bag filled with stuff hid the hazmat-suited body of her friend. The intercom hissed with a sing-songy voice and Rebecca's head popped up from behind the bag, "Hello? Good morning, goody delivery!"

"Where have you been?" Alex jumped up and stepped over to the window, both relieved and annoyed at the same time, "I am going out of my mind in here, and I don't know anything. What happened to Michael? What is going to happen to me?" Alex knew that even through the glass Rebecca sensed her anxiety because Rebecca didn't react with any of her usual sarcasm or defiance.

Rebecca tried to appear cheerful, though her face, shadowed and languid, revealed how worn out she was, "I am sorry Alex, but you need to have faith. You are a sister to me, and I am not going to let anything happen to you."

"I know you were busy but please," Alex paused to take a breath. Expressing her feelings had almost instantly restored her outlook and she was able to move rapidly past her night of dwelling in self-pity and fear, "Why do you look like hell?"

Rebecca's entire body sagged, and she pleaded, "Come on now, I spent all day and night processing the office and victim you identified. The whole incident is a huge deal, and all of D.C. is buzzing." She looked around the small room, and back at Alex, "Boy, your little room is stimulating."

"Yes, the palette of white on white, on more white really invigorates my mind, hence the irritable expression on my face."

"Really? I thought your joyful display could be credited to being poked and prodded then quarantined for exposure to a fatal pathogen. I know you thoroughly enjoyed it, so don't give me any more flack or I will march off with this bag of goodies I picked up for you."

Alex smiled, fully submitting to the relief she felt for Rebecca's normal snarky response. She wouldn't be so glib if Alex needed to worry, "I see chocolate, anything else to eat in there? I might ignore your long absence if you brought food to bribe me."

"Oh, I know you far too well." Rebecca pushed a couple bags through the wall chute identical to the one in David's little cell. One bag contained her pillow and blanket from home and the other had several of Alex's favorite kind of chocolates, protein bars, peanut butter crackers, and other snacks, her toothbrush, and other sundries, as well as her tablet, and an adult coloring book with colored pencils and a sharpener. Something to do! Both women turned at the sound of footsteps coming down the hall, as a technician wheeled a cart loaded with bags and water bottles toward them. The tech stopped near Rebecca and handed the bag and several water bottles through the chute. Alex held up her finger to Rebecca as she tore into the bag, it held a carton with eggs and toast, a container with fruit, a sealed pouch of juice and several snacks including an apple and protein bar. She couldn't wait to eat and instantly began shoveling it in. After several bites, she motioned for Rebecca to continue.

When Alex was hungry, nobody interfered because she was like a ravenous animal. Rebecca eyed Alex with a silly smirk while watching the obnoxious eating manners, "I guess you were hungry, try not to eat the plate, or you'll be poked and prodded for other reasons. I can download more books when you finish reading those."

Alex thumbed through the titles Rebecca had added to her tablet with one hand as she scooped food into her mouth with the other. "Thanks, these look good, can you upload more the day after tomorrow or will I be gone by then?"

Rebecca ignored the question, but Alex didn't mind, her gratitude for the food and entertainment outweighed her need for answers that Rebecca wouldn't be able to give anyway. Her friend knew her taste in books and loved to tease her about her voracious appetite for reading, and Rebecca chuckled, "Okay, Bookworm."

With a fork full of eggs and a mouth full of toast Alex temporarily paused shoveling food into her mouth, "Will you stay for a while?"

Rebecca sighed as she shook her head, "I don't have much time because I've been awake forever and there is far too much to do before I can get any sleep." She placed her hand over her heart and dramatically spoke like she was reciting a sonnet, "The couch in my office is calling my name, and I want to oblige it, but my love for you is so great I went to your house to pick up your stuff and came to see you instead of sleeping. I plan to catch a couple hours of shut-eye this afternoon."

Alex rolled her eyes, "You probably haven't slept since yesterday but I know you barely need it. You're the only person I know who sleeps less than I do, so quit complaining. Last night I stared at the walls and ceiling for hours, I never thought it would end."

Raising her eyebrows, Rebecca smiled, "Really? I may know something about nights that never end."

"Yes, but how many times were you trapped in a box with nothing to do for the night. I know I am being selfish and whiney but why didn't you come by sooner? This is Hell, and my only mistake was doing my job; specifically a task I despised doing in the first place."

"Yes, I know, I wanted to come yesterday, but I did work all night, except when I went to get your stuff this morning instead of sleeping because I am such a martyr. Now, I am going to use some of your logic on you regarding your whining. It is a good thing you went to that office, if you hadn't gone, with your knowledge of the pathogen's external effects, think about how many more people would now be exposed. As it is, every person who saw the victim and every person they saw is being rounded up. The situation is quickly spinning out of control yet it could have been far worse, so suck it up."

Alex scrunched up her face in a mock sneer, "Don't you hate when someone uses your own logic against you? Fine, I will stop complaining but I had better not get sick, or you will hear a lot more. Why can't you let me feel sorry for myself without injecting reason into the situation?"

Massively grinning, Rebecca tried to swipe the hair off her forehead but knocked the suit helmet instead, "Only returning a favor that you'd do for me."

"Yeah, like you ever feel sorry for yourself." Rebecca grunted in response but didn't say anything, so Alex continued, "Well, getting processed through here was fantastic, and I met your buddy Sonso. She has the warmth and caring of a cold fish. She didn't exhibit an ounce of manners or humor and didn't even bother to introduce herself. She scared the daylights out of her assistant, without even saying a word to her, and she was quite blunt about her displeasure in doing the task of a lowly tech by interviewing me." Alex narrowed her eyes in pause, "I can tell by the Cheshire cat grin on your face I don't want to hear whatever you're about to say."

"You must enjoy cold fish. Didn't you say she sounded quite a bit like me when I complained?"

Neither said or did anything for a moment, at first Rebecca snickered, and then Alex joined her until they both laughed wholly. Moments later both turned at the sound of footsteps padding down the hall and saw Brent, in a hazmat suit, walking toward them. He stopped directly in front of Alex's window, and both women waited for him to speak, "Hello ladies, did I hear laughter? I've come to check on our newest Dashcorp resident." Everyone scrunched up their faces at the poor taste of his overly cheerful joke, including Brent, "Uh yeah, that came out completely wrong."

Mocking Brent, Rebecca grimaced and began to walk away, "On that note, work is calling; enjoy a lovely visit with our newest resident." Then she turned and mouthed "I told you so," in Alex's direction. As Brent turned to glance in Rebecca's direction, Alex shook her head and rolled her eyes. The poor guy had no idea what he walked into with the two women.

The day looked much brighter after Rebecca's visit. Sometimes Alex let her fear and imagination get away from her. Of course, everything would be fine, and now she even had chocolate to eat and books to read. Neither Rebecca nor Brent stayed long, but they stopped by to check on her, which demonstrated their concern. She wished they had visited more separately. The day would go by more rapidly with more distractions, although, at least Rebecca had pulled her out of her dismal state before Brent came along. Alex carefully arranged the blanket on her bed and the contents of the bag on the desk. She plumped up her pillow from home, grabbed her tablet, sat on her bed, and slid under the comfort of her blanket. After reading for an hour or so, her stomach had finally settled from the quick inhalation of too much food, and Alex tore the wrapper off the top of the chocolate, and then took a tiny nibble. Savoring the taste, she closed her eyes and took a massive bite out of it. Overcome with the pleasure of the delicious treat she smiled and moaned in ecstasy.

Tap, tap, tap. She jumped, startled by the sudden interruption. Her eyes shot open and focused in on Brent, in a hazmat suit, standing in front of the window, holding up a small television. She didn't expect to see him again, so quickly, and tried to chew and swallow as she smirked and waved him in. She hopped up and hid the chocolate behind her back but realized how ridiculous she must look hiding candy, so she casually placed it on the desk and tried to straighten her scrubs. The clank of the electronic lock signaled the door opening and the technician she hadn't even noticed, standing with Brent, holding tools and swinging the door open, surprised her. The two walked in, and Brent put down the television on the desk beside her treats, "I brought you something to keep you entertained, but I see somebody beat me to it, I didn't even notice earlier."

Alex wondered how he missed all the stuff when he came by before and politely wiped her mouth before she spoke. Realizing it was covered in chocolate she tried to clean up but knew she looked ridiculous. Feeling juvenile and with chocolate still in her mouth, she mumbled, "Thank you! I saw one in Tristan, and David's rooms as well."

Already working on wiring the television to the wall the technician grunted, "Yeah, I had to install two others as well." Brent glared at the tech but didn't say anything.

"Oh, you mean these aren't part of every room?"

The technician sighed, apparently unhappy, "No, these rooms are usually used for temporary observation, and we don't bother."

"Oh yes, David said something about that the other day. You brought these over just for us?" Alex watched Brent grin and noticed his cheeks redden a little. She smiled back hoping chocolate wasn't still in her teeth, "Well, you better be careful, Tristan might take apart the television and obtain control over the entire building before anyone knows what's happening." Brent's face twisted into a serious expression of fear. Alex cackled to herself then stared with a straight face, "Don't worry unless you left him with a paper clip or something else he could use as a tool." She paused as Brent's mouth dropped, but continued the jest, "You don't give him metal silverware to eat did you?"

Brent closed his eyes and shook his head, "You're teasing me aren't you?" His laugh filled the room with a low, warm chuckle, and his eyes sparkled mischievously increasing his charm factor. Alex paused and thought to herself, don't get caught up in it, he's merely being kind, but he stared deeply into her eyes, throwing her off again, before speaking much more seriously to her, "I thought I might take you to go see your brother, but Sonso caught me on the way in here. They need to examine you again before you can go anywhere, to see if any symptoms developed overnight. Don't worry, you look great to me, and by the way you devoured most of that chocolate bar you must feel pretty well too." Alex looked down at her hands and felt her cheeks burning, nonchalantly wiping her mouth again.

A brusque voice interrupted the two, "All set here, the remote is on top and you can get most channels." Nodding in the technician's direction, she thanked the man before he gathered his tools and left.

"I should go as well. I'm not supposed to enter these isolation rooms, I am breaking protocol." Brent leaned in, "If I can't get back, another technician will take you down to visit your brother after your examination. I'll make sure of it."

Alex didn't know what to say but managed to croak out a thank you before he left the room.

Rebecca strode hastily down the hall, struggling to carry the coffee someone had mysteriously left on her desk while she scanned the reports in her hands. She abruptly slowed when she heard the hushed voices of Abe and Sonso in the lab around the corner. She took to calling Dr. Sonso only by her last name, and it caught on. Every Dashcorp employee joined in, except the CDC techs and Abe, the old softy, still referred to her as Doctor. Rebecca couldn't help enjoying the piqued expression on Sonso's face every time someone left the Doctor off too. All the other doctors at Dashcorp went by their first name. It brought more equality to the rest of the staff but Sonso hadn't conformed, and everyone noticed, so Sonso stuck. It served her right for holding on to such antiquated customs or formality.

Rebecca stopped short, just out of view and heard Sonso, "I know I ran a basic R-naught projection with latent incubation suppositions but I can't find them anywhere."

Abe's deep voice replied, "Would you like me to run another for you?"

"I don't think so Abe; it is the third missing report. It isn't in the paper or digital files, and I am missing protein damage reports on the carotid artery tissue that would back the current symptom progression hypothesis. The information is absent from the full tissue protein analysis. Is incompetence a common occurrence in Dashcorp labs?"

Never unhinged by even the most unpleasant person or situation, Abe soothingly assured her, "Now, now, we run our labs with the utmost efficiency."

"Maybe the missing information isn't apathy but intentional. I question Rebecca's acceptance of my presence in this lab."

"That is ridiculous. She may be a bit prickly but above all, she is a professional, and her main concern is her work. Her cooperativeness and dedication in an investigation are, unrivaled, and her reporting is quite fastidious, as is all of ours."

"I thought you might say that, which brings me to my next point. Beyond the members of our lab teams, the only other individuals with access to the missing information are your boss and Nithi."

Rebecca intentionally rounded the corner at that exact moment, causing both Abe and Sonso to recoil from the start, "Don't jump so quickly to blame others for missing information, many people, including the CDC, are working on this investigation. Maybe as lead, you should more vigilantly manage your own paperwork. If you need information try addressing me directly instead of one of my colleagues, as the negligence you accuse others of may be your own incompetence."

"You cannot speak to me in that manner! I should pull this investigation from Dashcorp access completely and handle it out of the CDC headquarters. We don't lose reports." Sonso's nostrils flared and her eyes bulged, the anger clear on her face.

Rebecca smiled inside; she intentionally overstepped with her tongue-lashing but needed to bring Sonso down to balance the playing field. She knew Sonso couldn't move the investigation now without a complete upheaval. Undoubtedly, Sonso had a considerable ego, yet her scientific expertise was not even close to the knowledge Rebecca possessed. She thought to herself before countering, break them down then build them back up, "Clearly, Dr. Sonso, you speak from your pride, not the logic that has gained you your stellar reputation. I am here working almost 20 or more hours a day, and while I am not a tech or a file clerk, I am sure if you tell me what you've misplaced, a perfectly logical explanation is available."

"Twenty hours?" Sonso raised her eyebrows and her jaw dropped a touch as she continued, "I need the R-naught projections, the protein damage reports on the carotid artery tissue, and WHO statistics of illness disclosure. You know, off the top of your head, the location of these reports and an explanation as to how they've gone missing digitally, as well as physically?"

With a severe stare, Rebecca peered into Sonso's eyes and nodded, "I remember everything I work on, every time. The R-naught projections are being reworked due to some subtle errors and were deleted from the digital stores to prevent anyone from working on erroneous data. The protein damage tests on the carotid artery tissue were corrupted in the lab and are being rerun. The WHO statistics on illness disclosure was never in our possession, as it is classified, and would help immensely by adding to the R-naught projections for more accurate incubation and transmission data."

Sonso gaped at Rebecca and stuttered, "I, I put together the projections and my work is always accurate." Again, Sonso's ego, but Rebecca could see Abe holding back a smirk in the background.

"I'll happily examine the mistakes with you. I saw no reason to point any of it out as the errors were subtle, and anyone could have made them."

Sonso pressed her lips together in a grimace then pumped her chin, subtly one time, "I must insist that you do show me the errors. I don't make careless mistakes; one of my techs must have erroneously input the data. I needed that protein damage information and the two days the test takes to run is going to set us back. I am sure I forwarded the WHO information to Nithi, he should have already uploaded it to the server." Sonso shook her head in disbelief.

Rebecca placed her hand on Sonso's shoulder, "Not to worry. We will figure this out." Sonso glared but yielded.

"The news is out, or at least it will be by this afternoon."

Sonso's announcement to Rebecca didn't surprise her, but she thought she would have more time, "What? Whose brilliant idea is it to send the world into a panic?"

Agreeing, Sonso nodded her head, "After yesterday it is already out there. The WHO is suspending all international travel to see if the pathogen can be contained in the countries already exposed and Brent is doing an interview with the bimbo news reporter to get ahead of it. The name is already going around as Kopvein virus because the German doctor working on it in the Congo kept calling it Kopvein pralles virus, which literally means 'bulging head vein virus.' In a few hours, the WHO will announce the travel suspension and travelers not already in their home country will be stranded and most likely quarantined."

Rebecca sank down into the closest chair, how did everything progress so quickly? Her audibly ragged breathing increased rapidly, and she gripped onto the edges of the chair until her knuckles turned white, then she started to hyperventilate. Everyone in the lab glanced or walked over to see the commotion, and stared in disbelief. She grasped at her chest and tried to slow down her breathing with deep cleansing breaths, but the apparent anxiety attack only intensified with the effort. Abe, witness to the entire scene, rushed over and spoke softly to Rebecca, reassuring her that together they would develop a cure to the pathogen.

Rebecca looked deeply into Abe's eyes and felt a sense of overwhelming guilt. She wrapped her arms around his neck, an uncharacteristic display for her and softly whispered, "It isn't supposed to happen this way."

"I know dearie," Abe embraced her and soothingly patted her back, "but ye can't expect ta figure out the answers to the unknowable immediately. It's just not possible, even for ye."

She pulled away from Abe's embrace, cupping her face in her hands, and her breathing finally slowed. Rebecca thought to herself that she looked foolish and the emotional display was a touch overdone. She had shown far too much vulnerability, but the situation was bizarre, and everyone experienced abnormal reactions, although, not usually her. After several minutes Rebecca looked up, and everyone in the lab still stood around staring, "All right everyone, back to work. We have several hours before all hell breaks loose and I want to show some progress or solutions. Incubation, transmission, anything!"

Several hours passed without a sound in the lab, each technician and doctor worked diligently trying to accomplish the impossible. Sonso approached the large television in the corner of the lab, and switched it on, "Here goes." Until now, the pathogen was known on a regional level only, but now the world was about to be upended. The stone-faced doctors and technicians shuffled begrudgingly over to the television and somberly watched, waiting, for their lives to change forever.

Christy appeared in her usual short skirt and tight, low cut shirt, with a slightly over made up face, but was as perky as always, "Christy Gallagher reporting directly from the lobby of Dashcorp Enterprises where I am about to conduct an exclusive interview with its CEO, Dr. Brent Adams. Dr. Adams what can you tell me about the illness that inflicted the inmates of the Fulton Penitentiary."

"Well, Ms. Gallagher,"

Christy interrupted and batted her eyes with a come-hither ogle before she placed her hand on his and said in a syrupy-sweet voice, "Please, call me Christy." Rebecca laughed at the overt flirt as several others in the lab also snickered.

Brent smiled with his undaunted charisma and continued, "Okay, Christy. Ten days ago, several men incarcerated at the Fulton State Penitentiary reported into the infirmary with cold or flu-like symptoms, a fact, which you seem already aware. After several days the men's symptoms progressed and more atypical, yet pronounced symptoms developed. At that time, we assigned a special committee to investigate.

"Why didn't Dashcorp bring the CDC into the investigation right away?"

"I personally notified the CDC at the time, but we first needed to test for the possibility of poisoning, and most symptoms were quite similar to flu, so nobody panicked. After eliminating poison as a cause, yet still unable to identify pathogens in the blood work, the hypothesis that a new strain of influenza had developed, and antivirals were administered."

"Couldn't you just look under a microscope and see it?"

She smiled seductively at Brent again and he seemed to enjoy the attention. Hmmm, maybe he wasn't interested in Alex. The reporter continued with her flirtations waiting for his response, "That is an excellent question, Christy. My team looked under a microscope for all known foreign infectious and bacterial material and found nothing unusual."

"Don't you have microscopes that can see things as small as blood cells and stuff?"

Brent laughed and grinned his charming, warm grin at her, "Yes, we can see substances even smaller than blood cells, a red blood cell is about 8 micrometers or 8000 nanometers. A virus is usually 10 to 250 nanometers in size, to give you an idea of how small that is, a nanometer is about 1 million times smaller than an ant. Enough with the science lesson, I don't want people to panic because I am under-explaining some very confusing information. The patients, after several days, developed new symptoms; most obvious was the striational veining that began to appear on the sides of the face and neck. Currently, we only have a handful of cases in the United States. We can prevent further spread of this pathogen with your cooperation." Brent looked directly into the camera, "If you develop any cold or flu-like symptoms, please stay home. Segregate yourself from the other members of your household and call the toll-free number at the bottom of the screen. Callers will receive instructions. If you have been exposed to anyone that develops veining on the sides of their face and neck, please follow the same procedures. "

"I am sorry to interrupt Dr. Adams, but a live report from the World Health Organization is about to begin."

"Thank you, Christy." The screen changed to a report from the WHO with the same information Brent provided, as well as the added news of the international travel suspension and that all passengers still in-flight would return to their departure sites or be escorted to quarantine sites.

Each person in the lab remained motionless around the television, saying nothing, and their eyes were filled with sadness. Rebecca did not need anyone else in the office breaking down, "Okay, now we have all seen the sensationalist cow throwing herself at our boss, we can't take her too seriously, can we?" Several techs and even doctors exhaled and snickered at Rebecca's joke. Alex would be proud, these people are responding to her as if she was a real people-person. She dismissed everything said during the news report with a clap of her hands, "All right everyone, back to work."

Several minutes later Brent marched up to the lab door, highly agitated, and gestured subtly with his head for Abe to come out into the hallway, "You saw what I had to do to get the information right? She wouldn't give me anything until the interview ended."

"And?"

"It was as we thought, but I need concrete proof."

"I'll do my best, sir."

Rebecca heard every word said in the hallway. She knew they had discovered the leak at Dashcorp. Did Brent let people overhear him on purpose? She didn't know whether to be excited or scared, but she knew Brent had allowed everyone to overhear his little hallway conversation on purpose. She had to tell Alex about the interview and the WHO report but dreaded it, so she decided to procrastinate, later.

CHAPTER 12

Day 9

Rebecca pulled her lab coat on and rubbed her face, trying to scour away the exhaustion that her short nap had not even begun to alleviate. The big meeting was about to begin, and Rebecca needed to prepare as much as possible, so she hurried. She gathered her files, the ones she chose to share, and then hastened over to the conference room. Brent, Sonso, Abe, Nithi, several other doctors, as well as Sonso's principal technicians, Josie and Hector waited, softly discussing the agenda. Rebecca strode in and slid into a seat near the door, but Brent motioned for her to relocate to the head of the table near Sonso. Rebecca preferred not to be in the forefront of a meeting unless she held all the control and felt her grip on the investigation still too precarious to seize command, but she reluctantly gathered her files and moved.

Each person wordlessly watched and waited for Rebecca to collect herself before the meeting started. Sonso, technically the lead, at least in name, paused before she took a deep breath and grimaced. The expression in Sonso's eyes communicated the words that nobody wanted to hear, yet all knew. She dove right into the meat of the meeting, not wasting time with unnecessary bureaucracy or evasion, "The quarantine process seems to have been initiated too late in the discovery of this virus. I don't believe that anything we do will stop the spread of the virus completely; therefore it is imperative we determine the incubation period and transmission determinants."

Sonso nodded to Rebecca for her to continue where she'd left off, "Even then, we don't know what is making the Pathogen attack some individuals and not others. We have at least determined how Kopvein is killing its victims. So far, 98% of all victims are male and autopsies reveal brain and thyroid, as well as lymph nodes in an abnormal state. Our hypothesis is that a viral type material in-bedded in the brain, thyroid, hypothalamus, pituitary gland, thyroid and parathyroid, adrenals, pineal body, and the reproductive glands. I say viral type material loosely. Kopvein is unlike any viral outbreak we or anyone has ever encountered in history. We can't find it in a petri dish, it hides and from what I can gather, it is a nanovirus." Rebecca paused to let the information sink in, and she saw the horror growing in each person's eyes. Talk and speculation persisted, but until now, their compartmentalized knowledge of the complete horror of what they faced shielded them. She almost wished she could take the knowledge back. Each staff member had worked on their aspect of the investigation and only she, Brent, and Sonso were privy to the entire spectrum of information.

Abe cleared his throat, "Rebecca didn't you spend time in the Antarctic studying prehistoric nanoviruses?"

Hopefully, each member of the meeting turned to Rebecca, who shook her head, "The nanoviruses I studied were extremely simple and easy to find, which is why I said the term viral material is a loose term."

Hector raised his hand afraid to speak out, and Rebecca nodded with a half-smile at his timidity, "How can we stop a pathogen if we can only see the end result and can't see it? Is the investigation going to change direction now?"

Both Rebecca and Sonso shook their heads in unison, but Rebecca gestured for Sonso take the lead on the question while she watched Hector. He listened to Sonso but kept glancing at Rebecca. Sonso's constant need to be identified as the individual in charge came through in her explanation, "The leadership and I agree that the best course of action is to determine how Kopvein is transmitted, who is most susceptible, and its incubation period. Once we've ascertained those parameters, we can halt or at least slow the transmission, and then more intense studies on Kopvein itself will be warranted."

"But wouldn't identifying the pathogen further our discovery of the transmission parameters." Hmmm, strong women do not intimidate Hector, or he would cower in his chair with the glare that Sonso gave him.

Rebecca sat back in her chair to let Sonso continue, "We aren't forgoing our investigation of Kopvein itself, our first concentration is escalation reduction in victim fatalities. Rebecca will lead a small team in the examination of Kopvein to further the rest of the teams' goals."

"Well, can I be on the examination team?"

Requesting reassignment during the meeting, especially when his attraction to Rebecca was undeniable, was bold. Rebecca hesitated in astonishment, as several others in the room snickered. Sonso peered over the rim of her glasses, annoyed at her own technician's hubris, "And why do you want to do that may I ask?"

Hector sat up, grinned and with a sharp nod blurted out, "Scientific curiosity of course." Several more people snickered, but it lightened the mood of the room enough that people started to discuss ideas instead of sitting glumly with horrified expressions that promised hours of useless commiserating. Sonso shook her head in disgust, but Hector didn't notice. He gazed at Rebecca as if nobody else was in the room. Rebecca needed to berate him, severely so he'd stop looking at her like she could do no wrong, but his tenacity was impressive. She had to give him that.

Sonso looked around the room as little groups discussed their end of the investigation, however, the meeting needed to continue to review the rest of the pertinent information. Brent smirked, "Okay folks, settle down. We have several other topics on the agenda to discuss then we can get back to doing the important work of figuring out how to contain this pathogen." With a wave, Sonso proceeded, but the pursed lips clearly expressed her displeasure. At Hector or her inability to control the meeting, Rebecca couldn't tell.

"Thank you Hector, for lightening the mood." Sonso's expression imparted an entirely different message, and Hector's little grin faded before she continued, "While we've kept the quarantine protocols for the on-site virus exposure subjects at an extreme isolation level, I think we can now proceed to normal isolation levels. Wear hazmats when in direct contact with the exposed subjects in isolation, review your protocols and when in doubt lean to the side of caution. If you expose yourself to any of these subjects, you will join them in isolation, and then we lose your skills in the investigation." She paused for a moment, "And if any of you contract this virus due to your own negligence I will personally fire you." Sonso smiled at her little joke not realizing that it sounded heartless but Rebecca cracked a smile, and Sonso shot her a look of appreciation. Rebecca's own jokes had often been misunderstood and she empathized with her colleague. As a woman who also had an imposing personality, Rebecca understood.

Alex appreciated that Brent had made special morning arrangements for her. Not only did she get to visit Tristan and David but also she got out of the tiny, cramped room for a while, even if she had to wear a hazmat suit. She'd become quite the expert on donning the suit and easily managed it now. As the trip down the identical white on white halls became more familiar, Alex knew she was merely a few rooms from David's little cell. On her arrival, she paused. David rocked back and forth, sitting on his bed and staring blankly at the television picture of a leopard in a tree. Alex watched him for a moment before turning on the intercom, wondering what thoughts bustled through his head. The sound of switching on the intercom didn't get his attention. He remained distracted, staring at the television, and rocking back and forth, although now she heard him mumbling. Upon closer inspection, she saw tears dripping off his face, "David? What's wrong? I am sorry for not visiting sooner, but I need all kinds of special approvals to leave my room."

Startled, he vaulted up from his bed and urgently scrambled to the window, so suddenly that Alex she jumped back in surprise before he whined at her, "It's all my fault, I am sorry, I am so sorry." In a dejected surrender, David put his hands in his face and sobbed.

Alex stared, dumbfounded, maybe he was having a breakdown, "David, calm down, what do you mean? What is your fault?" She put her gloved hand on the window, wishing she could go in to comfort him, "I don't understand. Why don't you tell me what is wrong." She'd never get him to talk coherently if he didn't calm down, although telling someone to calm down never usually worked, "David, please, take a deep breath and talk to me."

David weaved his head back and forth slowly, miserably, "Oh, sweet girl, when I tell ya; you ain't never gonna forgive me. I should have cleared 'em out, ages before it all happened and now, because of my indifference, we are both going to die." His body slumped as he hung his head and fell forward several inches until his forehead leaned against the window's glass.

Alex's stomach suddenly clenched into knots, "Oh, David, have you developed symptoms? Should I call a doctor?" David shook his head, rubbing it back and forth against the glass, squeaking as he did it. Distracted by the large smear mark he left on the glass she tried to get him to talk, "Then please, tell me what is bothering you because you're not making any sense, and it's worrying me."

David ran his finger against the glass and through the smear, "Ah Alex, it is all my fault. I coulda done something about it but didn't want to bother. Not my problem I said, and that's what ya get when you ignore a problem, it is all on me."

Glad to see he calmed down, but concerned about the melancholic expression in his eyes, Alex sighed, "You said that before but I still don't understand, please explain yourself. What you are talking about? Is this about Doug's death? You couldn't kn-"

Interrupting her, David, contorted his face into an annoyed expression, and snapped, "It ain't about Doug. I shoulda beat them down long before, but I didn't want the headache." Alex waited for him to explain and finally, he spit out the words, "That damn street gang."

117

"I still don't know what you are talking about. Do you mean under the bridge? There haven't been street gangs in the area for ages. What street gang?" Alex's emotions turned in her stomach as she thought about, yet held back what she wanted to say about the police clearing out the area after her attack.

David pounded against the glass, startling Alex again, "Not anymore there ain't!" Her escort looked up from his phone at the noise, but she waved him away, so he went back to punching awkwardly at the device with his gloved hands. David grunted, "The boys that got you. I shoulda chased them away before they hurt anyone. I saw them lurking around and knew they were up to no good, and then they got you. I don't expect you to forgive me, cuz I know your life woulda took a different path and then you wouldn't be in here with me now, if I had done something."

Alex gaped at David; he was the one? All this time and he was right in front of her, and she didn't recognize him, "I don't understand, you mean you chased away the boys who attacked me when I was fifteen?" Tears rolled down her cheeks but her hazmat suit helmet blocked her hands from wiping them away. They leaked out uncontrollably, rolling off her chin and nose, and down her neck, "You saved me? Why didn't you ever say anything to me about it?"

David hid his face from Alex, "How could I? I felt and still feel ashamed. I knew I shoulda done the right thing, and then it woulda never happened to ya."

Alex's heart pounded loudly in her chest, and she longed to sit down and process the information, but it wasn't an option at that moment. She had thought about him for years, but merely glimpsed the blurry shadow of her savior as she lay in the alley, and her foggy memory alluded to only unclear details of the attack, "Wait a minute, Rebecca saw you there too and said she didn't know anything about you. Why didn't she say anything? How could you both keep the secret from me all these years?" Alex wasn't sure whether to feel betrayed or relieved that her savior was safe and with her all these years. She struggled with both feelings but decided to lean toward relief about David. She would deal with Rebecca later.

David shrugged, "She came and found me after it happened, but I knew her already. She been down there a few times before your, well, you know. She bribed us with food to take blood samples and asked us questions about our past and such. We hungered for the food, so we tolerated her. She tried to get me to come forward but I told her I didn't want to go to the authorities. I don't trust the police anymore, but if they needed me, I woulda come. I was afraid they woulda locked me up for attacking them boys. I guess the little witch never said anything to ya, huh?"

Alex shook her head, not comprehending why he was apologizing to her, "David you saved me, Rebecca could never have stopped that group by herself. They almost killed me and if you had not shown up and chased them, away I wouldn't be alive. I've longed to thank you all these years but never knew who you were or how to find you. You're my guardian angel, and I've always loved you for it." Alex felt odd telling him that she loved him, but with the combination of her bizarre kinship with him and her years of gratefulness, she really did love him.

Still shaking his head, David's shame-filled face frowned again, "Nope. It is my fault they attacked you. You should curse me not thank me. All my fault, all my fault, and yet ya still fed me." David went back to weaving his head back and forth and moaning, and Alex's heart felt like it broke as she watched him.

He owed her nothing, yet he apologized to her. She wanted to reach out and hug him but settled for placing her hand up next to him on the window, "You aren't responsible for fixing the ills of the world like you did when you served. You couldn't have known what atrocities those boys had planned. No matter what occurred back then, I've always felt comforted in knowing my guardian angel watched over me because I am still here. Even as a small child I knew the direction my life would follow and coming down to that area or areas similar to it were always part of my plans, nothing would be different. Besides Rebecca will fix all this, she may be a witch but she is brilliant and practically a sister to me. She won't let anything happen to us, don't worry."

"I knew them boys were no good and I am responsible for fixing problems when I can see 'em right in front of me. I am so very sorry I did not stop those boys before they hurt you. I got so much from you every week with the food you brought and the conversations we had. You made me feel like a person again. Seeing you every week gave me such joy but also filled me with such guilt, please forgive me."

Time and love healed her, and now she could let her savior know, "No David, I am sorry that I never recognized you. You know, Rebecca is the one who suggested I go down there to bring food to you and the other residents there. She said it would help heal me and get over my fears, and she was right. Maybe my subconscious must have known you saved me because I always left there feeling mentally restored. I thought I just enjoyed helping others, but now I know that my mind sensed more."

"You weren't scared of comin' down there and of talkin' to me?"

Alex tilted her head and smiled through her tears, "At first I was terrified, but after a while only sometimes. It is a little dark under the bridge, but I knew YOU would never hurt me."

"Won't Alex be surprised!" Rebecca marched down the hall talking to herself and excited to be able to visit Alex without the cumbersome hazmat suit. She decided to pad the WHO announcement with the new much more lenient visitation protocols. Alex would probably break down and have an anxiety attack about the WHO announcement, so Rebecca practiced sounding cheerful, "With the new protocols for the investigation, we can speak to each other like people instead of wearing those annoying hazmat suits. You will be required to wear one when you leave the room, but as long as I don't enter the room we-" Rebecca paused mid-sentence, in front of Alex's window Brent sat in a chair donning only a mask. What was he doing there? She stomped up to him and scowled, "You ruined my surprise!"

Brent arrogantly faced her and smiled one of his charming mischief filled grins, one of the ones that Rebecca never fell for, "Good afternoon Rebecca. I ruined your surprise? Well, I enjoyed our visit Alex, but if I don't go now, someone will track me down for sure." He stood and nodded to both women before sauntering off, "Have a lovely day."

They watched Brent walk down the hall. Then, Alex got up from her chair, glared fiercely. Completely ignoring Rebecca, Alex turned and plopped down, backside up on her bed before putting her nose in her tablet. What now? Rebecca stared, completely confused, "What in the world? Alex, why are you acting so crazy? What did I do now? You seem annoyed or angry with me all the time lately. What is going on?"

Alex glowered over her shoulder and angrily sprung up from the bed practically throwing her tablet down, "You! You are supposed to be my friend! How could you keep it from me?"

"I see Brent told you about the announcement. I know you feel super emotional about everything, but why are you mad at me for it?" Rebecca would do anything for Alex, yet the woman asked for more.

Alex scrunched up her eyebrows in confusion, "What announcement? What are you talking about?" Gritting her teeth, Alex seethed and didn't let Rebecca respond, "All these years you knew and never said a word. You knew how much I wanted to find him, yet you kept it from me."

Rebecca bit her lip, ugh, Alex didn't know about the announcement yet, brave work there Brent. She visited with David earlier, and he must have told her. Keeping that secret from Alex all these years was far worse than procrastinating over the WHO announcement, which explained Alex's anger. She knew the secret of David's identity would one day reveal itself and that Alex would be furious Rebecca kept the information to herself, but her discovery couldn't have been timed worse, "David asked me to keep it private."

"Really? Are you his friend or mine?"

Rebecca started to roil with annoyance, "Oh stop, you aren't twelve, don't act like a child over this. We need to discuss much more important things than the past, and we can worry about our other trivial disagreements later."

Alex wasn't ready to let it go yet, "The police and the lawyers looked for him and you knew. The trial-"

With the volume of her voice, steadily increasing to match her aggravation Rebecca cut her off, "Telling you about David before now wouldn't have helped you or the situation in any way. Those animals went away without a hitch, without his testimony, so yes, I kept it from both you and the police, something you would have done. He was terrified of getting into trouble for beating those boys as severely as he did and I was protecting him. So just stop!"

Rebecca rarely raised her voice, yet Alex didn't stop, she merely hesitated before continuing, "Do you know how much guilt I felt over never finding him? All these years and he was living right under my nose."

Rebecca watched Alex breathing heavily, knowing she was only expressing her frustration, but she needed to defend herself, "Why do you think I suggested you go down and start 'helping others' in that area? It wasn't my altruism; it was to help you. I thought you'd figure it out, on your own, before now."

Alex sniffled, "Well, David told me when I saw him this morning. I don't understand you; sometimes you act like we're closer than sisters and other times you treat me without regard, like I am a stranger. You aren't stuck with me Rebecca, what do you want from me? You knew how much I wanted the information, yet you kept it from me, is our friendship that shallow? You didn't know me when you found me yet still you stuck around, why? What, did you need for some kind of little sister in your life?

Rebecca felt the discussion drifting over to one they'd avoided for years yet, much like the conversation about David, it never happened. She reached up and rubbed the pendant around her neck in anxiety but outwardly tried to remain as calm as possible, "I needed to help you, Alex, as much for you, as for me."

"But why did you do it? You spent every day in that hospital with me for weeks. You helped me eat and bathe, and even go to the bathroom when it made me cry. You were there as much as my own family. How did that help you?"

"Because Alex, sometimes doing things for others helps a person. I wasn't a saint, I was being selfish because it empowered me to assist someone I didn't know, and make a difference in your life. The fact that we remained friends, well that whole thing is a mystery to me."

"Staying friends is the only part that isn't a mystery to me. You hunger for someone to love you just as you are and you're not always that lovable." Rebecca grunted then looked away. As embarrassing as it was she knew her friend was right, Alex had become the most important person in the world to Rebecca. Alex's breathing had slowed, and her face lost its contorted ferociousness, as her usual self reemerged, "I can't believe we never had this conversation before. After all, we went through, I mean, come on, you wiped my butt."

"We never spoke of it because time needed to pass until the words became speakable. Now you are afraid for your life and so is David, which is probably why he told you. I knew you'd be angry with me for not saying anything, but it wasn't my secret to tell." She still needed to tell Alex about the WHO announcement and changing the conversation wasn't going to get any easier, so Rebecca decided to get it over with and blurted out, "The WHO announced a suspension to all international travel."

Alex gaped at Rebecca through the glass, "But that means that...?" She stopped in the middle of her sentence, put her hands on her face, and started to cry, deep, heavy sobs, "I know I am acting pathetically. I've been a complete psycho, but I am terrified Rebecca," Alex paused and gazed earnestly into her friend's eyes, "You saved me once before, and I need you to do it again."

Rebecca breathed deeply, glad that the previous drama settled as quickly as it did. She wished she could reach in and comfort her, but without a hazmat suit, she could only lean up against the window, "Alex, you have nothing to worry about. I always will look out for you, although this time, I will do because I need to do it for you, not me and I don't even have to wipe your butt, so it will be easy." Alex snorted a laugh and sputtered snot out her nose in the process and some of it hit the window. Rebecca contorted her face in disgust at the smear on the glass, "Now get some tissues and wipe up that mess. I came here for some fun banter, but instead, we've been having this extremely depressing conversation, and you know how much I hate dealing with all this emotion." Rebecca gave Alex a moment before she changed the subject, "I haven't even had the chance to tell you. I have a secret admirer."

Rolling her eyes, Alex sighed, "So what is new about that?"

Maybe Rebecca shouldn't have brought it up, but she'd desperately wanted to change the subject. "Well, this one leaves me cheese Danish and coffee each morning when I step away from my desk. I think I know who is doing it, but I really like cheese Danish so I won't say anything yet." Alex grinned ear to ear like she knew something, and now Rebecca really regretted bringing it up, "You look ridiculous, wipe your nose again, please. Oh, my parents asked after you, they were quite anxious when I told them what happened. They want to come in for a visit, and I am working on getting them clearance now."

Alex sniffled after blowing her nose, "I'd love that, I get bored in here."

"How can you get bored when Mister CEO brings you special lunches? That little spread there does not resemble the lunch leftovers of a standard Dashcorp cafeteria meal. Are those real dishes?" Alex smirked through her tear stained misery, relaying her forgiveness. Above all else, Rebecca knew the pathogen wouldn't take her friend, and she just wished she could convey it to Alex.

Judy fiddled with her new burner phone while she watched the news. Most of it just repeated yesterday's material, although now the WHO released the information on the countries affected first, which was leading to unrest. Reports from around the world, the U.S., Afghanistan, Pakistan, Turkey, the UK, the Republic of Congo, Sudan, Guatemala, India, and South Africa all reported mysterious deaths. Reported signs of Kopvein symptoms had spread in these and other countries, and now neo-Nazis, white supremacists, and other hate groups were speaking out against third-world disease and it was igniting their hate. The announcement from the WHO and the interview got Christy national attention. Hospitals and morgues all over the country promptly began reporting suspicious deaths, now known to be the pathogen and several agencies and private companies had joined the CDC, Dashcorp and the WHO, in the struggle.

She had not heard from Christy in over a day and waited for direction from the Viralist. So deep in thought, Judy almost fell out of her chair when the computer dinged, and a private chat room messenger came up, the only message, "The righteous person may have many troubles, but the LORD delivers him from them all: Psalm 34:14." She hated the cryptic messages and didn't know whether it was meant to comfort her or if she should be scared.

CHAPTER 13

Day 10

B rent stared out the glass wall of the conference room while he waited for Sonso to situate herself and spotted Rebecca striding down the hall. Watching her walk always entertained him, with her intense energy and long legs, she sped past those who meandered too slowly for her taste. Around the office, those who heard her coming knew to move to the side or she'd impatiently push past them and they'd get an abrupt 'excuse me,' like her business eclipsed everyone else's. Today, Rebecca seemed to be walking from place to place, her hands filled with files, and it frustrated him. She should use a tech to deliver information, although, she never had the patience to explain things especially if the tech might get it wrong. Some of her instructions took longer than delivering the material herself. Rebecca strode by the small conference room and glanced in, furrowing her eyebrows in a perplexed and suspicious expression. She paused momentarily. Brent worried she might barge in demanding to know why Brent was meeting with Dr. Sonso without including her, pretended not to see her. Lately, she'd been quite fidgety about everything that happened in the investigation, which was an unusual reaction for her. She usually kept to herself and didn't bother with anything but her work, but the gravity of Kopvein weighed heavily on them all.

Sonso, finally situated, sat down in front of carefully laid out piles of printed out reports. She wasted no time and dove into expressing her concerns, "I don't understand the hold up on the protein damage tests on the carotid artery tissue your facility has been working with it for over a week. The test and report should take only two days. The CDC should really do its own independent testing."

Brent breathed deeply, the tone of her voice grated on his nerves. He'd known this conversation was coming, but two could play at that game. In his most agitated voice, he ignored her complaint and sneered, "The WHO and the CDC showed no progress in their research on the pathogen because it is a complete unknown, the normal tests and scans reveal nothing. We pulled Rebecca, our most meticulous researcher, from her current projects to work on the investigation. She is also the person who noticed the corrupted tests and projection errors. You are being far too impatient."

Scrunching up her nose in an odd arrogant manner, Sonso sniffled, "Yet you still don't know anything."

Brent tried to control his breathing but felt his nostrils flare as rage swirled inside him, "You knew about Kopvein long before it affected our facility, yet you know nothing either. We found out it is viral instead of a poison, yet we wasted time on that theory because you withheld information. You know far more now than before you got involved with Dashcorp. Your boss had you move the center of the investigation here because our progress superseded your own. How long did the Ebola breakouts take to detect? And the Zika virus? All those reports from around the world and you found nothing until my researcher decisively identified the pathogen for what it was. I can see you are aiming for something, and I don't want a territorial battle at such a crucial time."

"I believe that someone on your team may be withholding information that both our teams could use in the investigation, the information you control, even though the CDC readily agreed to partner with you on this outbreak. You think you can keep doing the research here at your facility? Why, so you can control the vaccine or cure?"

It always came down to control with these bureaucratic organizations and Brent needed to squash it and get them working as a team. Sonso was probably agitated that everyone looked to Rebecca as the lead instead of her. He visibly managed to maintain his voice's volume and acted as if he wanted to scream, "You imply that Dashcorp is holding back so it can profit from the cure? As a research facility in a for-profit organization, we aren't hiding anything, and everyone will suffer if Kopvein is not contained. The CDC has not been forthcoming when we asked for their findings, yet you accuse my researchers? My facilities' team reported the first case of Kopvein directly, and it took plenty of time for the CDC's response. Why do you want us to repeat tests you've already performed? Do you know how much time you could have saved us all?"

Sonso shifted in her seat then looked away, showing signs of being uncomfortable and not wanting to relay information, "We required a look at your findings without our input, to make sure we hadn't overlooked anything."

Brent gritted his teeth. He hated the games people played all to maintain the visage of control. In a sarcastic, biting tone he sneered, "Relaying that information would have helped a great deal, but I can see how it is okay to waste my company's resources and not to mention the innocent lives, all to check your researcher's results. If I am going to continue to put my company's resources into this joint investigation, I need everything, processes, results, numbers, everything."

"Don't threaten me. I know you will work on it with me whether you want to or not. If you don't, it may be the worldwide pandemic that destroys us all. Your company won't exist if the situation gets out of control and we don't discover a solution quickly."

Sonso wasn't going to make it easy so Brent had to play dirty. He shrugged his shoulders and haughtily chuckled, "Or we could resolve to control everything, doling out vaccines and cures to those who can afford it creating the world we desire, exactly as you said."

Sonso's anger blazed across her face as she raised her voice, "I did not say it like that, and that attitude is exactly why the CDC prefers not to work with private companies like Dashcorp. Companies such as yours are always looking to increase their profit margin, to take advantage of those around them. All when they are needed the most. Where is your humanity?"

Brent leaned back in his chair and smiled, listening to the quiet of the room, satisfied he got his point across by getting a rise out of Sonso. He winked then flippantly replied, "I am not the one who began the battle of monopolizing information, and I didn't say we would monopolize our discoveries, but I may have implied that I prefer not to be forcefully compelled, especially when I control the majority of data and resources."

"Well, I don't like to be strong-armed either, this is not some game. People are dying-"

Brent cut her off, he had no desire to hear a lecture or excuses, "I am very well aware of that Dr. Sonso, maybe it is time you acted like that too. How many infected victims have you been in contact with? Do you know what Kopvein does to people? I saw it and worked on it. I'm not merely a paper pusher." She needed to realize that her assumptions, about him and his company, were wrong and that the CDC, as well as the world, needed his help.

Sonso quieted, the jabs successful enough to cease any more questions about his staff. Sonso sighed, shaking her head and relenting, "Fine. From here on out maybe we can both declare goodwill and transparency from both sides."

Rebecca reached the office unsure of what to expect from the last minute. She had seen Brent and Sonso earlier but that was hours before. On her arrival, Sonso was nowhere but Abe, Brent, and Judy sat around the desk. Brent motioned for her to have a seat, as they were already in the midst of a discussion, "I know you are no longer on the committee, but we thought you might have some insight into this matter."

Rebecca quietly watched and listened, trying to decipher where the meeting was going but had a pretty good idea. Brent and Abe discussed how accurate the news seemed with their reports and she smiled inside over the men's theatrics and tried not to let her satisfaction show. The little worm was finally about to get caught, and everyone in the room knew it, including Judy. Judy shifted uncomfortably in her seat, then glanced at each person in the room, "I- I- I- have no idea how the news is getting the information. Maybe the CDC has an information leak."

Brent's pleasant demeanor abruptly turned sour and the expression on his face shifted to an imposing glare, "You know, I considered that, but the leak started before the CDC came into our building. I sacrificed something important to me to find out about your loose conversations."

Sweat beaded up on Judy's forehead and her eyes darted around the room, "What does that mean? I don't know what to say."

Brent's eyes blazed with anger, "A hungry reporter will do anything for a good story these days won't they?"

Rebecca snorted her disgust at what he implied, wondering why would he tell her that. Judy first looked confused at Rebecca's response then she scrunched up her face in disbelief. She glanced around the room then back at Rebecca, and a look of terror and shock washed across her face. Her breathing increased, and she looked like she was about to say something, but she clamped her mouth shut and didn't say a word. Abe, Brent, and Rebecca stared imposingly at Judy, waiting for further argument, as the sweat on from her forehead now dripped down her face, and her ragged breathing reached a panting level, "I- I wish I could help you, but since I am no longer involved in the committee I don't have any information for you."

Suddenly, Brent jumped up from his chair, startling all of them, "Judy I know you leaked the information to Christy Gallagher!"

Judy avidly shook her head, "I-I-I swear, I never spoke to Christy about anything happening at work. We go to church together, that is all."

"You are lying Judy, and we all know it, so you may as well admit to it. Who is feeding you information? You need to tell me now!"

Rebecca would have preferred an old-fashioned waterboarding for this betrayal; they were far too easy on her. The woman was obviously leaking the information and had to be getting it from Nithi because who else would risk their careers to give help Judy. How could he not definitively know that? However, she sensed Judy knew something else, and Rebecca needed to hear it and whatever else she would tell Brent. Finally, Rebecca blurted out, "What are you hiding?"

Judy started to answer, but paused, then glared at Rebecca, and crossed her arms in defiance, "I am not saying anything to you, Rebecca."

Giving Brent a sharp nod, Rebecca didn't stop, "I think now is the perfect time to get to the point and ask her what you really mean."

Judy's expression turned like suddenly a light went off in her head, the corners of her mouth went up slightly, "Maybe I should wait for a lawyer before I say anything else."

Rebecca knew she should have stayed quiet when, at the word lawyer, Brent's expression morphed into something Rebecca had never seen. A look that told her he wanted to reach over and strangle both her and Judy but instead he only motioned for Rebecca to leave the room. Why have her come to the meeting if she was supposed to stay quiet? Judy, Abe, and Brent watched her go, and Judy now wore a satisfied expression on her face. She shouldn't look so smug. She could end up in jail. Whatever Judy knows will be passed on to the investigations team, so she should just get over herself. Rebecca knew she had pushed hard but wished she could be there or at least watch the rest of the questioning. If Brent thought he could control everything and leave her out of the loop, he was out of his mind. She would figure out everything that woman said, and Rebecca knew just how to him to relent. She thought about Brent's obsession with Alex. When Alex gave him the cold shoulder, Rebecca would beat him without having to play his little game his way. It was bad enough that Sonso held back, but her own team? He requested, no insisted on congruous teamwork, yet would withhold knowledge that might be essential to what she was doing.

The camera panned across a scene with emergency personnel and crying teenagers and distraught adults hugging each other, finally settling on the perky blond reporter, "This is Christy Gallagher reporting with breaking news from Anacostia High school in Washington D.C. Today, I am very sad to report a school shooting. At this time, there are eight reported dead with forty-three injured students and teachers in this horrible tragedy. The shooter attended the school three years prior and reportedly felt disgruntled with the way his life turned out after his tumultuous high school experience. The shooter left a note blaming the school, its staff and students, both former and present, for his misery. My sources say he also had connections to white supremacist groups that are making noise about the Kopvein virus. He entered the well-protected school carrying two automatic rapid-fire AR-15 weapons with ill intent in his heart and death in his eyes. Upon entering the school courtyard, he immediately shot several students enjoying their lunches on what had been a beautiful autumn day. He ran further into the courtyard as everyone ran for cover then cornered another few dozen students when his gun jammed. In the process of fixing his gun, students scattered and the shooter suffered a massive seizure then died in front of the very same students and teachers he was about to gun down. Witnesses state the shooter appeared to have strange markings down the side of his face and neck. Could the shooter be suffering from the symptoms of the new virus that is making its way through our world? Did he see no future for himself and decide to carry out one last act of desperation? And will the White House speak out about this tragedy or only tweet about it like the President has? Christy Gallagher reporting, more to come as the investigation unfolds."

Learning about the school shooting made Alex want to vomit. With all the horrible things happening in the world, this viral scare increased its volatility even more. She kicked her feet out on her bed then held the pillow over her face and screamed. She was locked up, trapped and unable to do anything useful from inside her little cell. A medical facility or not, this place gave her no privacy, with nothing to do but watch TV, exercise, or read. She waited to eat, spent her days counting down the minutes until the next one, and was in plain view for anyone walking by to see. It was a prison sentence. Dashcorp tried to make her imprisonment pleasant, but this little room remained her tiny cell. The pitiful rants she had to herself and

Rebecca made her feel weak and desperate. She was, but she couldn't stand the feeling. Each time someone came to bring her a meal, or when Brent visited or a doctor checked on her, she acted strong, courageous, and unconcerned, though inside, she felt anything but strong. Only Rebecca and the walls of her cell knew her true feelings.

Hearing an echoing down the hall, she turned to listen. Rebecca's was unmistakable, although this time the steps echoed with ferocity. She jumped up from her bed, not wanting to burden her friend with her pathetic feelings once again. Rebecca's respirator mask lifted away from her face, then sucked back to it with the intensity of her heavy breathing. Rebecca pulled up a chair and sat in front of Alex's window, and said nothing. Alex opened her mouth to ask her what had happened but snapped it shut, opposing the urge. Rebecca sat in the chair not moving but breathed heavily. Her face was a stone facade. Alex didn't smile or move, standing still as she waited for Rebecca to say something. The expression on Rebecca's face morphed several times conveying her deep thought process. Alex was accustomed to her usual bitchiness, but this felt different and she didn't know how to respond. It added to her anxiety but she waited, as quietly and patiently as possible.

Finally, Rebecca glanced up and smiled, "Why are you standing there that way? Pull up a chair." Alex's jaw dropped. Rebecca cocked her head to the side, confused, "What?"

"That wasn't the reaction I expected, from the way you marched up here." Alex cautiously pulled up her chair to the window and stood, gripping the back of it. Even with glass between them, she was wary, an outburst from Rebecca could radiate an entire room, and even if Alex wasn't the intended victim of the attack, it pained her to witness it.

A wave of Rebecca's hand dismissed the entire scene, "Work stuff, it has nothing to do with you." She stared down the hall, avoiding eye contact. There was more to the situation than Rebecca was acknowledging.

"Considering where I am standing at this moment, I think your work stuff has everything to do with me."

Leaning in, Rebecca resolutely peered into Alex's eyes, "Really, it is not related to you."

Alex narrowed her eyes, but acquiesced and sat down with a huff. She let it go, for now. Knowing whatever Rebecca had bouncing around in her head couldn't help Alex at the moment. She'd finesse it out of her later and address it then.

With folded arms, Rebecca leaned back in her chair, "What's the deal with you and Brent?"

Alex smirked, "What-what do you mean? I am behind glass, how could there be a deal with Brent?"

Rebecca snorted a half laugh, "I know how you think Alex. Behind glass, is the best way for you to let your guard down. He can't come near you, so it is easy to act like he is worthy when he is at a safe distance, right?"

Alex shook her head, but she knew her expression told Rebecca far more than she wanted it to, "I love how you think you know me so well. I haven't decided how or if I even think of Brent in that way. I already told you that."

"Well, I don't believe you, but if you truly don't know how you feel, you should forget about him."

She scrunched up her face in confusion, then weakly responded, "What? A few days ago you pushed me toward him?" Why reverse direction so suddenly?

"Yes, well, now I am starting to distrust the man. He thoroughly enjoyed flirting with that reporter Christy Gallagher in his interview. It was blatant and disgusting. I'm not sure about him and I'd feel better if you kept your distance for now, at least until we can figure out if he is trustworthy enough for you."

"You are out of your mind. For your information, he told me all about the interview and said he merely had a part to play for his job. I don't know why he felt the need to tell me anything about it at all. What has gotten into you? First, you show up looking like you're ready to rip someone's throat out, and now you tell me to forget about someone I haven't even been on a date with. You look like shit and are acting weird." Alex's scolding reverberated through her so intensely that her forehead almost collided with the glass as her finger jabbed the window.

"Why must you be so difficult Alex? Trusting a man who demonstrates a proclivity to lies proves you a fool!"

Alex did not know what to say to that comment or where it came from. Rebecca had left something meaningful out of this discussion, "Has he lied?"

Rebecca twitched, "I can't say."

Alex's eyebrows raised and she sat back in her chair, with her arms folded, "Can't or won't?

"Does it matter? I am only trying to protect you."

"Trying to protect me from what? I am stressed out enough by being stuck in here, and you know, about maybe having a fatal disease. Don't add to it by pushing me about an irrelevant possibility. You're talking about something ridiculous and useless. It is completely unlike you and I don't understand it."

The expression in Rebecca's eyes hardened as frustration grew on face, "Just stay away from him for a few days, would you?" Alex grimaced and threw her hands out toward the walls, gesturing around the cell with both of her hands because she wasn't going anywhere. Rebecca ignored it and shook her head, "Trust me, give him the cold shoulder. If he is interested in you, he won't be able to stay away, and if not, he'll take the hint, and at least you will know, okay?"

They sat in silence for several moments. Rebecca sounded like a psycho. Alex knew the agitation emanated from some other situation, one she hadn't disclosed. Rebecca was up to something but she just couldn't figure out what. She looked forward to her visits with Brent, it brightened her day, and now Rebecca wanted her to act aloof towards him. She hated playing games with men, which probably explained why she was still single. There must be a reason, maybe Brent had a secret fiancé or did more than flirt with the reporter, but he had no reason to lie. As long as she remained quarantined, she was untouchable. She refused to do as Rebecca asked, but now her mind couldn't dismiss all that Rebecca had said.

Finally, Rebecca interrupted Alex's thoughts, "I look like shit huh?"

CHAPTER 14

Day 11

A be and Brent simultaneously walked into the lab and glanced around. The lab echoed with their footsteps, and Rebecca glimpsed up from her station but went back to her work, ignoring them. She found it odd that both men came together. It was Saturday and her techs wouldn't stagger in until eight or nine, so every sound reverberated against the walls and equipment. The long weeks and even longer days since the beginning of the Kopvein investigation impeded on Rebecca's quiet time in the lab, and she needed to take advantage of the empty building before anyone came in. Abe checked his watch before addressing her, "Aye Rebecca, ye look like shite." Brent scowled at him, but Rebecca only grinned and went back to her work, saying nothing.

Of course, they came to the lab to speak with her, yet she made them wait. After disregarding them for several minutes, Rebecca, still focused on her work, addressed them, "Yes?"

Abe's voice sounded annoyed, "Come on Rebecca don't make this harder than it needs to be." Rebecca sighed, cast a dead-eyed look in Brent and Abe's direction, and continued to glare without uttering a word. Both men glanced at each other, but Abe took the lead, which seemed unusual in Brent's presence, "Ye know we are here to speak with ye."

She narrowed her eyes, "Yes and you're disturbing me, so what do you want?"

Brent cleared his throat before he verbally pounced on her, "Is something impeding your progress on this investigation?" Without waiting for a response, he continued, "I've seen you diagnose and develop a vaccine in two days when others can't crack it in a month. Yet with the world watching, and desperately waiting, you make no progress?"

Rebecca inhaled slowly, giving herself time to think. She felt a palpable anger burning in her eyes. She didn't have time for this and needed to adjourn the impromptu confrontation so she aggressively stepped toward them and instinctively they jerked back. Satisfied at their response, she laughed to herself. In a quiet, calm and intimidating tone of voice, Rebecca uttered, "You think that because I've had quick success in the past with small outbreaks that I should be able to decipher the solution to an unknown outbreak just as expeditiously? Those were simple problems and were to outbreaks that resembled previous pathogens. I merely put together solutions someone else had already developed. This pandemic is one like nobody has ever seen."

Abe looked away and rubbed the back of his neck, but Brent matched her belligerence and stepped toward her, stopping inches from her face and peering directly into her eyes. Matching her snarkiness, his reply reeked of irritation, "Rebecca, I thought your usual logical and efficient participation would deter the mess these multi-organizational investigations rile up, but Sonso says you are hindering the progress. She says you are investigating abstract disciplines that have nothing to do with the pathogen? What does that even mean? In Sonso's eyes, you are diverting the investigation with your investigative techniques."

She knew she could easily intimidate or at least quiet both Brent and even her old friend Abe with her anger, and it fueled her to press forward, "Really? And how am I possibly doing that? She doesn't understand this pathogen any more than anyone else does, and even LESS than I seem to. Her observations are transparent and her budding solutions shortsighted." Rebecca hastily reigned in her anger and indignation, and in a most matter of fact way, redirected their attention to the conversation she had overheard in the hallway, "Now we know the information leaks came from our team, we can also assume that the guilty party is probably responsible for hindering my progress. Maybe you should attack the real problem instead of the only person here working. I had suspected either someone from Sonso's team or Nithi, but apparently you already obtained a good lead, so I will defer to you."

"You suspected Nithi? Then why didn't you say anything about it?"

"You mean, state the obvious? I had no proof and didn't feel like wasting time on a witch-hunt when the investigation isn't much further today than it was last week. Information leaks affect Dashcorp management and the CDC, not the investigation."

"You are a member of Dashcorp management, remember?" Brent paused momentarily and combatively glared, "As of now, all of your theories led us down unsuccessful paths."

"How do you know that? I am not like those single-minded drones or you wouldn't be here right now. I am working on multiple aspects of the investigation at the same time. I am trying to figure out not only how it spread, but how it works, and trust me, I know my theories require a lot more work, but I am not finished with them. I am taking the investigation beyond epidemiology into what Sonso calls "abstract disciplines" and she doesn't understand my investigative techniques so I kept my theories to myself. I don't want the distraction of unnecessary interruptions. I came here this early to see what I could determine on my own before a dozen other voices hypothesize in my ear and waste my time with their disruptive questions. I also am desperately searching for how the virus works. We know what it does now, but not why or how." Rebecca's anger slowly crept in, again, "If you think I am not working hard enough, look around you, it is seven in the morning on a Saturday. I haven't gone home in days, and I haven't slept in my own bed in a week. I sleep in my office and shower in the locker room, then when I wake up and get right back to work. Nobody is as dedicated to figuring out this pathogen than I am. I am investigating abstract disciplines because that it the direction my investigation is leading me. If you want the normal investigative tactics, there is an entire lab of people who will be in shortly, talk to them."

Outraged desperation rose in Brent's throat, "Thousands of people are dying, and I need answers. It is growing out of control!"

Abe placed his hand on Brent's shoulder, "This isn't her fault man. She just hasn't unraveled this one, yet."

"You can yell and stomp your foot too, but throwing a fit isn't going to help me or the investigation." Rebecca tried to sound as empathetic as her stressed out brain would allow, "Listen, I've told you already, Kopvein is unlike anything anyone has ever encountered. It presents like a virus, but the makeup of it is,-is sophisticated and perplexing. I don't know what I am looking at, but like Abe said, YET. I am going where the research is leading me, and you need to let me do this my way. I always get results but I can't if I am not allowed to proceed in the way I see fit. I know it sounds arrogant, but nobody else here can do what I do. Now go away and let me work."

Brent hung his head. Abe patted him on the back, then they both staggered out. They couldn't say anything else, Rebecca was right, and she knew it.

Rebecca returned to her work but couldn't concentrate. When would Hector arrive with some coffee? She knew he was bringing her the coffee and Danish, and she needed a distraction after that useless confrontation.

She had a little talk to herself, it helped to separate her emotions from what she needed to do. She reminded herself nobody cared about her. Only results mattered. The choices people made benefitted them and padded their egos along the way. She knew she couldn't get caught up in the turbulence of emotion and self-doubt, it would merely alter her path. She refused to be deterred. Brent and everyone else here at Dashcorp only tolerated her and nothing more. Rebecca's skills met their needs, but they never saw her. Her entire purpose in life aimed to fix the real problems of the world, not deal with the drama of these people. Rebecca closed her eyes and sighed, vigilance, she said to herself, the answers are not always the final solution.

Brent walked back into his office consumed with distraction over the confrontation with Rebecca, so he sat at his desk, unable to get anything done. Abe said she always had a sixth sense about her investigations and research projects, and in his mind, he knew she was entirely in the right, but something felt off. Rebecca was probably the most intelligent person he had ever met, frighteningly so. He'd never worked closely with her on anything important, but could she really be that insightful? He should ask the one person who knew her best to find the answer, Alex. People already commented on Alex's special treatment, and now they would also say Brent made excuses to see her.

Brent walked, attempting to appear aloof, toward the isolation rooms. He knew the stress was starting to affect him but he didn't want others to notice. He needed to figure out the situation with Rebecca but he also hungered for another conversation with Alex. When he arrived, she was sitting back on her bed reading and snacking, and he silently watched for a moment. The woman could eat! There was something very intimate and possibly a little creepy about watching a person without their knowledge. Alex's strength and composure during everything she'd been put through surprised him. Most people would have broken down into crying disasters at all she was going through. He never saw any of it from her. He leaned forward and tapped on the glass, and Alex jumped from the start of it. He pointed to the intercom waiting for her consent, and then pulled up a chair.

Alex smiled waiting for Brent to say something and he smiled back but struggled to make it genuine, a fact she didn't seem to miss, "You're wearing the same look on your face my brother gets when something is wrong." He raised his eyebrows and pumped his chin to acknowledge what she said but he was having a difficult time opening up now that he was in front of her. Alex took the silence as an invitation to continue, "Tristan smiles, but I can tell when it is fake because his eyes give him away. Most people give themselves away with their eyes. What is wrong or can't you talk about it?"

Brent's smile faded, and he inhaled deeply, "You spend a lot of time trying to read people, don't you?"

She grinned knowingly at him, "And you spend a lot of time evading people's questions don't you? Or is that a prerequisite of your job?"

Brent pursed his lips, how could he admit to her that he thought he'd made a mess of everything and now people were dying because of it. If Brent unloaded his feelings to her, this pretty girl who he couldn't stop thinking about, she would know he failed and that he would probably fail her too. He couldn't bear the thought of it, and the look on her face grew more and more concerned as she waited for him to respond. Somehow, though, Brent knew if he could talk to anyone, Alex was the one. He leaned his head against the glass, unable to look her in the eye, "I feel I've made a mess of the whole Kopvein investigation and it is getting away from me."

She didn't reply, so he tentatively glanced up and saw her a wide grin had consumed her face, then she began gently chuckling, "Not to be insensitive but of course it is getting away from you, but that doesn't mean you made a mess of it. Look at what you're dealing with. It is beyond you and your company, or even this country. For some reason, Kopvein is taking over the world, and while the fatalities may only be a few thousand now, those fatalities are everywhere. Wouldn't the statistics of that fact alone lead a scientist to deduce that the spread is inevitable and unstoppable?"

Astonished at her insightfulness, Brent watched her for a moment, "Yes, but it happened under my watch, and every death is my responsibility. I feel like I should do more and I'll be quite frank with you Alex, I am afraid and my next step will either save lives or condemn us all."

Alex grunted, "I have to say, you always seemed confident and sure of yourself but I didn't realize you had a God complex."

Brent laughed for a moment, reassured by her teasing, "Am I that much of an arrogant ass?" His mirth faded, "Maybe sometimes but I am afraid I made too many mistakes in how I handled the entire investigation and now everyone is going to pay."

"Rebecca is working on the problem, isn't she? Well, I am her only friend so she can't let anything happen to me or she will get very lonely. So, I have complete confidence, that with Rebecca you will figure it out and save us all."

Brent started to smile, but then his face straightened into a somber stare, "But how many people are going to die before she figures it out?"

In the group lab, Rebecca felt like everyone came at her nonstop. Why did they think she had all the answers? Stupid question, she usually did, but this morning's confrontation with Brent and Abe still lingered in her mind. How long could she continue the charade of keeping it all together? Everyone around her, including Alex, continually pressed her for more. Rebecca couldn't pull herself out of the deep emotional hole she fell into after the morning's confrontation. It was an enemy that called itself friend, one that lurked with self-doubt and self-hatred, a hole she managed to climb out of in the past by planning and working hard. Rebecca could not vacillate over her choices now; she needed to press on. Without her contributions, she as a person would not matter and her life would remain irrelevant. Rebecca shook her head; her work would speak as it always did.

She realized she'd been staring off into space for the last several minutes and had been mumbling to herself, but she hoped it had been incoherent to others. As she turned to see if anyone had noticed, she saw Hector watching her with a starry-eyed gaze. What was his problem? He should hate her already for as hostile as she'd been to him, yet every time she barked an order, he smiled and practically skipped away, and each morning coffee and a Danish sat on her desk like he was rewarding her snarkiness. Every tech and even the doctors in the lab absolutely loved him, he charmed them all, and several of the women gazed at Hector the same way he stared at her. His pretty face and thin, athletic build was something she was attracted to, and he must be halfway intelligent to have a job at the CDC. Maybe she'd throw him a bone and be pleasant to him for the day, although, right now, she didn't feel like being polite to anyone, "Hector, I require assistance, I need you to come with me." He nodded and slid over toward her in a confident saunter, a mannerism she often appreciated in a person. Brent sauntered confidently, but he seemed to be laughing at her when he thought she didn't notice and they constantly butted heads. Brent's input and even his presence annoyed her thoroughly. Hector, on the other hand, seemed pleased by the requests and undaunted by her aggressive and sometimes abrupt tone. Too bad he wasn't a little older.

From her peripheral vision, she noticed several of the female techs flash her a jealous, death stare. Two doctors who saw rolled their eyes, but their reactions made taunting them cheer her up, "We are going down to the analysis lab to re-examine some samples, I will need these files, oh, and order lunch for the both of us, we'll eat together." Hector scooped up the flash drive, and paper files then followed her. Rebecca, hoping to also annoy Sonso, satisfactorily nodded to Sonso on her way out.

138

Working in the group lab was productive for sharing information, but she did her best thinking in peace, and Hector did not bother her, well most of the time, except for his undaunted lack of fear.

Stopping in the large conference room, Hector shot Rebecca an inquisitive look, she smiled, "I said analysis lab because I didn't want a whole entourage following us in here. I work better in the quiet." He put his finger over his lips in a silly gesture but remained quiet, which Rebecca appreciated. She carefully laid out the data using tape to section off information on the table and walls, and Hector seeing what she planned, jumped in to help and pushed some of the chairs out into the hallway to make room. Sometimes the digital models prevented scientists from viewing the whole picture, so she reverted to the old school paper route. Rebecca started ordering the victims, both domestically and internationally, by date of pathogen infection and death, and then individuals exposed to the victims in the number of days common that the pathogen incubated. A clear pattern emerged, "Have you noticed?" Still, without uttering a sound, Hector's head bobbed up and down in an emphatic nod. Her appreciation for him was growing.

"We didn't miss it before, but it was incomplete, and the two-dimensional digital model may limit further discovery. Sonso immediately noticed that almost all of the victims were male, but we originally hypothesized that because the victims were incarcerated or in male-led occupations, this model, however, tells a different story." The air shifted slightly, and both Rebecca and Hector turned around to see Nithi watching.

"I apologize if I startled you; this model you created is quite interesting. Should I contact Dr. Adams?" The man still refused to call his boss by his first name, although Brent preferred it.

Rebecca shook her head, "Not yet, we aren't ready to discuss the information since we still need to analyze it." She needed to delay revealing it until she had time to think about the what to do with information that this model divulged, "Perhaps you can configure the data into the holographic 3-D display as we laid it out here while we continue to work on it." Nithi nodded and left the room presumably to acquire a laptop or tablet.

Rebecca, accompanied by Hector, marched toward the group lab, annoyed that she left some of her work there. They paused to listen to the news as the annoying reporter Christy Gallagher announced with an inappropriate amount of enthusiasm, "A new player on this frightening war board of live or die with the Kopvein virus has made itself known. A group called the Viralists for Justice has released a statement, 'Brothers and sisters, God is just: He will punish those who do not obey the gospel. Those following the evolutionists and their heathen brethren will be punished with everlasting destruction but it is not too late. Repent and the Lord God will forgive you. Find solace in prayer and meditation, and whether here or in the heavens, you will be free to walk among the blessed. This petulance among us is the destruction of the profane and God's gift to His people.' The Viralist group claims that only the righteous will survive the Kopvein virus' cleansing and people are listening. The pews at St. Mary's chapel were full, and the service was standing room only, earlier this morning,"

"In a separate story, High ranking military officers were spotted entering the White House, presumably to speak to the President, who we have not seen in days. Is he hiding out from this virus? The world needs you now Mr. President. How are you going to help us?"

All the doctors and technicians in the lab stared at the television in disbelief as Rebecca turned down the sound, and Sonso snorted loudly, "Well, I am going to burst into flames then." Sonso smiled at her own joke, and Rebecca burst out in a shriek of laughter, followed by Hector. Then, the entire staff amused by the humor in Sonso's comment and entertained by the new fanatic faction's ridiculous claims joined in.

Rebecca clapped her hands together twice, "Alas my heathen colleagues, Sonso has spoken the real truth and we must work to save our fellow infidels." Rebecca shook her head and waved Hector over, "Can you believe the crazies that come out every time the wind blows the wrong way? What will they do next? " Hector grimaced as he shrugged what could he say?

CHAPTER 15

Day 12

Rebecca rolled over on her couch. Ugh, her back ached, and she longed to sleep in a real bed. What day was it? She glanced over at her desk and was shocked to see it read Sunday, nine o'clock. How late had she gone to bed, five or six? Exhaustion consumed her, and one decent stretch of sleep barely lightened its blunting physical effects. She laid for several more minutes before she stretched, rolled her weary body up, grabbed her bag and left the office to go down to the locker room for a shower. As she let the water roll down her neck and back, she developed a mental to-do list for the day. Planning her activities relaxed her. Probably most important on the list, a stop at the shared lab to evaluate yesterday's accomplishments, although they would have come down the hall and woken her with any dynamic discoveries. After that, she'd return to the quiet of the conference room with Hector and Nithi to finish what they'd started.

Refreshed from her shower, she ran her fingers through her damp hair and started thinking about the last couple of days. She felt connected to the team and was leading not only through fear and intimidation but also with comradery and a joint goal. Leave it to a disaster to help her discover that she could be precisely who Alex had said she was capable of the entire time. She and Sonso worked together reasonably well, a development she had never expected, the lab techs seemed to be enjoying her humor, and some even liked her. If only she'd seen it before now, the years she spent alone, making the choices she'd made,... yet now, those choices demanded that she remain on her fated path, no matter where it led. She sighed and shrugged her shoulders before pulling her damp hair back into a loose bun.

When Rebecca entered the lab nobody made eye contact with her. This couldn't be good, so much for her earlier optimism. She nervously rubbed the pendant on her necklace while deciding how to respond. She did not have the energy for guessing games, "Whatever it is, out with it." Hector swallowed hard before reluctantly waiving her over to her computer. He must have drawn the short straw and remained quiet but pulled up the interoffice email, and then pointed to the one that went out to everyone working on the investigation. Seth Mitchell died yesterday due to complications from the Kopvein virus. Hector gently patted her on the shoulder and walked away. They all knew about her friendship with Alex and that Seth caused Alex's quarantine. Now she needed to tell Alex and Rebecca's stomach clenched in knots, "Why didn't someone tell me about this sooner?"

Sonso stepped forward to throw Hector under the bus, "I apologize, yesterday was such a busy day that at Hector's request, I advised that everyone let you sleep. He said you were up late working on an aspect of the transmission, and not to disturb you."

Rebecca glanced over at Hector staring down at his shoes and found his concern endearing, "Good call, exhaustion clouds thinking, and I needed the sleep. Yesterday's work may prove invaluable in preventing further transmission of this pathogen. Where are you at Sonso?" Sonso tried to play games, and probably expected Rebecca to rip Hector a new one, but wouldn't let the woman manipulate her that way and she had needed the sleep. Every time she thought the two made progress in their relationship, Sonso did something to force a wedge between them. Rebecca realized that others probably thought that working with her was similar. No wonder everyone avoided her. She patiently listened to Sonso's abbreviated synopsis of their work yesterday. Sonso didn't overly explain every detail, which helped alleviate some of her testiness towards the woman. Rebecca wanted to deliver a few sarcastic blows to bring Sonso down a little but refrained for the sake of the rest of the lab. She looked around but didn't see Nithi; he must already be in the conference room. Rebecca half-smiled and winked at Hector, "I would appreciate your assistance again today. Would you mind getting me a coffee and maybe a little treat before we start?" Hector smirked and hurried out the door as Rebecca inwardly sneered and nodded to Sonso before she left.

Rebecca tried to escape to her private lab before settling back into the conference room, but as she snuck by the conference room doorway, she heard Nithi, "Yes, I know, but I can't get away today. I will try to call you later." He quickly hung up the phone when Rebecca walked in. He smiled innocently and said good morning before turning to his computer. Could he be talking to his wife? She looked and did not see a ring on his finger. At thirty, he is still young, so maybe a girlfriend? It couldn't be his mom, could it? Perhaps it was someone else, she shook her head, but the thought brought a smile to her face.

Judy didn't know what to do with herself during the days since her suspension from work. Her husband was quite angry with her, and they'd had a terrible fight. He didn't understand why she was suspended, and she couldn't explain it to him, but the man wouldn't appreciate the value of her decisions, so she kept her activities to herself. She might lose her job or even worse for what she revealed to Christy, and Brent didn't even know everything she'd been doing. The entire episode felt so mortifying, but she couldn't tell that to her husband either. She'd never tell anyone the full extent of her humiliation.

In her mind, she went back and forth about her choices and shook her head. Ultimately, Judy decided that she did what she thought was right. Helping the Viralists would lead her to her final standing in the world, and she couldn't falter. Her husband would be furious, yet no matter the cost, she needed to continue her work. Judy just hoped she could accomplish all her required deeds before time ran out. She spent hours browsing the news articles and the Viralist Justice Blog. Many people had joined the movement and supported it by commenting and chatting about the messages, and with each other on the site. She felt herself developing close relationships with several of the new Viralists, some local, and others around the country. They had sought her out.

The Viralist requested Judy check the website every day, at certain times for messages with pertinent information and instructions. In a private chat room with the Viralist, he delivered a troubling directive, one that scared her so much she jerked back her hands from the keyboard, abruptly, as if it burned her. So far, she'd had no visible contact with the Viralist movement, and changing that would transform everything for Judy. She typed back, "If I do this, my cover will be blown, and I will probably lose my job."

The reply arrived almost instantaneously, "God is just, sister, and the righteous person may have many troubles, but the LORD delivers. Your days in the shadows are over. You need to lead these followers and take the position you were meant to have, as a leader!" Judy gasped and almost fell out of her chair upon reading it, but felt validated and forgot her recent doubts. She kept reading, "You need the Gallagher woman to interview you, and I will even help you with the script."

She smiled to herself. Finally, a position she deserved, so with shaking hands, she slowly typed back, "How may I serve?"

Alex closed her tablet, tired of sitting in the same position. The days lingered and it was amplified by the monotony. She got up from her bed and stretched out, then rolled out the yoga mat that Rebecca had brought her. Fully focused on the meditative aspect of each pose, Alex jumped at the tap, tap, tap, on her glass window. Rebecca stood outside her window, and the expression on her face screamed of dread. Whatever news Rebecca had, it upset her enough that she let it show. What if her latest blood tests revealed that she'd contracted the disease? She interacted with David regularly, and he lived right near Doug. How would she survive the news? She wished she could go home and curl up in the comfort of her big couch in her cozy little apartment. Alex couldn't decide whether she wanted to know or not, but leaned toward getting it over with, so, she wiped the sweat from her brow and acknowledged her friend. Hesitantly, Rebecca activated the intercom, and Alex braced for whatever she was about to say, "Alex, you should sit down."

She felt her throat dry out and got a little woozy, then, Alex closed her eyes before replying, "Please just tell me. If I have the disease I'd rather just know, I think."

Rebecca sighed and shook her head, "No, it isn't you Alex; it is your friend Seth Mitchell. He passed away last night."

Alex gaped at her, silently for a moment and held back a smile. She shouldn't smile, and the gravity of a man's death pulled her back to the gloom of the news. Wait, friend? "I feel sorry for Seth's family, but that man wasn't a friend of mine."

"I am confused. I know you weren't looking forward to work that day, but you were so upset about Seth contracting the pathogen."

"I was upset because of the implications. Everyone in that office including Michael and I now stand the chance of contracting the disease. I know it seems heartless to speak ill of the dead but I couldn't stand Seth." Alex quickly added, "Not that I'd wish death on anyone, even that lowlife, but still, he was my least favorite person on Earth. That man had a rep for 'seducing' women,' many times against their will, yet he never took responsibility for it, unless of course, he was bragging.

As someone on the receiving end of his charms, I will tell you that he used his power to get what he wanted, and the more you resisted, the more determined he became."

Rebecca didn't say anything for a few moments, "I am sorry, I know we never discussed him after you were quarantined, but I assumed you were friends. Well, good riddance Seth."

"Rebecca!"

"Oh, you know I jest, but looking back, that information clears up a lot for me. The little creep hit on all the techs and had the gall to hit on me too, even on his deathbed. I thought he was reacting oddly to his meds for him to be so frisky so I lowered the dosage, but he begged for more. Now, I see it wasn't the meds."

Alex nodded her head, "That sounds exactly like Seth, but I am surprised he didn't crawl right into your hazmat suit to get you."

"Oh he tried, and not even my bitchiest stares or snarkiest comments and threats slowed him down either, which is why I thought his reaction to the medications made him crazy. No normal human would act like that, and so I ended up sedating him every time a woman had to be around him. How does someone like that even exist in the world today?"

Seth was the most horrible womanizer Alex knew, and it helped her feel better about her past dealings with him to vent, but she needed to change the subject, even if only for her mental well-being, "Your parents came to visit yesterday."

"Really? They saw you but not me, how lovely. How did I miss that?"

"Maybe if you came to see me more often, you could hear the excitement that goes on in my little cell sooner. The somber way you suddenly appeared, I thought my most recent blood tests came back infected and I was so terrified that I could barely even breathe."

"I told you nothing would happen to you; I won't let it. I can't believe my mom got my dad out of that stupid chair, and he didn't even come to say hello to me. What did they have to say?"

"Not much, they are concerned about me of course, but they mostly talked about you. They think you work too much, don't eat right, or sleep enough, and that you push yourself too hard. They told me not to worry because you'd figure out everything, and I think they are right on all accounts. Seriously, you look horrible."

"Everyone keeps saying that, but I am fine, just stressed, overworked, and trying to cure a fatal pathogen." Rebecca abruptly covered the mask over her mouth with her hand, "Sorry, as I said before, you have nothing to worry about." Alex stared at her for a while, opened her mouth to say something, but closed it without a word. Rebecca looked like she was struggling with something and finally pursed her lips before muttering, "I don't want to end the discussion like that, but after this morning's news my team went insane, so I can't stay. We are making progress on the pathogen, and my team is scurrying around like a bunch of headless chickens, so I need to go direct them."

Alex nodded although she wasn't thrilled, "I understand, get back to work so I can get out of here, I am going stir crazy." Rebecca trotted down the hall towards the lab doors, and Alex waved as she went, but as soon as her friend was out of sight, Alex plopped down on the bed. Her mind reeled, and she couldn't stop thinking her death loomed near, she glanced down at her hands and picked at her cuticles until they bled. Luckily, Rebecca included bandages in the package she brought over; she knew Alex too well. How much longer?

Rebecca tried to ignore the small ruckus in the hallway, but curiosity eventually overcame her concentration and she joined Sonso, Brent and several others from the lab at the window watching people lining up at the gated entry to the facility. Sonso turned to Brent, "That didn't take long. Are we safe?"

"I brought in extra security several days ago, but I think we need to push the fencing perimeter back tonight. Believe it or not, I got a heads up shortly before this afternoon's report aired that there would be protesting. Our lawyers are working on an injunction against the reporter and the news outlet. I guess I shouldn't have given that ambitious little girl an exclusive, it fueled the fire to blame this on someone."

Rebecca stood with her arms folded and tapped her chin deep in thought, "Or maybe you should give them another interview and show that we have nothing to hide. Give her a tour of the facility and the quarantine warehouse to show how well we work in conjunction with the CDC, tell her everything."

Sonso nodded her head, "It could work and then we wouldn't be nearly as interesting and we could get back to work unhindered without their distractions. We don't need this right now."

Brent thought for several moments, "Let me give the lawyers a call and run it by them." He walked away with his phone already in his hand.

Sonso and Rebecca quietly watched the growing crowds together, and then Hector materialized with a pair of binoculars and stared out the window. Sonso and Rebecca looked peculiarly at the man. Sonso opened her mouth to speak but nothing came out, and she shook her head, but Rebecca could suppress her curiosity, "Where did you even get a pair of binoculars?" Hector smirked and shrugged his shoulders but didn't answer. He handed the binoculars over to Rebecca, and she peered through with unbridled inquisitiveness. The number of people surrounding the gates of the compound seemed to swell as she watched, but the crowd was still small. Some in the crowd waved signs that said, 'Viralists for Jesus,' 'The Lord Delivers Us,' 'God is Just,' and 'The LORD delivers,' and some had even pitched tents. They were in it for the long haul. Dashcorp was located so far out in the boondocks, Rebecca wondered if they got wifi out there. They marched and she could see they were shouting on loudspeakers. Luckily, they couldn't hear the protestors inside the building, but anyone looking out a window would have no doubt about what was going on. Rebecca opened her eyes widely and practically yelled, "Hey isn't that Judy? She took this farther than I could have ever predicted."

Sonso and Hector appeared confused by her excitement, but only Sonso replied, "You really don't like her do you?"

She regained her composure as quickly as possible, "She is a bit of a self-righteous Bible thumper and by betraying her place of employment, and she obviously isn't a loyal person. Those kinds of hypocrites make me nauseous. Where is Brent? Hector, go find him and tell him that Judy is leading the little protest out there."

CHAPTER 16

Day 13

In the breakdown of material from more than a dozen autopsies and daily statistics they received, the techs and doctors discovered a little more each day. Rebecca gave the transmission team a big boost with her new model and would hand it back to them after the meeting. Those on the transmission prevention team had not achieved the progress levels of the pathogen examination team, but Rebecca led examination. She and her team discovered some of what the pathogen did to the body and the information would help both teams. Rebecca insisted that the samples go to the accelerator over Sonso's objections that it was a waste of time and even money, but her hypothesis proved correct, the returned material indicated invaluable discoveries. The information that came back required a thorough analysis as there was a collection of thousands of accelerator pictures. The cost shouldn't even be a consideration, because the pathogen was spreading at a pace much more rapidly than she or anyone else could have predicted. Rebecca wished she'd gone with the samples to begin the work immediately, but couldn't leave the investigation in Sonso's hands. When the results arrived late Sunday night, Rebecca first thanked the accelerator team for working so late on a weekend, but they were scared for their lives too. Then, she divided the information into groups for distribution the next morning. She assigned each collection to different team leaders, each with their own access to electron microscopes.

Sorting through the pictures for an effective division of labor took Rebecca most the night, thankfully the call she received announcing the results' completion helped her prepare, and she got right to work. She decided for her purposes, the most productive approach was to let Sonso and her team take the lead starting the image investigation while she got some sleep. She yielded to her exhaustion as her vision blurred and couldn't continue to survive and expect to accomplish anything on getting only two or three hours sleep a night. Rebecca stumbled over to her office and dropped onto the couch falling asleep before her head hit the small decorative pillow.

Several hours later, she awoke to a small commotion in the lab down the hall. When she glanced at the clock she could not believe the time, almost noon, and someone placed a blanket over her at some point. Her mind tried sifting through the grogginess she felt, but a little caffeine should cure that. She grunted, thinking that she'd fire any of her techs that let themselves get as run down as she appeared, and wanted to clean up a little before anyone saw her. Lab drama usually lasted quite a while and would still be there when she finished. She needed to take a trip to the bathroom and longed for a shower, but that little luxury would require waiting until later. She got up and grabbed her sundries bag to at least brush her teeth and splash water on her face before going to the lab and heard her phone ring as she walked out the door, but kept walking.

The cool water on her face woke her up, and she changed her shirt, but any more self-maintenance felt like an indulgence. Rebecca sighed before she walked into the lab and headed toward the heated debate between several. She was surprised to hear Hector passionately pleaded with Sonso, "The sequence looks more like a computer code than RNA, pull an air-gapped computer and plug in the sequencing. Ma'am I know it sounds crazy but with RNA being so malleable, it was only a matter of time before someone figured out how to electronically code onto living matter. The implications are phenomenal. Do you know what we could accomplish with that kind of information? Dr. Sonso, I spent two years working as a programmer after college before I decided to go back and pursue epidemiology, and I recognize it." Rebecca paused; well Hector was full of surprises.

Sonso shook her head, "Don't be ridiculous. You misunderstand; your comprehension of genetics is in its beginning stages. As you get your doctorate and more experience you will see it for what it is. RNA programming is not nearly far enough along to be used let alone employed as an integral strand of a viral infection agent."

"Viruses are not that complex, why won't you consider this a possibility? The technology has been around since the nineties, and who is to say that illegitimate scientific entities haven't experimented in a way that the legitimate entities have not yet broached. Isn't it at least worth a little investigation?"

Hector mumbled something that Rebecca couldn't hear. She felt terrible for him because computer code and viruses were not that different. One organic, one not and with RNA being as malleable as it was she wished she could support him. Instead, Rebecca shook her head, "Kopvein is viral-like material, and it is far more

149

sophisticated and difficult to deal with than what you are suggesting and as scientists, we aren't there yet. Sonso is correct Hector, I am sorry." He glared at her with a look she had not seen from him before, anger, but didn't debate with her. He stood brooding for a moment before stomping out the lab door with a passion she didn't know he possessed. Sonso opened her mouth to say something, but Rebecca put her hand up, "I will go speak with him."

Hector sat in the conference room with his arms crossed and the expression on his face a frenzied resentment. Rebecca shut the door behind her then closed the blinds to the office before sitting down next to him, "Listen, I understand your frustration. Many times on my way up the ladder my superiors wouldn't listen to me when I knew I was right."

"Were lives depending on your research though? Rebecca, I know I am right about my theory, once a programmer always a programmer, you recognize it anywhere."

She needed to get him off this topic so the investigation could get back on track with its current progress. They worked well together, and she knew he felt betrayed, partially because she hadn't backed him up. She sat quietly looking at him and wished she could consult with Alex at the moment for the right words to say, but her friend was in quarantine, and she had to figure it out on her own. Rebecca understood his anger and tried to be compassionate but needed his mind focused on the investigation, "Organic computer coding has not been created yet."

Anger clouded his clear green eyes, and he mumbled some more, "That we know of."

Her efforts were backfiring. Maybe she should let him brood and return to her work alone, but she enjoyed his assistance. While working together for less than a week, the number of hours added up to quite a substantial amount together and it made the relationship feel closer than she usually got with any man let alone a co-worker. He seemed to enjoy her assertive banter and sarcasm, which few even tolerated let alone appreciated. His natural charm and accommodating mannerism made his assistance easy to accept. He also followed her around like a puppy dog and stood up to Sonso several times on her behalf, even though he'd known her only a week. His allegiance was definitely to Rebecca. Knowing he'd back her up just because he liked her comforted her, something she'd failed to do for him. He might be the most desirable man she had ever met, and in a different situation, she might consider pursuing or letting him pursue her. No, she couldn't fool herself. In a different situation, she would lock herself away in her lab and never spend enough time with him to consider a romantic relationship.

She reached over, touched the side of his face, and played with his hair. At first, he flinched in surprise, but instead of turning away, he turned to Rebecca and pulled her right into his arms and into a very passionate kiss. Rebecca did not know how to respond, but she felt the intensity of his kiss from her mouth to her toes causing her to melt into it, and savor it. She was so lost in the kiss and his firm embrace that before she knew it, he had pulled her down to the floor with her on top, letting her know she controlled the situation, and Rebecca let herself go. She kissed him deeply, and he kissed her neck and down her front. Rebecca unbuckled his pants and slid her hand down them. Within minutes, they were completely wrapped in each other's embrace, moving desperately with each other's rhythm. Rebecca had not let a man touch her in ages, this man knew how to please her, and she ached for more. He touched her with gentle passion, like he'd known her for years and understood her every need. As they finished, she rolled off him and lay beside him looking at the ceiling. When she turned to look at him, he was gazing into her eyes but the stargazed look had changed, and now he looked lost in her presence. Maybe allowing this interlude had been a miscalculation on her part but her body told her it wasn't a mistake, it was the perfect stress reliever.

"So, are you ready to get back to work? Is your head all cleared up now, because mine certainly is." Rebecca smiled at her own joke.

Hector chuckled and clasped his fingers with hers, and in a tone slightly higher than he usually spoke, he confirmed, "I think my head is clear now."

Alex turned the television to the news that was focused on a protest right outside of the building she currently resided in, and Rebecca walked up to Alex's window and rolled her eyes at the television screen, "Christy Gallagher reporting from outside the gates of Dashcorp Enterprises. The company added extra security to protect them from what? These peaceful protestors? What is Dashcorp trying to hide from us? Here is the leader of the picketers now, hi I'm Christy Gallagher, can you tell me your name and are you the leader of this protest?"

The plump woman Alex recognized as Judy self-consciously brushed her hair back from her face, "I am Judy Samanski, and yes, I am the leader of these peaceful protestors, but only as a servant of righteous behavior. We are here to let the CDC and Dashcorp know that their continual concealment of the truth will not stop the Viralists from spreading their message. We will not leave until our message has been received."

Christy made sure the camera focused on her face even as she interviewed Judy, and she smiled sweetly before continuing, "Ma'am, what is your message, what do you want to say to the world?"

"Our message to the world is," Judy took a deep breath and hesitantly proceeded, "you brought this plague onto yourselves. The world will be cleansed if it doesn't change their ways. God is Just; the righteous person may have many troubles, but the LORD delivers-"

Alex switched off the television on Judy mid-sentence, and turned to her friend, "Do I want to know? A bunch of crazies surrounds us?"

Rebecca laughed almost giddily, and Alex's face contorted with a confused look but Rebecca managed to swallow her laughter, "Oh, I used to call her Twiddle Dee but now, especially after that, she will be known as Twiddle DUMB, I guess I mixed up the names originally. I knew she was religious but never figured her for a fanatic, but I guess fear brings out the crazy in people. Don't worry. We are fine. I watched them from the window, the crowd is quite small, and the cameras just panned over it in a way to sensationalize the event. All that reporter does is sensationalize. Now on to what I came here for, I have some confidential and much more interesting news." Rebecca smiled and told Alex what happened in the conference room, moments before.

"You didn't!"

Rebecca nodded her head, "I did, right in the conference room. I feel like a college student sneaking around and letting my urges take control of me."

Alex shook her head, "Well, no wonder you look so refreshed but come on, you never did anything like that in college."

"Well, I was only a nerdy 15 year old, so no, I didn't, but I should have. I was far too concerned with my work in school, and I should have had some more fun. Until now, sex has only been a necessity not so much fun. I feel much better than a couple of hours ago."

"Okay, how did this happen and with who?"

"You know the tech, Hector? I am not sure how it happened. I guess I was trying to comfort him, and one thing led to another."

Alex's mouth hung open, "Wait, you were trying to comfort him? What am I missing and what alien has taken over the body of my best friend?"

Rebecca sneered at Alex, "Very funny, but you always told me I had the capacity to comfort others. She grinned, "Somehow I don't think you were referring to this particular kind of comfort unless you see me as a prostitute." She lightheartedly laughed at her own joke, and Alex joined her.

Alex loved to see the severe expression on Rebecca's face lighten up; it thrilled her that even in the midst of the world falling apart, Rebecca had found some happiness. Your taste is impeccable; he is extremely handsome and charming. I've been up close to him when he did my blood work a few times, but isn't he my age?"

"Yep, and now I need to get back to work."

"Seriously? You come here to drop that bomb and then leave? Hey, come back here."

Rebecca laughed maniacally as she walked down the hall.

The lab reverberated with energy, or maybe Rebecca still felt the high of her hormones from earlier, but it didn't matter because nobody noticed as they worked at a frenzied pace in an equable rhythm. Sonso and her team examined the accelerator images and information. Rebecca, Hector, and Nithi put their final touches on the holographic transmission model before the meeting that was about to begin and before she knew it, it was time to share their model. The entire investigation team, as well as Brent, and many other departments all filed into the sizeable theater-style meeting room so as not to disturb Rebecca and Hector's model in the conference room. The projectors waited, and without a word, Rebecca flipped them on and let everyone absorb the information. Immediately, some started taking notes while others just stared at the data. The patterns Rebecca and Hector laid out were there but would still be difficult to detect for some.

"I would like to thank Hector and Nithi for all their hard work putting this model together. It more completely clarifies the transmission information, and we can look at the whole picture at once. I've been involved in the investigation of the pathogen now called the Kopvein virus for thirteen days. The CDC and Dashcorp joined forces on day five, marrying our resources. As you can see from the model Kopvein, is a global pandemic with clear transmission patterns. One prominent pattern we noticed but missed the importance of earlier is the male victim pattern and no prepubescent children, which is unusual. Many of the clusters began in male-dominated areas such as prisons, military facilities, and areas with high concentrations of the indigent population, so depending on the incubation period, which we still don't know, those statistics may change."

Rebecca paused again giving everyone time to find the patterns themselves. Hector and Nithi both stared at her; she hadn't taken credit for the model even though they had only assisted her. Rebecca didn't need to be stroked and praised right now for work that was expected. She had always known exactly how to proceed in the past and was shocked at her confused and doubtful state of mind over the last week. Rebecca preferred the confidence she now projected, but the self-doubt lingered and grew stronger each day, but she just wouldn't let it consume her, she had to finish this without breaking down.

"This airborne pathogen is striking its victims, and most see death within seven days. The pathogen begins like a cold with symptoms following the course of a fever one day, the next a slight flush, headaches, and the veining begins to appear on the side of their face on the third day but does not immediately develop into full Telangiectasia. At that point headaches increase and the eyes bulge, shortly after, the patient suffers a stroke and dies. The only exceptions are the fatalities in which an onset of violent outburst preceded the immediate stage three symptoms, stroke and death, such as the school shooter her in D.C. and the Fulton case, as well as a few survivors. Follow the track of our Fulton Penn survivor whose symptoms did not progress past the Telangiectasia, the headaches and other symptoms have faded.

Autopsies reveal brain and thyroid, as well as lymph nodes in an abnormal state. The damaged tissue is located in the brain and thyroid the hypothalamus, the pituitary gland, the thyroid and parathyroid, the adrenals, the pineal body, and the reproductive glands. The blood surrounding the glands has damaged materials in it as well. When I said viral type material, I mean it loosely. Kopvein is unlike any viral outbreak we or anyone has ever encountered. It is a pleomorphic nanovirus and hides and from what I can gather, it is also highly complex."

Thus far, the fatality rate of those who contract the disease is about ninety-eight percent."

CHAPTER 17

Day 14

Christy Gallagher peered into the camera. Her eyes were slightly swollen and her face was missing its usual animated expression. She appeared less perky and quite upset. Behind her was a church rectory with a small crowd of people holding candles with signs that said, 'Viralists for Jesus,' 'The Lord Delivers Us,' 'God is Just' and 'The LORD delivers.'

"This is Christy Gallagher reporting live from Hollister Street in the suburbs of D.C., and today I have more devastating news to report." She bowed her head to emphasize her sorrow, "A loved and beholden man, Pastor Murdock has contracted the dreaded Kopvein virus. He is known throughout the community for his outreach program with boys and young men. He holds a boy's summer program in which he works with these boys one on one, trying to groom them for the future, and congregation families feel very privileged when their boy is chosen to work with Pastor Murdock. His tutoring programs and college scholarships help these young men find a way out of one of the toughest and most forgotten communities in the U.S. and he works closely with these boys until they are grown up. A vigil is being held outside of his home as we speak, so send your prayers this way as Pastor Murdock struggles to stay alive."

Brent walked into the lab with Hector and Abe in tow and waved Sonso and Rebecca over to him. Hector had avoided Rebecca all morning and did not look her in the eye, maybe her assumptions about him and his feelings were wrong, and now he was embarrassed. Brent and Abe, however, both glared accusingly. She thought she knew why and it made her a little sick to her stomach. They wouldn't consider a sexual harassment suit in the middle of all this, would they? Brent pulled them all out into the hall then closed the door, "Our new tech has an interesting hypothesis about the extra RNA strands in the makeup of Kopvein."

Rebecca exhaled with relief at first, but then felt annoyance growing inside her, and ignored Hector to focus on Brent instead. Sonso glanced over to a frightened-looking Hector before she spoke with agitation in her already grating voice, "We discussed it yesterday and his hypothesis while interesting is not yet possible with our scientific capabilities. Rebecca agreed with me, so we went back to what we were working on. Scientifically it would be a phenomenal topic to study, but we don't have the time to waste on it right now."

Abe, stepped forward and peered directly at Rebecca, "This isn't like ye las, ye always jump on the most inane details and weave brilliance out of it but this ye dismiss? The boy explained his logic behind his theory, and if ye listened at all, ye'd agree it has merit, at least for discussion sake."

Rebecca's breath caught in her throat, as she stared haughtily at Abe, "If Sonso or I thought the idea worthy of examination, you know I'd have pursued it wholeheartedly. If however, you feel it needs closer scrutiny, I'll happily waste my time reviewing the merits of the idea more closely." She choked the words out, but at least they came out.

Brent nodded, "Give it a half day, but only use a small team, then send me a full report on the entire survey. Take it over to I.T. and isn't Tristan some master hacker? Maybe his insight into it will help if you don't get anywhere with I.T. Hector, you write up the report and have it on my desk as soon as possible." Hector, Sonso, Rebecca, and Abe all nodded before Brent sauntered off.

She didn't like to be challenged, and at first, didn't know how to contend with it, but held back her annoyance as she focused on Hector's shaking hands. To alleviate anyone's possible uncertainty, she decided to address the problem emphatically, "Well, you heard the man, but let's not waste time going to I.T. first, let's divide and conquer. Abe, you and Sonso bring the accelerator images and information Hector pointed out yesterday to I.T., and Hector and I will grab an air-gap then bring it down to Tristan." The development could be a blessing in disguise. She feared the pathogen's infection being too far beyond her control and maybe this was happening the way it was supposed to. Abe and Sonso simultaneously nodded, and then abruptly walked away. Hector for the first time since he'd met her did not bounce after Rebecca, but he slowly shuffled after her. With slumped shoulders and a drooped head, Hector appeared to be heading for his execution.

Down the hall, Rebecca stopped and turned to Hector. His face went white, but she kept her voice intentionally calm, "I had no idea you were the type to go over your boss' head, as well as mine." Imagining he was on her side, what foolish speculation. He was an opportunist and merely wanted a moment alone with her boss after he got what he wanted from her. Inside her stomach roiled with anger and a touch of betrayal, but two could play the game of exploitation, and unfortunately, she'd let her guard down.

Hector shook his head adamantly and grabbed her arms. He did not let go even when she tried to step back from him, "It isn't like that Rebecca, please don't be angry with me. I know I am right, but nobody would listen to me, otherwise, I'd never sidestep you."

Annoyed with herself for desiring him at that moment, she peered into his pleading eyes. Rebecca's emotions swung from rage and betrayal to confusion and disappointment. Something was wrong with her, and she tried to grasp onto the inner logic that ruled her life to better understand the situation but her emotional reaction to his little stunt, agitated her that her feelings were involved at all. As she thought about it, she'd have made the same decision in his position and gone to a set of listening ears. The look in his eyes reeked of sincerity, but she needed to keep yesterday's encounter separate from the work and view it as nothing more than stress relief, so she could disconnect from her emotions. The little sidestep wouldn't matter to her, "I am disappointed Hector, and your punishment will be severe." The expression on Hector's face at the comment confused her. He looked like she had just rewarded, and couldn't help but ask, "Are you a sadist? Most people would run out of the building if I said that to them."

"Nope, I am not a sadist, but you are still speaking with me, so," he shrugged, still grinning widely. Her outrage toward him fizzled out, and a whole scene flashed through Rebecca's mind that being angry with him was similar to being angry at a puppy, useless, although now she needed to alter her strategies, which she despised. Her mind already scoured through ideas, maybe something will develop that can help. She'd deal with her feelings on Hector's actions later, "Let's go see Tristan."

The trip down the white on white halls seemed to take forever, and Alex didn't understand why she and Tristan weren't moved closer together. With electronic locks on the doors, nobody was going anywhere. Security told her they needed to take precautions, but if she and Tristan were next to each other, they could leave their coms open and talk anytime they wanted. Alex decided to talk to Brent about it next time and skip the bureaucratic nonsense of dealing with the technicians. They probably hadn't even spoken to anyone each time she asked them. As she approached his room, Alex noticed Tristan's clenched jaw and jittering foot, "You look upset."

He stepped over to the intercom, and then looked up and down the hall, "I am afraid our visits are being recorded."

Alex smirked and grunted, "Now, why would you be afraid of that? You sound paranoid, and nobody wants to hear what we're talking about."

He shook his head before grabbing his hair with both hands, "I've searched everywhere in the room and even taken apart the com, but I can't find anything here, I think my past caught up to me."

"Wait, you took apart the intercom?"

Tristan nodded his head yes. His nervous ticks and wide eyes added to his crazy demeanor, but his expression remained completely serious. Either he was suffering from the beginnings of a nervous breakdown, or he was right and his shady dealings in the past had crept up on him. How that was possible in here, Alex didn't understand, but she kept her expression the same because she wanted to hide her disappointment in him, again. How could he find more trouble while being locked up? Tristan's eyes teared up, and he swallowed hard, "Alex, I did a job, a completely legal, albeit somewhat suspicious cloak and dagger job, but completely legal." Tristan paused to breathe, "This morning Rebecca and one of her techs with obvious expertise in coding came down here with some of my code. I recognized it, altered and now biological, but I know my code, I did it! They wouldn't tell me anything about their coding questions, but I am not stupid. I know it is connected to Kopvein, and now all those deaths are on me."

"Wait a minute, what are you are talking about? I don't understand. You couldn't have anything to do with the virus, you're a ha- I mean programming architect, not a biologist. Explain it from the beginning."

"I did a programming job a few years ago. The customer, whom I never met, described it as a small medical startup and explained, in detail, what they needed. I thought it would be used to monitor the processes of miscreant behavior nullification. I did the job, got paid and thought nothing more of it until today." The pallor on Tristan's face shifted to a greenish tint as if he was about to vomit, "I know my code, only I just don't know how they changed it. Rebecca and her tech came down with an air-gapped laptop that had images and information on it. The tech did most the talking while Rebecca stared at me. I think she knew. The look in her eyes, you know that cold, scary death stare. She said nothing, but she knew. I told them it didn't look like computer coding to me. Crap, Alex, what have I done? I've been watching the news, and I know what is going on out there. I couldn't face the end of the world or the virus blamed on me, so I lied, but I did it. Even if I survive this bloody thing I will go to prison for the rest of my life, and I deserve it. I murdered thousands and thousands of innocent people! I should say something, the job may have been one of the most abstract coding jobs I've ever done, and now it is hidden in biologics, so unless they know how to look for it or get lucky, they won't see it."

Alex inhaled and tried to settle her mind. What the hell! Maybe she could get Brent to help, "I still don't understand how computer coding could be part of a virus. You are wrong Tristan, and you haven't murdered thousands of people. If there is computer coding in the virus then it isn't naturally occurring. Somebody made it on purpose and whoever developed Kopvein set it loose on the world and murdered those people. You're as much a victim as the others, and they used you."

"With all the cloak and dagger garbage the customer pulled, I knew something shady was going on, but I brushed it off as nerds having fun, but I knew better. I am not innocent in this."

"Even though I know some of your jobs were questionable, you would never participate in something you knew would hurt or kill people."

"Alex, it is like a robbery. If someone dies in the midst of a crime, you're guilty of their death whether the death was intentional or not."

"No, I refuse to believe that you are guilty in this. I am going to speak with Brent, and maybe you can even help." Tristan nodded his head and stepped back to his bed, where he stayed and put his head in his hands. He did not look back up, and Alex knew he'd broken down in tears. She waved to the tech standing down the hall and told him she needed to speak with Dr. Adams immediately, that it was an emergency.

Sitting nervously on her bed, Alex picked at her already sore cuticles, waiting. When she heard footsteps running down the hall, Brent appeared and slid to a stop in front of the intercom switch. His eyes wide and wild, and he practically shouted, "Alex, what is wrong? Please tell me you aren't developing symptoms!" He was breathing heavily, as he spoke. Did he run the whole way?

She shook her head, but didn't know how to broach the subject with him, "No, I am fine."

Brent's face went slack with relief, and then filled with confusion, "Then what is the emergency?"

Alex's heart felt as if it would beat out of her chest at any moment, but she needed to get the conversation over with, no matter the consequence. Tentatively, she stepped over to the window, "I needed to speak with you immediately." His expression morphed from confusion to repressing annoyance, and she hoped he didn't think she took calling him like this lightly, but after the conversation they were about to have, he'd probably avoid her anyway. None of that mattered. What mattered was finding a cure and saving lives, "I am sorry to alarm you Brent, but it couldn't wait." His annoyance appeared to be growing, but he sighed and patiently waited. Alex felt her stomach whirling and that she might hurl at any moment but knew she'd made the right decision to speak with him, "I visited with my brother a few moments ago, and he said Rebecca and a tech visited him with a computer. They wanted him to look at some data and try to decipher it, to see if the information they had was computer coding."

Brent clenched his jaw and nodded, "Yes, I sent them."

Alex took another deep breath, "Well, it is a good thing you did because he recognized it."

Shaking his head, Brent shifted on his feet, "No, I already have the report on it; neither Tristan nor I.T. recognized it as computer coding. The tech that brought it to our attention felt humiliated for pushing the issue so hard, but I'd rather inspect all possible options than to overlook a clue that could help us."

She shook her head and felt tears welling up in her eyes, "Tristan lied to them. He said the information they showed him was an altered version of a code that he developed."

Alex told Brent about the whole conversation between her and Tristan and with each word, the expression on Brent's face grew more and more angry until, by the time Alex finished, his face had reddened several shades deeper. Alex knew that Tristan might spend his life in either an isolation cell or prison if he didn't die from the virus and she opened her mouth to plead with Brent, but he interrupted with an angry bark, "He should not have lied. Does his cowardice trump even his own self-preservation? He could die from Kopvein too! I don't understand how he could lie about it!"

Desperate, Alex put her hands on the window, wishing she could reach out to him, "Please Brent, he knows and is racked with guilt, but for the first time in his life, he was truly terrified, so he lied because he was shocked and afraid. This isn't his fault! Someone developed and released Kopvein on purpose. He said the job was perfectly legal, and he had no idea how the code would be used. I know Tristan can decipher the code even though it's been altered. He is desperate and not because he wants to save himself either. Tristan will help you if you allow him to, but he is calling himself a murderer, and he'd never hurt anyone. When it comes to code, you won't be able to find anyone who knows more, so please, help him, and let him help you. "

Brent's eyes softened and suddenly, the anger evaporated. Brent cleared his throat, "All right Alex. I believe you. I spoke to Tristan quite a few times, and I don't believe he would intentionally hurt anyone, but this is a big deal. Let's figure out the pathogen, and I will do my best to protect your brother along the way." He paused, but by the expression on his face, his mind was reeling. Alex stepped back in confusion. When had he and Tristan spoken and why did Tristan not mention it? Brent pursed his lips and peered at the ceiling, "Okay, I have an idea."

He turned to leave, but Alex rapped on the window, "Hey aren't you going to tell me about it?"

"No, and we never had this conversation, plausible deniability." He turned, hurried off, and did not look back.

CHAPTER 18

Day 15

The next morning, Rebecca, Sonso, Nithi, Hector, and Abe headed to Brent's office for a meeting. Lately, Rebecca appreciated a few minutes away from the lab as a welcome break, even if it was for a meeting. She walked down the hall, and couldn't help wonder why Brent had asked Hector to join them. All five filed in and immediately found seats around the conference table where Brent and several of the company's lawyers, some high-ranking uniformed military men and two other suited individuals who looked like lawyers awaited them. Now the military was involved? Introductions were made and the company's lawyers, two lawyers from the district attorney's office, a couple of generals, a colonel, and a major, all men, gawked at Rebecca when they met. While accustomed to men ogling her, Rebecca found the most interesting gawker was the bright blue-eyed Major Duffield. He couldn't stop eying her. Peripherally, Rebecca saw Hector notice and stiffen, so she smiled at Duffield with a subtle, yet alluring demeanor. It was cruel to flirt so blatantly in front of Hector but toying with the two men helped calm her nerves as she squirmed inside.

Brent waited for them to settle, played a gracious host and offered each of them a beverage. This whole situation reeked of catastrophe. He cleared his throat to start the meeting, "Before we get started, I need each of you to sign a very strict, nondisclosure for this meeting." Brent cast a pointed look at Rebecca and emphasized, "Information we speak about and anything related to it is not to be discussed with anyone, and I do mean anyone, from this point forward."

Rebecca settled back in her chair trying to appear nonchalant, but inside her heart beat so loudly she felt sure everyone in the room could hear it. She quickly reviewed the nondisclosure but had a difficult time concentrating. It seemed standard, yet something nagged at her. Even in her uneasiness, she signed anyway. What is the worst that could happen now? They were already locked in the building like prisoners 'for their own safety,' surrounded by a fatal viral outbreak, with crowds amassing outside the facility, some had been camped there for days. The national reserve had been called in to deter any possible disorder.

Rebecca pretended not to notice that Brent had been watching her intently before he turned his attention to the whole group, "The CDC technician, Hector, interpreted the accelerator pictures accurately. The extra RNA strand in Kopvein is a computer coded sequence." Chaos erupted as everyone talked at once, everyone except Brent, Nithi, and Rebecca. Nithi's jaw dropped and his eyes practically popped out of his head confirming his understanding of the implications. Rebecca wanted to scream but managed to maintain her composure, especially since Brent had not taken his eyes off of her. What was he thinking? She listened intently to the objections of Sonso and Abe, while Hector, occasionally glancing at Rebecca and Brent, tried to speak over them to support his evidence, again. As the situation escalated it got much more complicated and out of control until Brent stood up, effectively silencing the group.

Each one of them fidgeted in their seats, except Rebecca, she didn't move and tried to control her breathing. She knew it made her RBF flare but didn't care; she needed to maintain her calm. They all waited for Brent to start speaking because the expression on his face was unreadable, "The implications of this discovery are phenomenal and terrifying. Kopvein is now considered a deliberate full-fledged bio-terrorist act. We do not know who released it or why, as no terrorist groups have taken credit and no major nationality has been spared. While our new determination certainly adds even more terror to the outbreak, it also gives us a commencement point for significant progress in halting the progression of Kopvein, through understanding its origin."

Rebecca thought the meeting would be a short progress update but it ended up lasting over an hour. As the meeting broke, some of the attendees departed, silently stunned with the unfathomable realization pasted across their faces. Sonso and Hector wandered toward the cafeteria, Nithi retreated toward the outside gardens in back, and Rebecca drifted off for a walk to mentally prepare for the team meeting Sonso had called for that afternoon. This development changed her agenda, and she needed to think. Abe remained behind with Brent and the military. His involvement had been peripheral in the investigation since right after Alex was quarantined and she didn't understand why. Were they running a secondary investigation without her knowledge? They found out about Judy and dismissed her. But, security could not have hacked into her work computer by themselves nor understood the information involved in the investigation. Brent, Abe, I.T., and security? She had not foreseen that combination working together. What else was the secondary investigation looking for and why be so secretive about it, what did they suspect?

She absent-mindedly rubbed the pendant around her neck while considering the information, and the time slipped by. Rebecca stopped, leaned her back against the wall, deep in thought, and slid down it. As she wrapped her arms around her knees, to contemplate, Rebecca looked up and found she had wandered to the indoor gardens. Nithi must be around here somewhere. He regularly escaped down here to meditate and pray, and everyone usually left him alone to respect his devoutness. She listened intently and heard whispering, so as quietly as possible, she got up and crept around the corner. Nithi sat at the edge of the water fountain, whispering into his phone. Even with everything else going on around her, and all she needed to do, she couldn't resist and her curiosity overwhelmed her. She got as close as possible without him noticing but still couldn't figure out what he was saying. Not knowing might drive her crazy. She took out her phone and recorded it; maybe a digital sound separator could decipher it.

Moments later, Sonso and Hector strolled by, noticed Rebecca hunched over, and hiding behind some planters. A perplexed expression filled their faces and she motioned for them to get down, but Nithi must have heard them because he'd abruptly ended his conversation. She snuck out of sight just before he joined Hector and Sonso. They must have thought Rebecca was acting crazy but both pretended not to see her and said nothing about her strange behavior. They were better at taking hints than she thought and she hoped they would forget about it. Rebecca waited a few moments before standing up and walking toward the labs. She slipped the phone into her pocket and chuckled, Nithi seemed harmless, but she knew he was up to something. Now, she needed to get on with mentally preparing for the day and the meeting that afternoon. How to deal with the computer coding issue? If Hector and Tristan spent all their time decoding, she would have to figure out how to best utilize the development.

Brent pressed on his temple, thinking aloud, "I don't know gentlemen, I feel like something is off. We've overlooked something, but I can't put my finger on it."

General Ross raised his eyebrows, "Perhaps you are too close to the investigation to remain objective, and it is time Homeland security took over."

Abe stroked his beard and confidently leaned back in his chair, "Now gentlemen, this is a part of Dr. Adams' process, he was merely thinkin' aloud. He is figurin' out a problem ye don't even detect yet. He's led Dashcorp to great discoveries in the past, and bringin' in Homeland Security to lead the investigation, would be premature. Ye need to give it some time man."

"Yes, but the situation is quite volatile, especially now we suspect a biological terrorist. Homeland is much better equipped both with experience and reach than your company, it is what we do."

Brent knew the meeting would result in Homeland trying to assert its authority, but wasn't willing to lose control of the investigation. General or not, Brent did not hold back, "We huh? You don't have any idea what complications the investigation addresses. This isn't nerve gas dropped on an unsuspecting town, an outbreak of Ebola, or Ricin in the food supply; we are working against an unknown. The pathogen is embedded with technology that doesn't exist and is so unique it is only considered a virus-like material. You wouldn't know where to start. This investigation is of a scientific nature, not a military one. You are accustomed to dealing with known typicalities, whether it be a bomb or some existing killing agent. Taking us out of the equation will only impede the progress."

The general interrupted Brent, "You misunderstand Dr. Adams, we want you to continue working with the CDC, but we will direct all other aspects of the investigation."

Not what he wanted, but at least a start, so, with as much authority as he had, Brent spoke in a low controlled mutter so that everyone needed to lean in to hear better, "The CDC is working here because my lab and people are more qualified than any other in the world. One more example of how Dashcorp is better equipped to manage this outbreak than any other organization." Brent's thoughts pulsed. If the military inserted itself more into the investigation, the corrupt and powerful would be pulling the strings, but he remained calm and tried to project confidence, "How do you think I attract such talent? Segregating the investigation as you propose will completely interfere with its fluidity. My people interpreted the transmission path, and my people will break the code, with our resources we will uncover the source, as well as develop a cure and a vaccine. You won't be able to do any of that without a malleable control center, and the bureaucracy within a government agency, such as Homeland, will slow down our progress."

"I am going to disagree with you on that Dr. Adams; a CDC tech discovered the computer coding. You've been aware of Kopvein for over two weeks, and now the world is falling apart."

Brent slammed his fist onto the table, "Do you know how long it took the CDC to identify the pathogen as a viral material? They didn't, and we did, they needed our help. Do you know how long it took them to get involved? Weeks, we identified the pathogen in one of our facilities and notified them immediately, yet still, they took days to become involved, and in that time, we excluded the possibility of it being a poison. In the Ebola outbreaks, the deadliest known modern-day pathogen, until now, it took the CDC months to start getting some control over the outbreak, six months. In two weeks, Kopvein has already killed as many people as the largest Ebola outbreak did in a quarter of the time. You are mistaken to think your lead over this investigation will help. We don't have months for a bureaucracy to resolve the problem. We will all be dead in a year at the current transmission rate."

Not one military officer said a word at Brent's outburst because they knew he was correct. They were dealing with a global pandemic unlike any in the recorded history of humankind. Duffield cleared his throat, "Gentleman, I believe Dr. Adams is correct, at least for now. May I suggest we find a way to coordinate a joint effort and work together." The Generals and the Colonel appeared quite unhappy with his suggestion, but at least one of them remained sane enough to see logic and possibly the big picture. "Sirs, consider the implications of getting caught up to speed."

"But the President..."

Brent cut the General off, "Where is the president? Nobody has seen him, and normally his tweeting and social media presence blow up when anything he deems newsworthy circulates. Does he not think this matter requires his attention?" Brent wanted to add something like 'or is he too busy chasing tail and profiting from the panic to notice,' but he refrained, "The country needs his reassurances that the government and everyone else is working on a cure and not to panic." Their faces paled, both the colonel and General Carpenter looked out the window, and Duffield stared at the floor, emphasizing his forehead, which now glistened with sweat. General Ross peered directly at Brent, but nobody said anything. Brent's jaw dropped, "He contracted it didn't he?"

"We are not at liberty to say anything about the President."

"Well, you've said plenty with that response. Now I understand your sudden demand to be involved in the investigation. Why hasn't anyone contacted us about this until now?

"We thought he had a cold."

Brent knew he had regained control of the meeting and the investigation, and sighed deeply, "We all want the same thing, and that is to fix this, and ultimately to survive. Major Duffield and Colonel Ups with your medical field training background I believe you are the best candidates to continue working out of this facility, you will understand the medical protocols. You can help coordinate with Abe and be the liaison to Homeland Security. Please feel free to send a SMALL number of appropriate staffing to best capitalize on this joint effort and we will immediately begin vetting them." The Generals looked like they were about to object, but Brent knew his company was far too embedded in the investigation for Homeland to take over at this point. They all had too much at stake, and both Generals reluctantly nodded. Duffield and Ups stared white-faced at Brent. He knew the task ahead daunted even him, but these military men must feel like they are drowning.

Alex stared blank-faced at the wall. An entire day, no information for an entire day. She felt like her stomach had turned to mush and she would vomit any second. She switched off the news because seeing the bunch of crazies waving signs did not help to quiet her mind and it told her nothing new. It never seemed to stop. She couldn't eat, read, or even think about anything but her conversations with Tristan and Brent yesterday. If he went to jail for longer, he'd die in there, if they didn't all die here first. She became more and more confident each day that she hadn't been exposed to the virus, but she wasn't sure about her brother.

Alex heard footsteps coming down the hall; she'd left the intercom on for that purpose. She quickly picked up her tablet to act like she was reading. Rebecca appeared at the window, and her expression was veiled in stress. Under normal circumstances and with most people Alex preferred to maintain her composure, but it was Rebecca, so she dropped all pretense as well as her tablet and she jumped up to the window, "What is happening? What is going on with my brother?"

Rebecca stared at Alex completely blank-faced, "Tristan is fine, what do you mean?"

"You don't know about the whole computer code thing? I spoke to Brent, and I thought you would know what was happening." There is no way that Rebecca doesn't know about the computer code snafu, but maybe she is mad that Tristan lied and didn't want to say anything. Perhaps she got in trouble for saying too much one too many times. Whatever was happening, she was acting very strangely, even for her.

"I am not allowed to discuss anything at this point."

"What do you mean you can't discuss it? I am your best friend, and you can't discuss my brother's welfare?"

Rebecca sighed, "I told you he is fine, and I can't tell you anything else."

Alex stared at her friend, and even though Rebecca said Tristan was fine, not being allowed to discuss anything often meant confidential or classified. Maybe she just needed to ask better questions. Could Tristan be right and the conversations were being recorded? She thought carefully before asking Rebecca anything else and watched for her friend's reaction, "Is he still here?"

Rebecca nodded, "Please don't play this game; I know we've stretched the rules in the past, but now, everything is different."

The reply sounded like one of Rebecca's codes, and Alex didn't understand why she was visiting at all. It surely wasn't to talk because Rebecca stood there staring like a statue without saying a word, "Why did you come here if you aren't going to talk to me or tell me anything?" Alex quickly raised her hand to her mouth, she hadn't meant it that way, but annoyance supplanted reason and the wrong words slipped out before she could stop herself.

Stepping back Rebecca tried, unsuccessfully, not to react, "Maybe I shouldn't have come. You know, other people's lives are in danger and you expect everyone to bend to your desires. You are not the only one at risk here, and things here are, uh, this is a harrowing time for everyone. I am not endangering everything I've worked for just to appease you, so go ask your little boyfriend if you need to know something, you know, the one who I told you to watch out for."

Alex stared at Rebecca with a stone-faced expression and said nothing as her friend turned and walked away. The bizarre interaction boggled Alex's mind. The stress of everything must be getting to her.

CHAPTER 19

Day 16

The lab and even work itself felt more like a prison than its usual escape for Rebecca. She worked in her private lab so she could better concentrate. It gave her genuine privacy and only Brent, high-ranking security, and she had access to it. The quiet soothed her soul, and today, she longed for it. When she needed to think she'd lie on an empty table in her lab, a weird habit she shared with nobody. The day before had drained all of her mental energy. Everything that could go wrong seemed to, and on top of it, she and Alex had an extremely unpleasant visit. What happened yesterday with Alex gnawed at her, but she needed to separate herself from her friend if she planned to finish the job she had set out to do. Rebecca's emotions were too tied up in every interaction with Alex, and it sidetracked her. While she owed so much to her friend, a couple of days without visiting Alex gave her a reprieve from on all the emotional baggage. Alex came into her life and saved Rebecca even more than she saved Alex. She went down to that area to end it all but finding Alex turned everything around for her. Taking care of Alex when they were both broken gave Rebecca the clarity to follow her path. It seemed crazy and unattainable at the time, yet now here she was, in the lab where she'd always longed to be.

Rebecca sat up, glanced around at the sealed containment rooms and machinery, and sensed her entire face relax. Her lab terrified most of the doctors in the building, but she felt more at home there than anywhere, except maybe the mini lab at home in her tiny cottage. Nobody went down to it except Rebecca; it was hers and only hers. Alex had always compared her cottage to a little dollhouse and said it didn't really match her, but the location meant everything to her. She'd acquired the most serene outdoor view in all the burbs of D.C., which she loved but still, she preferred the lab. She stretched out onto the table on her back again to stare at the ceiling. Rebecca sighed deeply, knowing she needed to rejoin her colleagues, especially with everything escalating. She should have predicted the speed of its acceleration back at Fulton, but she couldn't change it now. The entire situation had blown up too far, and too fast. For now, she'd take another moment and bathe in the quiet of her space, and for several minutes, she did. Then, with a deep sigh, Rebecca rolled off the table, ready to return to the chaos.

As Rebecca strode from the solitude of her private lab to the pandemonium of the group, she caught Hector's eye, but he quickly turned back toward his work. Ha, he was trying to hide from her. She felt utterly alone, especially with how awfully she'd treated Alex, and she needed an ally. Determined to change her mood, Rebecca immediately strutted over to his workstation and stood directly behind him, exceedingly close, with her breasts rubbing up just slightly on his back. She smelled his clean soapy scent and breathed directly on his cheek, and her stance had its intended effect because she heard his breathing deepen, abruptly. She began reviewing some of the recent findings with him, asking him what he thought they should include in the model he'd started with Tristan. He stopped momentarily to look at her, which seemed awkward because her position required he lean his head back only from her. Turning around to face her would have been more comfortable but he didn't seem to want to move. In a quiet voice, almost a whisper he questioned her, "We never talked about what happened."

She cocked her head and pursed her lips in feigned confusion, "What do you mean?"

"Well, about me going behind your back to speak to your boss about my computer coding ideas. I thought you would be furious with me, especially after what happened in the conference room, and you acted like it never happened."

Rebecca leaned back her head and smiled, "You were right, and I was wrong. I'd have done the same thing in your position, and I have. Why would I be upset about that?"

"And what about the conference room?"

"Oh, I think we both knew what we were doing in there. Why would that change anything?"

His voice grew an octave higher, as well as a little louder, "It meant nothing to you?" Several people in the lab glanced over, everyone knew about his obsession with her but his emotional response made him look silly and weak. She wanted to control the situation, not emasculate him.

With a half-smile, a wink, and a soft whisper she leaned into him, "Of course, but we can't get distracted, not right now anyway."

His slow breathing betrayed his concentration on trying to remain calm, and he nodded as he looked toward his work, trying to act nonchalant, "I am worried there might not be a chance for us if we don't take it now."

Rebecca leaned in even closer with her breasts now smashed up against his back. She breathed softly down his neck and whispered right into his ear, "Don't worry, we will." He stood perfectly still for a moment and took a staggered breath, as a small smile curled up on his lips. Extremely aroused by the interaction, she didn't know how he was controlling himself, but at least she gained his attention and thought she might also have his devotion. Rebecca picked up the paper she'd been reviewing with him and continued speaking in low, breathy tones, but still stood very close. She watched him bite his lip and knew he wasn't hearing a word she was saying.

These kinds of meetings wasted Brent's time, especially with Homeland involved, and this one included General Ross only one day after they'd already met. He had hoped to avoid the time suck by suggesting that Duffield and Ups each tail a lead in the investigation, but some people he could not avoid. Ups tailed Sonso, and Duffield tailed Abe. Duffield originally requested more direct involvement in the research aspects of the investigation by requesting to tail Rebecca, but Brent saw the way the man eyed her. Brent did not have the time to smooth over ruffled feathers if Rebecca chose to chew Duffield up and spit him out, a scene he usually enjoyed, but Hector following her around like a puppy annoyed him enough. He only tolerated Hector because the tech didn't get easily distracted, and he saw what nobody else saw in the RNA strand. Hector even stood up to Rebecca when she dismissed his ideas, which was an extremely difficult task. He impressed Brent so much that when the Kopvein outbreak ended, Brent intended to make sure that Hector came to work for Dashcorp.

Brent shifted in his seat, as the topic turned more serious and he was unable to redirect their arguments, "What about the homeless, we can't conscionably send them out into the streets. Consider the safety of not only those they might expose but also their own." He couldn't send the quarantined home; they'd be helpless out there. The safest place was right where they were, and Brent hated that Homeland kept pushing their agenda. His thoughts drifted over to Alex and inside his stomach roiled in anxiety, "And what about Alex Donaghue? She is Rebecca's closest friend, and we can't let our best researcher get distracted."

"We need the rooms if we are going to keep the investigation based out of this facility and I believe Dr. Martin is a professional, she will act like it."

He sighed in an exasperated display, trying to get his point across, "Dr. Martin usually gets what she wants for a reason, and she will want her friend to stay here. We both know that you only want the room for your own political agents and they won't assist in this investigation in any way."

The general scowled at him, "It isn't just our men we are concerned with but the future as well. We need people here who can aid in recovery after a vaccine is developed, ones who can disseminate it throughout the world, attain order and help re-build."

As the general spoke, his intensity rose and spittle escaped from his lips with each strongly enunciated word. The man argued by flexing his military strength and waving Dashcorp's need for it over Brent's head, leaving an implied threat on the table for them all to understand. Brent felt control slipping through his fingers. He should never have let the military through the Dashcorp doors. After an hour of arguing back and forth, he felt himself desperately grasping at straws. He knew that he needed military cooperation, but the general was being increasingly stubborn and Brent felt the more he pushed the more the General took advantage of it. He needed to keep the families of the Dashcorp employees safe and on-site, "Gentlemen, I think you are looking at this the wrong way. We need to find some kind of a compromise that will suit us both." He explained his plans to the general trying to include Alex and David's asylum, but the General knew he had Brent trapped between the safety of his less technical employees and their families and Alex. "But I don't think Tristan Donaghue will be forthcoming with his assistance if he thinks his sister is in danger. He is probably the most talented hacker I've ever met, and we need him."

"We will make sure his sister gets home safely, and other than that he won't have a choice in the matter or he will spend the rest of his life in jail."

This man was a fool to think that threatening one of their best resources would get him what he wanted. Tristan did not seem like the kind of person who responded well to coercion. The General, however, wouldn't concede on any allowance that benefited Tristan and Brent slowly realized that saving Alex would only hurt dozens of other people that he was responsible for protecting. Knowing Homeland had him trapped, but trying not to sound desperate, Brent, in one last effort, muttered, "I don't know if that threat will work, we could all die tomorrow, and you don't understand how much help we will need from him. Wouldn't it just be easier to keep her here, maybe even offer an incentive, for example, moving them in together in a closed ward where they can live with one another?"

The glare that enveloped the general's face clarified his hostility toward Brent's ideas. There was a story behind them, one that neither the general or Tristan had divulged. The general didn't try to hide his feelings as he seethed out the words between his gritted teeth, "We aren't going to spend our time pandering to a known criminal."

Brent knew the fight fell on deaf ears and they'd reached a stalemate but felt he owed it to Alex and her brother to defend Tristan's honor, even if he was a criminal, "That known criminal has been assisting our investigation team to decipher the coding in the pathogen."

As the debate circled around to the same facts repeatedly, the others in the room lost interest yet remained quiet and respectful while the General delivered his final blow to the argument, "Really, because he is responsible for the coding in the first place, so unless he is a psychopath, he should WANT to fix his mistake."

"Don't be so shortsighted; he isn't responsible for what a terrorist does with his work. That is like saying Einstein is responsible for every act of nuclear misconduct since its discovery. In fact, we are lucky Tristan is the one who wrote original code because we are probably months closer, in a matter of days to understanding how Kopvein works, bringing us that much closer to developing a cure or vaccine. It is like he looks at code and understands it like it is written in English. I can't believe you haven't already recruited him for the NSA or CIA."

"Oh, we are well aware of Tristan Donaghue and his skill set."

"Is that what your objections are all about? You don't want to 'pander' to him because you couldn't recruit him? I am trying my best here, but maybe consider your goodwill a step in the direction of building some with Tristan by keeping his sister and his friend here."

With a sigh, Colonel Ups stood up and nodded pointedly, "I am sorry Dr. Adams. You won't win this one. Take your concessions as we've agreed upon and let's move on with the business of defending against the Kopvein pandemic." The General, used to getting his way, had won and Brent, crestfallen, nodded his acquiescence.

Josie wandered into the lab. Nobody had seen her all week, and if Rebecca hadn't known better, would have thought Sonso got rid of her. Sonso, annoyed with her simpering sent her off to do copious amounts of tedious comparison research. Josie wasn't really annoying as much as insecure and unsure of herself. Sonso assigned the poor girl to comb through every scientific publication, digital, microfiche, and paper, from the last several decades to try and find similarities to Kopvein. Rebecca chuckled; she loved to punish her techs similarly. Maybe Sonso did possess some admirable qualities. Josie's shoulders were practically up to her ears and she gripped the papers in her hands so tightly they looked cemented into her fingers. She couldn't tell if the girl's wide-eyes and body ticks were from agitation or excitement.

Josie hesitated, scanning the room, and her eyes stopped on Sonso. She advanced toward her but hesitated again, and Rebecca stepped in between them before Sonso noticed. She smiled at the girl to put her at ease, though Josie was wound so tightly, it probably wouldn't help, "We've missed you around here, what have you been up to?"

"Well, uh, you see, Doc- Doctor Sonso told me to do some research, and I, uh, I may have found something."

"Really?" Rebecca glanced over her shoulder, Sonso still concentrated on her work and hadn't even looked up one time. Rebecca, tried to put the girl at ease, smiled as warmly as she could, "I think she is in the middle of something. Would you like to show me? I will let you know if it is something you want to bring to her." Josie nodded then followed Rebecca over to her station, "Let's see what you found." Josie cautiously handed over a stack of notes and flash drive, Rebecca scanned the paperwork and admired the girl's fastidious approach to research, "Your work looks impeccable, maybe I should consider poaching you from the CDC when this is all over." Josie's face lit up from the compliment, and she relaxed, a little. Rebecca plugged in the flash drive, and when Hector began approaching the two women, she winked and gave him a half-smile before returning to the work in front of her. Luckily, he took the hint and went back to his station.

The information Josie had collected caused Rebecca's heart to flutter, and she didn't know what to say as she stared in disbelief. How did anyone find that dissertation? It had been forever and even Rebecca had forgotten about it. The notes referred to the paleoviral strand Greens Virus 06B, and she knew it too well. That little worm, Green, she worked with all those years ago in the Antarctic, the fool, desperate for recognition had arrogantly named it after himself. Her life was in such an upheaval after the terrorist attack in Israel that she transferred to the Antarctic to escape and work through her grief where encountered Green, an inadequate scientist with the soul of a puny man. She'd happily handed him her discovery and her work on it to get him off her back, or ass in this case, and he took all the credit. She didn't need it and it distracted him from the ass grabbing and pathetic attempts at flirting. Green was so thrilled with himself and the attention he received, that he completely left her alone. His audacity extended to writing his dissertation on his discovery. It was one of the most advantageous decisions she'd ever made for herself, but now it looked like Green may be connected to the pathogen.

Only a small similarity of the structure and the dsDNA connected it to Kopvein and Rebecca was shocked that Josie noticed it. Many techs completely missed such subtle relationships and their importance. She turned to the girl and nodded her head in approval, "What made you look into the paleoviral research?"

Josie shrugged, "I couldn't find any other pathogens that would support the separate RNA strands types of Kopvein that also possessed a double strand similar enough to build a viral pathogen from. Since the discovery of the coding, I thought the RNA while malleable enough to program, still required a base dsDNA with the adequate structure adhesion to code and build a viable pathogen with Kopvein's persistence. After days of sifting through current and historical pathogens, I decided to check the prehistoric database as any Pathogen with enough permanence to survive the arctic might possess the necessary traits to be a viable base for Kopvein." She hadn't taken a breath through her entire explanation.

Rebecca had to make herself consciously shut her jaw as it hung open then inhaled and slowly, deliberately exhaled, while Josie surveyed her reaction waiting for a response. She underestimated the girl a great deal, but Josie must have value or Sonso wouldn't have hired her. Rebecca needed to properly reveal this finding so Sonso couldn't take all the credit and to benefit Josie as well as herself, "Sonso," her voice much louder than necessary, "I think you are wasting your talent." Josie looked like she wanted to crawl under the table. Rebecca could have laughed at the intense glower Sonso shot her, but somehow kept the humor of it to herself. Sonso sighed heavily, pushed herself off her stool and ambled over to Rebecca's workstation and while Sonso reviewed Josie's research, Rebecca texted Brent and Abe.

"This is Christy Gallagher reporting live from outside the Department of Homeland Security Building in Southwest Washington D.C. and while I wasn't able to get a direct comment; my sources say that officers from the Department of Homeland security and several high ranking military officers connected to Homeland Security were observed at the Dashcorp main research facility. The Viralists movement has informed me that their fearless leader, Judy Samanski, will not stop until the world is safe. In a statement earlier today, Ms. Samanski said that the military involvement only proves that the core values of the movement are the best course of action if you want to survive the pandemic Kopvein."

CHAPTER 20

Day 17

Alex contemplated her strange interaction with Rebecca, non-stop since it had happened. Nobody visited, not even Brent. She'd only seen the medical techs who delivered her food, examined her, took blood samples, and they wouldn't or couldn't answer any of her questions. She knew Tristan was okay no matter how weird her friend had acted. That secret is one Rebecca wouldn't keep, no matter the consequences, even if she had to keep the details about it confidential. Alex had complete faith in her bitchy friend but started wondering if Rebecca felt the same. She made excuse after excuse, in her head about Rebecca's cold flippant treatment, but none made any sense. She really wanted to see Tristan again today, didn't think he would hold back from her, but perhaps he would too. Alex sighed sadly, doubting all notions and assumptions on her personal relationships, as more and more secrets came to light.

In the back of her mind, Alex thought that Brent probably wanted to avoid her now because she clearly had too much baggage. She missed their talks and was relieved that glass separated them because their conversations had become very intimate. Alex hated the feeling of losing control over herself but felt she could allow herself to relax with him. The way he gazed into her eyes, he appeared to look straight into the depths of her soul and bring out the fun, innocent girl she once was. He seemed confident and Alex hoped she'd get the chance to know him under normal circumstances, although life might never achieve any kind of normalcy again. Chaos may be the new normal, either way, she hoped they'd see and speak to each other without glass between them to discover if her feelings were real or merely a reflection of the situation they experienced together. He was a sought-after bachelor and she ultimately concluded that men don't usually give up women waiting in the wings for an interesting possibility, especially one with baggage. Why would he want her?

Lost in thought, Alex jumped when Brent suddenly appeared at her window and began speaking, "Do you always leave your intercom on?"

The flood of relief Alex felt at seeing Brent almost clouded her vision with joy. She forgot her usual reserved mannerism she saved for everyone but Rebecca and bounded to the window, "Holy cow you scared me! I leave it on so I can hear what is coming down the halls, but obviously, I wasn't paying attention today. How long have you been standing there?"

"Long enough to see you daydreaming,"

"Ha," she grunted, "No, I was just thinking."

"Hmm, profound thoughts? Because your face looked scary stern, almost as terrifying as a scientist we both know."

An unexpected giggle bubbled up, alleviating some of the tension built up in her stomach, "Yes well, I haven't stopped thinking about my brother, the med techs don't seem to know anything and Rebecca wouldn't tell me anything, except that he is fine. That was the day before yesterday, and I haven't seen anyone except the techs, who are bleeding me dry."

Brent stepped back and grinned, "Wow, this is the most excitable I've seen you since you got here." Alex glanced down at her hands and sensed her cheeks burning as Brent continued, a strange tone in his voice, "Your bother is fine and I am pleased to hear that Rebecca takes her job seriously. She has been under strict orders not to discuss any information regarding the latest findings with anyone, not even you." Alex gaped at him, stunned at the seriousness of his response. He usually tried charming her, especially when delivering unpleasant news. His face softened at her reaction, and he sighed, "I can't say anything either except that Homeland Security is now a part of the Kopvein investigation and while I can't give you details, I've taken care of an area you were quite concerned about."

Alex thought for a moment, okay, Tristan must be helping with the investigation. Her hopes soared, and the authorities would look positively at his assistance, "Vague, but I get it, and I can't thank you enough. May I go see Tristan today?"

His pallor paled and the muscles around Brent's mouth twitched. He stared down the hall as he responded, "I'm sorry Homeland is not allowing it. In fact," his voice cracked, "You may not get to see him for a while." He wouldn't make the eye contact and continued staring down the hall instead.

Alex slumped, all her previous hope flittered away. She knew she sounded miserable and whiney, yet no longer cared, "But why?"

Brent stepped closer to the window and tried to smile, but his discernable unhappiness transformed his mouth into a guilt-ridden grimace, "I am sorry Alex, since the investigation exposed a terrorist connection, Homeland is trying to control everything about it. All low-level risk quarantined will be released to their own homes."

His response overwhelmed Alex and in a pitch about three octaves higher than her normal voice, she screeched out, "What? I am going home?" Brent nodded but turned away as she breathed heavily, not knowing how to respond or what it meant. Queasiness developed in her stomach as she thought about how the news portrayed the severe turmoil on the streets and goosebumps formed on her arms. She hadn't realized how comfortable and safe the environment inside the walls of the Dashcorp facility felt as the outside world worsened.

"In fact, the military will escort you to your apartment and David to a secured homeless shelter, today. You and all the other...,"

She wanted to stop the influx of news Brent was methodically delivering so she abruptly interrupted him, "Wait for how long, and what do you mean a secured homeless shelter? You've seen him since he has been on his medication. He doesn't want to go back to that life and he won't tolerate being locked up in a homeless shelter. And what does that mean for the people working here?"

She swore tears were building up in his eyes, which contradicted with the impatient sound of his voice, "Alex, please let me finish, you will be required to wear an ankle transponder, and if you step one foot outside your apartment or David leaves the shelter, authorities will arrest and detain you at a secured general quarantine. It is almost like a jail without any of the privacy." Alex exhaled in disgust as Brent continued, "You don't understand what it is like out there. It isn't safe. Frenzied people took to the streets and intentional or not, pandemonium ensued. Please promise me you will stay home."

With terrified thoughts swimming through her head, she responded in a screechy panic, "Oh my God, then you shouldn't send us out; we're going to die out there. How will we eat or get the basics to live if we can't leave the apartment? How is this legal?" She paused to take a breath, she hated losing control of herself, but Alex stopped caring what Brent thought of her because she'd probably never see him again. David was doing so well, and his progress shocked her, "I can't let David go to that shelter. He will fall right back into the same place he was when he came here, and that can't happen especially now that I know who he is. I want him to come to my apartment with me."

Brent stepped back, "I've never seen you this flustered. You always seem so calm."

"Well, I'm not calm, and why would I be? I feel as if I am being turned loose into the unknown and without much of an explanation either."

"I will make sure you are okay, I swear," but he didn't sound confident.

Brent reached out a gloved hand and gingerly touched Alex's hand, grasping it tenderly for a moment before she spotted the tentative smile behind his helmet. Her heart fluttered, but she only nodded to him. Anything more and Alex would have lost control, jumped on top of him, then begged him to keep her there and safe with him. Over the last couple of hours, since no other solution seemed available, she'd developed some knight on white horse fantasies, but now reality was setting in. Glass and a fatal disease had separated them over the past week and a half, but now, as they stood closely, she realized how much she wanted him. Would she feel the same if the circumstances were different?

"Under penalty of arrest and incarceration, you must remain in your home at all times until your quarantine has been lifted. The required confinement period is a maximum period of 40 days, some of which you already served in isolation at the Dashcorp facility." The private in charge of the escort continued to drone on as he read a prepared statement to Alex, David, and several other quarantined individuals losing the safety of the Dashcorp facility to go back to their homes.

Brent handed bags to the private then assured Alex that he would bring her more supplies in the next week. With a concerned expression he stepped closer and peered down into her eyes then whispered, "I am worried Alex, I don't understand how can you take a homeless man you don't know into your house?"

With her sanity having returned, she was able to behave calmly and shrugged like she wasn't worried, but she could barely swallow the nervousness that stirred up her stomach, "Well, apparently I've known him since I was fifteen, and, he saved my life, so I think I will be okay. Do you know if Rebecca is coming to say goodbye? She knows I'm leaving today, right?"

Brent nodded his head but said nothing. Alex knew that Rebecca hated dealing with the emotional repercussions of anything difficult and saying goodbye would probably overwhelm her. She wasn't coming. Alex wanted to hug Brent goodbye but settled for smiles from behind the mask and a silent nod of the head, then she waited until the last moment in hopes that Rebecca would show, but she didn't. Alex entered the passenger van and took a seat next to David but still kept watch out the window searching for Rebecca.

The news hadn't prepared Alex for the reality of scenes from the outside world. The streets appeared deserted, and an eerie cast shadowed the landscape as the sun went down. Only a few cars speckled the roads, and the military escort dominated the road. No people wandered the streets, nobody sat at the cafés or coffee shops, most of the stores looked closed down, and some were even boarded up. The van transporting her and David slowed as it neared the apartment and she saw people peeking out the windows, but nobody came out.

A suited armed guard escorted them through the deserted courtyard to her front door. Alex fumbled with the keys her neighbor and Erika poked her head out of her apartment, "Alex where were you, I've been worried." She glanced over at the armed guard and the masks they wore, then at David, "Who are these guys and what are they doing here?"

The guard antagonistically stepped towards Erika, "I am sorry ma'am you must keep your distance."

"Who is this bozo? I will come over, and you can explain it to me over coffee."

The guard clasped his huge gun and aggressively moved in front of the door, "These individuals are under strict quarantine, and you must keep a safe distance. Step back inside!" Erika squeaked and slammed the door shut but the guard wasn't finished, he turned to David and Alex, "Must I remind you of the parameters of your quarantine?"

Alex shook her head and shouted to Erika's door, "I will call you later, by phone," she added. Erika was probably standing right there peeking through the eyehole, watching them. They all entered her apartment. She put her bag down then glanced around, at least the plants survived, thank goodness for Erika. David shifted from one foot to the other, looking uncomfortable and not taking his eyes off the guards. They were only doing their jobs, but they needn't act brutish, especially to her friend, it was rude and unnecessary. After the guards walked through her apartment then left, both she and David exhaled a breath of relief.

David, still shifting from one foot to the other, glanced around curiously, "You sure you're okay with me staying here? I mean I am a homeless guy, a stranger, and it feels weird like I am imposing. I haven't anything to offer you in return, and what if I get crazy again?" His voice sounded shaky and nervous, which matched Alex's feelings exactly, yet he appeared very sincere as he spoke, "I left everyone and hid under the bridge because I can hurt people, especially if I go crazy again."

She cared for him and tried not to let her nervousness show, "We've been over this. Of course, I want you to stay here, I am the one who insisted remember? And you aren't going to go crazy, you suffer from PTSD, not some untreatable psychosis, and you're on medication to calm your anxiety. Have you experienced any episodes since you went on the medication?" Alex waited for David's response, and he shook his head. She continued, "You save people, remember? I owe you my life, so I think that you staying at my place while the world is crazy is the best idea for both of us. If you start feeling anything unusual, let me know, and I will help."

David nodded then pointed to the corner with the potted orange tree in it, "I can take the corner over there."

"Don't be ridiculous, at least take the couch."

He looked down, his cheeks reddening, "I don't like all that padding, I spent the entire time in quarantine sleeping on the floor of that place."

Alex pressed her lips together and sighed before reluctantly nodding, "However you feel most comfortable, and feel free to watch TV or help yourself to some reading." She gave him a sleeping bag, some sheets, and a pillow before taking her stuff into her room then closing the door behind her. Alex locked the door as silently as she could. She felt strange having a man she barely knew stay with her in the house, but she didn't want to insult him, and she tried her best to be covert. She plopped down on the bed and rolled around for a minute, then stared up at her ceiling. How she missed her own bed.

"This is Christy Gallagher reporting from outside the Dashcorp Enterprises compound," the camera panned over Christy's shoulder, "As you can see a much larger military presence has grown overnight. Military vehicles, even tanks, and machine guns now occupy the field of this private company. Could this metamorphosis from private to military security be related to news that is too exceptional for me to wait until our evening edition? The question has arisen, where did the virus come from? Researchers suspect that the warming planet is the cause of not only an increase in temperatures around the world but a change in extreme weather events, an increase in the polar ice melt and rising sea levels. My sources tell me that all these planetary changes may have caused unknown, exceptionally dangerous viruses thousands and thousands of years old to seep from the polar regions of the world and visit their deadly horrors upon us now. That's right, the planet we live on could conceivably be retaliating against its inhumane treatment and set global warming loose to kill us all. Is this how the Neanderthals died out? Could the entire human race be next? As with all diseases, some individuals exposed to Kopvein have experienced no symptoms. Fulton Penitentiary is full of unaffected people, and according to this reporter's calculations, the entire prison population should now be feeling the symptoms of Kopvein.

"Dashcorp seems to be at the center of it all, so how is Dashcorp involved in this biological disaster? Did they know about Kopvein and do nothing to save these poor victims from this horrible disease? The latest number of U.S. Kopvein fatalities has grown to over 367,000 fatalities, all with the telltale sign of Kopvein, the dreaded veining marks on the sides of their faces and necks. Who will survive this horrendous blight on humanity?"

Rebecca had escaped to her private lab, again. An occurrence that seemed to happen more and more frequently, the longer the investigation stretched on. Figuring out the next move was critical, and the quiet calmed her. She needed to return to the group lab and slowly meandered down the hall with her mind deep in contemplation. Voices interrupted her thoughts, and she ducked into a conference room to avoid having to talk to anyone, yet.

Brent, Abe, and Duffield, the major with the beautiful blue eyes, came down the hall. Could they all be working together on the secondary investigation? Don't they think she noticed that Abe wasn't around most of the time, or did they not care that she knew? They debated an issue as they walked, and Duffield's clear, commanding baritone voice boomed as they approached, "Don't worry we are tracking down Green as we speak. He may be connected although I don't think he could have engineered the whole virus. Only a few people in the world with the multi-disciplinary knowledge necessary could have built a virus like Kopvein and one of them knew Green and is right here in this lab."

"Don't be daft, you're graspin' at straws, looking for a scapegoat. She's workin' harder than any of us to help cure Kopvein. Rebecca spent her life tryin' to fix the ills of the world. She is workin' like a dog to figure out a way to stop it." That a boy Abe, tell him.

"I know something is off, but I can't figure out what. Maybe she can spot what I am missing." At least Brent sort of defended her.

Damn, Homeland was already making her life more difficult and now, this man accused her of slacking. How dare they question her! She earned her distinguished reputation, one beyond reproach, but her thoughts shifted as Duffield continued, "She hasn't lived up to your promises, and now she seems to be folding under the pressure." They approached the door where she stood, "She studied biomolecular computing using circuit gates in Israel at the Weizmann Institute of Science. She also researched in the Antarctic at the time of the Green's prehistoric virus discovery. How do you not know about a discovery made while working at such a small research facility?"

Right at the moment they passed the door, Rebecca stepped out and blurted out, "The prehistoric virus wasn't my discovery; some prick named Green claimed it." Brent jumped, and Abe yelped. Only Duffield withheld his surprise at her sudden appearance. Her anger was thick and palpable, and she seethed, "I had no interest in him or his work. You wouldn't even care to speak with such a mediocre scientist."

Abe held his chest and breathed heavily, "Rebecca, we had no idea ye were there."

If fire could have burst from her orifices, it would have, "Obviously!" Rebecca paused a moment to gauge their reactions, "I went to the Antarctic to work while I dealt with my grief. Somehow, when I lived in Israel, I managed to survive a major terrorist bombing while I watched my best friend fall to the ground in pieces. Literally in pieces! My memories of that place still haunt me in my nightmares, so excuse me if I was oblivious to what happened at the institute while I researched there. I went to the Antarctic looking to hide, work, and clear my head, but Green wouldn't leave me alone. He thought I existed only as some kind of trinket, there to distract him when his boredom set in, so when he found some new virus he left me alone. Only then did I finally get to concentrate on my own research, as well as deal with my grief. I didn't look at his work; I ignored him and everything he did. I was thrilled when he left to go lecture about his little discovery. Circumstances curtailed my time and attention, and practically ruined both my education and my research and I almost gave up on it all. You have a lot of nerve questioning my intentions and trying to find a scapegoat when you need to get your ass out there and catch the terrorist responsible!" Finally, Rebecca stopped for a breath saw the men tense up with each new sentence out of her mouth, and then relax as she stopped yelling. She knew that her rant beat down their arrogance and suspicion.

At the sight of her word's impact, Rebecca's anger dissipated and she reclaimed her calm persona, "If you want to know why I haven't seemed to accomplish much, I can show you, but I warn you my theories appear ridiculous." She led them into her personal lab and brought them over to one of her worktables, "At the discovery of the coding within the RNA I started to think outside the box. Those lunatic Viralists gave me the idea with all their irrational claims and I investigated the victims." She thrust a handful of papers and files at each of the men, "These are all the reported unexplained and Kopvein deaths I can find. As I looked into some of the victims, we know of, a large number of them have criminal charges, and some are soldiers but many are upstanding members of society, religious leaders, and community service personnel. The people you'd most likely trust. I suspect there is an external component to the pathogen we are missing. Do you see where I am going with my hypothesis? Brent and Duffield look skeptically at Rebecca, but the ever-faithful Abe had already opened his mind to the possibility and started reading it. Irrepressible tears cascaded down in lines on Rebecca's cheeks, and she shook her head while wiping away some of the tears, "Look at the reports I wrote up!" Brent and Duffield, still apprehensive joined Abe reading the information Rebecca had compiled on the desk, carefully looking at each piece while Rebecca watched.

Finally, after what seemed like hours, Abe looked up, "Your theory sounds crazy, a pathogen with such an aggressive set of selective contagion perimeters? Ye are suggesting a designer pathogen on a massive global scale. This is a stretch, even for ye Rebecca."

"I know, but we still only possess a rudimentary knowledge of genetics and how the brain works, but someone obviously knows more than we do. My theory is the pathogen is fundamentally similar to a brain infection, although Kopvein isn't ordinary. It has computer coding for god sake! With what Tristan said about his original coding and the victim pathology, I think Kopvein attacks brains that exhibit the structural and hormonal combination, but I can't find the triggers. We might not know how it works, but maybe we can slow it down, just look at the prisoner who contracted it but is still alive. There must be a reason he escaped death.

"You mean that he has a natural immunity to it."

"Possibly, but we practically drained the man taking blood samples and took dozens of scans. Physically his genetic story is no different than yours or mine or even Doug's or any of the other fatalities."

"I can't consider such a crazy theory without some proof or at least a running theory of how it works."

Rebecca felt her inner loathing develop a palpable perimeter around her, as she scowled at Duffield and growled, "Why do you think I kept it from you?"

CHAPTER 21

Day 18

Birds chirped and Alex slowly fluttered her eyes open to allow them to adjust to the light and the sunshine that shown in through the window, illuminating the morning. She exhaled deeply and realized she had fallen asleep without dinner or even calling Erika. Alex stretched out then pulled herself to the edge of the bed. It was the longest, deepest night's sleep she'd had in years, all those sleepless nights at Dashcorp must have caught up to her. Quietly, as the dawn had barely broken, she opened the door and peeked out, David lay curled up in the corner with pillows behind his back and sheets draped over a chair similar to a fort like she used to make as a child. Now he wants a tent. He peered over some reading glasses and the book he read, "Good morning sleepy head." With a big grin, Alex walked the rest of her way out of the room, and David pointed to her phone, "Your friends called, but you seemed to need the sleep, so I answered your phone. The lady next door says she will drop off some fresh food, but keep the bug to yourself." Alex chuckled. He must mean Erika. "The witch and the TV man also called, I told them you were asleep, and you'd call em' back in the morning."

"TV man? Oh, you mean Brent and be careful, or I am going to tell Rebecca you go around calling her a witch."

"No, no, no, don't do that, or she'll curse me for sure," he chuckled; he was such a different man than the one she'd known under the bridge. He was clean, well groomed, and his eyes sparkled clearly, but it wasn't just his appearance, the medication calmed him and seeing him with a book he appeared so, so, normal. Nobody would guess he'd been homeless a couple of weeks ago, but suddenly, he hopped up and babbled, rapidly, like he felt nervous, "I unpacked that bag that TV man gave us. There are enough MRE's for each us for a week, and it also had other stuff like shampoo and toilet paper. I already helped myself to some food. I hope you don't mind, but I got used to eatin' three squares a day, and well, it called to me, so I ate a couple of the MRE's, but I didn't touch your stuff."

"David, we are stuck here for a while, so please eat whatever you want. If it is in the kitchen, it is fair game."

His face brightened, "Okay." He jogged past her, a difficult thing to do in her small apartment, then opened the freezer and pulled out some ice cream, "want some?" She laughed and shook her head, but opened the cupboard to hand him a bowl and spoon. He grabbed the spoon and eyed the bowl "Oh, uh sure, but there ain't much left, I planned on eatin' the whole thing."

Alex snickered, "I guess we won't have to wash the bowl then." She grabbed cereal out of the cupboard but realized she had no milk, so instead she fingered through the well-organized MRE's, apple maple oatmeal will work, and ate it right out of its bag. This was going to be a long month. Alex went into the bathroom and locked the door. It still would take a while not to feel a little odd and uncomfortable about having a stranger in the house, even if he saved her life at one time.

In the shower, she let the water run down her body, relishing the peaceful feeling and stayed in the shower until the water ran cold. Alex thought about the past two weeks spent in her tiny, little cell, mostly by herself. She read, slept, ate, exercised, watched television and waited, for a visitor, to visit Tristan or David, and for the time to pass. It was like she was on a vacation, an all-inclusive one confined to one room. For some reason, she confidently believed that she wasn't going to contract Kopvein from her exposure to Seth or Doug. The future, however, remained uncertain. How were they going to make it out of this mess alive? Rebecca told her Kopvein had a 98% fatality rate once contracted, but they didn't know what genetic traits made some people more resistant to it, yet. Rebecca always emphasized the 'yet' when she explained it to Alex, trying to reassure her.

Alex towel-dried body and hair then paused in front of the mirror and wiped away the condensation from the heat of her shower. She sighed as she stared at herself. She had needed a haircut before getting quarantined two weeks ago and her hair had grown far too long for her liking. Having the back of her hair too short for a ponytail gave her a sense of control. Nobody would ever grab her ponytail and drag her down again. She carefully combed it out and remembered how much she used to love her long hair and the time she devoted to brushing it until it felt like silk between her fingers, but that girl no longer existed. She pulled a pair of scissors from her bathroom drawer and grimaced. She wouldn't be able to schedule a real haircut for a long time. Alex picked up a piece in the back, held it up and snipped it off very short, about an inch long, then picked up the next section and continued cutting. When Alex approached the side of her head, she ran her finger along the scar on her cheek near her jawline. She wouldn't be able to hide it anymore, but it had become a part of her over the years, and she might as well accept it. Her flawless skin was stolen from her the same day she began feeling weak and helpless but now, she was no longer that vulnerable girl. She had spent years proving it in the bowels of the city trying to help those that everyone else forgot or ignored. She wasn't going to let Kopvein take away all the strength she'd gained and snipping the hair that covered her scar felt liberating, like loudly announcing her emancipation, from past troubles to the world.

Alex rubbed her hair with her towel and inspected her work. She nodded to herself and smiled. Her hairdresser would freak, but she liked it anyway. She'd always admired the super short pixie cut that so many women wore. They didn't have time for such frivolous concerns as playing with their hair and she wouldn't either. After dressing and walking out, Alex grabbed her tablet, fell back onto the couch, and curled her legs up under herself as she wedged herself into a corner. David peered over his reading and nodded his approval. She smiled inside and turned to where she'd left off.

The camera panned across the large building and over the empty streets, "This is Christy Gallagher, and today I am reporting from Capitol Hill. Congress should be in session but attendance is so low that neither the House or Senate has any representation, and everyone wants to know where the politicians are. Are they hiding when their people need them the most? Do they have the virus? Politicians, we are all afraid right now, but please show your faces, we need to hear from you."

Judy switched off the news and returned to the private chat room to continue her virtual meeting with the Viralist. She typed, "Wouldn't a riot go against all that the movement stands for?"

The Viralist typed back, "Sometimes you must break down the old before you it can be built anew. You will help with that by declaring to the world that they can no longer rule through corruption and intimidation. The people of your movement need you. You must go to the places I have told you, with your followers, tell them the end is coming, and then return to the center of it all, and begin to express your commitment to the movement physically. I am not a strong and inspiring leader like you, but together we can clear the path for Him to return to this world and you will be right by His side. Your followers are waiting for you to lead them."

Brent had been waiting for this moment. They finally confirmed the information leak. He had waited for what seemed like hours and tried to distract himself with other thoughts, and Alex's pretty little face kept drifting into his mind. He hadn't spoken to her but by text, and David had said the return home went smoothly. He imagined one of their many visits and how she smiled each time she saw him or the severe look of concentration on her face when she was focused on a topic. How at times her almost cold, matter of fact responses conflicted with her open and warm-hearted spirit. The little way she would self-consciously pull her short hair to cover the small scar on the side of her face and the way her pale blue eyes lit up when she thought of something that excited her. He also thought of how melancholic he felt since she left for home.

Security, the Homeland staff, Abe, Rebecca, and Sonso all filed in the door breaking up his little daydream. General Ross, in a blatant power play, took the head of the table, which Brent found amusing, but instead of reacting, he nodded and smiled at the man. Abe and Duffield, with the help of Tristan, and some Homeland security endorsed hacking, found out more than he thought possible, in a very short amount of time. Abe's angry expression buckled under Brent's scrutiny, and then his old friend grimaced and gave him a serious, almost unrecognizably small head shake. This can't be good. Duffield, whose ambitious nature would surely get him promoted soon, took the lead, "We found your leak and brought him in yesterday."

The announcement shocked him and Sonso, but Rebecca didn't flinch. She carefully looked around the room stopping on Brent. He stared intensely at her trying to decipher her reaction, and she shrugged her shoulders as she mouthed 'What' at him. He didn't know what to think or do, but he could tell she knew something about this. Duffield continued, "An anonymous source submitted a video that helped lead us to the information leak. Nithi Almeda was brought in yesterday for questioning and has admitted to leaking the status of the CDC's investigation into the Kopvein pathogen." Brent swallowed hard, great one of his own people. Homeland would surely use this fact as leverage against Dashcorp leadership. Duffield continued, "Mr. Almeda used a burner phone to call another burner phone, but the recipient of those calls is still an unknown. We have several leads and will continue to question Mr. Almeda. We suspect that the news reporter Christy Gallagher is directly involved since she is reporting the information from these leaks but she won't relinquish her source, and she could be getting the information secondarily."

No wonder Abe appeared overcome with rage. Brent felt it too, and it filled him to the brim. He wanted to throw a chair across the room, but instead, he silently seethed inside trying to show no emotion. Rebecca glared at him, as did Abe. She had mentioned Nithi before, but the idea seemed ridiculous to all of them, even her. One of his people deceived them all, betrayed them all, and made their investigation that much more difficult. With Nithi's strong administrative and technical abilities, they let him in on so many aspects of the investigation. There was no way he could have masterminded the leak though, somebody much smarter and more devious hid at the root of this betrayal. Brent cleared his throat to interject, "Christy Gallagher might make a deal. I offered her an exclusive interview in the past, and she easily rolled on her source. We caught and dismissed Judy Samanski for speaking to the Gallagher woman, so maybe she will deal again."

Duffield shook his head, "That probably won't work. The nation-wide hysteria and immeasurable fear of the outbreak is enveloping all of the United States, and smaller news stations all over the country are already shutting down. We don't know how long the news will be a viable information delivery system, so it wouldn't be an enticement."

Rebecca spoke up, "Why don't you offer her a job? She could have direct access to the information we give her, and our satellite systems to broadcast. With the state of the world she may feel safer in here at the facility, but keep her down on the first floor where she only has minimal access and feed her the information you want her to have."

"You mean reward her for-"

"Doing her job? Yes, that is exactly what I mean. She is ambitious, but simply caught a lucky break then dug her heels in after she was assigned to the Fulton shut down. She is like a dog with a bone, relentless but still, isn't the sharpest knife in the drawer if you know what I mean. You could control the information."

The air in the lab sizzled with anxiety and for many, the sting of betrayal. Some mourned the loss of a trusted colleague, even though Nithi still lived, his duplicity hurt. The comradery that had developed over the past couple of weeks while working closely together for so many hours had evaporated. Since Nithi leaked the information, the CDC staff was wary, and the Dashcorp staff felt trapped. Sonso looked at all the Dashcorp employees with suspicion, and Dashcorp staff bowed their heads, in shame or anger, or both, but each person sensed the reproachful look of the CDC staff. Both groups worked in utter silence, and the atmosphere of the lab's stillness crept under Rebecca's skin. The noise and chattering usually annoyed her, but this quiet wasn't peaceful. It rang of treachery, and her heart wept inside, but she knew they all stood in the path of even more heartbreak that was about to barrel down in their direction.

Only Duffield knew the truth of the video Rebecca had taken of Nithi, but Hector and Sonso probably suspected. They had seen her when she videoed Nithi, though neither said anything to her. Maybe they suspected, but Brent's accusatorial stare spoke loudly of his assumptions. Rebecca needed to change the mood now before it brought the lab crashing down into a sparring match. Homeland might get involved in the dispute and interrupt everything. Those military types annoyed her, and she didn't want them in her lab. The time to say something would never get better than that moment, and Sonso, as the supposed lead should do it, but her retracted feelings and doubt in Dashcorp probably only fed her anger. She wouldn't be able to convincingly get the lab back on track. Besides, Rebecca's connection to Hector lightened people's viewpoint about her over the last week and a half. Everyone liked and respected him, and it bled over into their feelings about her. She wasn't used to having people openly like her, and it filled her with a sense of empowerment. What to say and how to say it? Alex inspired others much better than she, but her friend had returned home and she was on her own, "All right everyone, I know you all feel the sting of what has happened here, but as much as I hate to say it, it was for the best." All attention abruptly shifted to her, and some of the lab techs even glared, "But we are a team, no, we are 'the' team who is going to save the world. Now we know who to trust. You are here for a reason, and one weak spot does not take away from all we have and will accomplish together. So brush it off and let's get back to work."

Alex would undoubtedly have been able to warm their hearts with an encouraging, heartfelt plea for fellowship, but Rebecca wasn't that person. Hector came over and kissed her on the cheek, "Thank you that is just what we needed to hear." Surprise and a small thrill consumed her. Usually, a display of affection at the workplace would have been completely inappropriate, but this time, it encouraged her. She hoped nobody here got Kopvein. She hadn't been with Hector since the conference room, but today she might show him her private lab. Brent walked in at that moment and the thought dissolved, seeing him expunged it immediately. He'd been acting quite peculiarly the last couple of days, and it worried her. She sighed deeply, and Hector noticed and promptly returned to his workstation.

Brent marched over and watched Rebecca but she ignored him. His demeanor made her antsy. Mostly because her state of mind already teetered on the edge of breaking, but she couldn't allow him to see it. She had too many people to worry about and too much at stake to let his behavior alter her dedication to her task. From her peripheral vision, she picked up Brent crossing his arms, waiting for something and finally, she caved and turned to him, "May I help you with something? As you can see we're all quite busy in here."

"Yes, I demand an accounting of yesterday."

The lab did not need to see Dashcorp's leader jumping down the throat of the person who just moments ago encouraged their teamwork. Brent's eyes betrayed an incensed passion she did not understand. He must know about the video, the timing was too coincidental. She peered a little deeper; could there be more to it? Rebecca gestured for him to follow her into the hallway, and his stiffness screamed to his state of mind as he barked, "What is going on?"

Rebecca met his aggressiveness with belligerence, "I don't know, why don't you tell me. You are the one acting like I killed your dog. Is this about the video?"

"No, I knew you gave it to Homeland instead of running it through Abe or me the moment it was mentioned. Now Duffield thinks we don't work as a unit and he will work to dichotomize our team for Homeland's benefit instead of resolving the Kopvein issue. It is all about power with them, and you definitely hindered our progress with that little move, but I am not here about that. I know I am missing something and I think you know what it is, and you are withholding. The video stunt proves it to me."

She pursed her lips and sighed, "I am sorry about the video, I wasn't thinking of it in that way. I wanted to keep Duffield out of my hair and thought his trust in me would go a long way."

Brent leaned in closer, "Yeah, I don't really believe you, since when do you not see every angle, of a move you make, especially when pulling some sneaky little stunt. I think you knew exactly what you were doing. In addition, since when do you think any of your ideas are too ridiculous to share? I've seen you make grown men cry when they were completely in the right. Now you treat your ideas flaccidly? "

Rebecca stepped back. His continued combativeness startled her. She had definitely miscalculated with the video. She had never seen him so furious, but the overwhelming stress must be debilitating his control too and she decided to use that to deflect this accusatory confrontation. She pleadingly peered into his eyes, "No, I just, just think all the stress is getting to me, and I am not thinking straight." His anger didn't change or dissipate at all, so she felt compelled to continue, "I just barely kept the lab from a full mutiny a moment ago, and I need to keep them happy so let's not get paranoid here. I don't know what I was thinking, and I guess I played it wrong. I wish I'd brought the video to you or Abe, instead. Again, I apologize and won't try anything like that again."

Brent glared at her, "Rebecca, you need to divulge whatever is circling your brain soon if not immediately! I've spent the last several years giving you cart blanch on your research, but you still work for Dashcorp, and I won't allow you to follow your own agenda, especially not when dealing with a tragedy. Develop a useful model from your collection of data, use whomever you need to help you, and I want it by tomorrow." He scowled for several seconds, sighed and shook his head before walking away.

Rebecca grimaced, the stress, the guilt, all of it almost overwhelmed her at that moment. She leaned against the wall and repressed her tears. How could she continue?

CHAPTER 22

Day 19

Rebecca, Hector, Sonso, and several other techs worked through the night building a model from the information she, Josie, and the others had collected. She preferred working with a smaller group but the expression on Brent's face shocked and daunted her. She speculated about what ran through his head and none of it worked in her favor. Major Duffield arrived in the lab a few hours into the evening, "I heard you are developing your theory about who is most susceptible to Kopvein into a model to work from."

Rebecca detested dealing with the military, and though Duffield was a pretty thing to look at with his dark hair, blue eyes, and perfectly fit body, she didn't think he exhibited much mental depth. Like most military men, he probably saw life in the straight lines of order and stability. He also gawked at her the way most men did, the way Hector did, but Hector possessed something intriguing behind the pretty face. She needed to manipulate the man to her own benefit, so she feigned modesty and looked down, like her embarrassment overwhelmed her, "Yes, I thought the theory was nothing more than a sidestep," then she paused and peered up into his eyes, "until I showed you, Brent, and Abe." If Alex were here she'd probably laugh so hard she'd pee herself, but she wished Sonso and Hector weren't witness the act. She quickly glanced in their direction and saw the tight smile that Sonso hid on her lips but Hector's wrinkled brow revealed his hurt.

Duffield leaned in as he tried to reassure her, "At this point, we shouldn't ignore any theories, even unique, seemingly impossible ones. I am glad you showed it to us." She smiled sweetly up towards him. If she hadn't been acting, the condescending comment would normally be too much for her to ignore, but now it played right into her agenda. From the corner of her eye, Rebecca saw Sonso bite her lip to stop the laughter from bursting out and she kicked Hector in the shin to prevent him from reacting. Sonso knew exactly what Rebecca was doing. Duffield nodded, and the hunger in his eyes intensified with each moment, "Well, keep up the good work and don't keep any more theories to yourself, no matter how obscure."

Rebecca gazed as earnestly as possible into his eyes, in the way most men couldn't resist, and placed one hand on his shoulder, then in her most sincerest, deferential tone of voice, "Thank you, Major, I appreciate your support in the matter." Duffield smiled, his eyes filled with yearning and probably a few other places as well, yep she had succeeded. Hopefully, he'd stay out of their way now. Now to seal the deal, with a smile and a tiny headshake, "Oh, I am sorry, I shouldn't let myself get so distracted. Please excuse me; I really need to focus on my work. There are lives to save."

"Oh yes, Ma'am," he quickly nodded, turned and marched with his straight-backed walk out of the room.

Hector stared at Rebecca, his eyes filled with confusion and betrayal. She felt a little guilty and now, if she needed to manipulate him in the future, he'd already know her tricks. Sonso lightly slapped the back of his head and laughed, "She took one for the team you silly, lovesick boy! A military man like that will never jeopardize work to flirt with a woman. He is going to avoid the lab and stay out of our hair now so Rebecca can," Sonso air-quoted the word as she said it, "concentrate. Duffield probably marked his calendar when he'd revisit the situation and pursue her." She glanced over to Rebecca as she gestured toward Hector and teased, "Are you sure you can handle this lovesick pup? Maybe you'd be better off with an older man, one more your age. I think this one here is clueless."

Snickering, Rebecca shrugged her shoulders and winked at Hector. His cheeks grew bright red and he quickly returned his attention to his work. Later, in the early morning hours, when they all took a break, Rebecca gave Hector a tour of her private lab and an intimate explanation of her interest in him. She sealed his fate with the intensity of her passion. As she lay next to him, her naked breasts pressing against him, she could see by his gratified, loving expression and his heart was lost to her. Any doubts in his mind had been chased away.

Alex already missed her brother, Rebecca, and even Brent's visits and discussions. Luckily, David continued to be good company. She couldn't believe how calm and coherent his medication made him. He kept to himself in the little corner behind her plant, quite a bit, not in an antisocial way, but in a way respectful of her space. He made fun, intelligent conversation, and she saw him taking his medication each day for which she was grateful, but still, she missed Rebecca and her crabby little comments, Tristan's dreamy discussions, and Brent's explorative dialogue into each other's lives and thoughts. She despised the idea of seeming needy, and hadn't called Brent yet, but texted him and Rebecca to apprise them of her safe arrival. She couldn't call Tristan since all his electronic access needed supervision but asked both Rebecca and Brent to relay messages for her.

Alex sat on the couch staring out the window looking at the empty streets, and wondering what was happening outside her walls, but couldn't stand to listen to the news anymore. She saw David watching her out of the corner of her eye, and to get Alex's attention, he cleared his throat, "You know, being here is not much different than living in a box. Well, except you have a roof, food, and safety, but seriously, I spent much of my time living in my own thoughts. It makes me realize that not having a job or anything important to me kept me trapped, kind of like being here under quarantine. I couldn't get out of my own way, and while my suffering wasn't to addiction, as it is for many of the homeless, my mind endured being lost and trapped at the same time. I had no hope and no way to find it. Watching you stare out the window at the emptiness just now yielded the same lonely feeling. It's the heartache in your eyes that does it."

Alex smiled sadly, "David, I can't imagine surviving with what you experienced out there, and I hope that if we make it through all this, your life can move forward with some hope and beauty in it. You deserve it for sure. Now that I know who my guardian angel was, I know you protected me more times than I care to think about. Did you watch me every time I went near Doug to deliver food? I saw you sometimes but didn't understand why." David's cheeks reddened and he pressed his lips together, then nodded his head and lowered his eyes. Alex stared at him curiously, "Why do you respond like that when you answer questions that reflect positively on you?"

David continued to look down, "Guilt. I know I should do more with my life, but my aimless state of being is disconcerting for me too. I feel like my head is clearing up and I don't want to go back to that box under the bridge. I just don't know what to do now."

Maybe David would be able to make a change in his life for the better. Alex's stomach whirled with both guilt and excitement, "You are good at helping and protecting people." She hoped, she hadn't said too much with his current mindset being so tentative and fragile still.

He nodded and returned to his reading, then from behind a smile, and without looking up, he said, "You should call that boy, he really likes you."

"Ha!" Alex picked up her phone, and retreated to her bedroom, then fell haphazardly onto her bed. She stared at the phone and thought, wouldn't he call me if he found the time? Alex felt like a coward but didn't know what to do. Her reluctance seemed stupid and weak. She wasn't a young teenage girl, but she felt like it. She made a bold statement to herself when she chopped off all her hair the day before, but ignoring men, her usual reaction, was so much easier. Trapped in that little cell, she couldn't ignore him, especially when he came for his visits and smiled that charming grin. She didn't want to disregard him or his attention, even as all the alarms went off in her head. With his charm and good looks, he could have anyone he wanted, why would he want her? Not only was she damaged goods, but she feared she'd get her heart broken. If she ever told him about what happened to her, surely his interest would wane, unless he was some kind of a masochist. She lived with too much baggage to be worth the work for him, and she refused to be some kind of charity case he could use to boost his ego. Maybe her hair cutting liberation extended only to her own psyche as a declaration of independence from her past, not that she was ready to include others in her life. Alex sighed deeply and knew she had talked herself out of calling him.

Brent peered up at the much larger, and somewhat taller Scotsman, Abe's imposing size always impressed him while growing up. He'd still call him uncle sometimes, which they both seemed to love, he respected the man, but Brent wasn't sure why Abe thought the way he did, "You really think this will work?"

Abe nodded, "Aye, Rebecca has always been a bit of an odd duck, and whatever is in her head she isn't executing the investigation with her usual vigor. I saw glimpses of it back at Fulton when we first started, but I can normally watch her face and see her brain workin' as she develops a plan then pursues it. Lately, I watch the expression on her face and she only seems to be flounderin'."

How could such a difficult woman change so much based on the presence of one person? Brent didn't think it was possible, but shrugged, "She's buckling, and we've put all our hopes in her abilities, which is a mistake I'm sure, but we don't have much of a choice in the matter. We need all the help we can get, and Rebecca is an integral part of the solution."

"Ye sound like you are tryin' to convince yourself."

Every scientist in the world was working diligently toward a cure, vaccine or both for Kopvein, but none saw things as clearly as Rebecca did, even in her current mental state. The fact that she seemed to stall with some aspects of the investigation worried both him and Abe because she wasn't the type to hesitate when working on complex problems, but Kopvein perplexed everyone. They'd spoken to her about the delays in her research, which wasn't fair to her when nobody else identified anything else helpful. They still couldn't definitively identify Kopvein and even Rebecca appeared bewildered. Brent sighed and grimaced, before answering his colleague, knowing they were grasping at straws, "Convince myself about it being too much for her or needing her?

Delivering a knowing, pointed glance, Abe grimaced in return, "Both."

"That woman is a genuine pain in the ass, but I always ignored it, even enjoyed the show of it, due to her unique combination of skills and problem-solving abilities. Her interpersonal skills, or lack of them, always remained secondary because, well, she is a scientist and they don't always fit a normal mold, but I feel like I am missing something that might help us. She follows her intuition, I also follow mine, and something has to help her over the hump she is stuck on. More people are dying every day, and it is beyond my own as well as every other scientist's abilities to fix it. I've always been a mediocre scientist. My skills excel in management."

"I agree with ye that somethin' is off with the girl, and she definitely needs help, but we all seem off. Nobody has taken a day off in more than two weeks and the days wear on forever. I've found a couple of techs asleep on their feet standin' up. Everyone is utterly exhausted. Her mother has always been able to focus her and her energies and Rebecca has a soft spot for that dad of hers. Even when she kept runnin' into tragedy after tragedy in her life, her mother helped her deal with the pain by challengin' her to follow her scientific curiosities. Although, if we'd kept Alex here I think she'd focus better, I am sure she will feel relieved her parents are safe inside the compound; maybe it will alleviate some of her stress. How do you want to tell her?"

Shaking his head, Brent looked down at his feet, hoping his desperation didn't show in his voice, "I agree, we should have kept Alex here, but Homeland needed to win a battle. They think punishing people is a motivator, so I had to sacrifice Alex to keep all our employees and their families under military protection. Luckily, Homeland views Dr. Martin's experience in the lab as a boon, and I brought Rebecca's mother up to the lab a short time ago. Her Dad is on one of the public floors comfortably watching the news, she will it figure out when she gets in there."

"Where is the girl?"

"Rebecca said she needed to sneak in a few hours of sleep, so she is probably in her office or lab. I am bettin' she will wake up soon. I don't know how the woman survives on almost no sleep. I am going to get somethin' to eat and I'll be in the cafeteria if you need anythin'." Abe nodded and walked away, probably headed over to greet his old colleague.

Brent strolled over to the cafeteria and grabbed some food, then sat in the corner to think. Rebecca wasn't the problem, the situation outside was the real problem, and his constant impatience impeded progress more than it helped. He wanted to help everyone sure, but he treasured life and he was too young to die. Immediately a picture of Alex's pretty face popped into his head. He longed for them both to survive, but couldn't keep allowing thoughts of her to interrupt his focus. What were her intentions? Was their attraction inspired by the dire situation and their fear of dying? He strongly desired to be with her and the glass separating them, the virus, and now the physical distance broke his heart. Other than the text yesterday, he hadn't heard from her, and he missed not only their conversations but even the chance to look at her. He hated to appear overbearing or worse, desperate; she would probably run from both. He needed to be somewhere in between, but the question remained, should he call or wait for her? Brent's thoughts reminded him of his sixteen-year-old self, and he felt ridiculous. He never doubted himself with women, so why did he hesitate with her? Because she matters you dimwit, he told himself, slapping himself on his forehead. Then, he quickly glanced around to make sure nobody saw him slap himself. He wouldn't care if she didn't matter, yet she distracted him from what he needed to do, and he thought about her all the time. He wanted to touch her face, press his lips onto hers, be with her intimately, passionately, and the more he thought about it, the more aroused he became. Call the girl. Just don't be too needy.

Brent pulled his phone from his pocket and stared at it for a moment, then dialed, closed his eyes and imagined her face, wondering what her apartment looked like and how she kept busy at home, "Alex?"

She answered immediately, "Brent?" She sounded excited but also hesitant.

As calmly as possible, Brent tried to sound like his normal self, "Yes, are you and David faring well?" However, it came out a little clinical and extremely stuffy, and he felt like an old man stuck in the nineteen-fifties.

She didn't answer for a moment, and then slowly responded, "We are, thank you. David is a very respectful houseguest. How is the investigation proceeding?"

Brent shifted uncomfortably in his seat wishing he'd gone back to his office to shut the door before making the call, and glanced around again to make sure he remained alone. The call seemed forced, and Brent panicked. Trapped in that little observation room she was unable to escape his visits. Maybe he imagined the attraction between them. Try professional and courteous, he thought to himself, "All is well as could be expected; we continue to move forward with some new theories."

"Really? Anything you can tell me about?"

He tried to evaluate the progress of the call by the sound of her voice, but only felt more inadequate as he listened to himself, "Unfortunately not. Neither you nor David developed any symptoms, have you? No cold or flu-like symptoms?"

Again she hesitated, "Uh no, is that why you called?"

Brent felt like a boy asking a girl to prom and failing miserably, "Well, I want to see how you were doing and that you are both healthy." He shook his head because he sounded like such an ass.

"Yes," she said curtly, she must feel the awkwardness too, "we are both fine." Then, she said nothing at all, and the curse of awkward silence screamed loudly to him.

Time to save the call, "Okay, well, I will check on you both tomorrow and maybe we will have more time to talk," or maybe not.

After hanging up, Brent put his forehead in his hands as he tapped the phone against his head, "I am such an idiot." He looked around again and saw a couple of techs looking at him from a table barely out of earshot, so he smiled and nodded to them. If anything could kill his distraction, looking like a fool would do it. Back to work, try again tomorrow and maybe the conversation will be less awkward, hopefully.

"Christy Gallagher reporting live, from Capitol Hill as the late afternoon shadows paint an eerie picture, protestors gather here, demanding their government take action. Congress still has not made an appearance, and we are all left to ask, who is running our country? Nobody has seen the president in almost a week, and the Secret Service reported that he has remanded himself to the Presidential Emergency Operations Center, PEOC, in response to the Kopvein viral outbreak. Why hasn't he broadcasted any messages to his people from there? Where do the citizens of the United States stand in this situation? The Viralist movement is growing stronger in response and continues its protest from several key areas of D.C., as well as from here at Dashcorp headquarters."

As the screen scanned over to the scene of the crowd, she abruptly inhaled, "Is that? What? Oh my, please re-roll the last section of tape for our viewers." She quickly scribbled a note for her producer, "What we seem to be witnessing is the leader of the Viralist movement, Judy Samanski, being handcuffed and taken away. Who is the arresting military officer and why was she arrested? These are seemingly peaceful protestors only want to see justice handed out to those responsible for Kopvein and while Dashcorp facilities were not the first infected with the virus, they seem to be in the center of the investigation, and we want to know why. My producer has just identified the arresting officer as Major Fitz Duffield, seen with several high-ranking Homeland Security officers at Dashcorp merely four days ago. I will try to reach someone for comment and keep you apprised. This is Christy Gallagher reporting live from Capitol Hill."

CHAPTER 23

Day 20

The questioning continued all night long, and Judy, exhausted from sleep deprivation tried answering question after question but begged to be allowed to sleep. Her usual bedtime was 8:30 and it wasn't right for them to keep her up all night, and he kept yelling about bombs. She didn't know what the man was talking about, the Viralists wouldn't use bombs, but Duffield insisted they had found dozens. Finally, after hours of interrogation, Judy broke down. She yearned to make a difference, but she never thought bombs were part of the equation. Her will was weak, and she'd let her ego make decisions for her, but she wasn't a murderer and no matter what Duffield said she had nothing to do with any bombs. Judy told him the Viralist's plans to riot around Washington D.C. and several other metropolitan areas in the country, as well as the names of the other Viralist leaders involved, "I swear the Viralists are mostly pacifists, I only found out about the riots yesterday, and bombs were not part of the plan."

"Do you expect anyone to believe that? All across the country and the world, Judy Samanski is touted as the leader of the Viralist movement, and you are trying to tell me you didn't know about the bombs."

"I had no idea, those kinds of things take advanced planning, and I wasn't even aware of the Viralists until two weeks ago." She pleaded desperately, "Check my computer please, I told you everything I know. Whoever is really leading the Viralist group contacted me through a private message board. It is all on my computer."

"Oh Mrs. Samanski, we've known about the bombs for hours, the information was all on your computer, and each one was placed exactly where you said a riot would occur. You must know you can't escape your part in this."

Judy sobbed loudly, "I wanted to do some good. I wanted to prove that I was more than just some mediocre middle manager, and thought I could be a hero and lead people to God. It was only supposed to be riots."

"Nobody believes you and condoning riots is still hurting people. Fanaticism is fanaticism, no matter how you look at it. You think wounding and killing all those people would be Godly work?" The volume of Duffield's voice steadily rose, "Do you how many people would have died or been hurt if those bombs had exploded? Three thousand died from the 911 terrorist attacks, and these bombs were rigged to kill ten times that number. Many were placed near where prominent public figures and military personnel gather, not to mention the thousands of innocents that would have been killed or injured." His yell had escalated to a scream, and his anger raged so intensely his hands shook, and spit flew as he spoke. No one had ever been so furious with Judy and terror swept over her, but Duffield wasn't finished, "Are there any more? You are out of chances to do the right thing!" Judy felt warmth filling her seat and running down her leg as she peed herself. Her head shook so fiercely she felt like she was seizing, and her fear intensified. Duffield turned on the television and stuck his finger in her face, "Look at the catastrophe you led," he briefly glared at her, his nostrils flared, then he marched out of the room with Judy shaking in her seat and urine dripping down her leg.

The news featured Christy Gallagher, although she wore a faded smile and had developed dark circles and bags under her eyes. Her demeanor now seemed very jumpy, "Christy Gallagher reporting from Capitol Hill, and Homeland Security informed me that several explosive devices were safely removed without incident from this and other populated areas of Washington D.C., as well as dozens of metropolitan areas across the country. At least 73 individuals have been detained for questioning, many claiming links to the Viralist movement. While the world falls apart around us, Homeland Security continues to protect us from terrorist threats, foreign and domestic. The military deployed troops to help maintain the peace as citizens resist during this harrowing time. How much can these heroes of our armed forces accomplish? Monsters continue to plague us even with the virus-like pathogen, Kopvein, ravaging our population."

Cool water ran down the sides of Brent's face and neck while he splashed water on his face. He sighed and looked into the bathroom mirror. Three weeks ago, the world bent to his will or at least it seemed to, and now he felt no control over anything. Judy? And Nithi too? Brent mentally outlined to all the years Judy had worked for him. She'd been quite a competent manager, endearing all those she worked with, all except for Rebecca. Rebecca lacked patience for Judy's passive-aggressive approach to dealing with problems, but he reasoned, sometimes a lighter touch was required to deal with individual personalities. Rebecca could never tolerate her and it turned out she was right.

Why did Judy suddenly turn on Dashcorp and the world? Did she think she wouldn't get caught? Before the bombs, Judy and Nithi might have received a slap on the wrist but now they'd find themselves incarcerated in federal prison for a very long time if they made it through the whole Kopvein disaster. She said she knew nothing about the bombs, and that there was only supposed to be a small upheaval in the crowds, but the evidence was all on her computer. She told Duffield to look there but Tristan had already hacked it, and they knew everything they needed to know, both to bring her in and stop the terrorist bombings. Brent was consumed with disgust at Judy's involvement in the incendiary plots. Her foolishness got her sucked into the Viralists' little ploy and she moved about as their little pawn. She was a fanatic and deserved whatever punishment she got.

Many of the terrorists detained already exhibited symptoms of Kopvein when they were apprehended and must have felt they had nothing left to lose. Others developed symptoms after being brought in. Maybe they would have been safe if they hadn't associated with their infected collaborators. None of them would live to be convicted of any crimes. Kopvein's fatality rate of 98%, baffled everyone, but not everyone exposed to it contracted it. Judy and Nithi were still both symptom-free. If only they could discover the natural immunity factor, they'd be able to replicate it and develop a vaccine or cure.

Brent dried his hands and face, and strode through the hall to an empty cubicle and plunked himself down into the chair. Whoever this office belonged to seriously needed to tidy up. He picked up a framed photograph on the desk and studied it; he knew her, Jessie and her family. She was a sweet lady. He wondered how they were doing and would check on them later. Brent wished he'd gotten a photograph of Alex. He knew Rebecca would likely share one with him but she would also mercilessly tease him about it, so he refrained for now. He should have snapped one with his phone while she read, but hadn't because it felt invasive. Something about Alex reading stuck out in his mind. At a moment when she thought nobody was around and she became completely herself, completely vulnerable, not hiding anything. He felt he'd barely scratched the surface of who she was and noticed that she had somehow learned a lot about him in their time together. If he survived this biological disaster he'd wasted enough time, he needed to pick up the phone and speak with her, like a man. He stared at the phone sitting in his hand, no more stalling, either she would or she wouldn't.

Alex answered the phone after one ring and Brent barely got out a greeting. She instantly started to relay their physical state to him, babbling on like she was in a race to get all her information out. Brent listened to her ramble before he found his voice, then he tried to act upbeat and charming, "Alex, thank goodness you're both still symptom-free and safe."

"We're perfectly fine. I saw the news, and while the city streets look crazy, ours seems to be empty."

Brent sighed, "Yes, but how are you, really?" He thought he heard her smile through the phone line, which helped his entire body loosen from its stiff posture. "I am worried about you. I know that Homeland remanded all the quarantined back to their homes, but we should get you back here. Rebecca isn't focusing and then I could also keep an eye on you."

She giggled, the tension, gone from her voice, "Keep an eye on me, eh? I think that little window allowed everyone to keep an eye on me and you want to watch me more? No seriously, I am perfectly all right, although I felt safer in there. I didn't ask to leave, you know."

Brent heard himself chuckle and knew he was too obsessed with her by the crazy thoughts that swirled through his head. Some of which, was that if Alex could read his mind, she might think he was a stalker, "We're in the process of converting several of the office floors and lounges as well as those lovely little medical observation rooms to living quarters for the staff and their families. In fact, I brought Rebecca's parents here yesterday.

"How is Tristan?"

"Ahh, he is still considered a prisoner and Homeland is particularly interested in him right now."

The tone of Alex's voice changed again and got a little shaky, "What? Why?"

"Oh no, don't worry. I am probably going to get busted for saying too much, Homeland is probably monitoring the call, but I can say that he is fine and not in any trouble." Again, Homeland only made the investigation more difficult. She almost sounded back to herself, like the woman he got to know through the window of her observation room. Brent ached to explain how his feelings, which was a heavy conversation he'd rather have in person, but over the phone was their only option. Therefore, rather than wait, he plowed headfirst into the discussion, "Alex, I want to apologize for yesterday's call."

"Really? Why is that?" Her reply sounded curt and businesslike again, and all the tension in her voice had returned. Today's call was only going a little better than yesterday, but he decided to let her know all he felt and stop wasting time.

"Come on now, you know why. It felt awkward and forced, and I don't know why. I enjoy talking to you and it always came naturally. Yesterday was only a small hiccup in our relationship, I promise." Holy cow, the words just slipped out. They had never discussed the status of their connection. He sounded desperate, and she probably thought he was a fool to believe they were in a relationship.

"Relationship, huh?"

Either she was interested or not, but he was determined to find out today, on this call. With nothing to lose, except his pride, he continued, "I am sorry, I know I am being presumptuous, but yes relationship, at least that is what I hope it can be." He held his breath waiting for her response. Usually, the thought of her aroused him, but the uncertainty of her feelings killed his excitement. Now, his apprehension took over, and his ego was crumbling waiting for her answer.

"I-I don't know what to say." Brent closed his eyes and wanted to smash the phone against the wall. But, Alex said more, "I've enjoyed talking to you every day too, but-, I mean you were considered one of the top fifty bachelors last year, and I assumed you dated a lot."

Relief washed over him. She didn't say no, which meant it wasn't a hopeless pursuit, "That stupid article made me the butt of jokes at work for the past year! And trust me Rebecca seemed to have the most fun with it. At first, I blew it off, thinking it helped with marketing Dashcorp's image as young and trendy, but it has been nothing more than an annoyance." He realized how angry he sounded and worried about the absence of her reply. In the background, he heard the muffled snickering and sighed in exasperation, "You're laughing at me, aren't you?"

Alex released a burst of laughter that sounded like a cross between a cackle and a little bell, "I am sorry, but I thought you wore that title with pride. I had no idea it was such a sore spot."

Brent didn't know whether to laugh or cry because she still hadn't answered him. His time was limited and he needed to get back to pressing matters, but he couldn't do so it until he knew one way or the other, "I am glad you find my pain so amusing, but do you feel the same way that I do?"

Her laughter abruptly stopped, and the silence once again drove him crazy, until she quietly answered, "I like you Brent, and I'd be interested in seeing where this odd little connection between us leads when this catastrophe is all over, of course."

Brent found himself very aroused at the possibility of getting closer to Alex and one day, hopefully soon, being able to touch her intimately and physically express all he'd repressed since meeting her. He sensed her hesitancy, but that cautiousness seemed like part of her more than indecisiveness, "Okay then, I want to end this call on a high note and need to go. I hope that Homeland Security is enjoying my awkwardness on this call and does not let it reflect in their dealings with me in the future."

Alex lied back on her bed, and her heart beat so rapidly that she could barely catch her breath. He actually asked to pursue her. Rebecca would enjoy rubbing that fact in her face for a while, if they had a while, of course. She yearned to run out and tell David since he had seen Brent's intentions too, but telling him might feel a little embarrassing. Alex stared at the ceiling feeling the huge grin pasted across her face. She began imagining them spending time together without a sheet of glass between them and felt her face burning. She knew she was acting like a schoolgirl with a crush, but she'd kept men at a distance and never got to know them well enough to trust them as anything more than friends. Even those friendships had remained tentative, based on keeping them at arm's length.

The hours she'd spent talking to Brent made the entire situation different with him, but she still hoped he wasn't the player she suspected he might be. Rebecca said he worked all the time, but he made time to visit her in her cell, so she didn't know what to think. She did not want to open herself up to someone who'd leave her the moment she got comfortable with him, although the excitement she experienced being around him made her want to risk it. Alex went back and forth in her head about him, he seemed genuine, but the appearance of sincerity was part of his charm. She wanted to kick herself for not dating more in college. If she had, maybe she'd better understand how she should act and feel about him.

Suddenly, she shot up in bed. What was she thinking? The country, no, the world was in the middle of falling apart, and she was in her room daydreaming about a man. She shook her head at her foolish thoughts. People were dying, bombs were being planted, nobody knew what tomorrow would bring, and she was sitting around worried that the man might hurt her feelings? Alex realized she needed to stop being scared and follow her heart. She spent her entire life, since the attack, afraid that someone would hurt her again and limited herself to what she felt comfortable with. Now the world was about to end and what had she really experienced in her life? She fed a few homeless and helped inform a few families about some housing possibilities? If she got hurt emotionally or physically, neither mattered because at least she'd be alive to experience it. Her fear of taking on more significant challenges in her charitable undertakings now seemed ridiculous. She could die, be raped, beaten and none of it mattered if she helped someone else lived a better life. She'd already proved she could survive almost anything. If the man she cared for tossed her away like trash, so what, as long as she enjoyed her time with him. She leaned back, hearts like bodies healed, and the revelation shocked her. If she and the ones she cared about survived this Kopvein virus, nothing could stop her.

Why did she feel brave all of a sudden? The insight stunned her, but she knew she needed to survive and do better with the life she'd been given, first by her parents, then by David and Rebecca when they saved her, and now by surviving the virus. Ha! Now her attitude matched her hair, confident.

Rebecca waited for Hector in her private lab while she finished writing, and she concentrated so fiercely that when the Hector rang the buzzer to come in, she jumped and let out a startled breath. Her stomach roiled at the contradictions she felt about all that was happening, both with her and the world outside Dashcorp. Quickly stashing her work, she pulled Hector in the door, and the silly grin on his face told her what he hungered for, but she dismissed it, urgently needing to speak with him, "Hector if I did something that you questioned or didn't understand, would you still trust in me?"

Looking disappointed and slightly confused, Hector scrunched up his face, "What do you mean by that?"

She slipped closer to him then traced the side of his face with her finger, a blatant manipulation that both enjoyed, "There is no easy way to put it, but I am worried. With the troop requirements building up and my best friend being out there, I may ask you to do something that could get us both in trouble. I want you to leave with me."

Hector looked appalled at her question, maybe asking him was a mistake, "I am shocked Rebecca. I never thought you would be one to run from a fight, of any kind, ever, I don't know what to think."

Wishing Hector would go with her, both because his presence would make the trip more manageable, but also because Rebecca wanted him and his company. She could not have him wrecking her plans and knew to ask him posed exposure but decided the possibility was worth it, "Don't kid yourself, I only take calculated risks. I can't focus on my work right now and those Viralists scare me with all their religious admonishment. I'm getting nowhere with a cure right now and probably hindering the progress in fact." Looking to give herself an out, she sat and looked up at him, then started tearing up, "I don't know maybe you are right, and I'm not thinking clearly. Both my body and my mind are listless, desperate for little rest."

Hector knelt down and peered deeply into her eyes and kissed her tear as it ran down her cheek, then tenderly kissed each closed eyelid, "What do you need?"

As quickly as the tears started, they stopped with his question, "Well, for one thing, I need to know my friend Alex is safe. Will you go with me to get her?"

"Of course."

Rebecca played as innocently as possible even though her plans were set, and she merely waited for his acceptance to participate, "We could get into trouble because we can't tell anyone we are going. They will try to stop us."

He shook his head, "I don't think so. I saw the way Brent's eyes lit up at the mention of Alex's name. I think he'd support your idea wholeheartedly, and might even go along."

She adamantly shook her head, "I can't risk it. If he or Homeland stepped in to stop me, I'd be stuck." Rebecca hesitated, she needed to push the issue for him to either reject or wholeheartedly accept her plans, "Oh never mind, I don't want you to get into trouble. You don't have to go, and I can go by myself. Don't worry, I'll be fine." The exploitation was quite apparent, but she thought it the best way to understand what he wanted from her, as well as his mindset.

Hector tenderly took her hand and kissed it, "That isn't what I said. I never answered your question before, and by now, I thought my feelings about you were pretty clear. I will unquestionably drive through the military and a bunch of crazies, and risk getting locked up to help you or make you happy. It doesn't matter where you go or for how long. You go, I follow."

Rebecca placed her hands around his neck and pulled his head into her chest before kissing the top of Hector's little curls. Smiling, she rested her cheek on his head, and tears formed in her eyes for real this time, but he didn't need to see them. He was already hers.

Several moments later Hector mumbled, "While there is no place my face would rather be, I am about to suffocate." Rebecca's laugh rang with relief throughout her lab bouncing off the bare floors and sterile equipment.

CHAPTER 24

Day 21

L ate the night before, the call came in and Rebecca's voice had sounded frantic, an odd behavior for her, "Get back to my place, it is halfway to the facility, and we'll come to get you tomorrow. Just don't say anything, not even to Brent. He needs to act innocent in this, and I think Homeland is monitoring his calls."

Rebecca was coming to get her? Maybe Brent decided to go against Homeland's orders, but she couldn't believe that Brent would allow Rebecca, their best scientist, to leave the facility to go on a dangerous rescue mission. Alex told Brent that both she and David were okay for now and she couldn't fathom why Rebecca suddenly needed to come get her. She hadn't even said goodbye, but maybe something had changed, "Did Brent tell you to call me?"

"Shhh, we've got an armored Humvee."

Rebecca abruptly hung up and Alex's confusion increased with each moment, and she thought about it until morning. Something must be happening and not even the news was reporting it. Her anxiety swelled. They must be closing off the city and the military wouldn't allow Brent out of the facility for much longer. Homeland mustn't be aware of what Rebecca and Brent were planning, so they had to do it secretly. That reason explained why Brent would allow Rebecca to risk her own safety but still, she would need to find a way to her friend's house. By morning, Alex no longer cared about the risk or reasons why and decided to do what it took to get to safety. Alex's car wasn't at her apartment since the whole quarantine started. Erika! Erika had a car, If she hadn't already left the city. She called her up, "Erika! Are you still at home?"

"Yes!" Erika sounded like she had been sobbing, practically hysterically, "I don't have anywhere to go. My fiancé is visiting his family in Mexico, and my other friends already left. When I got off my shift at the hospital, everyone had already left. They left me behind."

Alex had almost left Erika behind too, and the thought made her a little queasy. She was so completely caught up in her own drama that Alex felt ashamed that she almost forgot about her friend, "Well, I am still here, and we need to leave, now before they close off the city. Grab a bag, and we'll get you in two minutes." David, alerted by overhearing the telephone call, had already grabbed a bag with some food and a blanket and waited for her by the door, his eyes wide and alert. Without hesitation, she grabbed a couple of surgical masks, her phone charger, and David's arm before heading out the door. Pausing at the door, she glanced around and sighed, all her plants would die.

Amazed and unaware of the hysteria and fear that seized the civilized town she lived in, some of the stores were already looted, and the streets deserted, changing its appearance and atmosphere to a picture of a war-torn country. Alex thought they might run into a problem crossing the Wilson but other than the slow speed and a few broken down cars, it was uneventful. The problem came when they approached Livingston Road, a mob wielding a large cross and signs barricaded the road and was inspecting vehicles. Alex saw the churches right off the highway and figured the mob must be part of the fanatical Viralists, "Get off here, I know a way around, we cannot miss Rebecca." Erika complied and drove right over the grass behind the Chinese food place. Alex sucked in her breath at the abrupt change of direction and grabbed the dashboard. Luckily, Erika not known for her fantastic driving skills didn't crash into anything. Unfortunately, the sudden change in direction and the speed of the car alerted the mob that someone had escaped their blockade and some of the mob pursued. Alex turned to Erika, still a little shaken from the unexpected off-roading, "We should stop and let them see we aren't hiding anything."

David's booming voice erupted from the back seat, "Don't do it, girl, they're in a frenzy and they might attack us for going around them. A mob willing to chase you may do much worse." Erika looked at David in the rearview mirror and nodded but remained quiet and kept driving, following directions around the takeout place and barbershop and right into another crowd of people. Just as David had predicted they were riled up and tried to get into the car. They pounded on the roof and pulled at the door handles. Erika shrieked the whole time and cursed in Spanish. She leaned on the horn and stepped on the gas without concern for who was in front of them. Suddenly, with an unexpected force that threw Alex sideways and caused the airbags to inflate in their faces, a large truck rammed into the side of their vehicle.

Alex's head slammed into the side window and the world around her grew foggy and spun. She heard glass break, and large hands grabbed her shoulders forcibly pulling her from the vehicle. Several blows battered her body, and she heard Erika screaming. Each punch to her body brought her back to that day in the alley but Alex, no longer a helpless young girl, not weak or vulnerable, started swinging and kicking back. She didn't know who or what she hit, but the world swayed and her body pulsed. Suddenly, Alex felt adrenalin take over her mind and body and she began to see straighter and aimed her blows more directly. She ducked and landed her own punches and kicks, hitting the men all over, including in their private parts, debilitating them. As her attackers writhed on the ground she ran toward the screaming, but David was already pulling men off Erika, and Alex joined him by delivering a kick from behind, straight into a man's kidneys. The attacker instantly fell to the ground and dropped a knife as he fell, then convulsed in front of them. The disease and the marks from it branded him as a victim of Kopvein, yet he had been attacking them. Alex saw David bleeding on his side, but he didn't seem to notice. Frantically, he grabbed Erika and Alex's hands and started running off the road, toward the woods.

She thought they were about to get away when the sudden sound of a gunshot brought all three of them down to the ground. Alex looked over and saw David bleeding from his leg. Without warning, he brandished a knife, one already covered in blood, from the back of his pants, "Go on, I will hold them off, stay to the woods and run!"

Alex pleaded with her savior, "I can help you fight them off."

"There are only a few of them, and I can't concentrate on them with you here. I will catch up to you; I got the directions in my head."

"But you've been shot, Erika can patch you up."

"At the house, it is only a flesh wound, and I didn't go through all this just to watch you get hurt. My job is to protect. All those people in Afghanistan I couldn't save but I saved you, and it will all be for naught if you don't go. Please!" Erika pulled her arm, and Alex glanced back and forth between the two of them, torn and terrified, but she let Erika pull her away. They ran alongside but far enough from the road that they could hide. If they hadn't been running for their lives, the smell of pine and beauty of the dark shadows sculpted by the waves of light peeking through the branches would normally have taken her breath away, but for now, it hid their presence from anyone on the road. If they had been followed, Alex didn't see them, so she focused on not tripping over the roots or stepping in animal holes. A sob stuck in her throat as she realized David might have just sacrificed himself for her and Erika.

They gave a wide birth to another church that they saw in the distance and crept past the area as quietly as possible, afraid they'd run into another frantic mob.

They might be Viralists, and she did not want to find out. Upon reaching a safe distance and circumventing the church, they continued to run in the direction of Rebecca's house. Alex could barely breathe and noticed Erika struggling when they finally reached Rebecca's house. She recognized it from the side, a good distance off the road, tucked into the woods. She stopped Erika as she ducked down behind a bush and she put her finger to her lips. They crouched down waiting, watching and recovering from the three-mile run. She had accompanied Rebecca many times on the run from her house to town, where they'd gorge themselves on copious amounts of donuts and ice cream before slowly stumbling home, high on sugar and carbs, but today it seemed much further. Running through the woods, terrified for her life had worn her out. All she wanted to do was curl up in a ball, cry, and take a nap but she needed to hold it together, for now. She already heard Erika trying to stifle her sniffles.

Making it to Rebecca's felt like a hollow victory. They'd lost David. The area appeared quiet and clear, so Alex gave Erika the signal to stay hidden and quietly snuck up to the back of the house to peek into the windows. She punched the key code into the electronic door lock and snuck in. After checking the entire house, she went to the back door and waved Erika in.

Leaving Dashcorp shouldn't have been as easy of a task as it was, but people were trying to sneak in, not out. Rebecca and Hector waited until mid-afternoon when they saw a slowdown in the comings and goings of the military to leave. A missing vehicle wouldn't be noticed if nobody demanded its use. She had 'procured' an armored Humvee, as well as an army uniform for Hector, and when the guards stopped them, he easily charmed his way through the checkpoints. The road out of the Dashcorp compound looked entirely different, no longer the scenic scape of a tree-lined street and rolling hills of meadow and landscaping, it resembled an area preparing for war. The natural grasses were torn up from vehicles and people marching on them, the landscaped bushes and flowers were strewn with articles of clothing thrown over them, and in the trees sat snipers. Tents speckled the area, new fencing, military vehicles, and barricades lined the perimeter near the exit where an additional fence had been erected. Hector's breathing rate increased as he spotted the machine guns mounted on top of the barriers at regular intervals, "Do you think getting back in will be difficult?"

Rebecca tried to smile reassuringly, "I left a note and will call Brent, but only after we find Alex." He nodded but did not look as confident as Rebecca thought she would make him feel.

The crowds at the exit scared her, they blocked the road, but luckily, Hector had found his calm and they slowly parted. Her insides now roiled with anxiety. Usually, the angst stimulated her creativity as she planned scenarios out, right down to each minuscule detail, but a crowd of people could turn unpredictable and violent without a moment's notice. The crowd had lightened at the news of bombs, many didn't want any connection to a violent terrorist group, but that meant the remaining people weren't opposed to it. If the crowd reacted in any way, the military might step in, and she'd end up stuck inside the facility. She saw some of the people in the crowd had pale complexions and sweat dripped off them, a sure sign of their bodies were fighting off a cold or flu, the first indicator of Kopvein. Maybe leaving in the night would have been the better plan, but looking suspicious to Homeland remained their highest risk. The crowd may be unpredictable, but odds leaned in their favor as long as the military did not stop them. She wondered about the crowd's reaction when one of their compatriots developed symptoms. She hoped the victims found the wisdom to sneak off into the night or the group might forcibly dispel them, possibly killing them in the process. If such a violent disruption occurred, the military might shoot civilians to maintain control.

Hector peered over with concern all on his face, and Rebecca longed to reach over and pat his leg to reassure him, but he needed to focus on the road and the crowds around them, "I can see what you're thinking Hector, but as long as we remain calm, everything will go according to plan." Again, he nodded, but Hector's breathing grew erratic and revealed his true feelings. As many news reports as she had watched and times she had imagined it, her mind never accurately portrayed the scene she now encountered. Its destitution and trepidation revealed the uncertainty and sorrow of the world's future. No wonder Christy Gallagher reported from this location, but her reports only glimpsed the terror that she and Hector felt as they traveled through the crowd.

Finally passing safely through the crowd, Hector sped up the Humvee and headed in the direction Rebecca told him to go. They passed by the lone restaurant and the oddly placed funeral home. Rebecca never understood how they managed to stay in business in an area so secluded. No traffic clogged the rural roads, only military checkpoints until they approached the Indian Head highway south of Accokeek. A large group of men and women barricaded the way and held signs that said 'Viralists for Jesus' 'The Lord Delivers Us and 'God is Just' and 'the LORD delivers.' Rebecca scowled and muttered under her breath, "Judge not, lest ye be judged assholes."

Hector glanced over at Rebecca with a confused expression, "Do you want me to go around them?"

Rebecca pursed her lips at the daunting thought of facing unpredictable possibly volatile crowds. She pulled off her lab coat and shoved it under her seat while buttoning up her blouse to her neck, "Roll down your window and wave them over." Panic struck Hector's face, but he complied, and when a large man with a gun approached their car, she smiled sweetly and confidently, "God is Just, brother. The righteous person may have many troubles, but the LORD delivers him." The man gestured to Hector, but Rebecca interjected, "Brother, we are everywhere." He smiled back, whistled loudly, then waved them through, the crowd parted and waved as they passed, while other cars, being searched, waited.

"How did you know?"

"Haven't you seen all those signs on the news? When I heard the Viralists debut with a bible verse I looked it up, and it wasn't hard to put together."

Hector visibly shook, "So you guessed?"

"I formed an educated deduction from the information available."

He looked like he might vomit, "Did you see how big that gun was? That man could easily have killed us, and you guessed that we'd get through. He stared at me like I was a juicy steak and he wanted to eat me alive."

Rebecca narrowed her eyes and arrogantly barked, "You knew the trip would be dangerous. I prepare for all contingencies, and you should trust me more."

"If I didn't trust you, I wouldn't have agreed to come, but I've never even been up close to a gun that big."

She needed to overlook his angst because the devastation of the Kopvein outbreak had barely begun, and they would both see much worse before the catastrophe ended. Rebecca appreciated him and feared she'd never get to explain how she felt, "Listen, Hector whatever happens from here on out, I have enjoyed our time together."

"What is that supposed to mean?"

"The world is in an upheaval, and people will say or do things, unpredictable things. You are a good man, and I don't want you to regret the time we spent together."

"You aren't making any sense."

"I know, I guess I am scared too. With you, I've let my defenses down, and I don't want to lose you."

Rebecca couldn't tell if Hector's eyes were filled with panic or regret, but he quickly expelled a grunted breath, "Little chance of that now."

The camera panned slowly over the Viralist protestors outside the gates of Dashcorp and settled on a group seated several dozen yards from the Viralist group. It focused onto the small blonde reporter, now dressed in yoga pants, a thick jacket, and baseball cap, "Christy Gallagher reporting again from outside the Dashcorp facility front gates where a rival group protesting the Viralist movement sits, in what looks like meditative poses, perfectly still, chanting quietly. If we weren't approaching the end of 2019, I'd think we'd taken a time machine back to the sixties. This growing rival group claims they have no name and their goal is peaceful resistance. One such protester calling herself only Lakshmi had this to say in an earlier interview."

Christy knelt down next to a line of seated men and women, who were meditating and pushed her microphone toward an average looking girl with no makeup, a ponytail, a thick blanket wrapped around her, and sitting on a small printed carpet. The girl spoke with an emphatic tone, "These Viralists declare their belief in justified murder, that they are pure and the virus is removing whoever does not match the definition of how they think mankind should live. Sometimes, they even escalated to attempted murder themselves as we saw with the bombing attempts. True evil takes on many personas. Adopting the role of judge, jury, and executioner, no matter how pure the original intent, is still the action of a vigilante. They want beauty, compassion, and kindness but those ideals are choices, not an absolute that can be forced. They try to force people to bow to their ideals, but the victims of Kopvein are just that, victims. The Viralists took on the persona of a God and judged us all, and we come here today in peaceful resistance to spread the message of peace and love." The woman bowed her head and mumbled Namaste to Christy, before returning to her meditation.

Christy began speaking back into the microphone, "Lakshmi appears to be the only protestor of the peaceful resistance, as she called their group, willing to voice anything besides their gentle chants. Nearer to the gates, the Viralists have not reacted negatively to the newer protesters, but many still shouted their messages and waved their signs. Christy Gallagher reporting, with more to come as the story unfolds."

Rebecca instructed Hector to pull off the highway where Livingston Road crossed back over and straight onto a small overgrown deer path in the woods. The twenty-one-mile drive that typically took less than thirty minutes lasted over two hours. Rebecca told Hector to park directly behind an odd outcropping of rocks grown over with bushes and vines that was north of her house to approach it from behind. As they moved toward the house, Hector's lack of outdoor and woods experience became apparent by the amount of noise he made. Rebecca pulled him to a stop and placed her finger over her lips, then showed him how if he stepped on roots, rocks and dirt patches he wouldn't make as much noise. It was slow going as Hector's inexperience walking in that manner curtailed speed, but was much quieter. When they approached the clearing to the house, Rebecca squatted down and pulled Hector down with her. He opened his mouth to say something, but Rebecca quickly hushed him with her finger over her lips again.

In the distance, they heard vehicles and men shouting. They watched silently and noticed some movement in the house. Rebecca quickly recognized Alex's silhouette in the kitchen window, and motioned them forward, to go in through the back door. Alex, shocked by Rebecca and Hector's sudden appearance nearly dropped the glass she was holding, and she practically screamed. Rebecca quickly hushed her and reached for her hand, shocked by the bruises that covered her friend's arms and that her eyes and face were also swollen and bruised, "Alex what happened to you?" The noises outside grew closer, visibly scaring both Alex and Rebecca. They turned and noticed the sultry looking shadow in the hallway, and Alex abruptly pulled the panicked looking woman down to the floor. Rebecca recognized her, but couldn't place her. She pointed to her ear and then toward the direction the noise came. Quickly and quietly, Rebecca shut off the one small light coming from the bathroom and began closing all the drapes in the house, and they all jumped up to help before crouching back down in the kitchen.

Alex frantically looked around, then whispered, "You exposed yourself, what are you thinking?"

"I think we both know you don't have it, but that isn't our immediate concern. The Viralists started hunting down people, probably sick people or anyone who doesn't agree with their ideas."

Nodding, Alex pursed her lips, "Yes, we were chased down by some. That is what happened to us and how we lost David." She started to weep at the mention of it.

"You lost David? What does that even mean?" Alex explained what happened between the occasional sobs and tears that were now flowing. Rebecca quietly nodded and took in the information, then asked, "Did they get a good look at you?" Alex and the woman nodded. She too had bruises and a black eye. Rebecca thought for a moment before asking, "You didn't think to have your friend wear a mask to protect herself?"

Alex shrugged and sadly responded, "She's exposed now. Some of the men who ambushed us were showing symptoms and our masks were lost in the struggle."

Rebecca eyed Erika, then gently grabbed Alex's chin and inspected the marks on her face, "Did you return the favor?" Alex snorted out a quiet laugh and nodded as Rebecca gently ran her hand through her friend's hair, "What happened to your hair?"

Self-consciously, Alex stroked the side of her now super short hair and looked up like she could see the hair on her head, "You like it?"

"I do. You won't be able to play with it the way you used to. Why does she," Rebecca pointed to Erika, look so familiar?"

Erika pursed her lips and sighed, "Because we've met, probably a dozen times. I am Erika, Alex's Neighbor."

"Ohh," Rebecca tried to cover, "the stress of our current situation must be getting to me and has destroyed my memory." Erika's face portrayed a look that told Rebecca she wasn't buying it, but Rebecca often unintentionally offended people, so she ignored her expression, "What are you doing here?"

Alex answered for her, "I don't have a car, and Erika was left behind, so she drove us here. She's got nowhere else to go, and I don't want her out there alone, it is too dangerous."

"Okay. I didn't see a car, did you hide it?" As she said the words, Rebecca figured out the answer to her own question, they lost David. She refused to think about losing him and continued before either answered her, "The idiots are spending their time looking for someone to blame for Kopvein, and we'd be the perfect targets. The locals can't stand me. We won't be able to sneak around them tonight because they will spot our headlights, so I think we should stay here until morning. The dark of the night often brings out the beast in people, especially when they are in a mob, and I don't want to risk it."

Alex's eyes grew wide and she anxiously peered toward the window, still wide-eyed, "Won't they find us?"

A plan slowly began to develop in Rebecca's head, she just needed a little more time to figure out the details, "Not if we keep the lights off and stay quiet, we can all sleep in the office and on the kitchen floor near the back door, and one of us can take watch at all times. If anything happens, we will slip out the back door and run to the car. We parked the Humvee about a couple of miles back in the woods behind the rock cropping. I need time to think."

Alex cocked her head in confusion and crinkled up her pale blue eyes. Rebecca always felt she could accomplish anything as she looked into her best friend's pretty eyes. They were like little pools filled with endless compassion that sparkled in the dim light. But Alex interrupted her thought "Think about what?"

"About how we can manage all this, with an unexpected person here."

Erika glanced down and studied the floor, looking scared and guilty, while Alex glared at Rebecca. The tone in her voice went from grateful to annoyed, "Always the charmer Rebecca. Erika is a nurse and if you need to talk Brent into it, I am sure he wouldn't mind an extra pair of hands to help." Rebecca glared back at Alex but remained quiet; they often butted heads, so their reaction to each other wasn't a surprise. Alex's bewildered expression returned, "I thought Brent would come with you?"

Rebecca shook her head, astonished Alex had waited to ask about him. She probably wanted to race back to Dashcorp to see Brent and hide behind the battalions of military guarding the place. Knowing that Alex wouldn't appreciate Rebecca's answer she weighed the pros and cons of telling her, but eventually decide to tell Alex the truth, "No, he doesn't exactly know I'm here, or he might not, I left a note in case they started to look for me."

Rebecca scrutinized Hector who had remained quiet while she and Alex sorted out their feelings and the situation. Then, she glanced back at Alex and couldn't tell if the expression on her face revealed fear over lack of military support, or disappointment, over not seeing Brent there, but her response dripped with anxiety, "What? I thought you said 'we' are coming to get you?"

"You assumed I meant Brent, but I meant Hector and I wasn't taking the chance that he or Homeland would say no. I never planned to tell him and Homeland would never take a chance with a valued asset, me, leaving the facility. There was no way I could wait another moment with you out here alone, no matter how I acted toward you before you left. If you contracted Kopvein, I wouldn't have a good reason to keep working." She didn't want to explain herself any further, and she changed the subject, "The fool fanatics will probably give up hunting for victims to torture sometime during the night. I know it is early right now, but it has been a harrowing day and we should all get some rest then leave before dawn."

CHAPTER 25

Day 22

Rebecca took the first watch. She required the least amount of sleep, and she needed time to think. She believed she had planned everything out down to the last detail with every imaginable contingency, but unexpected circumstances kept derailing her. Now, all these unanticipated variables surrounded her and she didn't think she could make it all work together. It was supposed to be just Alex and her. Alex's attachment to David and Brent completely blew up her plans, although Hector was a pleasant surprise. She supposed she would need to accept whatever decisions Alex made, but it would break her heart to leave her best friend behind. After several hours, she shook Hector's shoulder and put her hand over his mouth to prevent him from waking anyone else. She motioned him over to the bathroom, "I don't know what to do, I didn't plan for Erika, and I know Alex will never leave her behind."

"Why wouldn't Brent let her come to the facility, she is a nurse."

"Hector, I never planned on going back, I am going to leave. I planned on doing that with you and Alex and figured David as well, but I don't think this is going to work."

"Why wouldn't you go back? We have work to do."

"My work there is done, I am not going back. I couldn't leave Alex behind, but I may have to now."

Hector grabbed her arms and shook her, "What are you talking about? You need to do the right thing, and go back to find the cure."

Tears streamed down Rebecca's face, she shook her head and abruptly brush them away, "No, I know I'm doing the right thing." For years, she felt that if she disappeared off the face of the earth nobody would notice, and only wonder why things weren't being done. "I lived invisibly you know. I know my parents loved me, but they never saw me or my pain. After 911, the world fell apart, humanity had reached a tipping point, and I couldn't stand the world we lived in, that day changed everything for the world, but hit me even closer to home."

"My uncle and grandfather died in the tower that day, and my father suffered a heart attack on the floor of our family room that morning. My dad's spirit died, and I lost him forever that day. My anger and devastation over the loss of the three most important men in my life turned my heart. I was angry at them for leaving me, at the government for not stopping it, and also at the terrorists. They took my father's life without killing him, a fate crueler than death and they had no right. They were beasts, and nobody will ever truly get redemption for those atrocities. They escaped by choosing death instead of facing what they didn't like or agree with."

Hector's face contorted into a more confused expression and he tried to interrupt but Rebecca held up her hand so she could continue her rant, "Each step I took toward forgiveness was irrevocably altered by further terror and heartbreak. The very culture from which those animals reign encourages subjugation over of half its community and weak, spineless little men rule that culture. The brave want to escape their destitution and our own country turns them away, out of what, fear? Our country is mirroring their behavior, and even our own president is a misogynist bully, concerned only with personal profit and benefit. There is no changing that kind of man or the countries that support him. My father now lives as an observer, a man with no spirit, and no life of his own. It may be a weakness on his part, but he may as well have died. The wretched monsters always won while the innocents suffered at their brutality and with each horrific experience, I developed more insight into their depravity.

"The day I found Alex, beaten and broken, I thought that ripping my own heart from my chest more tolerable than watching her suffer. All so I could stop feeling her pain. I went to the bridge that day to end my suffering and die when I heard the most monstrous sounds coming from the alley. What happened there made me scream. David chased off the monsters, beating them senseless and my single action to help was to hold her head and cry. As I cradled her head in my lap, every memory, every disaster I experienced and witnessed, flashed through my mind and helped me to develop my plan. She saved me, through the broken bones, bruises, and blood, the young girl in my arms saved me, as well as every other worthwhile soul that walks the earth. I knew I'd find the way to stop the monsters that leech off of all of us and destroy the beauty in our world." Rebecca stopped momentarily to sob, "It was the last incident that I needed to find the courage in my soul, to rid the world of the monsters, so the innocents could live in peace."

"Now, I've set it loose and it will cleanse the world. The first animals to die were the monsters that hurt me the most and nobody even noticed as they rotted in the sun. I never wanted to hurt anyone, but a world without brutality will be worth it." Rebecca cupped Hector's bewildered face with her hands, "I don't regret it, but I never expected to meet you. Mostly, I never expected my emotions to get as caught up in the horror of it and in wanting to cure it prematurely either. In the midst of my time involved in the investigation, I thought I'd fall apart. Putting down those beasts and monsters shouldn't be as difficult as it was, but I can't let my will bend. They will never find the cure for Kopvein until all the monsters have been destroyed."

Hector pulled away from her and looked at her in horror, "What are you saying?"

They heard noises coming from outside and also a gasp from outside the bathroom. Alex stared at them; her face twisted in what Rebecca assumed was absolute fear. Rebecca didn't know how much she'd heard of her and Hector's conversation but they all heard the commotion outside. The Viralists had found them. The roar of large trucks, and men talking in loud voices, boomed. She, Hector, and Alex froze and she noticed Erika stiffly sit up, her face overcome with alarm.

Rebecca recognized the voice outside. It was some redneck from town who worked at the gas station and always hit on her and she wasn't kind in her rejections. In his annoying twang, he spat out, "Oh, I know the wench that lives in this here house well enough, and if she's in there, well-."

They heard someone else ask, "You think she's infected?"

"That bitch won't let nobody on her land and besides the one girl; I ain't never seen her talk to nobody. She's been living here over a decade and never graced not one of the churches with her presence. If anyone's got it, she does."

It wouldn't matter if they were infected or not, the fool from town wanted his revenge, but she knew how to save them. Rebecca crawled over to her study, reached into the bookcase in the middle of the wall, and pulled a latch, and then she pulled the bookcase out to reveal a steel door with an electronic lock. She quickly punched in the code. Hector still stared at her his mouth agape, "What the hell?"

"Nobody was ever supposed to see this, but we're in trouble, so unless you want to die, go." Erika went through the door first, without hesitation, down the spiral staircase, Hector followed, and Alex scowled at Rebecca, her expression filled with a hateful rage but she also followed.

◆ ◆ ◆

Christy Gallagher no longer looked or felt perky. She gave up wearing makeup and pulled her hair back into a bun. Now, she wore pants and a loose shirt in case she needed to move quickly, but she wasn't willing to give up on the story, "This is Christy Gallagher reporting from the Dashcorp research facility, the center of the research for a cure and the news is grim. The military and the government have declared martial law, but folks, the curfew in effect is not the only thing keeping the streets clear. The brave men and women of the U.S. military were deployed to help you." She knew she had flipped on her opinions of the military, but her audience needed some hope and she loved the new deal she had with Dashcorp and Homeland security, "In fact, I saw two fully armed military trucks race out of the Dashcorp facility just this morning, and they're coming to protect you. We are all afraid, but viewers, you must have faith, we will make it through this, together. I will be with you, following the news where the story takes us, and please, be kind to your fellow man as the men and women of the military try to keep order. They want to help you and keep you as safe as possible." At first, she couldn't believe her luck in making a deal with Dashcorp, but Christy didn't know if she could trust them. She held on to the hope that working behind the scenes at the Dashcorp facility would lead to the heart of the story. Unfortunately, though, she had to include some of their propaganda in her reports, so she sighed before saying, "Remember to call the CDC hotline or go onto the CDC website to report suspicious symptoms. Check with this station's website for updates and instructions in your area. We are still here for you. Christy Gallagher, reporting, with live updates from dawn until dusk, every hour, on the hour." She closed out the report with another sigh; at least she was able to retreat safely behind the guarded Dashcorp facility walls when she wanted. Well, it was safe for now.

The bumps and turns in the road jostled the men in the truck around, but their solemn quiet cried with anguish and distress. Brent glanced at Abe's face to see his eyes brimming with tears, and his heart clearly broken, "Sir, aye just don't get it, ay've known the girl her whole life and aye don't see how she could leave us this way. We need to get her back to Dashcorp safely both for her own protection and to help us find the cure."

The rage in Brent's heart accompanied his fear, fear for the world, fear for themselves, and fear for Alex, "I'm sorry old friend but her message was clear. The note was in her own handwriting, and I can't believe she'd do this either, but she did. Why do you think Alex would leave her house? Do you think she knows anything?" The question about Alex should not have been spoken aloud, the military might perceive it as subjectivity, but it weighed on him heavily.

Abe shook his head, "I don't know, but we all turn desperate when our lives are at stake. Rebecca made this decision without thinking of the consequences; maybe she couldn't survive without her friend. She isn't always as tough as she lets on, aye, maybe I don't know anything." Abe put his head in his hands and wept his fear for Rebecca's safety evident and Brent's heart went out to him. He'd come along with Brent and Duffield to make sure nothing happened to Rebecca, but Duffield's rage surpassed even his own. There was no telling how the man would react when they caught up to her. Luckily, they needed Rebecca, and if Sonso hadn't needed a question answered, they'd have never looked in her lab and found the note. Rebecca's lab was now overrun with techs, doctors, and military, all looking for answers as to why she'd risk leaving the facility at all. Brent was planning to go get Alex, but Rebecca just wouldn't wait until he figured it out. Now, they raced toward Rebecca's house where Alex's ankle bracelet last transmitted, in hopes that the two met up there and both women were safe.

A large crowd bearing Viralists' signs, trucks, and people with guns blocked the approach to the house. He feared the crowd would turn on them, but it parted instead, and a large bearded man with a rifle strapped to his back approached the truck convoy. Brent lowered his window as several military men jumped out and pointed their guns in the direction of the crowd and the bearded man, but Brent put up his hand to speak, "Sir, we need to get through to the property beyond, we are looking for a couple of women."

The man put his hands on his hips, shook his head, "Sorry sir, we've scoured the house and the property, and the wench that lives here is nowhere to be found, and we haven't seen anyone else on the property either."

Duffield exited the vehicle, approached the bearded man and saluted, "Sir, thank you for upholding your citizen's duties, but we need the area cleared, forthright."

The bearded man returned the salute and delivered an abrupt, 'yes sir' before he directed the crowd and trucks to clear the area. When Duffield returned to the truck Brent looked questioningly at him, and the man shrugged, "I saw the tattoos on the man and could tell he had served, a former military man. I knew he'd comply."

The search of the small house did not take long, and the bearded man with the Viralists was correct, there were no people or even clues as to where Rebecca might have gone. The transponder from Alex's ankle monitor stopped and left no signs as to where she went. As Duffield and his military searched the property, Brent sat down in the study to look through the desk, but he found nothing helpful. He turned and leaned forward in his chair, put his head in his hands and felt the tears building up inside his eyes. The silence of the little home crept eerily into his mind, especially compared to the noise of the men outside. The only sound was Abe breathing heavily in the other room. Suddenly, Brent heard a startling clicking noise, and his head shot up.

Rebecca descended the staircase, talking as she went down, "I thought we'd have more time, but don't worry the lab is completely fire resistant and has its own ventilation system, in case the fools upstairs get any ideas." When she got to the bottom, Hector and Alex gawked at her, and Erika screamed. In one hand, Rebecca held a Taser and the other she held a gun, "Oh these aren't for you, they're for our protection."

Erika gasped with relief then began eying the vastness of the lab. Alex knew better and felt her insides about to spill out onto the floor. She had heard Rebecca's entire confession to Hector. Her best friend in the world, a woman she loved more than anyone else hid a monster inside herself, one that endangered not only the people Rebecca supposedly loved but the rest of the world as well. Did Rebecca even comprehend love? Alex knew about the atrocities she'd faced as a young woman, but always thought they had caused Rebecca to hide her true emotions of love and compassion. She'd seen signs of Rebecca's giant heart many times over the years, but no person with empathy decided to kill the world, which meant Alex had deluded herself all these years. Alex felt empty inside and saw through Rebecca's stare, then she waved her hands and shrieked, "How could you do this?"

Alex made a grab for the weapons, but Hector blocked her, and Rebecca rolled her eyes, seemingly annoyed at the reaction, "You weren't supposed to find out this way. Thank you, Hector, I guess you've decided you are with me, I am glad you're here. Alex, why are you reacting violently? You know I'd never hurt you. In fact, I did it all for you and people like you. In the end, you'll be grateful."

"Rebecca, your friend is acting crazy. I'm so sorry. I had no idea you experienced such horrors in your life, but it sounds like you were leading up to having something to do with Kopvein."

Alex struggled against Hector, but his arms grasped hers too tightly for her to get away. She growled at him, "Are you a complete moron? Did you listen to a word she said, of course she did."

Hector scrutinized Rebecca and sighed, "I'm trying to interpret my feelings right now, but nobody needs to get hurt. I don't know enough about you Rebecca to understand what you were telling me, but I can't believe the beautiful woman I fell in love with is capable of such monstrosity."

Erika sat down on the couch and watched the three of them, appearing confused, "What is going on?"

Still being held back by Hector, Alex shifted her weight to turn toward Erika, "She is the cause of it all, I heard her admit it to Hector. I just don't understand why."

Poor Erika looked like she had stepped into the middle of a dogfight without knowing any of the rules. She cluelessly called too much attention to herself, and Alex worried that she might not survive the struggle, but Erika's curiosity and fear overtook her common sense, "The cause of what?"

Luckily, Rebecca ignored Erika and focused all her attention on Alex and Hector, "You know I love you Alex, and I am sorry I kept it from you, but I needed to know you'd accept my choices before I said anything. I'm glad I held back, because I knew there was a chance your bleeding heart wouldn't allow you to make the tough decisions, and believe me the choice bordered on impossible, but I saw no other way."

Jumping up, Erika insisted on understanding the conversation, "What is going on? The cause of what?"

As they cowered in Rebecca's secret lab, hiding from the men upstairs, Alex considered how the Viralist uprising must have subverted Rebecca's plans. How long had this lab been here? She scoffed at the idea of a clandestine lab, but answered Erika, hoping her friend would escape injury, "Kopvein! Rebecca created Kopvein." Alex then turned to Rebecca and spat, "You're right, I'd have stopped you."

Erika paused and contemplated what Alex had told her, "That is impossible, how could she create-." She couldn't choke out the words to finish the sentence as comprehension came over her face and she reached for the wall next to her, to stop herself from falling. She leaned against it and slowly slid down it, missing the couch to land on the floor.

Alex gaped at Hector, "You know Hector, this makes her a homicidal serial killer. I am so blind! You were my best friend. You came and took care of me when my own mother couldn't stand to look at me, and my brother's guilt drove him further from me. I've seen such kindness in your heart," Alex started screaming, "Please; tell me how you could choose to destroy the world?"

"Innocents aren't the ones dying here! You once told me that my heart was so huge that I couldn't handle all the emotions they threw at me, and I shut them down and acted cold. That realization helped me. The pain I felt will always live within me, but those atrocities don't need to continue to happen to others."

Hector forcibly held Alex back as she pulled toward Rebecca, but being unable to move didn't prevent her from yelling, "Whoever gave you that right? Why do you get to decide who lives or dies?"

"I developed a plan and used it to make the world a better place. Unlike all the other disasters of the earth that have cleansed it in the past, my solution does not leave the wealthiest, most unworthy and vicious at the top, and it leaves the ones who should oversee the world and will do it with compassion."

Alex sank into Hector's arms and cried, desperate sobs, "What is that even supposed to mean?"

Rebecca's voice cracked as it came out, "I am sorry, I never wanted you to hurt and I am sorry you cannot see the justice in my choices."

Hector brought Alex over to a chair and lowered her into it. Alex cried and studied the room. It was partially finished and surrounded by huge rocks and decorated in a style that matched Rebecca much more than her cottage upstairs. It contained a bedroom, a bathroom, a small control center and kitchen near the couch in the main living area at the bottom of the spiral staircase. The living area was connected to a pressurized set of glass and steel doors that led to a hazmat room and a lab. No wonder Rebecca loved her little dollhouse so much; she lived in the lab below it. Alex numbly watched Rebecca turn on security cameras and open the steel door to the hazmat suit room. Rebecca peered at the three of them while she bustled around pulling bags and a few boxes down from shelves, "Hector, remember that statement you made to me, where you go I follow, is that still how you feel?" Hector eyed her sadly and hesitantly nodded before she continued, "Your life just got much more difficult, and now the world will pursue us. I knew that Alex might not accept my choices, but now she knows and she'll open her big mouth to everyone. I never thought I'd meet someone like you, someone I respect that also seems to love me for who I am, no matter my crimes and I do realize that my actions are crimes, but it needed to happen."

Alex sighed a big breath of relief, at least Rebecca wasn't planning to kill her, or she wouldn't worry about anyone finding out. Alex thought that a person crazy enough to claim she released a deadly virus onto the world, would kill them too. For some reason, Rebecca refrained from doing it. Too weak to stand from the shock of all she'd just learned, Alex couldn't believe that Hector was accepting what Rebecca had done. He seemed so kind and compassionate, why wasn't he trying to stop her?

Alex looked over to Hector's heartbroken face still filled with love when he gazed at Rebecca, and he sighed deeply before replying to her, "Yes, I am in too deep. My heart is broken from what you did, but I don't think I can stand any more heartbreak. Watching you leave would surely kill me on the spot. Our time is probably limited before Kopvein gets us anyway and as abhorrent as your choices may be, my heart still wants you."

Rebecca nodded, not exactly pleased with his answer, but accepted it as she continued bustling around. Each minute crept by slowly, and on the security cameras, the night's darkness lifted as morning drifted in. The crowd of men parted and cleared for two large military trucks pulling up into the front yard. Brent exited one of them, and Alex noticed immediately but tried not to react. Unfortunately, Rebecca saw it too. Viciously, Rebecca turned to the screen, "I told him not to come. Why would he put himself and the others at risk?"

Alex jumped up and screamed, "Brent is here to rescue us, and you won't get away. You can still fix it, Rebecca. If you devised the whole thing, I know you created a cure. PLEASE, nobody has to know that you did it."

Hector hopefully turned to Rebecca, but she ignored Alex and in calm, controlled manner faced Hector, "If they're here they might already know what I've done, and if they don't, they will when they find Alex. Hector, take these bags out through the lab to the other side, you will find a cave tunnel. It leads to a hidden exit, and I will give you the code to get out. Don't take your suit off because I need you to come back through and help me. The exit is in the outcropping of rocks and vegetation where our vehicle is parked, put the bags on the other side of the doors and come back. I will gather a few more things from the lab, but hurry, I want you to help me set fire to the whole thing."

Hector's disappointment in Rebecca's complete dismissal of Alex's plea filled the room with a palpable sadness. He pointed at the other two women, "What about?"

"They obviously aren't coming with us, but don't worry the chamber is fire safe, and they won't get hurt as long as they stay in here. The fire will fry the electrical components, and it is set up to disengage in case of a fire, they'll be fine." Hector donned a hazmat suit, and wearily picked up the two duffle bags and went through the doors. Rebecca grabbed some small items and placed them inside the doors of the hazmat areas, not taking her hand off the Taser or her eyes off the women. She donned her hazmat suit and pushed the boxes through the second set of doors into the lab with her foot. Then, she quickly moved around in the lab but Alex couldn't see what she was doing. Alex jumped up and went through the first set of doors, then grabbed the last Hazmat suit to put on. She had to try to stop her. Through the intercom, she heard Rebecca's voice, "You can't come in here without protection. Don't take such a stupid risk; I've smashed all the viral samples and cures.

Alex gasped and tried to hurry to put on the suit, "I knew it! I knew there were cures."

"Alex, you won't have time, please don't come in here, the lab is swarming with the viral compound," Rebecca glanced over and watched the door on the opposite side of the lab open. Hector had already returned to the lab and was breathing heavily. She and Hector squirted down the research with a hose coming from a canister and Alex saw the first tendrils of smoke rising. The canister must have contained some kind of accelerant because the boxes they had squirted suddenly burst into flames and it rapidly spread. Alex, now quite efficient at donning a hazmat suit on her own, was finished. She heard Rebecca over the intercom, "Hector's already lit a fire to my research, you won't find anything."

Alex turned when she heard Brent noisily clamoring down the spiral staircase. Rebecca wasn't lying, the locks disengaged when the electrical systems detected the fire. He stepped back in shock when he saw Alex, "What is this place? The house appeared empty, but I heard the bookcase and saw it opened a few inches, so I decided to investigate. Are you okay? What is going on here?"

"Rebecca has the cure," he dashed toward the doors, but she put her hand up, "You can't come in here without a suit; the lab is filled with Kopvein."

Alex raced through the doors following Rebecca, "Rebecca, please! Don't do this!" She saw Rebecca about to put a tiny glass vial into a small case, "I knew it. That is the cure isn't it?"

Rebecca abruptly turned from Alex to run, dropping the case but still clasping the vial, as smoke filled the lab, "The virus needs to carry out its purpose before I can allow anyone to stop me. Not you nor anybody else will ever get the antidote or my research." Alex grabbed for the vial in Rebecca's hand, and Rebecca tried to push her away, but Alex had clutched the vial tightly. Dozens of other glass vials, broken in pieces, were scattered across the floor. Rebecca probably held the only dose of the cure left, and she was trying to keep control of it. They struggled, and as they wrestled, the vial slipped out of both of their hands and smashed on the floor. Rebecca glimpsed over Alex's shoulder, they both saw Brent, standing at the doors beating them with his fist. Rebecca pushed Alex desperately trying to get her off of her, and the noise that came next was deafening in its finality, the ripping sound caused both women to freeze. Both Rebecca and Alex gawked downward to see whose suit had torn, but Hector appeared and grabbed Rebecca's arm. He pulled her out the cave side door, sealing and locking it behind them.

Are you ready for the next part of Alex and Rebecca's story?

HOUR OF TRIAL

Dear Reader,

Thank you for taking time to read **Hour of Trial**. If you enjoyed the book, I would greatly appreciate if you would take another moment to rate and review the book on Amazon. Every review helps others to discover **Hour of Trial**.

Look for the next segment of Alex and Rebecca's story in

Viralist Series Book 2, Unknown Hours available for pre-order now and release on June 27th 2019.

Sign up on **www.LenaRobinWrites.com** for updates on the newest releases.

230

ACKNOWLEDGMENTS

I would like to take the time to express my sincerest gratitude to all the wonderful people in my life who encouraged and supported me. I would like to give a special thanks to my readers: Lisa, Kristi, Becky, and my sister Valerie. I am grateful to Liz Laquidara, a.k.a. Liz Alexander and Diane Abdo for inspiring me to take up the pen and pursue my dream wholeheartedly. I could not have done it without my friends Melissa, Myleia, and Stephanie for taking my girls on playdates so I could write. Thank you, DD for pushing me and always being there when I need you.

ABOUT THE AUTHOR

Lena is a fifth-generation Floridian who was raised sailing and riding horses but does not know much about either. She is married with two children and has an early start on her crazy cat lady collection. Her undergraduate degree in Fine Art and MBA are from Florida Atlantic University and she has been a certified yoga teacher since 2009. Lena loves practicing yoga with her cats when she isn't eating too many sweets or writing.

CPSIA information can be obtained
at www.ICGtesting.com
Printed in the USA
FSHW011302020320
67723FS